EVOLUTION

Stalker/s, Book Two

L.J. Hasbrouck

A NineStar Press Publication

Published by NineStar Press
P.O. Box 91792,
Albuquerque, New Mexico, 87199 USA.
www.ninestarpress.com

Evolution

Warning: This book contains sexual content, which may only be suitable for mature readers, scenes of horror and gore, suicidal ideation, references to past trauma and deceased family members, guns, and the deaths of prominent characters.

Brian Jameson left behind a world of chaos—vicious Stalkers, ruthless survivors, and an unforgiving landscape of bitter cold and snow—and escaped to an idyllic island paradise with the love of his life. But now he must abandon everything he fought for and return to the warped remnants of America, land of the lost and the home of the depraved.

His sizzling affair with hotheaded Cajun Louis Lavellé came to a boil when Louis's secrets surfaced: among them, the fact that he left his sister in the clutches of a twisted, infected psychopath and let Brian think she was dead. Unable to bear Louis's betrayal or the enigma of Eva's fate, Brian flees the island—without Louis—and returns to New Orleans to begin his search for the missing girl.

If Brian can find his friends, gregarious D and her badass brother, Antoine, he thinks he might have a shot of fighting his way back to Eva's last known location. But the Stalkers haven't died out—in fact, they're exhibiting frightening new patterns of behavior. And memories of Louis continue to torment Brian...along with the strong probability that Louis hasn't forgotten *him* either.

Hopes and fears of reuniting with the Lavellé twins drive Brian as he navigates through familiar but shifting surroundings and obstacles. Sweltering heat has melted the snow, revealing once-buried horrors and allowing both Stalkers and other survivors to emerge from hiding. Everything Brian thought he knew about this warped world is shaken by mounting revelations, and each one chips away at his hopes for a happy ending.

But at this point, he doesn't even *know* what his version of a happy ending could be.

Chapter One

The Return

3/9, New Orleans, Louisiana, Orleans Marina, 12:37 a.m.

There are no happy endings. Because when a book ends, the story's not over. The characters continue to exist in their illusory world, kept alive by the readers long after the author has moved on. Our own existence lacks such perpetuity. We're born, we live, we die. I'm still wondering when my end will come. All I know is this chapter has ended and a new one is beginning.

Brian closed the journal over his pencil and slid his palm across the warped image of Van Gogh's *The Starry Night*. A real-life starry night twinkled outside the boat cabin. When he'd been behind the wheel and spotted the Louisiana shoreline, a surge of triumph had lit him with such heat he imagined himself glowing. But the realization there was no one to share the moment with had extinguished his flare of elation.

Flyers and photos stuck out from the pages of his journal. Brian slid them out, craving company in whatever form he could get. He swiped away a smiling man with a deer.

Dead.

A pair of actors in '20s garb facing off on a poster for *Chicago*.

Gone.

A freckled girl bathed in light, young and beautiful.

Abandoned.

A dark-skinned woman in a colorful robe and turban advertising psychic services while an orange tabby napped behind her.

Safe—I hope.

His grandfather caught in a rare moment of laughter with his dog, Rocky, cradled in his lap.

Murdered.

A Polaroid of an Adonis crafted with the same perfection as the marble chiseled by the masters. And the same deceptive impenetrability.

Gone but never forgotten.

Brian swept a thumb over the photo and sighed, regret swelling within his gurgling stomach. He shoved the photos and flyers back into the journal.

After tearing into a tasteless strip of dried fish and following it with water that retained a faint seaweed flavor, he abandoned the kitchen table and descended into the cabin. He crawled into bed and tugged the sheets to his nose. The scent of suntan lotion and burnt wood transported him to a less desolate night.

Brian curled onto his side and embraced the bare pillow beside him. *What a hollow victory, returning to the place I tried to escape from.*

Alone.

When Brian woke, he couldn't identify whether it was day or night. A quick look at the watch he'd stolen from Louis told him it was 10:37 a.m. He glanced at the bedside table, making sure the revolver remained there, and got out of bed. After tugging a worn pair of jeans over his boxers, he pulled on a scratchy long-sleeved shirt, then slipped on a light jacket and zipped it to his neck. Gloves, socks, and cracked leather boots finished out the ensemble.

Brian tucked the gun into his waistband and returned to his journal. He flipped it open to examine the scant inventory list within it.

Inventory P.I. (Post-Island):
Backpacks, 2 (1 waterproof)
Journal (Starry Night), 1
Pencil, 2
Poppa's bow
Quiver with arrows, 7
Magnum Revolver (6 bullets)
Cans of assorted food, 16
Boxed food, 4½

Strips of fish jerky, 14
Coffee cans, 2
Bottles of water, 3
Empty bottles, 6
2 pairs of boots
3 pairs of socks
3 short-sleeved shirts
1 undershirt
2 long-sleeved shirts
2 pairs of jeans
2 pairs of shorts
4 boxers
Pop-up tent, 1
Sleeping bag, 1
Compass, 1
Louis's map (even has all the old pencil marks)
Suntan lotion, 2 tubes
Bug spray, 1 bottle (half empty)
Matches, 2 boxes
Lantern, 1
D batteries, 8
Boat key, Orleans Marina
First-aid kit, 1 (missing some odds and ends thanks to Lou's
*   boo-boo)*
"Murder Comes Knocking" (finished, predictable)
Flyers of D/Jonesy and Parker/Spike
Photos of Poppa, Henry, Eva, Louis

Brian closed the journal and tucked it into his bag before those photos tempted him again. He pulled on the backpack, bow, and quiver of arrows, and then put his second backpack on his chest as if it carried a baby, not invaluable supplies. Revolver in hand, he ascended the steps and left behind a cabin saturated with bittersweet memories.

When he stepped into the open air, the blinding light reminded him of the time he'd emerged from the tornado shelter into the wintry landscape of Poppa's farm. A sheen of snow had hidden the hellish ruins awaiting him, such a brilliant white he saw red when he blinked.

Brian squinted, breathing in salty sea air as a seagull squawked nearby. The water lapping at the dock evoked a misleading sense of tranquility.

I don't have Grimes to ride. I don't have Louis to watch my back. No D, no Antoine. All I have are the skills Poppa taught me—and the lessons I learned from everyone else.

Beads of sweat pooled on his skin. His nerves tingled like pretest jitters times a billion. But *this* test would kill him if he failed.

I doubt Antoine and D are still at his house, but it wouldn't hurt to check.

He sighed: he couldn't avoid going through the city without taking a gigantic detour. Anything could have popped up while he was on the island. Stalkers would only hide for so long before their hunger forced them to follow the scents and sounds of their quarry.

The gruesome creatures were no longer as predictable as they'd once been. Brian used to think they'd been solitary, predominantly active during the day. But now he knew they worked together—even if they sometimes ate each other—and also hunted at night. They were adapting to the shifting patterns of their prey.

But the one on the ship spoke to us. And I killed it. So who's really *predator and prey here?*

Brian didn't look back at the boat, tried not to think of the island; he forced himself to stare ahead at the expanse of land and buildings beyond the docks. The snow and ice had given way to mild, pleasant weather.

Winter was over; spring was on the way.

He raised the bow and crept behind buildings, staying low to the ground. Everything around him remained still and silent. The world seemed to have frozen in his absence.

I need a bike. I'll even take a pink tricycle. Hell, a unicycle, or maybe skates.

He suppressed a laugh at the thought of trying to brake on rollerblades while a Stalker jumped out at him. He'd taken numerous childhood tumbles on them and doubted age would turn him into some rollerblading prodigy. And Louis wasn't there to snag his hand and stop him from careening into a wall.

Sweeping the buildings along the way would be too dangerous. But he hadn't forgotten the sniper and her father; it was equally dangerous to be out in the open. One shot and it was all over. One bite, one scratch.

Brian continued through the streets, scanning cars for passengers before he slunk behind them for cover. He glanced at broken windows in the homes of suburban neighborhoods, searching for a flash of metal or the glint of a scope. A bird chirped as it flew overhead. With most of humanity gone, nature would thrive and reclaim Earth—the Stalkers would become another predator in the food chain.

Silence surrounded him once more: the bird had moved on. His boots crunched into the gravel. He avoided the Garden District, where they'd had the close scrape with the ambushing Stalkers in the condo. Instead, he took a detour he'd planned using Louis's old map, following Robert E. Lee Boulevard to a golf course called Bayou Oaks.

It took us an hour to get here from the condo. It should take me two or three to make it to the cathedral.

Like pages in a photo album, his mind flipped to the image of the young girl's body splattered on the cobblestone. *Kill or be killed. I had to do it.*

Escaping his memories and the suburbs, he headed for trees with budding leaves and hills coated with sprouting grass. The verdant vista reminded him of the golf course he'd gone to with D and Louis—and Grimes's disappointment with the fake turf grass.

Brian shook the thought off and focused on traversing the course behind the sporadic coverage of trees. The exposure of the grassy hills put him on edge, but he preferred it to the clutter of houses and cars. The soothing sight of swans swimming in ponds reassured him life went on regardless of whatever calamities befell the world.

He cut across Filmore Avenue and passed a park surrounded by lush forest. It surprised him that natural beauty and open land existed in a once-bustling city like New Orleans. When a rabbit bounced by in search of food, he stopped to watch it, comforted by the simplicity of its routine.

It just wants to eat in peace and not be bothered by predators. I can relate.

He moved on, leaving the rabbit to pick at strands of grass. He had food—for now.

His passive jaunt ended when he reached a highway littered with cars piled into signs, light poles, and each other. Several had pulled over in the emergency lane or rolled onto the side of the road. Broken glass twinkled from the asphalt. A skeletal arm dangled out of one smashed doorframe, beckoning to anyone who passed by.

Brian sank an arrow into a face grinning at him from one of the busted car windows. Blood dripped into crevices between flesh-knotted teeth as he jerked his arrow out and cleaned it. The creature's dying chortle faded into a final whimper.

Killing had become as thoughtless to him as lifting a fork to his mouth. As normal as eating salty canned food or drinking tepid water or dunking into a murky river for a bath. But Brian didn't have time to mull over this unsettling realization—nothing about this life resembled the life he'd led before his mother's infection. He'd bid that version of himself farewell while he stared into Poppa and Nana's bedroom mirror, trying to ignore the intertwined bodies he'd put down moments before.

If I stayed the same sheltered, naïve kid I was, I'd be dead now.

Once he crossed to the other side of the highway, he followed Wisner Boulevard south alongside the river. He stopped beside a sign sent from the heavens: "Wheel Fun Rentals."

"Cute pun," he muttered. The absence of a reply reminded him he was alone, so he moved on.

Wheel Fun Rentals sat next to a lake. A bloated body floated within the algae-coated water, too decomposed to identify. The thought of some submerged Stalker leaping forth from the water's edge made a shudder ripple through his flesh and kept him from lingering near the lake.

The inside of the building had been wrecked. Apparently, everyone else thought a bike would be a good idea too. He found only a tandem bike missing a tire and a cruiser with a deflated one.

But Brian had time on his side. Everyone had been in a panic, rushing to grab a bike and go, so they hadn't stopped to fix the tire. Nor had they taken all the repair kits and pumps lining the shelves.

Brian worked quickly to air the tire and patch it with rubber and adhesive. Once the rubber dried, he rolled the bike out with a satisfied grin. He strapped the backpack from his chest onto both handlebars, relieved to ditch some weight.

Anticipation and trepidation dueled within him as he pedaled along Wisner and Carrollton. Carrollton took him to Conti, the road leading to Antoine's house. Without Louis and D by his side, the enormity and silence of the city overwhelmed Brian. He continued past buildings and landmarks he recognized, including the cathedral and park where D and Antoine had reunited. Brian avoided the road where the body had fallen, not wanting to see what had become of it.

The pink house with the iron gate sent a swell of relief through Brian. The blue SUV remained behind it, and particleboard still covered the entrances. He climbed off the bike and leaned it against the fence before approaching the gate. It creaked open beneath the gentle pressure of his hand—but Antoine had locked it before they left for the Garden District.

It doesn't look like someone busted it open. Maybe they made it back and left it unlocked for me.

Brian rolled the bike through the gate and closed it. He spied a small white object in the corner of the SUV's windshield which hadn't been there before. The door opened easily and sent the odor of leather and vinyl wafting into his nose. Another benefit of Antoine's Powerball winnings. After inspecting the vehicle, he climbed into the seat, shut the door, and locked it.

He grabbed and unfolded the paper with eager hands.

To B from D: I left this just in case you got tired of louise and came back for us. We gone to evergreen, brought grimes and jones too. I don't want to write it here in case someone not you is reading this but theres a way to get into Bros place here if you look for it. we couldnt take all the swag so feel free to crash and relax, eat up and such before you come see us at evergreen. If you readin this just know we love you baby boy and we been thinkin about you. XO Scarecrow, The Tin Man, and The Cowardly Kitty

Smiling, he folded the note and tucked it into his backpack. He scoured the SUV, shuffling through a book on self-defense, a box of Black & Milds, a pair of cheap sunglasses, and numerous empty fast food bags until he found a key wrapped in the napkin of a grease-spotted Arby's bag.

His head flopped back against the seat cushion as he exhaled and held the gleaming key in front of him. *It's like I'm playing a video game and unlocked the next level.*

He didn't have time to sit and bathe in his achievement; he hurried out of the SUV and shut the door before rolling his bike with him to the side of Antoine's condo. He tried the doorknob to see if it was locked and slid the key in. It twisted with a satisfying *click.* Enter, shut, lock.

The house still possessed a lived-in quality, but the space felt empty without the Etiennes' boisterous chatter. Brian walked past the worn kitchen table they'd eaten at and slid his palm along the dusty wood. *I hope they made it to Evergreen.*

He performed a quick inspection of the house but was relieved to find it as pristine as the day he'd left it. Even better: he found a pantry filled with canned and boxed food and a gallon of water. Antoine had even gotten a shopping cart from a Piggly-Wiggly and loaded it with *more* food.

Brian tore into as much as he could. He'd grown used to suppressing or ignoring his hunger and thirst, and he'd lost several pounds because of it—but since he could eat as much as he wanted now, he was positively gluttonous.

After he finished, he unbuttoned his jeans and collapsed into the chair behind the kitchen table, gazing at the stairs. He'd bounded up them after Antoine and D with Louis behind him, Jonesy weaving in and out of all four pairs of feet. He'd lost his footing at one point trying to avoid Jonesy's tail, but Louis had been there to catch him.

Not anymore.

Brian retraced his steps up the stairs and set his belongings on the bedroom floor. He kept his gun in his hand as he flopped onto the bed and caught a whiff of Antoine's overpowering cologne. *Strong stuff. Louis wore something more subtle—or maybe it was just* him. *He always smelled good somehow, like burning wood and leather. And cinnamon...*

He groaned and rolled onto his side, swatting a pillow with his arm and imagining who might have slept beside Antoine in the double bed. The space he'd once loved in his bed at home now seemed agonizingly bare. As much as he sprawled over it, nothing could fill the void.

Unable to keep his eyes closed, he stared at the cream ceiling and studied the cracks and stains. He was more content with moving, keeping his thoughts occupied with the possibility of encountering Stalkers or strangers, and finding shelter and food. This moment of repose transitioned into torturous languor.

I'm not tired. I have no one to talk to, my tablet's low on power, I finished Nana's book, and I'm scared to open my journal because I'll just look at those damn photos.

Brian screwed his eyes shut and tried to force himself to sleep. It didn't work. He wandered around Antoine's home and nosed into every nook and cranny. He learned Antoine had an interest in gardening and cooking and found several jazz records beside an old-fashioned phonograph. Antoine's DVD shelf had movies ranging from *The Shawshank Redemption* to *Machete*.

He stole back to the bed with several of Antoine's books and flipped through them, but he gave up on reading after his eyes swept past the same paragraph a dozen times and his brain remained too occupied to comprehend the words.

After stacking the books into a pile on the table next to his handgun, he raked his hands through his bangs with an irritated groan. *I'm not as good at entertaining myself as I thought. I got spoiled having Louis around to talk to and play games with. Among other things.*

His anger toward Louis hadn't dissipated, but neither had the desire for his company. Brian found this infuriating opposition of emotions impossible to resolve. He dug out his journal and gave in to temptation. He peeked at the perfect body preserved in the Polaroid and relived all the sensations he associated with it. But the image was a spectral echo of Louis's presence, only catering to one of Brian's senses when all of them craved appeasement.

He stuck his pencil between his teeth and gnawed on the eraser, then flipped to a blank page and pressed the lead tip against it. *Dunno if I'll ever read this again—or if anyone else will—but what the hell else am I going to do?*

There and back again. I'm seeing the same places, doing the same things. Riding the same rollercoaster—but without anyone in the seat beside me.

On the boat, I felt free for the first time in my life. The ocean was around me, an infinite expanse of possibility. No one could tell me where to go or what to do. I was safe and happy.

Making it to the boat, to the island, was an accomplishment. It gave me purpose. I have a purpose now—to get back to Evergreen, to look for Eva—but I don't feel the same drive.

It's because he isn't here.

I guess he was the first thing I ever wanted so badly. No, I convinced myself I needed him. And for some crazy reason, he wanted me too. But when it all went to shit, I ran away from him. Sometimes I wonder if I did the right thing. He never abandoned me, but I abandoned him. Despite everything he did, I still worry he's angry at me for leaving, and I still think about going back to him.

It's ridiculous, isn't it? But it's complicated. The entire thing still feels like a dream: the pandemic, the island, and everything in between. A nightmare and a fantasy twisted together. We went through so much together, first when we were growing up, then when we were trying to survive, falling into that bottomless pit of love... I guess I wish I'd stayed long enough to talk with him more, but I was angry, scared, hurt—

And deep down, I knew if I didn't leave then, I never would.

So what now? We're both alone, both miserable. The only way I can be with him is in my mind, in concrete memories and abstract fantasies. That's the same way I "visit" my family, having imaginary conversations with them about things they'll never know and reliving the times we shared before that awful Christmas.

I guess I'll stop writing and go close my eyes. I might not sleep, but at least I'll be with them all again.

Chapter Two

Hello!

3/10, New Orleans, Louisiana, Antoine Etienne's home, 11:42 a.m.

Brian woke several times, but he shut his eyes and forced himself back to sleep. He wanted to keep dreaming, to avoid the reality awaiting him outside his mind—not to mention the daunting task of traveling through New Orleans. He'd been lucky to make it to Antoine's, but there was no way he'd ride that far without bumping into at least one Stalker.

Out in the open he either avoided them or killed them with a well-placed arrow. But people were another story. Each encounter would be a coin flip: heads, someone competent and chill like D, or tails, some maniac like the King. Brian wasn't as ruthless as Poppa or Louis, so he'd probably duck out of sight to avoid the dilemma. *They go their way, I go mine. No one dies.*

There came a point where his eyes would no longer stay shut, so he meandered to the bathroom. The plumbing didn't work, but the toilet bowl served its purpose regardless.

He leaned over the sink and brushed his teeth with an old toothbrush and chalky, flavorless toothpaste. While he glanced into the mirror, he combed his bedhead with his fingers to untangle it. He thought he looked skinnier, but the burnished tan of his skin had returned on the island. A pale line remained in his lower lip: a reminder of Louis's sharp eyetooth, but not permanent like the scar Brian had left him all those years ago. He spat the toothpaste out and dragged a thumb along his lip. It still stung.

He dressed and ate a hearty breakfast with Antoine's leftovers. His backpack soon bulged with the rest. Aside from a photo of Antoine and D wearing Mardi Gras beads and toasting with plastic martini glasses, he took nothing else. D had the same bone structure and smile, but her sturdy figure was less curvaceous. It was obviously an old picture.

Once he collected everything, he moved his bike out and locked the door behind him. He lingered behind the safety of the iron gate, surveying the cluttered but lifeless streets of the French Quarter.

He rolled his shoulders and cracked his neck. *Here goes nothing.*

Brian walked through the gate and climbed onto the bicycle. A liberating breeze cooled his face while he pedaled over bumpy, narrow streets past two-story buildings once home to restaurants, bars, and other businesses. One sign proudly displayed the title: "Rev. Zombie's Voodoo Shop." This whimsy was now a poignant reflection of the levity with which people had once observed the dead.

A strange part of him wished the apocalyptic event had been nuclear instead of viral: he wanted to explore these buildings without worrying about Stalkers lurking in the shadows. But he supposed the selective nature of the pandemic had spared him when a bomb would've obliterated him and everyone he cared about without them even knowing the end was coming.

The passenger of a derelict Corvette Stingray leaped out at him, but Brian maneuvered the bike around the corner onto Basin Street and outpaced it. The shock of adrenaline quickly faded; the sight of a lone Stalker no longer frightened him. Since he had a bike, he could save ammo by avoiding them. Although he'd killed most Stalkers he encountered, none of the surviving ones followed him. The sneaky bastards preferred hiding when they were alone.

Just like me.

Dark clouds hung overhead, swollen with the threat of rain. He passed buildings interspersed with foliage fighting back to life. Another business called Opp Poo Pa Doo caught his eye, and he smiled when he imagined the jokes D would've made. This shifted into a frown when he reached an intersection with a green sign for St. Louis Street.

"Ironic name for a saint," he muttered. Instead of strangely named businesses, he continued past suburbs and parks. The colors surrounding him composed a palette of drab grays, murky browns, and a sickly chartreuse. Not much of a step up from the austere white and bleak russet of winter.

Maybe one day I'll make it out of the South, go somewhere with mountains and tree leaves that actually change color.

Brian's legs ached by the time he made it to his next turn near a huge apartment building. Something moved in the distance. He skidded, burning rubber. A group of people marched down a sidewalk across the street.

Fuck! I hope they didn't see me—

He took the only opening: the door into Blue Plate Artist Lofts.

Brian steered his bike inside with him and scanned the lobby. A pair of parted elevator doors gleamed in the corner. The shattered remains of a glass table lay alongside busted phones and computers. He didn't block the front door; if they came after him, they'd know someone was inside.

Not much cover. But if I take the stairs, they'll be my only way back. I'm not jumping through a fucking window and twisting my ankle—or worse.

He kneeled in front of one of the barricaded windows and peered through a gap in the boards. The group crossed the street and headed straight for him.

They were armed. And they were big.

The elevator—I can squeeze in there. They can't.

Brian took the bicycle with him to the elevator doors. He glimpsed two partially skeletal bodies curled in the corner. An unpleasant scent clung to the stagnant air.

They either fled from Stalkers or people like the assholes headed this way. Must've killed themselves or starved. Fucking depressing.

He pushed the bicycle through, unwilling to leave it for some burly man to steal—even if the image of one riding it amused him. He squeezed in behind it and kneeled beside the elevator doors out of sight.

Occasionally, he leaned around to check the lobby for the men. But he needn't have bothered—he heard them before he saw them. They were laughing and chatting like they owned the world.

Heavy boots crunched the glass outside the elevator. A thick Southern accent drifted into the empty lobby. "This place is spiffy. Bet you the people who lived here had money."

"I thought it was a real art gallery. Kinda wanted to see some pretty paintin's."

Their footsteps ceased.

"Larry, you scared of those things?"

"Nope. Why you ask?"

"Just a lot of floors here. Lots of rooms. Lots of l'il hidey-holes."

"Shit, man—I hate it when they jump at you. But once that's outta the way, puttin' 'em down is easy."

"I don't like when they talk. The laughin's bad enough—but sometimes it sounds like they're *sayin'* stuff..."

Brian peeked between the elevator doors. Three men stood in the lobby, dressed in makeshift protective gear incorporating motorcycle helmets and combat boots. One held a shotgun over his shoulder. Another had a revolver tucked in the back of his dirty jeans. The third had a rifle slung over his chest. The weapons and gear tempted Brian, but the men outnumbered him.

Even if they look like Mad Max *rejects, they're too hard to take down.*

The man with the rifle groaned. "I don't like the thought of lookin' around in here, man. Let's get outta here and go someplace smaller."

The man with the shotgun grinned, his eyes hidden behind sunglasses. "Pfft. Pussy."

"I gotta take a leak," the pistol-packing man declared. The others waved him off, snickering. He turned toward the elevator—Brian tucked his head inside and held his breath.

Weighty footsteps headed his way. The disgusting sound of spit being sucked in and spat out followed. The man passed the elevator and disappeared into the corner of the walls. Brian crinkled his nose as the steady stream of the man's piss soaked into the carpet.

Pistol-Packer shook the rest off and zipped up. His footsteps faded away. When all three pairs of feet crunched back through the front door, Brian tipped the back of his head against the elevator door and exhaled. He was in no hurry to follow them out—even if the scent of urine and decay made him want to hold his breath again.

It doesn't matter who they are or what they want—I need to avoid them and move on.

After about five minutes, Brian emerged from the elevator with his bike in tow. He peeked through the window, making sure the coast was clear, then whipped onto the road and pedaled until his feet couldn't take it anymore. He ate his lunch in a diner, tucked in a plush red corner booth surrounded by dead neon lights and chrome accents. Out of habit, he clicked the buttons of a powerless jukebox.

As he glanced at framed portraits of classic Hollywood stars, it occurred to him people had always yearned for the past. Especially a past they'd never lived in—after all, nothing could go wrong in such halcyon-laced dreams.

Despite his awareness of this, the same imaginary time machine sucked Brian into it, sending him back to the occasions he'd eaten at diners with his family. Poppa and Nana had been especially fond of them.

His appetite disappeared, so he put the rest of his food and water away. Apparitions of his smiling grandparents filled the empty booth across from him, and the space beside him burned with the imaginary heat of his sister.

You can't go back. This moment is already the past.

Brian slid out of the booth and left the diner behind.

Brian biked alongside the Mississippi River for what seemed like an endless stretch of time and space. The long silences before had been agonizing, but *this* was hellish. With no one to cover him, he couldn't even listen to music. He had no one to talk to, no one to remind him he wasn't alone in the world.

He followed the river until he heard something—some*one*.

"Hello!"

The way they spoke resembled a parrot miming. Brian shook his head. *It's just phantom noise like I hear sometimes when I'm trying to fall asleep.*

He kept moving. The cheery voice didn't greet him again.

I've only been on the road an hour. Six more and I'll imagine entire conversations!

Brian passed more drab suburbs until an oil refinery disrupted the monotony. The structure towered over the small block buildings with imposing superiority. Thoughts of humanity's future sped through his mind—of creating new power sources, of managing waste, of cleaning water.

Will people ever work together again? Or are we back to being warring Neanderthals?

Were we ever anything more?

When he emerged onto a dirt road surrounded by barren plains, he imagined he was in the past before people even existed. As a child, he'd enjoyed picturing dinosaurs walking amongst civilization, long-necked herbivores munching on trees in yards while carnivores chased cars on roads. He once read someone looking at Earth from a distant planet would see it at the point in history where dinosaurs still roamed. This was a difficult fact to wrap his mind around and made his entire existence seem so pointless.

Great time for an existential crisis, Brian. You're gonna go nuts for real if you don't find other people.

He continued past a drying lake with an alligator sunning beside it. The reptile grinned indifferently; Brian imagined it asking, *"How's your day going? I'm enjoying the sun! Bye-bye!"*

"Now I'm making animals talk too," he muttered, scratching his head with the butt of the revolver.

When he passed a road called Etienne Street, he ached with loneliness. He longed for D's cheery voice, and even though he hadn't gotten to know Antoine well, he missed the man's contagious smile. Everywhere he went, he passed reminders of people he'd known and strangers he'd never meet.

He stopped to relieve himself and heard it again. "Hello!"

Brian zipped his jeans and whipped around, putting his back to the river. A light gust shook the emerging blades of grass. Then silence and stillness again.

He climbed onto his bike and pedaled away. *Did some parrot escape from a zoo? Maybe the "Get out!" parrot from Cayo Levisa followed me.*

Yeah, right. You still have quite the imagination—just like Louis liked to say.

God, I miss his snaggle-toothed smirk.

Brian continued past barren stretches of land until civilization's remnants came into view once more. Plantations were stereotypically prevalent here. An RV park reminded him of raccoons, hot showers, and card games.

Forward, not back. You can never go back.

More houses, more boats, more industrial complexes, more nothing. When he crossed a bridge over the river called Sunshine Bridge, he sighed.

Please be okay, D. All of you.

"Hello!"

He braked hard at the other side of the bridge and glanced behind him. That time, the voice had come from right behind a car parked on the bridge.

It's not in my head. It can't be. Dad wasn't paranoid, just suicidal.

He considered replying, but he pressed on—why would someone waste time following and harassing him? And if they did, they weren't anyone he wanted to meet.

When he turned onto Fourth Street and entered a suburb, something scampered below a wooden fence. He didn't stop to see what; for all he knew, it was a squirrel. His stops needed to be infrequent—moving kept him safe.

"Hello!"

"Oh, for fuck's sake!" His head snapped toward the lawn where the voice had come from. "Leave me alone!"

A child kneeled in front of the steps. Stunned, Brian squeezed the brake and put his feet on the ground. The kid giggled. "Hello!"

This kid's been following me? There's no way it could keep up. Something is really fucking off about this...

But he couldn't leave a child behind. Thoughts of his sister and his inability to save her still haunted him.

"Hey," Brian called, keeping the handgun ahead of him, "are you okay?"

The child dashed into the bushes next to the house. Brian wasn't curious enough to follow. He hurried away, bothered by what he'd witnessed.

Am *I hallucinating?*

While he pedaled along a highway surrounded by forest on one side and yellowed fields of grass on the other, his mind drifted from the uncanny encounter with the giggling child. His feet were shot, and the pain in his nerves crept from his tailbone into his spine.

He stopped to eat and scurried into a small farmhouse next to an elementary school. He sat at an aged wooden table covered with dust and set his things down to give his arms and back a break. When he sank into the chair with a groan, the chair creaked in agreement.

While he ate the tasteless food and chugged the faintly salty water, he glanced through the window. He doubted the men who'd come into the Artist Lofts would've doubled back and caught up to him by now, but he couldn't be sure they didn't have friends lurking within the state.

He tugged at the clothes clinging to his sweaty skin. The cool air had been the only nice thing about winter; now the air was warm and moist during the day. Brian *despised* sweating. He'd gotten used to feeling dirtier than he liked, but sweat made him feel gross.

He swatted at the stagnant air—but his hand froze when a figure stirred in the school parking lot.

Brian stared, not moving a muscle. The small figure hurtled away and vanished.

He rubbed his eyes. *I'm going nuts. I wish someone else was here so I had proof that kid was really there.*

It was time to go, anyway. He packed his things and scooted the chair back under the table out of habit.

"Hello!"

"*Fuck.*" He spun and pressed his back to the table, trying to catch his breath in his thudding chest. He'd shoved a desk in front of the door, but the knob jiggled above it.

It stopped. A knock took its place.

"Hello!"

"I'm losing it…" Brian swept his wet bangs out of his face, vowing to trim them if he found a sharp pair of scissors and some downtime.

The knocking stopped. He crept over to the window and peered through it, keeping a tight grip around his revolver. Although he couldn't spot anything in the bushes, the glass muffled childish giggles.

I don't like it. No kid would be happy to be alone out here. No kid would follow me and harp "hello" like a fucking parrot.

No normal *kid.*

His foot shifted. The child's head jerked out of the bushes.

Brian swallowed. He'd suspected what it was before, but he'd been in denial. He didn't want to imagine what had happened to the children, of what would've happened to his sister. But the black chunk gouged out of the scrawny neck left him unable to deny it.

He had to take care of the kid. It might be playing with him, but it was still dangerous.

As soon as I move, it's gone. Can I lure it?

He jogged upstairs and headed into the bedroom directly above the kitchen. He lifted the window and glanced down. The bushes rustled, but the child was gone.

Figures.

He grabbed a baseball from the bedside table and tossed it into the yard, watching and waiting. This time, he aimed an arrow through the window.

The tiny figure bounced out from behind a tractor and pounced. Brian watched it bend over to grab the ball, draped in a frilly dress. She seemed so human—but even from here, he distinguished flakes of skin peeling from her stretched grin.

Not "she," not "her"—"it."

The arrow sailed into the child's forehead. She slumped into a limp pile, and the ball rolled out of her outstretched hand. *"It," damn it. It it it—*

Brian's eyes stung and blurred as he lowered the bow. A small part of him withered away inside. He had to sit on the bed for a long time, on the verge of tears he never let fall.

He finally forced himself to leave the house and approach the body to retrieve the arrow. He averted his gaze from those glazed, staring eyes and jerked it out of the smiling face with a sickening crunch. Soul-crushing guilt filled the void of his indifference.

It was playing with me, just like a real child. Something remains, at least for some of them. The King changed, but his mind stayed the same. Maybe this—

If he stood there arguing with himself all day, he'd get nowhere. He left the small body behind and cycled back onto the road.

Brian's heavy heart lightened when he rolled up to the wooden fence surrounding Evergreen Plantation. Marie was right: once the leaves returned, the oak trees were truly majestic. A gentle current drifted through the air, tickling his sweat-sticky skin as the leaves rustled and swayed.

An ear-piercing whinny broke the silence. A brown horse with a white spot on its head trotted out to meet him at the gate. Brian scrambled over to meet her, abandoning his metal steed for a flesh-and-blood one.

"Grimes! You remember me, girl?" He pressed his hands to her face and scratched her cheeks. Her snort blew hot air onto him. "D and Antoine made it back with you then, thank God—"

Someone armed with a rifle approached. Brian didn't recognize him, so he moved his hand to the gun tucked into his jeans. The strange man lifted his weapon. "Hold up, kid: I don't know you."

"I'm looking for my friends, D and Antoine. I've been here before—Jacque, Marie, and Cecilia ring any bells for you?"

The man spat to the side, a beacon of stereotypical Southern manliness. His stomach bulged over faded jeans from beneath a "Don't Tread on Me" rattlesnake shirt. "Yeah, I know Jacque and Marie. They keep a roof over my head, and I keep an eye out for Stalkers and strangers. What's your name?"

"Brian Jameson."

The man sniffed. His hair was cut into something resembling a mullet, and he smelled like Poppa's Skoal tobacco. "You're still a l'il bitty baby; how you make it this long?"

Brian's eyes narrowed as he suppressed a smart reply to being called a baby. "Listen, man, I don't have time to stand here telling you the whole story. Just go get someone I mentioned."

Grimes whinnied and nudged the man as if trying to reinforce Brian's point. The man slapped her hard on the nose. "Get outta here, horse!"

Brian's adrenaline spiked as his hand twitched against his gun. "I found her alone in a stable; all the other horses were dead. I wouldn't be here without her, so back off and show her some respect."

The man's thin lips curled into a smirk. "She's just a damn animal. Hold your horses, kid—I'll get one of your buddies." He walked off, snickering as if he'd amused himself with his pun.

Brian glared after him, stroking Grimes's nose when she hung her head over the fence. "I know. He's a jackass. I'll bet D and Antoine hate him. Louis probably would've shot him"—he pressed his nose to hers—"and I woulda loved it."

Eventually, the man reappeared in the driveway with a diminutive figure beside him. When Brian caught the glint of straw-blonde hair in the sun, the brewing bubble of tension within him popped. Cecilia and the redneck guard unlocked the gate.

"I'll be fine," she assured the man with a sweet smile. He grunted and walked away; when she looked at Brian, her smile shrank. She rolled her eyes. "Ugh, I'm sorry you had to deal with Chad. He's new. He's like a caricature, isn't he? There's a Chad everywhere. But you know how Jacque and Marie are—"

Brian wrapped his arms around her, relieved to see a familiar face. Her embrace wasn't strong and comforting like D's, nor did it send pleasurable shivers through his spine like Louis's, but it warmed his soul all the same.

"I'm glad to see you too," she said as they parted. She glanced around, taking in the fallen bike—and Louis's absence. Far too considerate to mention it, Cecilia curled her arm through Brian's and led him through the gate. "Let's get you settled. You probably want a bath, right?"

He groaned, leading his bike with his free arm. "God, yes. Is it bad I almost miss winter?"

She laughed musically. "The humidity *is* quite miserable now." They walked arm in arm with Grimes at their heels. The light shining through the tree leaves created dappled shadows on the ground. The atmosphere evoked the sensation of drifting through a dream.

When they reached the Big House, a tinny trilling escalated into an insistent meow. An orange cat zoomed into view and weaved around Brian's legs. He let go of Cecilia and kneeled to ruffle Jonesy's fur. "Jones! I missed you, you furry jerk!" He looked at Cecilia with a hesitant smile. "D and Antoine are here, right?"

Cecilia nodded. "D's helping with supper, and Antoine's working with the animals." When she helped him up, his entire body ached. "They're so lovely. We were happy they arrived, but we still worried about you. They explained where you went, so I hoped for the best." She led him into the house—after Jonesy dashed in and nearly tripped them both—and escorted him to the bathroom. "I'll take your things and put them in your old cabin for you. While you're bathing, I'll let everyone know you're back."

"No matter what"—Brian reached for her arm as she retrieved his bags—"don't let D bust in here, okay? She'll try. We're good friends, but I don't exactly want her to catch an eyeful."

Cecilia laughed. "I'll keep her busy, but I can't make any promises." She winked and headed for the door, bearing the burden of his belongings. She paused while she pulled the door shut behind her. "I'm beyond glad to see you again, Brian. I prayed to the Good God on your behalf. If this isn't proof he answers those prayers, I don't know what is."

She shut the door. Brian set up the bath and sank into the warm water, practically feeling the dirt, sweat, and stress melt away. Unfortunate echoes remained of his time here with Louis, but there were pleasant memories of Cecilia and D to balance it out.

They're all here... I can't believe it.

He pinched himself. For once, pain was a welcome relief.

Drawing Blood

Chapter Three

Evergreen, Redux

3/10, Edgard, Louisiana, Evergreen Plantation, 5:47 p.m.

As soon as Brian entered his old cabin, a pair of dark arms ensnared him and crushed the air out of his lungs. "Sunshine!" D withdrew, scrutinizing him while he sucked in a sharp gasp of air. "You look skinny, baby! That island not all it was cracked up to be?"

Brian struggled to catch his breath; the embrace of the Etiennes was not to be underestimated. "I...guess not. But...my ribs...might be."

"Boy, I didn't crack no ribs—well, maybe your back." D curled a hand around her hip and arched her eyebrows. "Cill said you was alone. Where's Louis?"

Straight to the point, as always. Thanks, D.

Brian glanced at the wall where he'd been unable to resist Louis's flustered pout. He pressed his lips together, a phantom flush of heat burning his cheeks and chest. "I left him."

D clicked her tongue. "That's vague. I'm gonna need deets."

"I think it's best if I tell everybody at once. They'll ask, and I'd rather not tell the same story a zillion times."

D's tight curls bounced when she shook her head. She managed a strained smile. "Well, supper's about ready anyhow. Jacque and Marie'll want to see you."

They walked out and shut the door, leaving the cabin with its haunts. "How long it take you to get here?" D asked. "And how long you tough it out on Gilligan's Island?"

"About three weeks, maybe four. It took me another week to make it back here." He gripped her arm. "Thanks for leaving me the key and stuff."

She patted his hand. "Call it women's intuition, but I had a feeling you'd be itchin' to get back before long. Cabin fever, island fever—same thing. No one likes to feel trapped."

They padded through lush grass until they climbed up the stairs into the Big House. They walked into the dining room while the dishes and utensils were being set. A few faces Brian recognized saw him and smiled. He smiled back, but he wasn't as happy as he should've been.

Eva should've been here. She would've liked it. She would've liked them, liked D and Antoine, and the animals too.

Time and distance allowed Brian to acknowledge his grandfather's presence would have prevented him from forming friendships with many of the people he'd met. He didn't want to think about what Poppa might have done to D or anyone else—about what Louis rightfully suspected Poppa would have done to *him*. Brian could justify what Louis had done to Poppa as preemptive self-defense, but Eva was another story entirely.

But I didn't give Louis enough time to tell it.

"Sit a spell." D urged him over to a chair. "You been on the move for a while. We can talk while I help them."

"How long ago did you get here?" Brian asked as D buzzed around the room assisting the others. He grazed his fingers along the utensils before him, realizing how lucky he was to be back.

"About five days after you set sail on the Love Boat." D looked up and caught Brian's glare. "Are these TV Land references goin' over your little blond head?" He arched his eyebrows and lifted his hand, urging her to continue. "Okay, *okay*! Well, Bro and I made it back to his place, packed, set things up for you, and left—didn't want to waste no time. Gettin' here wasn't too tricky: just had to bump off a few nasties but no groups or nothin'. Good ol' Grimes and Missus Periwinkle—that's what I named my bike—done a good job keepin' us movin'."

"How are things here?"

"Not much different; we ain't had to go lookin' for no Turned yet, but we helped 'em scavenge a few places. Tougher now, though; everything's picked clean around here."

"I saw people. Three guys armed and dressed in jury-rigged armor."

D paused, a fork still in her hand. "How close?"

"Not far from New Orleans. They were on foot."

She set the fork down. "They got a couple new Guardians. Cill said you met Chad. Salty little cracker, ain't he?" She finished helping with the place settings and walked behind him to give his shoulders a reassuring squeeze. "I know it won't be easy to adjust. But you have us. We'll help you."

"He's not *dead*," Brian blurted with an unintentional edge to his voice. He said nothing else since more people were settling at the table.

D sat in silence beside him. Cecilia entered the room and offered a consolatory smile as she sat at his other side. Antoine slipped through the front door not long after, but before Brian could even wave at him, D jumped and nearly knocked her chair down.

"Bro! Look who's back!"

"I know, Dee-Dee—Cill told me." Antoine held out his arms as he approached them. "Boy, get over here and give me a hug!"

Brian obliged him. There was something inherently reassuring in the strong embrace of a kind man like Antoine. He wanted to sink into it and escape his thoughts, but he retreated and sat.

He didn't get to sit for long: Marie and Jacque entered with broad smiles and outstretched arms. He embraced them, supposing he should be happy people cared enough to want to hug him—and that he even had people *to* hug.

"What a surprise and a pleasure to see you again, my child!" When Marie parted from him, a sweet scent tickled his nose.

Jacque gripped Brian's shoulders; his rich and earthy scent contrasted with Marie's. "You've lost weight, son! Sit, eat—we'll speak during supper."

Brian sat for the final time and watched the group bring in the serving dishes. *How long will they have enough food to sustain them? They have animals and a greenhouse, and since spring is around the corner, the gardens will grow... But what if bad people come here?*

Or worse.

They joined hands. D gripped Brian's left hand like before, but Cecilia's soft, lukewarm palm replaced Louis's threaded fingers and the slight stroke of his thumb. Over time, Brian had grown so accustomed to the intimacy between them he didn't notice it. But once Louis was gone, it became clear to Brian nothing could replace him.

Jacque and Marie blessed the dinner. Everyone ate after a communal "Amen."

While Brian was working on a mouthful of beans, Marie spoke. "So, Brian, what brings you back? And if I may ask, where is your companion?"

He held up a finger while he tried to rush his chewing. Once he swallowed the lump, he answered, figuring he might as well air his dirty laundry before anyone dug through it. "We made it to the island, but I left him there." He dropped his fork onto his plate, his appetite diminishing. "It meant different things to us. I thought it'd be an escape, but I ended up needing to escape *him*."

"He seemed terribly insecure." Marie offered Brian a gracious smile. "It was obvious he feared losing you more than anything. It isn't bad to have someone care for you so strongly."

Brian took a swig of room-temperature water; he found the lack of salty aftertaste refreshing. "Did he really, though? When his parents wouldn't let us hang out anymore because I got mad and cut his face during a birthday party, he set fire to their house and they burned to death. The grandfather who took him in used to beat him and threatened to rob me and my grandfather after everything went to hell, so he used a Stalker attack as an excuse to say his grandfather was infected and take him out. And when we fled those robbers in Missouri, he let me think his sister was dead so he could leave her behind. I'm still not entirely sure *why*—maybe because he was tired of looking after her, maybe because he resented her, maybe because she liked me and he didn't like *that*." Brian hid his hands beneath the table and dug underneath his fingernails. "We were already on the island when he got drunk and told me all this. Said he couldn't keep it from me anymore. I couldn't trust him, so I had to leave. I have to go back for Eva."

No one said anything for a while. The only sounds in the room were the scrapes of knives and forks against ceramic.

A thoughtful expression spread across Marie's face. "It sounds to me like you left your mark on him long before you reunited. You're the motivation behind most of his actions. If anything, it's a case of caring too *much*."

This implication both overwhelmed and intimidated Brian to the point where he couldn't form a reply, only give Marie a stupefied look and pick at his stolen watch underneath the table.

Sensing this, Jacque changed the subject. "When will you leave to look for Eva?"

"Not right away. I need to think about some things, unwind, resupply." Brian gave the watch a final twist and tilted his head back. He studied the cobweb-coated ceiling, imagining all the history those beams of wood were a silent witness to. "Kids turn too. I killed one about two hours out from here."

The ambient conversation cut off completely, replaced by several stunned murmurs.

"It talked to me. Said 'hello' over and over like some parrot." Brian returned his attention to his dining companions. "It followed me. Hid, like it was playing a game. I don't know if it's because it was a kid, but I don't think they're all gone inside. Not always. One broke into our bungalow on the island, stole a can of SPAM, and ran for it. It made a nest in a ship, had been eating all the other people on the island and some of the wildlife. When we found it, it held its hands over its face and said 'no' like it didn't want us to kill it."

A grave expression creased Jacque's dignified face. "I read the disease eats at a certain portion of the brain. But others remain such as motor control. I never understood why the bodies degrade so rapidly, if it's to do with neglect or biology. Perhaps in some, the affected areas are less impacted—or not at all."

"It's been over a year now," Brian said. "They're still around, and their patterns are changing. Did D and Antoine tell you about the group that ambushed us?"

Marie and Jacque nodded.

"If they're intelligent enough to plan, to form groups, they're just as bad as people." Brian shoved his chair back with a grating squeak. "What you have here is nice, but between the Stalkers and other survivors, it won't last. You should move on. You're too close to Baton Rouge, and I saw armed men when I passed through New Orleans."

D nodded. "Resources are gonna run out faster than you can make 'em. I know you wanna help people, but that well water's gonna dry out unless a damn hurricane hits again. People and Stalkers are venturing out now since the snow's all gone, and sooner or later they gonna find this place. I'm gonna go with Brian and see if we can find somewhere else to set up."

"I'm goin' with her," Antoine said before Brian could object to D's declaration. "I ain't gonna worry about her again like I done while I was waitin' on her in New Orleans."

Brian met the determined gazes of the Etienne siblings. "Guys, you don't need to go with me. I can look for a place, and you never even met Eva—"

D cleared her throat and laced her hands atop the table. "There's no way I'd ever let you leave here without going with you."

"Brian and D are right: one way or another, the Turned or other survivors will come for us—not all of them good." Cecilia's gentle voice sounded hushed even in the silence. "I'd like to help them look for Louis's sister, and if we find somewhere else to go, we can come back and guide you to it."

Jacque and Marie shared a glance and a resigned smile.

"Of course you can go, Cecilia," Marie said. "You're right: we've been here far too long without anything coming for us. Best not push our luck. We have the bus in the back and a reserve of fuel for emergencies. But we'll wait for you to return and prepare in the meantime. I imagine it might take you several weeks to travel there and back, given all goes well."

Brian's exhaustion kicked in since his stomach was full. He lost all interest in discussing this weighty topic and gained an interest in flopping onto his old bed. "May I be excused? I'm beat."

Marie flashed him a sympathetic smile. "Certainly."

"Thanks for everything." Brian pushed his chair in and lifted his dirty dishes. He bussed them back to the kitchen after bidding the group good night.

When he returned to his cabin, he dug into his backpack and retrieved the map. He retraced the path he and Louis had taken after running from the fairground. Trying not to live in the past was difficult while literally revisiting it.

Before long, someone knocked on the door. "It's Cecilia. May I come in?"

He twirled the pencil in his fingers. "Go ahead."

She opened the door and walked in, shutting it after an intrusive orange guest forced his way in. Jonesy pounced onto the bed and instantly attempted to curl onto Brian's map. Cecilia sat opposite Brian with Jonesy in the middle, right where he wanted to be. He curled onto his back and swatted at Brian's toes.

"He missed you," Cecilia said. "So did Grimes. She used to stand near the driveway watching for you, right where she was when I came to meet you."

"I should go see her." Brian scratched Jonesy's soft white belly. "I missed her. And you too, Jones—even if you're ruining my map." He glanced at Cecilia. "You really don't have to come with me. I don't think I can change D's mind—and Antoine, by proxy—but you're safer here. Plus, these are the people you know and love. It'll be hard to leave them."

Cecilia looked at the ceiling, lips pressed together. A sigh fluttered through them. "Brian, you miss him, don't you?"

His hand froze on Jonesy's belly. He stared at Cecilia through narrowed eyes. "Why're you asking me that?"

She let another sigh slip out, this time more exasperated. "Listen, even if D *hadn't* said anything to me, it was pretty obvious you guys were more than friends. The day you left, I bumped into him coming out of your cabin as I was coming out of mine. Serendipitous timing, I suppose, for him to give me a boastful smirk while he waltzed into his cabin with no shirt, unbuttoned jeans, and a bad case of bedhead."

Brian recalled this morning with vivid clarity. He glanced at Jonesy's twitching tail and the bed they sat on, which was the same bed he'd shared with Louis the night before they left Evergreen. "Do you want me to tell you every sordid detail or what? I already had to deal with D sticking *her* nose into it."

Cecilia poked his foot with hers. "Don't get fussy with me!" She glanced at the image of twilight-dappled trees framed by the window. A moment of silence passed, allowing Brian's prickly temper to dull. "Was he your first?"

"First *what*?" Brian's eyebrows arched. "Time? Boyfriend? Breakup? All of the above."

Cecilia tilted her head, straight blonde hair cascading over her shoulder. "I broke up with Matthew, my first and only boyfriend. His love for me was so strong it suffocated me. I couldn't believe things hadn't worked out, but I went back and forth trying to convince myself it was for the best, that our codependency was unhealthy. I missed him so much it *hurt*. I just wanted to lie in bed listening to sad songs. Sometimes I'd pull up his number on my phone, finger hovering over the screen, because I wanted to hear his voice again. But I didn't call him until after the outbreak, and he didn't pick up. I listened to his voicemail greeting and cried until every muscle in my body ached."

She let the silence linger so Brian could absorb what she'd said. Jonesy jumped off the bed in pursuit of some invisible bug.

"I'll never know if I made the right decision." Cecilia sniffed, eyes glinting, tightening her fingers into the sheets. "Living with regret is a struggle every day. And it's not just limited to him: there are things I wish I'd said to my parents, to my brother, to my friends... And I never got the chance to."

Brian leaned forward to embrace her. Her body trembled, but she didn't break down. His shoulder muffled her shaky sighs until she withdrew and wiped her eyes dry with enviable strength and composure.

"At least you know where he is," she said. "Not knowing is the worst part."

Insects buzzed outside the window as the descending sun cast dim orange radiance onto everything in the room.

"You know the feeling you get when you've just had company over and you've gotten used to them being there?" Brian searched Cecilia's patient gaze. "When they leave and there's this emptiness and silence where they should be? I feel it all the time now."

Cecilia flopped back on the bed and laced her fingers over the swell of her stomach. "I don't know if I would've made it without Jacque and Marie. The connections we make in this world are everything; they provide more nourishment than food and water."

Brian lay beside her and stared at the ceiling—the last time he'd stared at it, Louis's head had been buried in his shoulder. Although Cecilia was lying next to him, he couldn't bring himself to reach out and touch her. His stomach ached when he thought, *I'll never be that close to anyone again.*

Instead, she reached for him. She curled her hand around his, but their fingers didn't intertwine. "He might have done some horrible things, but at least he told you. It was a way for him to bare his soul to you, you know. I'm not trying to make excuses for him, but it shows whatever you had with him was real. So don't beat yourself up over it."

Brian wormed his hand out from hers and held it tight to his side, unable to bear the inferior substitution of her grip. "He killed my grandfather, Cecilia. He shot him in the dark, let me think a group of raiders did it. He said he was scared my grandfather would kill him, that he didn't believe Louis's story about why he killed *his* grandfather. I hate myself for thinking it, but he was probably right. My grandfather slit a woman's throat right in front of me and slaughtered unarmed villagers in Vietnam to keep himself alive. But he was my grandfather, the man who protected me after I lost the rest of my family, and Louis kept it from me for months. He looked into my eyes and told me he loved me even though he knew he'd done these awful things." Brian finally forced his stinging eyes to meet Cecilia's. "How could he do that?"

Cecilia's brow furrowed, and her pale lips parted, but she didn't answer until an agonizing moment of silence passed. "Well, maybe he didn't know he loved you when he did those things. And when he realized he *did*, he knew it was the right thing to tell you. He knew it would drive you away—probably the one thing he feared most—but he did it anyway because you don't hide the truth from someone you love."

This time Brian allowed the silence to linger.

"He did a good job of hiding it for a while, but he's an intensely emotional person," Cecilia said. "I think everything he did until that point was out of fear. We were all scared after what happened—most of us still *are*. I'm terrified to lose any of my friends. And you... Well, you were everything to him. And now he's lost you. If he's half as clever as I think he is, he'll have learned something from this. And if he's half as determined as I *know* he is, he won't stay on that island for long."

When Cecilia voiced the possibility Brian had been mulling over, his heart fluttered. The prospect of reuniting with Louis at some point both thrilled and intimidated him beyond measure.

"I have no doubt he'd be able to find you again," Cecilia said. "He'd look here first. But do you want him to?"

Brian's heavy eyelids fluttered, blocking the wooden ceiling beams he'd been studying. While he contemplated the answer to her question, the soothing void of sleep beckoned to him.

The bedsprings creaked as Cecilia leaned over and pressed a light kiss to Brian's forehead. Her hair tickled his skin. The floral scent of shampoo reminded him of when his mother used to tuck him into bed after her baths.

By the time he arrived at the answer to Cecilia's question, she'd left. He descended into the abyss with it lingering in his mind: *Yes, I'd want to see him—because I can only be with my family in my dreams, and I don't want to keep dreaming about* him.

Out of habit, Brian checked his watch when he woke. His eyes widened as the significance of the date clicked in his groggy mind.

It's my birthday.

He'd spent his last birthday with Nana, Poppa, and Rocky. It was hard for him to believe a year had passed since then, that a devastating pandemic had wiped out most of the population and all his relatives. That he'd encountered Louis, Eva, and all the others between then and now. The past year felt longer and more meaningful than the entirety of his life before it.

Brian turned and pulled the covers over him. The brilliance of the outside world beckoned to him, begging him to wake and greet the day, but he longed to linger in the world of memories and shadows.

I can't stay here forever. Everything ends eventually: life, the universe, my time in this bed.

Brian threw the sheet off and sat, still dressed in his clothes from the day before. Cecilia had been too modest to undress him. D would've just torn everything off.

He stepped outside and puttered across the yard without a thought in his mind other than the need to use the outhouse. Everything seemed quiet—*too* quiet. He reached for the revolver in the waistband of his jeans.

Everyone's probably in the Big House eating breakfast.

Inhaling, he flung the outhouse door open—but nothing jumped out at him, so he finished his business and crossed the lawn into the Big House.

The unusual silence and stillness of the building alarmed him. He kept his handgun in front of him as he pushed the dining room doors open. Dozens of figures popped up from under the table like whack-a-mole targets. He aimed his gun to the tune of a "*Surprise!*" which rapidly dwindled in enthusiasm.

"What the *fuck*?" He lowered it when he recognized their faces.

D jogged over to him, cringing as she put her hands on his tensed shoulders. "You okay? We thought you'd feel safe here!"

"I don't feel safe *anywhere*!" He tucked the gun into his jeans and dragged his hands down his face. "Why am I being surprised?"

"It's yo' birthday, isn't it? I thought the timin' worked out, that the Good God got you back here right on time for you to celebrate it. And it was my job to make sure you had one worth celebratin'!"

Brian's hands fell from his face. "How did you know?"

"It came up in conversation with Louis-boy one time. We was talkin' about zodiac signs and all that. Figures he's a Scorpio and you're a Pisces..."

She prattled on; Brian was still hung up on the fact Louis remembered his birthday and he and D had carried on a civil conversation at some point.

"I'm sorry I aimed a gun at you." Brian streaked his hand through his bangs while he absorbed the sight of a breakfast banquet on the table with a cake smack-dab in the middle. "A cake? Wow. Just...wow. Who made it?"

Antoine clapped a hand onto Cecilia's slender shoulder. "Your girl Cill stayed up all night bakin' it."

"Shush!" Cecilia slapped his hand, but a bashful grin broke out on her face as she looked back at Brian. "D mentioned your birthday was today, so I thought it'd be nice to have a cake. Jacque and Marie agreed. The chickens have been laying eggs, and we have a butter-churn here, so..."

"They practically Amish!" D enthused.

Yet again, Brian pinched himself; these joyful occasions were more unrealistic than the dreary world he'd acclimated to. "Woah. Thanks. All of you. I don't really deserve it, but..."

"You put up with Louis's ass for months." D curled an arm around his shoulder. "Even if you *got* some ass in the end, that shit wasn't exactly even-steven. Trust me: you deserve it." She led him to a chair in front of the cake and made him sit, fussing at Jonesy when he tried to jump onto the table.

Reassured they weren't going to be shot, everyone bustled about, some sitting in their seats while others ran to the kitchen. Two crappy plastic candles jutted out from the cake. There was no frosting, but something once taken for granted was a luxury now—as many things were.

Marie ran over to it, brandishing a box of matches. She struck one and brought it to the candles. "We didn't have many, so imagine each one represents ten."

The fluttering flame cast warmth in his direction. "Thank you—" A swell of panic made Brian freeze and stare up at her. "Please don't sing. Really. I'll cover my face and dive under the table."

Marie smiled, assuming he was joking. The longer she stared, the more her smile shrank. She gripped his shoulder. "We won't sing if you don't want us to, but please know we're glad we can be here with you to celebrate another year of survival."

"There's an old saying: 'Cry at birth, laugh at death.' You have already shed your tears, son." Jacque dug into the pocket of his slacks and dropped something into Brian's hand, and then leaned close to his ear. "In voodoo, carrying a lucky coin protects you from evil spirits. Take this and put it in your pocket; show it to no one."

Brian thought this was part of the mysticism of the tradition—but when he opened his fist, he knew why Jacque didn't want him to show it to anyone. Inside was a gold coin with foreign characters and people posed in sexual positions.

He stuffed the coin in his pocket and looked at Jacque. "Thanks. Where, uh, where did you get that?"

Jacque grinned and elbowed him. "I used to sell 'em back in the day at the voodoo shop."

Brian almost asked if Jacque had been Reverend Zombie himself, but Marie sat at his other side and gave Jacque a wry smile. "My gift to you is more traditional." She passed Brian a golden cross on a chain and folded his hand over it. "It's your choice whether you wear it or not, but I want it to remind you I pray for your well-being."

He smiled and looked between the two. "I can't thank you enough—for everything."

Their hands on his shoulders filled him with a warm swell of reassurance. Foregoing the pomp of the "Happy Birthday" song, Brian prepared to blow out the candles to a chorus of supportive claps.

I hope everyone here will be okay while we're gone, and we find a safe place for them somewhere. That nothing happens to D, 'Toine, and Cill on the way. That we find Eva and she's okay.

Louis crossed his mind, but Brian gripped the cross and blew before he could wish for anything else.

Everyone sank into a food coma, just like Brian's family at Thanksgiving. He spent the rest of the day trying to relax and eventually succeeding. Each smile he shared with D and the others reinforced how lucky he was to have them, to be here, to be *present* in this existence. No matter what horrors awaited him outside, the bonds he shared with his friends nourished him exactly as Cecilia said.

Over the next week and a half, Brian worked out a plan with D and Antoine, mapping out their route back to Joplin. He went with them to procure supplies for the B.E.N., bringing Cecilia to acclimate her to their routine. She managed to kill a Stalker in a grocery store, though Brian's astonishment shamed him. This sexism was more characteristic of Louis.

He wasn't really sexist—he just didn't think anyone was competent except for himself. I had to fight for him to let me do anything.

While they were gone, the B.E.N. would build their supplies and begin planning to relocate. Brian suggested they set some of the traps Poppa had taught him. He left the notes for them and helped build two pits with what they had, but until they found more, they lacked supplies for anything more complicated. They agreed to wait for six weeks for Brian's group to return; if they didn't arrive by then, Marie and Jacque would uproot to an old school Marie worked at in Northern Louisiana.

Brian felt guilty for taking Cecilia and the Etiennes from them, but Marie and Jacque insisted they'd be fine. They remained unerringly supportive. Jacque reminded Brian, with a wink, about the stock of good-luck coins he still owned. Brian smiled and studied Marie's exasperated reaction, recalling his parents' interactions when things had been better between them.

I guess this pandemic brought all sorts of people together. Maybe some good came from it—or we made something good out of it, at least.

After the B.E.N. were comfortably outfitted, Brian and the others focused on equipping themselves. D, Antoine, and Cecilia all possessed their own belongings from before their time at Evergreen, though they had to stock up on food and water. Brian had his bike, and Cecilia would take Missus Periwinkle while D and Antoine rode Grimes. Jonesy wouldn't be coming along this time; they had to shut him indoors to keep him from following them.

"I can hear him meowin'." D sniffed back tears. "He's clawin' at the door for me!"

Antoine's expression was a pitch-perfect copy of D's "boy, please" face. "He wants the horse, not you."

"It's strange to leave it all behind." Cecilia sighed. "This place has been my home for nearly a year, and these people have become my family."

"You can turn back," Brian said. "I'll understand."

Cecilia glared at him as a dandelion tuft floated by her pale face. "You're family too. Besides, it's good to get out and have something to do for a change. I may not be as skilled as the rest of you, but I'm no helpless damsel."

There was no arguing with her, so Brian let it go with a smile. "There's no shame in being a helpless damsel. *I* even felt like one for a while."

Grimes trotted on Brian's other side beneath the shade of overlapping oak limbs. "Only 'cause *someone* treated you like one," D said. "I ain't gonna baby your ass like he did. You either, Cill—we all got to be equals here, look out for each other."

"You got it!" Cecilia held up her palm. D slapped it, making both women giggle with shared glee. Antoine shook his head, but he caught Brian's gaze and grinned back at him.

The sun beamed before them with the promise of brighter days, highlighting sprouts of life breaking through the once-frozen earth.

Au revoir, Evergreen. I hope I'll see you again.

Chapter Four

Shadows

3/21, Outskirts of Baton Rouge, Louisiana, late afternoon

The oppressive afternoon heat made Brian long for the dry chill of winter. He wiped his brow, unable to ignore the tickle of trickling sweat and the throbbing ache in his legs—not to mention the numbness of his ass. Despite any compliments once directed at it, it wasn't cushioned enough to comfortably endure hours stuck on a bike seat.

Northern Louisiana might as well be Arkansas: farmland, churches, and not a whole lot else. I need a break.

When they stopped to eat and refresh themselves outside town, Antoine wandered off alone to relieve his bladder, a prideful man not unlike Poppa. Brian remained with Grimes and the bicycles while D and Cecilia took care of themselves.

They returned before Antoine. D's nonexistent patience made her fold her arms, fidget, and finally let out an exaggerated sigh. "He must be droppin' a deuce. I should go check on his ass. Literally."

Cecilia's nose crinkled. "Thanks for the visual, D."

Grimes nickered and pawed the ground. Brian studied the thicket Antoine had disappeared behind but didn't see anything awry.

D straightened her back and cracked her neck. She hefted the shotgun. "Y'all stay here. You'll hear me hollerin' or shootin' if I need help—or toilet paper."

"Are you sure—?"

D cut Brian off with a firm look. "Stay here with Cill. I got this." She marched off with an assured expression, but Brian spotted her underlying concern.

Cecilia frowned while she brushed Grimes's haunch. "I have a bad feeling about this."

As D disappeared into the foliage, a slight breeze cooled their sticky skin and made the blades of grass around their feet ripple. A bluebird chased a yellow butterfly, chirping with determination.

Brian was about to go after D when she burst forth from the woods waving her arms. They dropped their bikes and rushed over to her. Despite D's panicked demeanor, she appeared unhurt.

"Someone took him!" she said, out of breath. "I seen the footprints—they fresh. At least three pairs. Musta caught him off guard."

I knew *I should've gone with him.* Brian tried to contain his frustration. "Do the footprints lead anywhere?"

D nodded. "I know it's gonna take you off your path, slow you down—"

"I'm the reason he came." Brian started for the clearing. "Let's go."

D and Cecilia followed him into the woods. Cracked twigs and bent bushes were scattered around the prints she pointed out. If a group of Stalkers had attacked, there would have been a frenzy of noise: yelling, cackling, gunfire. People had taken him, probably snuck up on him, held a gun to him, and told him to be quiet—but *why*?

After doubling back for their transportation, they tracked the footprints and disturbances in the earth to the outskirts of an old dairy farm. Fields of grass stretched over flat land surrounded by a faded wooden fence, broken in places from livestock forcing their way out.

Cecilia peeked through a rifle Jacque had loaned her. "There's a barn with a silo, an old farmhouse, and a windmill." She elbowed Brian and handed him the rifle. "Quick—look right."

He took it and stared through the scope at another building, maybe an old schoolhouse. A row of four or five people filed in and out. They carried something, but Brian couldn't identify what.

He handed the rifle to D while he tried to plan. When Louis was around, Brian usually agreed to everything he suggested. Now he had to think not only for himself but for D and Cecilia. Antoine's safety depended on them.

"We shouldn't make a move until nightfall," Brian said. "The sun sets in about an hour; they'll lower their guards because they'll assume no one's followed by then." He placed a hand on D's arm. "I know it'll be hard to wait, D, but if we rush in now, we might put him in more danger. It's better to find him first, keep an eye on him."

"No, you right." D smoothed her hands over her glistening face. "When it's dark, we can sneak up close, hide. These fields don't give no cover. And if they try anything before then, we'll go in with guns blazin'."

Brian nodded. "Let's tie Grimes up here so they don't see her. We'll hide the bikes in the bushes. We'd have to make our getaway on foot, but I think we'll end up having to kill them anyway."

"What about negotiating?" Cecilia asked.

Brian shook his head. "I don't know what they want Antoine for, but I doubt anyone who runs around abducting people is going to negotiate. They'd ask us to lower our weapons or give them up, and we can't risk it. And if we leave them alive, they'll probably come after us."

"You did learn *somethin'* good from that boy..." D winced and swatted at a fly. It buzzed away frantically. "Brian's right: we don't negotiate. We get close, see what their setup is and how many there are, then get 'Toine out and kill these pricks."

"We'll move for the barn first, hug the buildings," Brian said. "Search the farmhouse last—it's probably where they'll be."

They hid Grimes and the bikes, then scurried over to the barn in the fading auburn glow of the sun. Cecilia kept the rifle slung over her shoulder and grasped a semiauto pistol. D clutched the shotgun in both hands while Brian held the bow in front of him. It took him about a second to withdraw and string an arrow by this point.

They huddled underneath a high window on the side of the barn facing away from the farmhouse. Brian hefted Cecilia onto his shoulders so she could look through while D watched out for them.

Cecilia tapped his shoulder. When he lowered her to the ground, she whispered, "Hay and troughs with nasty water in them. Nothing else."

They moved to the schoolhouse. The windows were lower, so they were able to peek through them as a group. Cecilia gasped while D and Brian struggled to make out the scene before them.

Several children sat in rows of desks lit by the flickering radiance of an oil lantern. They were duct-taped to the chairs and bags covered their heads. *There are only two reasons: to keep them from seeing something or to keep them from being seen.*

A horrified expression contorted D's face. Cecilia's eyes were practically the size of small saucers. Brian's thoughts flashed to the "hello" child and Becky, but he wouldn't allow fear to freeze him.

He gestured to the farmhouse with a jerk of his head. "Let's look for Antoine there."

They scurried over as the last rays of sunlight faded into the shadows. The dull blush of moonlight soon illuminated the sparse field. When they reached the farmhouse, they leaned against the brick wall beneath the window. Brian glanced through, surveying a rustic kitchen which seemed deceptively innocuous—until someone stepped through the doorway.

He ducked below the window. The trio flattened themselves against the wall and held their breath.

"Ah," a deep male voice echoed from inside, "fresh evenin' air."

"Just need a pie on the sill," a female joined in. Their voices drifted away.

Brian clung to the bow with sweating hands.

Footsteps squeaked, and dishes clattered inside. "How are the kids?"

"Quiet. I think they're bored."

"Good thing we brought them some presents."

Silence settled over the kitchen.

Brian poked his head over the cracked window. The kitchen was tidy despite the dust clinging to most of its contents. Beyond it, a lantern illuminated a set of stairs and the front door of the house. A plank of wood kept it wedged shut from the inside.

A pair of feet appeared on the stairs, descending from the second floor. Brian ducked his head as footsteps thundered onto the floorboards. Someone lifted the plank and pushed the front door open.

Brian's group scurried to the side of the farmhouse. Shadow-cloaked figures trekked over to the schoolhouse. One was clearly being shoved along against their will.

"We gotta follow them," D said.

Brian grabbed her arm. "We should check inside the house while it's clear."

D narrowed her eyes. "I need eyes on my bro. You go on ahead. Take Cill."

"We won't leave you alone—" Cecilia started to say, but D tapped her hand against her shotgun.

"If you hear this, come runnin'. Best make sure no one's gonna get the drop on us, anyway. If they all in that schoolhouse, we can take 'em out in one go."

Brian grabbed Cecilia's arm while D hurried to the schoolhouse. He tugged her back to the cracked window, pushed it up, and climbed through. When he helped her in after him, the wooden floor groaned under their combined weight.

Cecilia withdrew a flashlight from her backpack and clicked it on. They swept the first floor, creeping past ceramic knickknacks of pigs and chickens, photographs of a smiling elderly couple, and an award for Best of Show tacked to a framed photo of a shining black cow. Thoughts of Agnes and Hildy tormented Brian; he never thought he'd mourn the loss of a cow as much as the loss of a person.

Brian and Cecilia left behind the dusty rocking chairs and embroidered throw pillows and headed up the stairs. Cecilia handed Brian the flashlight and stayed in the hall to keep an eye out while he inspected the rooms.

An old bedroom, the blanket swept back and a teddy bear tossed onto the floor. A bathroom with a ceramic tub, no shower curtain—*Thank God*. A spare room with a loom and a washing tub in it for laundry. All of it empty, save for the reminders of an elderly couple who'd lived a simple but proud life.

No bodies. Either they died elsewhere, or they left.

"Brian!" Cecilia hissed. He turned with an arrow aimed at her face. Without another word, she shoved him into the bedroom and shut the door. She squeezed into a cramped closet between him and folded linens.

"Someone's coming up," she whispered. Her slender body quivered against his, reminding him of the closet in Earl's house with Eva.

Brian focused on the approaching footsteps. They creaked in the hall outside the bedroom. When he turned off the flashlight, pitch-black darkness swallowed them.

The bedroom door squeaked open. A sliver of light lit the gap under the closet door. Cecilia aimed her pistol, the contours of her heart-shaped face glowing from the light slipping through the crack in the closet. Brian barely had enough room to pull the bowstring back.

"I knew I was forgettin' somethin'," a male voice muttered, thick with a Louisiana accent. A shadow sliced the bright slit under the closet door. It retreated, footsteps moving into the bedroom again.

Brian swept the closet door open and sent a swift arrow into the back of the man's neck. He hunched forward, a lantern tumbling to the ground alongside the teddy bear. The stranger spun and clawed at the arrow tip emerging from his throat, gurgling as blood spurted between his fingers.

Cecilia's wide eyes moved to Brian's. "Why... Why did you do that?"

"One less to worry about." He moved closer to the middle-aged man's dirty body. Blood pooled around his neck and head as his mouth opened and closed. Brian conjured images of fish flopping on a dock, struggling to breathe. He waited until the man was still to retrieve his arrow.

He snagged the lantern and gestured for Cecilia to follow him, noticing her stunned expression but not dwelling on it. They hurried back to D, who remained crouched under the schoolhouse window. Brian peered through the window beside her. The children wriggled, fighting to get out of their chairs. Some had fallen over onto their sides. Eyeholes were cut into the sacks covering their faces, and smiles were painted over where their mouths would be.

Two adults stood in front of the group of seated children. Another lingered near a chair: a figure dressed in a Santa costume was taped to it like the children were taped to theirs. Despite the poor lighting and fake beard, Brian distinguished Antoine's dark skin and bright glare.

Why bother dressing him up and putting him in front of a bunch of children? The King and his group wouldn't bother with kids; the Stalker in the rabbit costume was just their sick version of humor.

Brian couldn't make out what the people were saying. They kept pointing at a lumpy knapsack between Antoine's feet. Brian ducked before the kidnappers could notice him.

"Cecilia," he whispered, "take the rifle and shoot the lantern."

D's eyes flashed in the dark. "What if the fire gets 'Toine?"

"We get them first while they're distracted. Plus, he's strong enough to bust out of the chair while they're busy looking for who fired the gun."

Cecilia backed away and lifted the scope to her eye. "What about the kids, Brian?"

"The fire won't reach them right away. If they're even healthy, we'd have time to save them." He hesitated. "But what would we do with a group of kids?"

"Take them back to Evergreen," Cecilia said.

"We don't have time for that," he hissed. "Just shoot, Cill!"

She took the shot. The window shattered, and she fell back onto her rear. Inside the schoolhouse, the lantern oil had spilled all over the ground around Antoine and his abductors. The excited children squealed, struggling to wiggle out of the chairs.

Antoine broke free from the duct tape and swung his chair into a heavyset man. He snatched a knife from the dazed man, buried it in his chest, and then jerked it free and raked it across another man's throat before he even knew what hit him. The lone woman made a break for it and ran to escape the blazing building and Antoine's wrath.

Antoine bent to snatch a shotgun from one of the fallen men and followed her, stripping the beard from his face and tossing it to the ground. While D rushed to assist him, Brian and Cecilia entered the building to help the children. Searing heat rippled throughout the air, and wood crackled in the building flames.

Brian held Cecilia back with one arm. "Let me see if they're even healthy." He lifted one up, chair and all, and circled behind it to jerk the burlap sack from its head. Cecilia's face told him all he needed to know.

"D-do you think they're all...like that?" she whispered.

Brian dropped the kid and snagged her arm instead. "We have to get out of here. Let them burn."

He had to drag Cecilia's feet to make her move. Once he shoved her out into the field, he twisted the lock and shut the door. He forced his mind off the gaggle of children burning to death and headed straight for D, Antoine, and the surviving woman.

She kneeled across from D and Antoine, who both had shotguns trained on her. Her vacant brown eyes stared at the burning building while children screamed from inside it.

Brian stepped up alongside Antoine while Cecilia waited behind D. He put a hand on Antoine's red velvet arm. "You okay, Antoine?"

"I'm fine, but what we gonna do about this crazy bitch?"

Brian stood between the Etiennes. He withdrew the bow and aimed an arrow at the woman. "Why did you take our friend? And why did you have a group of infected children tied up in there?"

When the bedraggled woman spoke, her voice was as indifferent as her gaze. "You killed my family."

"You fuckin' *abducted* me!" Antoine's enraged voice startled Brian, who'd never seen him lose his cool even when he dispatched Stalkers. "What'd you mean when you said, 'The last present is the best of all'? Huh? What was in that bag? What was you gonna do to me?"

The woman's lips stretched into a tight smile. A chill ran through Brian as she started singing a Christmas song—the same one which had been playing in the truck while he waited for his father, while his mother and sister were dying.

"It's beginning to look a lot like Christmas…"

He drew his arm back and pulled the bowstring taut. "We're not gonna get anything out of you, are we?"

She kept singing until he couldn't take it anymore.

He let go. The woman tumbled to the grassy ground in a puddle of spreading blood, empty eyes staring at the night sky. D and Antoine backed away from her body. Cecilia stared at Brian as if she was looking at a ghost.

Brian moved to retrieve his arrow and inspect the woman's body for supplies. "That's the last of them. We should stay here for the night; it's too dark and too dangerous to travel. The house is clear and clean. We'll get Grimes and the bikes, take them in."

Antoine nodded and tore off the Santa suit. He was dressed in his normal clothes underneath. D curled an arm around Cecilia while the fire raged behind them. The familiar scent of burning flesh crept into the sweltering air.

They retrieved Grimes and the bikes and walked back to the farmhouse in silence, watching stacks of smoke swirl into the stars. While D pulled Antoine into the kitchen to fuss at him for going off on his own, Cecilia and Brian waited in the living room on a worn fabric couch. She curled against the arm of the couch and stared at the wall, her face drained of color and expression.

"Are you okay, Cill?"

She turned her head slowly to face him. "Are you?"

Her accusatory tone betrayed the true intention of this question.

"Cecilia, we couldn't save those kids. I'm sorry."

She cradled her hands in her lap. "You said to 'let them burn' with such a cold voice—almost like it wasn't *you* speaking. And the way you killed those people… You didn't even give them a chance."

"You don't have a problem with burning Stalkers at those Cleansing ceremonies." Brian picked at a rip in one cushion and swallowed the bitterness rising in him. "If your Good God or whatever's going to judge me for what I do, so be it. But you don't get to."

Cecilia slammed a fist into the cushion between them. "I'm not judging you—I'm *worried* about you! You seem so different from the boy I first met—"

"The song she was singing played on the radio while I sat in my dad's truck and let my family die." Brian winced when he conjured the painful memory. "I can't be the kid who sits back and does nothing anymore."

Cecilia's eyes skirted his, moving to the fingers she twisted in the fabric of her jeans. "Are you sure you aren't doing what you think Louis would do?"

"No." Brian sighed and pulled his legs onto the couch. He tucked his chin into his knees. "But we were all wrapped up in each other, tangled into knots I still haven't undone."

D and Antoine returned to the living room. D wedged herself into the space between Cecilia and Brian while Antoine flopped into a creaking rocking chair. They stared at a soot-seared fireplace with charred logs still in it and tried not to picture the flames consuming those tiny bodies.

When they woke, the group continued along back roads until they emerged onto a divided highway surrounded by isolated patches of farmland. Their return to the edge of the Mississippi River led them into middle-class suburbs and small towns.

They stopped for lunch inside Big Boy's diner. Brian was glad to sit next to Cecilia instead of his sister's phantom and across from D and Antoine instead of Poppa and Nana's spectral visages. The red vinyl booth transported him into the past, to the times Poppa's rude belches made Becky giggle and embarrassed Nana, to when he'd scold Becky for not eating the crusts of her sandwiches and the deadpan way he'd say Becks and Nana were ladies any time a server referred to the group as "guys."

Who knew that man could slit a woman's throat in front of his grandson? Who knew he'd helped slaughter a village of innocent civilians?

Antoine practically inhaled his food, but Cecilia only nipped at a granola bar. D kept glancing through the window while they ate. Eventually, she leaned over the table and gestured for the others to huddle in close to her.

"Someone's followin' us," she whispered, resting her arms on their collected backpacks and bags.

"You're just paranoid, Dee-Dee," Antoine said. "We killed all those weirdos with the kids. You think a new batch of messed-up motherfuckers done popped up to replace 'em? Is some hillbilly gonna come after us with a chainsaw?"

D clenched the shotgun draped over her knees. "Maybe the fire drew Stalkers to us. Maybe they creepin' after us, waitin' for the best time to pounce."

A faint electrical spark made the hairs on the back of Brian's neck and arms prickle.

Brian met Antoine's gaze across the table. "It's not out of the realm of possibility the gang I encountered might've made their way down here."

"I don't think they were part of no gang," Antoine said. "From what I overheard, they was pickin' up children like they was adoptin' stray animals. I think all those dudes was with the woman. Had their own little family."

D scrunched her nose next to him. "Sounds like freaky cult shit to me."

"Freakier than armed men with masks painted to look like Stalkers?" Brian asked. Cecilia stared through the window from his side.

D reached across the table to squeeze Brian's arm. "Look at the bright side, Sunshine: if that gang *did* move down, they might have Eva with 'em. But we best find them before they find us, so let's get moving."

The group left Big Boy's and continued through town. They passed uninterrupted stretches of pastoral farmland, the grass now a vivid green instead of sickly yellow. An inviting farmhouse beckoned on occasion, offering refuge from the ominous storm clouds hovering above them. Soon, farmland transitioned into forests. Bare tree limbs clawed for the ashen skies, begging the clouds to release the rain. The moisture of the heavy air clung to their skin. This suffocating ambiance brought to mind every horror movie Brian had ever seen set in the rural South.

They remained enshrouded in this dreary atmosphere as it thickened in both humidity and intensity. Crickets chirped with the cooling air, and the low sun glimmered whenever it pierced the darkening clouds. Every now and again, Brian checked for phantom Stalkers, but he only glimpsed the shadows of trees shaking in the breeze.

By dusk, both night and rain verged upon falling. When the group arrived at a collection of industrial buildings, they decided they shouldn't risk traveling any farther. They stopped and let Grimes drink from a nearby lake.

D licked a finger and held it up to the wind. "It's gonna rain any minute. Best get inside and eat."

Something moved in the corner of Brian's eye. He followed the motion to the edge of a building—a pair of bloodshot eyes met his before slinking into the shadows. He dropped his water bottle and swapped it for the bow. "Guys—"

A spine-tingling peal of thunder shook the ground. Grimes squealed and backed away with D and Antoine still atop her. A plump drop of water hit Brian on the cheek, rolling with agonizing slowness.

The hairs on the back of Brian's neck stood on end. *Something's behind me.* He swiveled with an arrow pulled taut—and locked gazes with a grinning face peeking out from the edge of a building. It giggled like a child saying, "You caught me!"

The Stalker plunged back with the impact of his arrow. The boom of shotguns and the pop of a pistol pierced the saturated air as Stalkers emerged from behind the buildings and skittered up from the road. They were all adults—a more potent threat than the children, especially in a group.

D's right: they must've sensed the commotion at the farmhouse and followed us like that fucking kid followed me.

He ran out of arrows, so he switched to his revolver. Their weapons made short work of the prowling creatures. Several turned tail and disappeared into the outskirts of the woods. The rest lay scattered, snickers escaping on their dying breaths as if the whole thing had been a joke.

One remained. It scrambled for them, deciding who it wanted to go for. D and Antoine were too far away, still struggling to wrangle a panicked Grimes. The Stalker angled for Cecilia instead. She fired, but the shot only clipped its shoulder. It dashed toward her, jagged claws outstretched, cackling through chattering teeth. Brian rushed to her side and shoved her out of the way, but those nails dug into his arm, pulled him down—

The Stalker dropped instead of Brian. A spray of gore and blood stained the muddy ground behind it in a scattered streak. Pungent smoke mingled with the scents of moist earth and coppery blood.

He pulled Cecilia to her feet. She fumbled for his arm with shaking hands and inspected his sleeve for tears. The material hadn't ripped—but a shadow warped the ground alongside them.

Brian spun to face the silhouette looming from the roof of a nearby building. He steadied his revolver when something glinted in the tarnished light of the setting sun. "Who are you and what do you want?"

"That's a funny way to thank someone, Brian."

The voice froze time, sent shivers through his spine. All he needed was one word—no, one *syllable*—to know who it belonged to.

Chapter Five

A Dangerous Pair

3/22, Vidalia, Louisiana, dusk

"Here we are again, at the end of each other's gun barrels. We gotta stop meetin' this way."

Louis slipped out of the shadows. Even at this distance, the sight of him knocked the breath out of Brian. He replied once it returned to him. "Lower yours and I'll lower mine."

"I wanted to make sure no more Stalkers popped out first." Louis lifted a shirttail and tucked a handgun into his jeans. "Why don't I come down and we'll talk face-to-face? Preferably somewhere dry."

Even though his fingertips stung and his stomach had soured, Brian had to deal with this. "I'll come around back. If you try anything—"

"Brian, come on—I didn't save you just to shoot you. Keep those trigger fingers steady, Scooby Gang."

Antoine's focused gaze and shotgun barrel followed Louis down the metal staircase at the side of the building. Cecilia trained her pistol on him, but her grip shook. Brian wasn't sure if she felt guilty aiming it at another person or if Louis unnerved her.

D approached Brian and gave him a stern look. "You're doin' fine without him, baby—don't sink back into the quicksand."

Brian swallowed the lump in his throat and walked away with the revolver in front of him. The rain soaked through his clothes and cooled his skin, but scorching heat pulsed beneath it. Parting clouds revealed the radiant sun in all its glory.

When he rounded the corner and glimpsed Louis bathed in golden light, his heart skipped a beat like a swooning character in some cheesy romance novel. None of the words swirling in his jumbled mind were sensible. Aggravated by his weakness, he tapped his revolver against his thigh while those intimidating eyes scanned him at length.

"We always seem to get caught up in these storms, don't we?" The persisting downpour accentuated their silence. Louis stepped toward Brian and reached for his arm. "I couldn't think of a good way to approach you, but I was scared that fucker might take you down. Tell me I wasn't too late."

Brian retreated from Louis's outstretched hand and slunk beneath the building's overhang. "Too early, if anything. I figured you'd come after me, but not *this* quickly. I guess I underestimated you again." He cupped his right arm where the Stalker had grabbed it. "It didn't get me. I guess I should thank you, but I don't really know what to make of all this."

Louis leaned against the chipped brick wall and smoothed his wet bangs out of his forehead. "After you left, I laid there all tied up. My neck ached. My chest hurt. I couldn't breathe. When I saw the knife you left me, I had two choices: end my misery, or go after you. I didn't sit around feelin' sorry for myself for long. I cut myself loose and kept busy fixin' up the other boat. All that Boy Scout bullshit paid off."

Brian glanced away from Louis's penetrating stare. "Your resolve is almost scary." He sighed. "Will you ever give up?"

"On what?"

Brian's eyes darted back to Louis's. "What do you think?"

"I knew you needed to be alone, but I was worried, okay? I didn't plan on showin' myself so early—"

Brian scoffed. "So you were just going to follow me and leave me in the dark again? That's a little creepy, don't you think?"

"Hell, Brian, I didn't know how pissed you might be. I half thought you'd take a shot at me if you saw me. And if you didn't, D woulda been happy to try." Louis fought to keep his expression neutral, but Brian caught the quirks and twitches of his facial muscles. "You said it yourself—you knew I'd find you eventually. What else was I gonna do?"

Brian thought back to his conversation with Cecilia. "You went to Evergreen, didn't you? They must've told you what route I planned on taking. What sob story did you tell them?"

"That you left me." Louis's gaze drifted from Brian's, then returned to it with an electric jolt. "Said I couldn't eat or sleep because I could only think about how bad I fucked things up. I asked them how to fix it. They said I needed to atone for what I did, that I owed Eva, and helpin' you find her would make things better with you too."

Brian forced a neutral expression, but he suspected Louis saw through it as easily as Brian saw through *him*. "I'm not buying it. You hate them and everything they stand for. Why would you listen to them?"

Louis stepped forward and snatched Brian's hand. He tugged the muzzle of the revolver to his forehead above a deeply furrowed brow. "If you wanna end this thing, end it. But if a fraction of what you felt was real, give me the chance to make things up to you and Eva. I'm not gonna fuck you over again, I swear it."

The dull pulse of Brian's frayed nerves spiked. He let out a dazed chuckle. "You're crazy."

"We both knew that already." The wry twinkle in Louis's eyes faded. The contradiction of warm hands and cool metal trapped Brian in a place between desire and anger. He yearned to cut this twisted thread knotted between them, but even if Louis ceased to exist, he'd live on. He was in Brian's blood like an infection.

Thunder rumbled, reminding Brian other people existed besides him and Louis—and he'd left them hanging.

Brian withdrew his hand from Louis's and lowered the revolver. "We need to get inside. If you try anything—"

Louis pulled down the collar of his black turtleneck, revealing a fading bruise on his throat. "Trust me—I know what you're capable of. That punch hurt like a motherfucker." He launched himself from the wall with his foot. "Let's go."

Brian lingered behind Louis, watching his familiar strut with a groan rumbling low in his throat. He had to pinch himself. It hurt, but the pain blended with the tingling nerves in the tips of his toes and fingers.

They returned to the others, who'd taken shelter underneath the overhang on the front of the large brick building. The broad range of dramatic expressions on their faces would've made quite the Renaissance painting.

"You were over there long enough," D said. "I coulda finished a whole *Lord of the Rings* movie! Probably a damn book, even!"

Louis scoffed. "Am I still Gollum?"

"An underhanded little bastard who fucked everything up because he wanted to own a pretty thing?" D kept her shotgun aimed at Louis. "Damn straight you are!"

Louis remained unfazed by this as he was by most things. "Glad to see you haven't changed. Your *chat* run off again?"

D jerked the shotgun up. "Get yo' ass into that building, *ti zozo*."

Antoine made a face indicating he knew exactly what this insult meant, but if Louis did, he didn't let it show. He marched ahead of the others and boldly parted the sliding metal doors.

They entered the darkness with flashlights drawn and weapons aimed. Blood stained the floors and walls of what appeared to be an old slaughterhouse. Grimes whickered, unsettled by the scent of blood lingering in the stagnant air.

Louis pulled the metal doors shut behind them with a startling *clang*. "Let's inspect the place—"

"Give me your gun." Brian held out a hand and kept his eyes level with Louis's.

Louis handed his pistol over. "Wanna frisk me for other weapons?"

"I'll just shoot you if you try to pull anything out."

D cleared her throat. "Me and 'Toine got this. You two need to talk out some of the shit you got hoverin' between you. Stuff is so thick even *I* can feel it—or is that just humidity?" She looked at Brian for approval. He nodded. "A'ight, Cill—aim the flashlight for me and Bro. We got you covered, girl."

Louis watched them walk away while Grimes nosed around. He tugged off his backpack and soaked shirt and knelt to dig around for something in the pack. "I don't wanna sit around in wet clothes. You can change too, if you want."

"No, thanks."

Louis dug out a dry black shirt and slid it on. "You ain't got nothin' I ain't already seen. We've both exposed ourselves to each other in every way possible." He finished buttoning his shirt and stood. "I wanted to spend the rest of my life with you, you know. However long or short that might be."

Brian's hands tightened around Louis's pistol as a lump formed in his dry throat. "You don't mean it."

"I do. But I understand why you'd think everythin' I ever said was a lie." Louis's eyes softened into a plaintive expression. He slumped against the brick wall and dragged his hands down his face, exhaling. "Tell me what I need to do to fix this—*please*."

His vulnerable body language reminded Brian of that stormy night in the cabin at Evergreen. It threw him, looped him back toward urges he could no longer indulge. "It... It's not something you can just slap a Band-Aid on. It's not something I think you *can* fix."

Louis's Adam's apple bobbed, the fading bruise on his neck bared by the button-down shirt. "I know you can't slap a Band-Aid on this, but even if it's just fuckin' superglue and we can still see the cracks, let's *try*. Maybe everythin' else in my life was bullshit, but what happened between us wasn't. You're the only person I ever felt anythin' like that with. I don't wanna lose that. I don't wanna lose *you*."

Louis pinched the bridge of his nose, eyes aimed at the ceiling. His breath hissed out of him at a controlled pace. Brian's eyes ached with the sting of tears fighting their way out. Sympathy, regret, resentment—any of it or all of it.

The others returned before either Brian or Louis could crumble.

D wedged herself between them. "It's all clear. So now what? This asshole followed you all the way here—you ain't gonna shake him. You gonna put him outta his misery?"

Antoine and Cecilia returned before Brian could give an answer he didn't have. Antoine nodded at Louis with characteristic courtesy while Cecilia visibly struggled with her own reaction. The sting of Louis's cruelty toward her hadn't faded over time.

"You made it here fast." Cecilia rubbed one arm, forcing her eyes to stay locked on Louis's. "Did you ride a bike or something?"

Louis's shining eyes and quivering lips had transformed into his usual apathetic gaze and condescending smirk. "You're a mess, girl. You should get outta those muddy clothes. Got it in your nice blonde hair too."

"Just answer my question, creep."

Louis quirked his eyebrows. "Your pals at the plantation loaned me one, told me Brian had been there and you all left with him. I figured he'd take our original path back to Missouri, but I didn't catch up to you until the diner. I didn't plan on meetin' like this, but I couldn't let that thing get Brian while he was tryin' to save *your* muddy ass."

Cecilia tucked her hair behind her ear, fingers prying at the mud clinging to it. "You didn't exactly jump in to help the rest of us."

Louis clicked his tongue. "The ones I shot for you were the ones you didn't see comin'. And I used a silenced pistol, *chére*." He scratched his arm—a sign he was bored or uncomfortable. "Look, I've never been a people person, but I'm tryin' here. Either give me a shot or put one in my head and call it a day."

"That's extreme even for your ass," D said. "Option three is we send you packin'."

Louis remained with his back to the wall, unarmed. This atypical vulnerability concerned Brian—not to mention the casual way he kept suggesting his own death. "If Brian wants to be sure I'm not gonna be a problem for him anymore or he wants some kinda revenge, I'll give him that. But I'm tellin' you now, there's no way I can stay away if you try to make me leave."

D spun to face Brian so Louis couldn't see her expression: arched eyebrows, wide eyes, and a slack jaw. She mouthed "ohmygod" at him. Cecilia's hardened expression wilted into pity while Antoine shook his head. His face implied begrudging admiration for Louis's stoic conviction.

The weight of a crucial decision descended upon Brian's shoulders. All four pairs of eyes fell on him, awaiting this pronouncement. He balanced the scales in his mind—negatives versus positives, logic versus emotion, what he *should* want versus what he wanted.

By the time he arrived at a conclusion, all the energy had drained from him. "If I give you this chance, don't make me regret it."

Brian detected the subtle slump of Louis's chest signifying a substantial sense of relief. Cecilia kept her lips in a tight line while Antoine shook his head in a sort of "Well, okay then," but D spun toward Brian and thrust a finger in his face. "You better keep your ex in line, baby boy, or I'll shoot him myself."

Brian had acclimated to Louis's frequent flashes of intimidation, but the scarcity of D's made them all the more potent when they occurred. He swallowed but didn't back down from her. "I think D's hangry, so let's eat, okay?"

They formed a circle and unpacked their food. Grimes nosed at Brian's back, reminding him she was hungry too. The sounds of jars unscrewing and boxes tearing echoed within the spacious warehouse. Grimes crunched into an apple, her ears perking at the reverberating noise. Various pairs of eyes met and parted. Brian stared into Louis's, trying to read him. They maintained this eye contact for an uncomfortable amount of time.

"Okay, this awkward as hell." D shoved away a jar of peanut butter. "I can't eat with y'all eye fuckin' in front of me. I had enough of it the first time around."

Cecilia sighed and packed her untouched bag of trail mix. "Brian, are you really going to be okay with this? I know you still care for him, but those feelings might be clouding your judgment—"

"I thought you were worried I was too merciless." Brian met Cecilia's clear blue eyes; the dark circles underneath them hadn't been there before. "You heard him—either it's this or I shoot him. Would you prefer that?"

An uneasy tension enveloped the group. No one knew what to say or where to look, so they all stared at the floor and kept quiet.

Louis sat forward and jabbed a fork into an open can of beans, his chest swelling and collapsing with a heavy breath. "Brian, if you're gonna be like that, just put me outta my misery now."

"*Your* misery, huh? How about my grandfather's misery while he bled out? Or Eva's when you choked her and left her behind? How about mine after I found out I was lied to by the one person I loved more than anything in the world?" Brian snatched his bags and stood. "If you wanna die so bad, go ahead and put a bullet in your brain—but don't lay that shit on *me*."

He withdrew the pistol and tossed it at Louis's feet before he turned and stalked away to set up his sleeping bag. He wasn't tired, but he wanted to disappear like a moth in a cocoon and forget he'd ever been Louis's butterfly in a jar.

After a tense breakfast, Brian salvaged his arrows from the Stalkers' corpses and headed back onto the road with his crew. D and Antoine chatted like nothing had changed. Brian and Cecilia smiled at their banter, but Louis kept his lips shut tight and his eyes on the road. Brian knew he felt like the outcast in the group, and his prior intimacy with Brian amplified this disparity.

He faltered between regret and satisfaction at his outburst the previous night. He didn't enjoy being cruel, but Louis needed to experience a penetrating ache throughout his body, not just the sting of a rebuke and a figurative finger waggling in his face as if he'd been a naughty child.

When evening settled over them, they headed for an isolated house at the end of a long dirt road. They let Grimes roam and propped the bikes against the porch. Louis looked between D and Brian. "You want her to give me my gun back or what, Brian?"

"I took it last night before he could blow *anyone's* brains out," D explained. "It's up to you—you wanna keep an eye on him *and* Stalkers?"

Brian shook his head. "Keep it for now."

A wounded expression shifted Louis's features for an instant, but he quickly corrected it. Dissatisfied by this affected indifference, Brian dug deeper.

"You have the pocketknife, Louis," he said in a superficially saccharine tone. "Just don't go stabbing anyone in the back with it."

D rolled her eyes. "Oh, here we go." She cocked her head toward the front door of the house. "Let's drop this petty shit and hurry up, a'ight? Y'all can rip shirt buttons and punch each other once we inside."

She pressed the muzzle of her shotgun against the door. It creaked open with no resistance. Brian shoved a flashlight into Louis's face. "Light duty it is."

Louis snatched it with a surly glare and clicked the beam on while Brian and Antoine backed D up. Cecilia wandered between Brian and Louis, caught in the same riptide of tension Eva and Louis had once trapped Brian in.

The house wasn't barricaded or modified to eliminate hiding spaces for Stalkers. The dining area contained a round table with a glass of moldy orange juice and a bowl of soggy cereal floating in a putrid mess of milky chunks. Brian smoothed a hand along a yellowed newspaper bearing the headline: *BIZARRE ATTACKS IN KANSAS SPREAD SOUTH.* The kitchen sink held a pile of dishes with food crusted onto them; a bowl of uneaten dog food remained on the floor beneath it.

Hoarded belongings filled one bedroom, covering the floor and bed and allowing just enough room to enter and stand inside. A spread book rested on the bathroom sink beside an unflushed toilet. Flies buzzed inside the room, drawn to the pungent odor. Brian swiftly shut the door to lock in the smell and the swarming insects.

D pushed open the final door and swiftly recoiled into Brian. "Eugh!"

Brian peered around her: a corpse in a wedding gown hung from a light fixture. The desiccated carcass of an animal—probably the dog—lay at the foot of the bed. Louis shoved past them and approached the dangling body. He nudged a lacy veil up with the tip of the pocketknife.

"She's been dead a while." The veil fell. "Guess we're campin' out in the livin' room."

"Did she leave a note?" Cecilia asked as Louis edged past her. "Maybe we should bury her..."

He shrugged. "Who cares? She sure as shit doesn't."

While he slipped into the living room, Cecilia entered the master bedroom. She carefully skirted the body and searched for a note, but she came up empty-handed. Instead, she kneeled in front of the gently swaying body and prayed. Brian let her be and returned to the living room with the others.

"Depressing shit," Antoine muttered as he set his backpack on the ground beside a mottled, floral-patterned couch. "Wonder if her old man went before or after the outbreak?"

"Only one side of the bed looked slept in." Brian lowered his bags beside Antoine's. "It was just her and the dog. I guess it stopped eating and starved to death after she hung herself."

"Poor things." D slipped her backpack over her arms. "They both gave up, lost their reason to live. I came close with Gus, but Jones needed me and I didn't want 'Toine to wait for someone who wasn't gonna show."

Louis dropped his bag to the floor next to the couch without bothering to make eye contact with any of them. He stared into the distance with disquieting intensity.

"Let's get our bikes and set up for the night," Brian said, eager to move on.

Once they wheeled in the bicycles, they separated to barricade the windows and doors throughout the house with whatever furniture they could find. Cecilia returned to the living room while Brian was pushing the couch against windows covered by dusty curtains. She set her bag beside Brian's and rummaged for a drink.

Brian placed a hand on her slender shoulder, feeling bone beneath her soft skin. "You going to eat something tonight?"

Cecilia shrugged, almost as diffident as Louis.

"Hey"—Louis's voice cut the silence—"can I talk to you?"

Brian nearly answered, but Louis was focused on Cecilia. Brian felt as dumbfounded as she looked.

She scratched above a pale eyebrow. "Um, what about?"

Louis dug into his jeans for the pocketknife and set it on an end table. "I'm not gonna try anythin'. I just have some shit on my mind. You majored in sociology, right? Isn't that like the cousin of psychology or somethin'?"

She stood, her ponytail catching the sunlight seeping through the windows. "Uh, sure. We can talk in the spare room." She followed Louis in and shut the door to a crack behind her.

Brian stared at the door, completely at a loss. *What could he want to talk to* her *about?*

He collapsed onto the couch and twiddled his fingers atop his knees. Part of him wanted to eavesdrop on their conversation, but D would inevitably pop up behind him and ask what he was doing at the top of her lungs.

When the Etiennes wandered into the room, they sat on either side of him and cocooned him with their warmth. "Where's Cill and Louis?" D asked.

"He wanted to talk to her about something." Brian waved his hand. "He left his knife and we're all here, so I think she'll be okay."

"Oh, he's just all butthurt 'cause you didn't welcome him back with some passionate clench." D hugged her own arms and writhed while Antoine snickered. Their smiles faded when Brian's failed to appear. "It's good to be cold to him, but you ain't gotta be *mean*—it's just diggin' the wound deeper, you know?"

Brian leaned forward and clasped his hands atop his knees. "It *needs* to go deep." His knees bounced while he glared at the door obscuring Cecilia and Louis from view.

"Listen, Brian." D's somber tone caught him off guard. "Etiennes are known for three things: givin' good hugs, tellin' it to you straight, and stickin' with our friends. When you stayed with me to look for Jonesy, you made a friend for life."

"And you made another one when you got D back to me." Antoine patted Brian's back. "All the shit I won from the Powerball don't mean nothin' now—people are the only thing that matters. And boy, you is *flush*, you got me?"

"In other words"—D gave Brian's shoulder a light shake—"me, 'Toine, and Cill are here for you no matter what, so stop broodin' over him—he ain't worth it."

Brian's lips parted to reply—but something hit the window behind him with a *thunk*.

They leaped to their feet and scrambled for their weapons. Brian made the bold move of peering through the window, but the yard remained as still as a picture. The wind wasn't even blowing.

D and Antoine glanced through the other window. They looked at Brian and shook their heads. The trio huddled in the center of the living room, far away from the windows.

"What you think that was?" D whispered.

"It wasn't the wind," Brian said. "Could be another Stalker messing around. If we stay quiet, maybe it'll get bored and move on."

"Stalkers don't throw shit, though." Antoine cradled the shotgun in his arms. "Unless they doin' somethin' *else* new. Maybe it's one of those kids. I still ain't figured out why we seein' them now when I barely seen any before."

D frowned. "I got this weird feeling it's 'cause they all lost their parents, so they ain't got no one to protect them. Probably get ambushed and run away, turn into those things. Or maybe that crazy bitch hoarded them all and one got loose, wandered down south. Who knows? I don't like thinkin' 'bout it."

The Etiennes and Brian dragged their bags to the center of the room and ate in troubled silence until Louis and Cecilia emerged from the spare room. Brian tried to ignore Louis throughout the evening, but Cecilia curled up in her sleeping bag and fell asleep before Brian could ask what Louis wanted to talk to her about. D passed out not long after. Antoine offered to stay up with Brian so he wasn't alone with Louis, but Brian insisted he'd be fine—Louis stirred a lot of feelings in him, but fear wasn't among them.

Soon D and Antoine snored like motors beside one another, creating a complementary melody. The sounds drove Brian nuts, but the silence between him and Louis was worse. Unbearable, even.

He fiddled with his tablet and fidgeted on the couch, listening to music with lyrics which always seemed relevant to his situation. It only drove the nail deeper, so he switched it off and yanked the earbuds from his ears. "What did you and Cecilia talk about?"

Louis looked at him as if it just occurred to him Brian was in the room. "That's between me and her. Doctor-patient confidentiality."

This bothered Brian a good deal more than he was comfortable with. He pulled his knees to his chest and pressed his lips together to fight back an aggravated reply. Once, conversation had come so easily to them. Now they were practically strangers.

Louis fiddled with his fingertips. He sat in an uncomfortable-looking easy chair, his head hung and face hidden by the curtains of his bangs.

Brian cleared his throat. "Did you see any Stalkers when you were alone?"

Louis nodded and flicked something at the ground. Brian caught the glint of a knife; Louis was cleaning his nails with the tip. "Nothin' I couldn't handle."

"I think they might be evolving."

Louis scoffed and glanced at him. "Their brains and bodies are deterioratin', Brian, not improvin'."

D or Antoine stuttered in their sleep. Cecilia moaned gently.

Brian skirted Louis's condescending gaze. He tried to follow D's advice by ignoring the snide reply he *wanted* to give Louis. "Something banged on the window while you and Cecilia were in the room doing whatever it was you were doing."

Louis slid the knife into his jeans and straightened in the easy chair. "You're *jealous*, aren't you? You never were any good at hidin' your feel—"

Brian hurled a couch cushion into Louis's face. It bounced off onto Antoine, who stopped snoring and brushed it off with an annoyed grunt. "I'm done talking to you. I shouldn't have even *started* the fucking conversation." He stood, urged by the building pressure in the room— but there was nowhere to go. It was dangerous outside, one bedroom had a dead body in it, the bathroom stank, and he'd barely be able to squeeze into the other bedroom.

Before Brian could decide where to go, Louis closed the gap between them and snatched Brian's arm in a lightning-swift motion. "I get it— you're fuckin' pissed at me. I would be too. But don't throw a gun at me and tell me to kill myself one night, then try to shoot the shit with me the next. Pick one and stick with it."

Worried about disrupting the others' sleep, Brian lowered his voice and tried to step away from them. "Louis, let go of my arm."

"Why? Are you scared of me now?"

Brian jerked his arm free and pressed it against Louis's bruised throat. He backed Louis into the moonlit wall and pinned him to it, his pulse thumping with a surge of adrenaline, the high of control—the thrill of contact, of a taut, warm body pressed against his.

Louis grabbed Brian's arm with both hands but made no attempt to pry it free. His pupils expanded until his eyes were so dark Brian glimpsed his own reflection in them.

He relaxed his arm but kept it against Louis's collarbones. "I don't know—am I?"

Louis glanced down. "Doesn't feel that way."

Brian retreated from Louis, frustrated by the passion his body betrayed. He raked his fingers through his hair, his cheeks burning as his racing heart finally slowed. "You're dangerous. *This* is dangerous." He searched for something more to say, but he struggled to put his complex feelings into sensible sentences.

Louis rubbed his neck with one hand and stepped forward from the wall. Menacing sensuality radiated from him, stronger than before; he was now the fruit Brian wasn't supposed to pluck from the garden. "My heart aches and my body burns for you. If you asked me to plunge that knife into my heart and twist it, I would." He gripped his shirt and wrung it for emphasis. "Do you understand who's dangerous now?"

"The two of us together." Brian held his ground, neither backing away nor closing the scant distance between them. "Which is why this isn't happening. So let's find another way to kill the time."

Louis brushed past Brian and flopped onto the couch. The sensation of static electricity clung to Brian while Louis unbuttoned his shirt and tugged the zipper of his jeans down. True, it was hot, but Brian knew Louis did this more to make Brian *un*comfortable than for his own comfort.

He lifted Brian's tablet from the table and punched in the code. "You don't mind if I use this, do you? I can listen to your shitty music."

Brian glared at Louis, though he was relieved anger took the place of some of the other emotions fighting their way through him. "If it's so shitty, why listen to it?"

"Fine—what I really want is to see if you kept all your photos." Louis's face glowed in the white light cast by the screen. He dragged the fingers of his left hand along it, the same corded bracelet dangling from his wrist.

Brian kneeled to rummage through his backpack for his journal. "Why?"

"You really wanna know?"

"*Gross.*"

Louis scoffed. "I wouldn't do that in a roomful of people—and we both know you don't think it's gross, so don't talk like we're kids peepin' at porno mags again." He sighed, eyes softening but still focused on the screen. "I just wanted to see what photos you couldn't bear to part with, or if there were any I haven't seen."

More like you want to see if I kept photos of you *on there. Which I did.* Brian sat on the floor between the couch and table and opened the journal. If he tipped his head back, it'd brush Louis's wriggling leg. *I'm just torturing myself. Probably him too. But I guess I just want to be able to remind myself he's really there.*

"Why're you so interested in what I find important?"

"I just like bein' in your head a whole lot better than mine is all." Louis stuck Brian's earbuds into his ears and turned on the music.

Brian overheard the gentle thump of a familiar song while he flipped his pencil between his fingers and stared at the lonely lines waiting to be filled. The entries hidden in the previous pages taunted him with their presence: his description of the events which would change his life forever; the entries chronicling the fall of civilization; his musings on the various people who entered and departed his life thereafter; and sketches of landmarks they passed during their journey south.

And the flowery prose detailing the first tendrils of love taking hold.

Stirring with resentment and regret, he wrote the same thing in swirling cursive over and over, not caring if Louis happened to glance at it.

Je te hais, mon amour.

Dynamite Diva

Chapter Six

Empty Guns

3/24, Clayton, Louisiana, morning

Intense beams of light woke Brian. He ate breakfast with the others before returning to the road. The minimal airflow and scant tree leaves left them prone to the intense heat and light. During the winter, they'd been bundled in layers for warmth which also offered protection from Stalkers. Since it was hot now, comfort meant sacrificing safety. Gloves were a necessity, and Brian could live with wearing jeans, but long-sleeved shirts were still stifling in this heat. It made Louis's turtleneck seem even more impractical—though it was probably to hide the fading bruise on his neck.

I shouldn't feel guilty and I won't. When he looks at it, it'll remind him of all the horrible shit he did.

Few Stalkers hid on the side of the road, which didn't provide much cover for them. Some jumped out from cars, so Brian gave them a wide berth when passing. Although dispatching them didn't take much effort, they didn't waste ammo unless it was necessary. The B.E.N. had grown and stored food, but they didn't exactly have boxes and magazines of ammo lying around.

Their aching legs and grumbling stomachs forced them to stop at a quaint rest area with a single building for bathrooms. Grimes trotted to a nearby river to ease her own thirst and hunger while they settled at a picnic bench, covered by the rare shade of a tree with ample leaves.

Since they were exposed, they ate in silence. None of them were eager to eat in the restrooms. Somebody had barricaded one from the outside, which seemed a little strange.

While they were eating, the leaves above them rustled. Something fell and collided with the tabletop. Louis swatted away the offending object—an acorn—and glared at the perpetrator. *"Couillon."*

A squirrel chattered and scurried higher up the tree. Cecilia hid a grin, amused by Louis's aggravated scowl. It shrank when a noise came from behind her and Brian, a *creak* like the straining of wood.

The bathrooms? Maybe whatever was barricaded inside—

Louis got up from the bench and held his hand out. "Give me a gun, Brian—don't be stubborn about this."

He's faster on his feet than any of us. Impeccable aim and instincts—dangerous even without a weapon, but deadly with one.

Brian made a quick decision: "Cill, give him your rifle."

While everyone else stood and shoved their belongings into their backpacks, she withdrew the rifle from her shoulder and handed it to Louis. A twig cracked from across the road before anyone else could withdraw their weapons, but Louis swiveled the rifle toward it and aimed through the scope. "There's one in the bushes. If we run, it's on us. If we shoot it, more might pop out. The barricade's strainin'—make the call, Brian."

The restroom door behind them rattled. Wood splintered. Antoine and D pumped their shotguns and aimed them at the door. Cecilia clenched her pistol in both hands, unsure what to do with it.

Fuck. *I'm so used to him taking the lead when he's around. I can't fall back into the same old shit.*

Brian pulled the bow from the table, reached back for an arrow, and nocked it. "We need high ground. I'll take the Stalker out while the rest of you find a way onto the roof. Go!"

Everyone else rushed to the building while Brian kept an eye on the pale form concealed within the bushes. As soon as it moved, Brian released the bowstring. The arrow sailed across the road and knocked the Stalker back—but several more appeared. When he turned to dash for the building, the barricade shattered with a deafening *crack*, and the door slammed against the brick wall. A huge black blur dashed out—a bear, either starving or sick.

A bear on one side and Stalkers on the other. I'm so fucked.

He withdrew his revolver; the bear's thick hide would make his arrows feel like ant bites. A symphony of gunshots overwhelmed a low, guttural growl and the hysterical laughter building behind him. The bear stood on its hind legs until a shot knocked it onto all fours. Blood matted its fur, but it kept going, lunging with claws the length of steak knives.

Another gunshot cracked the air. The bear made a sound between a whimper and a groan, and then stumbled back onto its rear. Cecilia leaned over the side of the roof with her hand outstretched. "Hurry, Brian!"

He ran for her, shuddering when Louis sent another bullet through the bear's skull. It slumped to the side and deflated into a pitiful pile.

Brian grasped Cecilia's hand. Several others snagged his clothes and pulled him up; someone dragged him back by the collar of his shirt so roughly the top two buttons broke. His ears were ringing too much to hear anything, but the rooftop vibrated with each shot. Brian stood on wobbly feet, trying to survey the state of things around them.

A group of Stalkers had emerged from the woods. Some were kneeling by the bear's corpse and tearing into it with claws and teeth through fur and flesh. They worked in solemn silence like a flock of vultures, their laughter stifled by the meat sliding down their gullets.

But others weren't interested in the bear. They ran for the building and scrambled up the sides, their nails breaking as they tried to dig into the crevices between the bricks. Louis crushed the skulls of any Stalkers who made it with the heels of his boots. Antoine and D blew them away with the force of their shotguns. Cecilia used her pistol, her sweat-beaded brow furrowed in determination. Brian moved from corner to corner to pick off the swarming Stalkers until his shoulder and arms ached.

By the time the gunshots stopped and all the Stalkers were dead, smoke and rotten flesh churned inside Brian's nose, and a lingering vibration trembled throughout his body. He drooped to his knees and splayed out atop the roof, weak-limbed and breathless like he'd just worked out or had mind-blowing sex.

He stared at the cloudless sky and covered his forehead with his arm. *Except one of those is fun. This was the fucking* opposite *of fun.*

The weight of the others sank around him, Louis to his left and Cecilia to his right. D flopped onto the edge of the roof, but Antoine tapped her shoulder. "Pull your legs up, Dee-Dee—don't want a straggler snatchin' 'em like some monster under the bed."

D jerked her legs up. Antoine grinned at Brian while he sat beside his sister, sweat gleaming from his dark brow. He pumped out a final shell from his gun. "Got no more ammo, but I'm good otherwise. How're the rest of y'all?"

D inspected her gun. "Got two more shells and no injuries."

Cecilia's rifle hovered over Brian as Louis handed it back to her. "I used all five, so it's empty. Sorry."

"I used my whole clip too"—she wiped her forehead with her arm—"but at least all yours hit. Brian made the right call to give it to you."

Brian swiveled his head to face Louis. "You get the bear?"

Louis's eyebrows arched. "What do you think?"

Brian rolled his eyes. "You make it really fucking hard to thank you, you know. Jesus." He sat up, skin sticky, muscles throbbing from head to toe, and flustered by the scrape he'd barely pulled through. He wiped his face and dried his hand on his jeans. "Thanks for covering me, guys. That was fucking terrifying. I've never even seen a bear at a *zoo*."

"Or bison and elk," Louis muttered as he sat and scrunched his fingers through his sticky hair. He shook it out, ran a hand through it, and got to his feet. "Since we've all recovered, let's get outta here before any more show up."

"Good news is we probably drew most of the Stalkers in from 'round us." Antoine folded his arms and surveyed the area around the rest stop. "And I doubt there's more rabid bears and shit."

"It's crazy how many there were." Brian stood alongside Louis and extended a hand to Cecilia. He glared at Louis when he did the same, but Cecilia took both their hands and let them pull her to her feet. "That group was following us when Louis showed up, and something hit the window at that house—now this?" A frightening realization interrupted his thoughts. "My mother blocked the bedroom door to keep me from getting to my sister. Someone obviously barricaded the bathroom to keep the bear in, but what if it was a Stalker? Or even a group of them? Maybe the bear was a decoy and the Stalker I took out was keeping watch, or—"

"You got plenty of time to spin your gears once we find Grimes and roll outta here," Louis said. He jumped to the ground and helped Cecilia after him. As usual, he rebounded from stressful encounters like a rubber band snapping back into shape.

Antoine gave D a hand, but she planted with far less grace than the dainty Cecilia. While they wandered in search of Grimes, Brian walked around jerking his arrows out of corpses. He dwelled on his theory about the Stalkers using the bear as a distraction—or bait—but it bordered on outlandish for a group of Stalkers to work together to trap a bear and barricade it, and then wait for people to happen onto the rest stop. It would remain another unanswered question for Brian, one of many "what-ifs" he'd encountered during his travels.

Brian cradled the gory bundle of arrows and meandered over to the nearby river to cleanse it. The others were in sight, and he was too exhausted to worry about more Stalkers or bears. Like Antoine said, they had probably cleared out the area.

When a hand curled around his shoulder, he shivered and nearly dropped the arrow he was dragging through the water.

"Sorry, it's only me." Cecilia sat beside him while he finished cleaning the arrow. "Louis said you shouldn't be alone and he'd be fine, so here I am." She shrugged and gave him a cute, dimpled smile.

Brian slipped the arrow into his quiver and sank onto his rear. "I didn't mean to snap at you after what happened at the farm. I know seeing all that was hard for you—"

"I know it was hard for you too." Cecilia reached out and squeezed his arm. "When I told Louis, even he seemed surprised. He said you were too sweet to do such horrible things—"

Brian tried too late to suppress a glare. "Why would you tell him that?"

She dragged her fingers through her tangled ponytail. Her hair and skin were a startling white in the harsh sun. "Brian, look at the sky—let it remind you there's more out there than this."

Insects buzzed around them as delicate gusts rustled the tree leaves. Brian glanced at the azure sky, trying to see if any of the clouds resembled anything other than puffy white masses. "You think there's really a Heaven up there?"

Cecilia sighed. "Not really. But it doesn't mean I don't believe in God. There's *something* out there, something more than us. God may not be a person capable of thought, but more like a large cog connected to smaller ones by something we can't see. There's too much we can't explain—and many things we'll never know."

Brian scratched his head when an itch struck him. "Why'd you change the subject from Louis to God?"

"I guess I wanted to help you find some perspective. After talking to him, I know how damaged he is. You both are. Maybe you did more damage to each other, but it doesn't mean you can't heal." Her eyes sparkled in the sun, a more vivid blue than the sky. "Hatred is a waste of emotion and effort, Brian. Life is short, so don't hold on to this bitterness. People deserve a chance at forgiveness—and I know it's a cheesy saying, but true love conquers all."

Brian's face crinkled into a skeptical expression bordering on irritated. He opened his mouth to retort that this was, in fact, a cheesy *and* incorrect saying, but Antoine strolled up behind them with Grimes in tow. Grimes nickered a greeting and meandered to the edge of the water for a drink.

D waddled up with an abundance of toilet paper rolls clutched against her bosom. "Look at the *bounty* I found in the restrooms! Get it?"

"That's a paper towel brand, Dee-Dee!" Antoine corrected with a shake of his head and a chuckle.

"Oh—you right! Ain't it the one with that lumberjack dude straight outta some '70s porno?"

Brian's lips lifted into a bittersweet smile; the siblings' banter touched him but also reminded him of his failure to save Becky. Sometimes the pain struck him from out of the blue, but he usually numbed it. The fact Louis had a sister he was so willing to throw away rubbed salt in Brian's wound, which made the healing Cecilia spoke of impossible.

"Where is he?" he asked the Etiennes, reminded of Louis's absence.

D kneeled and shoved her toilet paper into her backpack. She gestured for Antoine's once she stuffed hers to the brim. "We switchin' to 'He-Who-Shall-Not-Be-Named'? 'Cause I could go for that."

"He's fillin' bottles with water to boil later," Antoine answered.

Brian scrambled to his feet. "You left him alone? Did you give him his gun, D?"

D's eyebrow arched into her Pretend Psychologist expression. "Why? You worried he has it or he doesn't?" She sighed when the only answer Brian gave her was a glare. "I don't do nothin' without askin' you. 'Sides, he said he don't need it. If he wants to go off on his own and die, that's *his* problem."

"D!" Cecilia stood alongside Brian and crossed her arms. She tried to force her gentle features into a scolding expression. "Stop pretending you'd be okay with that. You don't want to suffer more losses. None of us do."

"You his best friend all of a sudden, Cill?" D asked. "What'd he *do* to you in that bedroom?"

Brian bristled at this implication but tensed every muscle to keep this hidden from D, who'd latch on to it and try to yank it out from him.

"Good *God*, D—I'm just a person and so is he. Do I need to preach to you about compassion?" Cecilia strolled off in a huff—or as much of a huff as a petite girl like her could manage.

Antoine arched his eyebrows and cocked his head. "You know she's right, Dee-Dee. Two wrongs don't make a right. You helped me work through *my* mistakes."

"With tough love!" D snapped back. "Cill's too dang nice! You weren't there at Evergreen when He-Who-Shall-Not-Be-Named 2.0 was bein' all kinds of nasty to her! Besides, I can't stand it when people pull the 'if I can't get what I want I'd rather die' card. Life's a gift; it shouldn't be thrown away!"

"D," Antoine hissed, gripping D's shoulders, "the boy ain't right in the head. Cill understands that. Ain't everyone as lucky as you to know themselves so well."

Her shoulders sagged beneath Antoine's hands. "Well, I guess I'm salty 'cause I didn't wanna deal with his ass again." Her eyes met Brian's, glinting like gold in the sunlight. "I see the dirty look you givin' me, but I'm only sayin' to your face what most people'd say behind your back: when you said you'd give him another chance, I thought you were just as crazy as he is. And now he's suckered Cill somehow... I hope he didn't get to her the same way he got to you."

Brian forced a mocking smile. "I don't think she's as stupid as I obviously am."

"Brian—" Antoine tried to grab Brian by the shoulder, but Brian jerked free and stomped toward the picnic bench where they'd left their bikes. Cecilia and Louis were sitting on opposite sides of the table, engaged in deep conversation. Her small hand was curled around his.

The muscles in Brian's face twitched as he attempted to control his knee-jerk reaction to this. He walked over to his bike, aggravated at everyone but Antoine, and pushed his strained muscles to the breaking point by pedaling onto the road.

The others rushed after Brian as soon as they saw him leave, but when they caught up to him, he stuffed his earbuds into his ears and blasted music so he couldn't hear their admonishments.

A few Stalkers popped out from the scant rusted cars left on the road. Others emerged from the undergrowth and coppices on either side of the highway. Brian cruised past them, firing a potshot at any who got too close. Their rotten bodies moved with the tenacity of terminators.

His lips curled into a sneer as he thought of Cecilia's idyllic musings on God and life. *No benevolent God would do this to His creations. Maybe the Devil, but that's all bullshit too. This was just bad luck, and I'm still not sure I'm lucky I survived. I should've died with the rest of my family.*

What's the point to it all, anyway?

Brian didn't stop until his legs gave out. By this time, the sunlight shone through the jagged shadows of trees, and they were still in the middle of nowhere with a view to a foggy bayou vista. A large brown-and-white sign informed him it was a wildlife refuge.

Before he could finish plucking his earbuds free, someone jerked his arm so hard he stumbled off his bike. It clattered to the ground, but he caught his balance and stepped back. "What the *hell*?"

"I should ask you the same thing!" Louis glared at him with unnerving ferocity. "You ran off and left us all in the dust; then you wouldn't listen to anyone when we tried to talk to you! Not to mention you pickin' and choosin' which Stalkers you wanted to kill or leave for the rest of us to deal with! What the fuck is *wrong* with you?"

Brian scoffed and jerked his arm free. "That's gold coming from you. Really. Am I not allowed to pull the crazy card too?" He smacked the side of his head. "I'm not right in here, either! Even D thinks so!"

"Oh, Jesus, take the wheel," D muttered. Brian remained tangentially aware of her, Antoine, and Cecilia's presence, but he focused on Louis. D tried to step forward, but Antoine held her back.

"Don't you snap on me like you did in the Ozarks," Louis said, lowering his voice and arching his eyebrows. "You're tired, right? We all need some sleep after that shit back there. Let's just set the tents up—"

"You keep saying you'd rather die than go without me, so let's test it." Brian withdrew the revolver and aimed it at Louis. Somebody gasped. He jerked the muzzle down, eyes fixed on Louis's. "Get on your knees."

The stink of stagnant water hung heavy in the air. Insects buzzed discordantly, and a pair of egrets soared overhead. Sweat trickled down Brian's skin, making his clothes stick to it. He could make out the murmurs of the others trying to decide if they should intervene.

"This is what you want, right, D?" Brian didn't look at her; he watched Louis sink to his knees, his hands curled onto them like a member of the congregation about to receive confirmation. "You thought I should've done this to begin with."

For once, D couldn't find anything to say—or knew she *shouldn't* say anything.

Louis's eyes angled to the side; he shook his head gently as if to warn someone against doing something. When his eyes returned to Brian's, Brian pressed the muzzle of the gun against his forehead.

"Would you really be okay with dying this way?"

Louis nodded.

"Why?"

"Because I deserve it, and you earned the right to do it."

Brian shook his head. "No, I didn't. Eva did. You share the same blood. You and I only fucked around a few times."

"You know it was more than that." The first hint of emotion crossed Louis's face: frustration, not fear. "So are you gonna shoot me, or are you gonna save me for Eva?"

"If you had any last words, what would they be?"

Louis didn't hesitate or even blink. "I love you. And I'm sorry."

Brian pulled the trigger. Louis didn't jump when it clicked, but the others did.

"I already used all the bullets." Brian stuffed the revolver into his jeans. "Don't you *ever* threaten me with any suicidal bullshit again. You have no excuse to feel sorry for yourself after what you did. You're lucky you're even here with us—don't throw this opportunity away, and don't cheat Eva of the chance to confront you. If we even find her."

Louis sighed, eyes averting Brian's for the first time since he'd cautioned the others. "You're right." He leaned forward, the front of his head bumping into Brian's loins. Something about this submission doused the embers lingering within Brian. The thought of benediction loomed in his mind, but the gesture also carried a sexual charge which made this display uncomfortably intimate.

Brian didn't shove Louis away, but he stepped back and let Louis slump forward onto his palms. Brian strolled past the others and retrieved the camping supplies from Grimes's saddle. She swished her tail at the flitting gnats trying to settle on her for a sip of salt. "Let's set this stuff up and get some sleep."

Antoine and D helped him without a word. Cecilia went to Louis and kneeled at his side. She patted his back with the consolatory kindness of a parent reassuring their child.

Once they assembled the tents, they let Grimes forage for food and rolled their bicycles behind tree cover. They shared a silent supper, the violet shadows hugging their bodies darkening to black once the sun hid beyond the bayou.

Brian noticed the others avoided making eye contact with him. Even Louis was shaken by what had happened—which was the result Brian had been going for. He hadn't intended to rattle Antoine, but he had wanted to challenge Cecilia's resolute faith and D's judgmental nature. Not to mention the opinion they'd all formed of him being some lovestruck, spineless pushover.

Scaring them had been an inadvertent side effect. Reflecting on it, he'd even scared *himself*. But pride kept his teeth tight around his tongue. He bit it until it bled, reminded of the way Louis's tooth always drew blood when he'd kissed him. Always suffering for the pleasure.

Sweet little Cecilia offered to keep Louis company while the Etiennes and Brian slept. D and Antoine shared a tent, but Brian kept to himself—at least until someone stepped in wielding the blinding white light of a lantern.

"Are you done throwin' your little tantrum?" D preferred to confront her problems head-on, as usual.

Brian sat and blocked his eyes with one arm. "Get the light outta my eyes, D."

She plopped down in front of him and set the lantern at her side, decreasing the brightness. Her eyes scanned his from beneath deep-set brows. "What pushed you to this?"

"Everything."

"Well, that just answered all my questions." D rolled her eyes and shook her head. "I'm tryin' to help you here. Why else you think I'm here puttin' up with your shit when I could be back at Evergreen havin' a bath and eatin' a hot meal?"

Brian buried his face in his hands, trying to hide the frustrated tears building in his eyes. "I don't know. I don't know why any of you bother. I don't even know why Eva liked me, or why Louis is so goddamn obsessed with me."

"'Cause the feeling's mutual, obviously." D reached out to grab Brian's knee. "I'm sure there's more to it. But to be honest with you, that shit you pulled shook me—and he was *willin'* to let you do it! I thought he was just sayin' it to say it, but it really seems like you're the only thing he lives for."

Brian's hands fell from his wet cheeks. "*Why?*"

D threw her hands up. "I don't know—what happened between y'all was between y'all. But I can tell you why the *rest* of us love you: you got a good heart. Even if you run off and sulk now and again and have questionable taste in men, you'd back each of us up in a heartbeat. You went outta your way to help me find Jones and 'Toine, and you and Cill always had those long-ass conversations in your cabin. She told me how nice it was to have someone listen, to offer her a shoulder to cry on. And she didn't have to worry about you hittin' on her."

Brian whapped D's shoulder and laughed. "Shut up! She didn't say that!"

As always, D knew the right way to lighten the mood. And he loved her for it.

D reached for his hand. "No, she didn't. But she said the rest. And you're worth it, okay? You're not crazy, and I'm sorry if it seemed like I thought you was. You just young, went through too much shit, fell hard and fast for a problematic person."

"It's the most confusing feeling in the world to hate someone you love."

"It's enough to make anyone *feel* crazy, I'm sure." D sighed and tapped the side of her head with purple nails. "I miss bein' in love. Well, I guess I still love Gus—I always will. But he ain't there to love me back. In a weird way, even though y'all got some fucked-up love, I'm jealous. I'm lucky to have you and Cill, and findin' 'Toine was more than I could've hoped for, but it ain't the same without my Gus."

Brian wiped underneath his eyes and sniffed, trying to suppress his self-pity so he could comfort D. "I can't imagine all the things you went through *before* the apocalypse. The worst thing I had to deal with was my dad being depressed and trying to kill himself. But my mom was strong. She would've liked you."

"I'm sure I woulda liked her too. She done a good job raisin' you." D's eyes glimmered in the lambent light. Shadows rippled along the canvas of the tent. "You and me both lost a lot. We all have."

Brian curled his fingers into the fabric of his sleeping bag. "Does it help you to remember the people you lost? It still hurts too much for me. I dream about them. Sometimes I wake up crying, but it happens less now than it did before."

D pressed her lips together and tilted her head. "Aw, baby, so do I. Dreams are the worst 'cause they tease you, make you think *this* been the dream all along. But I'll take this reality over nothin' at all. When I get to thinkin' 'bout what I lost, I remind myself of what I got."

Ashamed by his earlier behavior, Brian skirted D's gaze. "I'm sorry I spoke to you that way. It hurt my feelings when you said I was crazy. I felt kinda like you were judging me when you're supposed to be the person who has my back."

"I'm sorry too. I just don't wanna see you get hurt again." D shrugged. "But you *are* an adult, and you can make the bed you lie in. And choose who lays in it with you, I guess." Her eyes narrowed, and her lips parted—her "should I say this or not?" tell. "You know Cill's bein' nice 'cause that's how she is, right? I shouldn't've said that shit, made insinuations about her sleepin' with him. I just run my smart mouth sometimes. And I guess I worry 'bout her too—I don't want him to find a weakness and latch on to it, twist her so she can talk him back onto your good side."

Brian sighed. "I don't think either of us gives her enough credit. I forget she's older than me. And she's clever—if he was bullshitting her, she'd see through it. Just because she believes in something doesn't make her naïve. I shouldn't judge her for it."

D slapped his knee. "Believin' in something just makes dealing with this shit easier. I wouldn't have made it if I didn't believe Gus was out there somewhere in the universe watchin' out for me. I mean, look at me—I met you and the folks at Evergreen, my cat's still around, and I found my brother alive. Either I got the best damn luck in the world or someone's makin' sure I do."

Brian leaned forward and wrapped his arms around her neck. He buried his face in her frizzy curls and inhaled the scent of lavender from some shampoo or perfume. Her arms tightened around him. "Don't pull any more weird shit, okay? If you want Louis to get on his knees and put his head near your dick, do it in private. I'm sure *someone* would wanna watch, but it ain't me."

He scoffed and withdrew from D. "As I recall, you asked me, 'Does he know how to work a dick as good as he works a gun?' So I don't wanna hear it."

D shrugged and looked away with a little smile. "Guilty." She stood and patted the top of his head. "I was just jealous you was gettin' some, I guess. Gotta live vicariously through you."

Brian flopped back into his sleeping bag. He caught a phantom whiff of cinnamon and took in a deep breath. "Well, I'm in the same boat as you now, so tough luck." He sighed and shut his eyes. "Good night, D. Thanks for talking to me. Love you."

"Love you too, Sunshine. Remember: shake the creamer, don't stir the sugar."

She slipped through the tent flap and zipped it shut before he could ask her what the euphemism meant. It made him long for iced coffee.

As if hyped up by the phantom thought of coffee, his mind struggled to shut down. His body pulsed with frustration, skin sticky with sweat. He kept tossing and turning atop his sleeping bag, aggravated by the faint sounds of voices outside.

Although his conversation with D bolstered his friendship with her, he still owed Cecilia and Antoine apologies for his irrational behavior. And the divide between him and Louis had stretched into a breaking point.

They'd ended the worst argument they had before this by literally kissing and making up. Which was exactly the wrong memory to relive before his mind gave in to his exhaustion and allowed him to dream.

Brian offered Cecilia and Antoine brief yet sincere apologies in the morning, but he couldn't bring himself to say anything to Louis. In fact, both avoided even *looking* at each other. Brian didn't know if he'd finally made Louis hate him, or if Louis hating him would be a bad or a good thing.

They retrieved their bicycles and pushed on in the ascending sun. Within a few hours, they encountered ruined buildings and wrecked automobiles—signs of a lost civilization. Any bodies left behind in the chaos had either decomposed or been devoured and scattered by predators. Despite the missing bodies, the violent struggles which had occurred left their mark on the battered windows of buildings and cars. Spray-painted images and phrases—"WE'RE ALL DEAD," "SEND MY LOVE TO MY FAMILY," "GOD HATES US ALL," and "THE EARTH JUST REBOOTED"—accompanied names and ages of people who wanted to be remembered when there was nothing else left of them.

In search of ammo to replenish what they wasted at the rest stop, they took a chance on a police academy. Blossoming trees and half-empty parking lots surrounded the modest brick building. Particleboard guarded the windows but not the front door. When they tried it, it didn't budge.

"Someone still in there?" D whispered.

Antoine shook his head. "Maybe they locked themselves in, tried to wait it out."

"We can't stand here all day," Brian said. "We have to kick it down or find another way in."

"Might be able to pry the board and push Cill in through a window," D said. Cecilia shot her an irritated look. "Shit, girl—*my* ass ain't fittin'!"

Brian narrowed his eyes. "No one's going in the window. We should stick with the door. Antoine, give it a go, all right?"

Antoine launched his foot into the area above the doorknob. The wooden door cracked but stayed shut. When Louis moved to help Antoine kick, it crashed open. Curved white lines scuffed the linoleum floor; they'd shifted the desk blocking the door.

They scrambled to get inside and push the desk back against the door, and then surveyed the dark lobby with sweeps of their flashlights and lanterns. Framed photos of cadets smiled at them from the walls. Broken pieces of benches and chairs littered the floor alongside a bloodstained United States flag. The pole once attached to it was cracked in two, perhaps used as a weapon. The entirety of the lobby gave off the impression it had been the scene of a last stand.

They froze in unison, grouped together in a circle. Their shared glances conveyed an unspoken consensus: *We're in here now. Might as well push forward.*

A metal detector gleamed within the hallway beyond the lobby. Even though there was no power, Brian still tensed when he walked past it and imagined a disapproving buzz.

The narrow hallways forced them to move in pairs. Antoine took the odd position in front with Louis and D behind him and Cecilia and Brian holding up the rear. When D's shoulder brushed a glinting photograph, Cecilia cringed and scrambled to catch it before it fell.

The short hallway split into a T at the end. They followed it right until they reached a series of doors. To Brian, they'd once been meaningless squares of wood on hinges that opened and shut; now they were a barrier protecting them from the unknown. He still had a phobia of Porta-potties and wouldn't go near them.

Brian stopped and reached for the closest door, which had a plaque with a woman's silhouette on it. Unprepared for the stench of festering feces, he gagged and muffled his mouth and nose with his arm, and then stumbled back into the hall. Antoine edged in with the guidance of D's flashlight, but it highlighted nothing more than shit and blood smeared all over the walls and mirror.

Antoine popped out and shook his head, taking in a gasp of air before they approached the men's room. Rinse, repeat, awful smell, awful sight. They hurried on, the rancid stench trapped in Brian's nose and mouth.

Brian twisted the knob of the next door, relieved by the *whoosh* of clean air which escaped when he nudged it open. He half expected to see the glinting barrel of a gun or a Stalker's bloodshot eyes—but it was only another silent room filled with reminders of lives once lived. Lockers lined the walls on either side, but they were meant for personal belongings, not weapons. Flimsy padlocks secured some. Coats still hung from a rack in the back.

Antoine shut the door and moved a bench in front of it. Still on guard but not as tense, they rifled through the lockers in search of anything: deodorant, toothpaste, shoes, underwear. And food, if they were lucky. They shoved anything remotely desirable into their backpacks.

A whine carried from the back of the room. They stopped what they were doing and dropped the loot in their hands. *It sounded like an animal. Is it trapped in one of the lockers?*

Brian held his breath. His heart throbbed in his ear.

No more animals bursting out of doors would be nice.

The locker rattled.

"All right," Louis said, "we can fuckin' hear you. Come out or we'll shoot you *through* the locker."

The locker door scraped open. A disheveled woman stepped out and held her hands up. Her defiant hazel eyes resembled Eva's. "Don't shoot."

"What the hell you doin' in there?" Antoine moved beside Louis, aiming the hijacked PPK. Louis spun the pocketknife in his hand, his dark eyes fixed on the woman while Antoine spoke. "You the one who pushed the desk against the door? Barricaded the windows?"

"I pushed the desk over, but the windows were already boarded. When I heard you come in, I hid in the locker. Those Stalker things are smart enough to move stuff out of the way. I wasn't sure if it was one of them or regular people. Still not sure which is worse."

"It's okay"—Cecilia squeezed between Antoine and Louis—"we're just looking for supplies. We're not going to hurt you."

"All it takes is one second before she pulls out a gun and plugs one of us." Brian pulled Cecilia back and studied the woman. Her black hair hung in tangles around her face, done up in a loose ponytail. She might've been pretty with a bath and a good night's sleep, but the harsh climate had taken its toll on her. "Empty your pockets and let one of us pat you down."

"Fine." The woman jammed her hands into her pockets and tugged them inside out. She turned. "There's a gun in the back of my pants. Don't get handsy."

D stepped forward. "You don't got to worry about that with me, lady." She reached in, took the gun out, and ejected the clip from the pistol. After she patted the woman, D came up with a shrug and empty hands. "She's clean. Just the gun."

"You have anything else stashed in here?" Brian asked.

The woman's eyes shifted to the side. *She's hiding something.*

Brian approached the locker adjacent to the one the woman had emerged from. He glanced at her, noticing her body tense up. When he reached for the door, the woman stepped forward—but Louis threw her back against a locker and kept her pinned to it, his knife pressed to her throat. "If you so much as poke him with a finger, you're dead."

The woman's throat bobbed against the edge of Louis's knife. Louis's shrewdness impressed Brian—and reminded him he was essentially traveling with a short-fused stick of dynamite.

Brian pulled the locker door open, anticipating a hoard of food or guns. Instead, a little girl cowered in the corner. He backed away, fearing she might be another infected child, one this woman couldn't bear to part with—but her complexion was unblemished. She covered her mouth to muffle the sobs shaking her slight body.

"Is this your daughter?"

The woman nodded. "Don't you touch her. And take your arm off me, asshole."

Brian met Louis's furious eyes and jerked his head. Louis backed away and lowered his arm, but he kept his knife angled toward the glaring woman while she caressed her throat.

Brian kneeled in front of the sobbing girl. *She's not much older than Becks—maybe even the same age.* He didn't reach out to her, trying to give her space and time to calm down. "Hey, don't be scared—we won't hurt you. You know what? We're scared too. Those things out there are pretty creepy, huh? Kinda like super ugly clowns." He stood and fixed his gaze on the bedraggled woman. "You should've told us she was in there… But I understand why you wouldn't. What's your name?"

"Sarah. Can I go to her?"

Brian nodded.

Sarah moved to the open locker and cradled her daughter in her arms. A frilly skirt covered purple leggings and sparkly tennis shoes. The little girl buried her face in her mother's chest and curled a hand into her flannel shirt.

"What were you doin' in here?" D's eyes softened as she watched Sarah stroke her daughter's strawberry-blonde curls. This time Brian thought of his mother—especially the way she'd soothed Becky the night of the attack. It was the last night she'd truly been herself.

"We haven't been in here long," Sarah said. "We ran in because we saw a group of people roaming around."

"How many?" Brian asked. "Were they armed?"

"We didn't stay to find out." Sarah tucked her chin onto the top of her daughter's head. "I think there were three. Maybe four."

Goose bumps rippled along Brian's flesh. "Where'd you see them?"

"An apartment complex about ten blocks from here. They were darting in and out of the apartments, probably looking for supplies. We'd been staying there for a few nights without any trouble, but we heard them this morning and slipped past while they were in one of the apartments below us."

Brian let a trace of doubt cross his mind. *How did they make it this long?* The sight of a young mother and her daughter reminded him of Cassandra and Bailey, Parker's sister and niece. For all he knew, this woman was another prisoner or actress under some gang's employ.

But he didn't doubt a mother's resiliency. It was entirely possible Sarah had gotten by with sharp instincts and a strong protective streak.

Sarah's eyes softened slightly as her daughter's frantic cries slowed to labored gasps for air. The little girl pried her head from her mother's chest, her bleary eyes widening with curiosity as she surveyed Brian's group.

D smiled at her. "Hey there, baby girl—I'm Dionne, but you can call me D. What's your name?"

The young girl sniffled and rubbed her eyes with her sleeve. "K-Katie, but my momma calls me Kat sometimes."

"Kat, huh? Well, back home, I got a kitty-cat named Jonesy!" D gestured over her shoulder with her thumb. "This is my brother, Antoine—but we call him 'Toine."

"T-the big bald guy?"

D snickered as a grinning Antoine waved. "That's him. He looks scary, but he's a big ol' teddy bear." D made her hands into mock claws. "Not the kind that goes 'rawr'! Trust me: they *nasty*."

Katie still gripped her mother's shirt, but she peered around D. "W-who're the blonde girl and boy? Are they brother and sister too?"

Cecilia moved next to D and offered Katie a gentle smile. "I'm Cecilia, and that's Brian. We're not related—just good friends."

When Katie's sparkling blue eyes moved to Louis, she buried her face in her mother's chest again. D frowned at Louis. "Louis Lavellé, you put that thing away! You scarin' her!"

Louis slipped the knife somewhere behind his back, but a slight smirk curled his lips.

Katie withdrew her face from Sarah's chest. "Puh-please don't hurt my mommy."

Louis's eyebrow quirked. "Listen, kid, she made a move for my *copain* first—long as she doesn't do it again, I won't touch her."

Katie scrunched her nose. "Why do you talk so funny?"

He scoffed. "I'm part Cajun. You're in the South; you should know what that is."

"Spicy food?"

"Do I *look* like spicy food?" Louis shrugged. "Well, maybe for Stalkers I am... Anyway, Cajuns are people who came over from France and settled in Louisiana. If you ever got to go to middle school, they probably woulda taught you that."

"You're from *France*? Do you speak French?"

Louis shook his head and scratched it with his free hand, an ineffable combination of amusement and aggravation contorting his face. "*Je ne suis pas de France, mais je le parle, peeshwank.*"

Katie's expression—impressed yet confused—made her mother smile. Louis had taught Brian enough for him to distinguish what Louis said as "I'm not from France, but I speak it, runt." Brian's fondness for these tutoring sessions and the way Louis spoke French gave him a regrettable case of the *frissons*—essentially, the chills, but Louis described it as being like a skin orgasm, which had made Brian bust up laughing at the time.

"We shouldn't stay here long," Sarah said. "If you'll give me my things, we'll get out of your hair."

Katie's face drooped with disappointment. "We're gonna be all alone again, Mommy?"

Cecilia pulled Brian back and whispered to him, "Should we tell them about Evergreen? I mean, she could be lying...but it seems like they're really struggling. I can't bring myself to leave them without offering any help."

"I wouldn't tell them about Evergreen yet," Brian whispered back, "but I don't see the harm in letting them travel with us—we outnumber them, five adults to one woman and a kid."

Cecilia relayed the decision to D and Antoine. Louis frowned; he knew it was coming whether he wanted it or not.

Brian sighed and faced the hesitant mother and dejected daughter. "Listen, it's tough out there for us—I can't imagine what it's been like for you. You can come with us if you want. We're heading north, looking for a friend. We all have our own supplies—water, food, sleeping bags—and we have transportation. Do you? Or have you been moving on foot?"

Sarah's dry lips parted before she stammered a reply. "R-really? It'd be so nice for Katie to be around other people. Um, we have bicycles."

"Us too!" D boasted with a proud smile. "And a horse! You like horses, Kat?"

Katie nodded, her face brightening. Louis rolled his eyes at D's generous attitude toward sharing information.

Sarah stuck her hand out toward Brian. "Thank you, Brian."

Brian took her hand and shook it, thinking of Spike and Parker. But Sarah was easier to read, not putting on a flashy act. "You really don't need to thank me. I'm not in charge or anything—we're a group, and now you're part of it."

Sarah lowered her hand from his. She set Katie down and tousled the top of her hair. "I hate to ask, but what are you going to do about my weapons? If you want to keep them, I understand—but I need to know my daughter will be okay." She looked at Katie, who'd been taking in the conversation. Her eyes kept drifting back to Louis, who seemed to fascinate her. Brian understood why, of course: he had a commanding presence despite his Abercrombie model good looks.

"You can have them back." Brian gestured to D, giving her the okay. She handed Sarah the items she'd taken from her. Louis reached behind his back but didn't withdraw the knife. His reflexes were quick enough to take Sarah out before she could lift her gun, much less aim it.

Sarah shoved the pistol into the back of her jeans and smiled at Katie. "You wanna travel with these nice people, kiddo?"

Katie looked at her mother, smiling with a warmth which could thaw nearly any frozen heart. "Yeah, Mommy!"

D and Cecilia shared an "Aw, isn't she precious?" look. Antoine smiled, an easygoing man who was too big and strong for much to scare him—especially not a disheveled woman and a little girl. Louis watched Katie, one eyebrow arched slightly, but he gave no emotion away.

He's not happy. He hates kids. He hates strangers. He hates people.

Louis caught Brian analyzing his expression. It shifted from unreadable to pissed.

After Antoine moved the bench blocking the door, the group filed back into the hall. Louis lingered in the locker room and gripped Brian's sleeve before he could join the others. "We're long overdue for a talk."

Brian shook his arm free and glared at Louis, but it was better to get it over with—in private this time. He sighed and called out to D, "Wait out in the lobby, okay? We'll be there in a few minutes."

D lifted an eyebrow and tucked her chin into her chest, her wordless, "If you say so."

Louis reached past Brian and shut the door. "Who went and elected you sheriff, huh? What the fuck are you thinkin' takin' on a woman and a kid? We aren't babysitters!"

Brian folded his arms, fingers digging into his biceps. "Everyone else is okay with it."

Louis pressed a hand to his chest. "*I'm* a part of the 'everyone else' too, Brian!"

"Not really. You're on probation, if you think about it. We have to see if you'll act up again before we let you out with the rest of the population."

Louis's jaw tightened. The corner of one eye twitched: his tell when he passed from irritated to furious. "The rest of the population is fucked! I'm one of a few people who can keep you alive, but I don't even have a gun—and need I remind you you sent me to my knees and pretended to put a bullet in my forehead? So don't give me shit about actin' up, 'cause you do it too."

Brian glanced away from Louis, attempting to ignore the perpetual electricity crackling between them. "I might trust you with a gun if I didn't think you'd shoot one of them with it like you shot my grandfather. And my dad used to manipulate my mom with that suicidal crap—he'd tell her if she ever left him, he'd have nothing to live for anymore. So I needed to know you weren't manipulating me, or at least that you'd put your money where your mouth was."

Louis shook his head. "Fine, I get it, but in front of everyone? I mean, fuck, I can do it right here if you want—I'll do anythin' you fuckin' ask. But you scared the shit outta them. Cecilia was about to fuckin' cry!"

"Since when do you care if Cecilia cries or not? You're the one who called her a bitch and treated her like shit at Evergreen."

"I know—I told her I was sorry. And you know why I was an ass to her: I was bein' a jealous idiot. She's a nice girl—probably nicer than anyone I've ever met. Why the fuck else would she listen to me talk about how fuckin' fucked up I am?"

Louis's normally ruddy cheeks had deepened to the color of beets. His dusky eyes gleamed, and he kept sniffing while he waited for Brian to say something.

Eventually, Louis collapsed onto one of the benches and hid his face behind his arms, fingers bunching into his hair. "You were always on my side before—you and me against the world, not you against *me*. I can't do anythin' right if I keep bein' reminded of how wrong I've been. So tell me what the fuck I'm supposed to *do*."

Brian walked over to Louis and stood in front of him. He considered kneeling in front of him like he had Katie, but Louis wasn't a child and Brian didn't want to baby him. He needed to hold his ground with the person who once held so much sway over him. "I'll give you your gun back, but don't shoot anything unless it's coming at you or one of us." He pointed a cautioning finger toward Louis. "You've got one chance, Louis—don't blow it."

The way Louis looked at Brian resembled a skittish animal seeking approval. He reached out for Brian's hand and held it in both of his. "*Je promets, mon bien-aimé.*"

Brian clicked his tongue and glanced away from Louis's enticing gaze. "Don't try to loosen me up with your French. It's not fair to use my weakness against me."

Louis tugged Brian's glove from his hand. "Your weakness is nothin' compared to mine." He lifted Brian's hand to his lips, maintaining eye contact. It sent an electric current down Brian's spine. His fingertips barely brushed the soft heat of Louis's lips, but the skin-on-skin contact made him feel like the room was spinning.

He jerked his hand away from Louis and stepped back, trying to regain his center of gravity. "Don't. It'll only torment us both."

Louis bit his lip and stood, averting his eyes from Brian's. He only exposed this vulnerable mien to Brian, which made it a rare gift, hard to refuse. "I just wanted to touch your skin. I'm sorry." He looked at Brian and lifted the glove he'd pulled off. "May I?"

Brian held his hand between them and allowed Louis to replace the glove, staring at their hands instead of Louis's eyes. Their foreheads brushed, generating a spark of static electricity which spiked Brian's already rapid pulse.

So much for standing my ground. I'm putty in his hands.

Louis slipped the last finger on. "We shouldn't be alone together; I don't know about you, but it's too much temptation for me. I'm at the limit of my self-restraint as it is."

Brian backed toward the locker room door and fumbled for the knob with his hand. "I'm sure you could find another way to satisfy those urges."

"That what you thought I was doin' with Cecilia?"

Brian twisted the knob. "I didn't mean that."

"You're just like me, jealous and needy and insecure, imaginin' things that make you boil inside." Louis stepped forward. "If you want me to move on, tell me. Tell me you never want me to touch you again, that you'll never forgive me, thanks for the memories, *adieu*. I'll disappear and you'll never have to worry about me again."

When Brian's lips parted, no words came to the tip of his tongue. Trapped between the inability to forget or forgive, Brian answered Louis with a fatigued shake of his head and a frustrated sigh.

Louis's expression betrayed neither relief nor disappointment. "That was your last chance to kill this love, just so you know." He pointed a finger at Brian, and then mimed the pull of a trigger with a click of his tongue. "You blew it."

Bothered by the implications of what Louis said—and what he couldn't bring *himself* to say—Brian squeezed through the door and hurried into the hall. He rubbed the hand Louis had kissed, trying to scrub away the poison left by his lips—

But he only ended up spreading it.

Chapter Seven

Interference

3/26, Arkansas-Louisiana border, afternoon

They traversed past murky Louisiana bogs and sprawling Cyprus trees until they reached a weathered wooden sign on the side of the road. Katie stooped and attempted to pronounce it: "Well-come to Are-can-sass."

While Sarah corrected her, Brian flashed back to the conflicting feelings of triumph and defeat he'd experienced when he'd seen it for the first time. *It was just the two of us. Eva was already gone. The island was the only thing keeping me going.*

But it was only a metaphor for him.

Brian examined the bronze profile of Louis's face, catching a glimmer of recognition in his dusky eyes. His lips pressed together and his brow furrowed—an attempt at repressing something, maybe swallowing words on the tip of his tongue.

Since he'd been rewarded for his good behavior with a gun, he was far less churlish. Instead of the silenced pistol, which he insisted Antoine keep until they found more ammo, he borrowed Cecilia's rifle. Louis had the uncanny ability to quickfire with it and hit targets up close, but Brian doubted more and more this would include any of his companions.

Mostly because it was harder to shoot a group in broad daylight than an elderly man in the dark. But also because Brian *wanted* Louis to be better.

They traveled past the sign and continued along desolate Arkansas roads no different from the ones in northern Louisiana. D made conversation with Sarah while Brian's tablet entertained Katie. "So how'd y'all end up in Louisiana? You don't sound like you from there."

"We were in Alabama when the reports started." Sarah pedaled a green mountain bike with Katie in tow behind her. "We tried to get out, but the military blocked the roads. Then they herded everyone into a quarantine zone. That didn't last long. People fought back. We took advantage of the confusion and ran. I figured it was better to try it on our own. We ended up in a motel, a Best Western or something, but we weren't the only ones there. Back then, there were people all over—not like this. They were trying to escape, to find sanctuary. But there is no sanctuary anymore. Eventually, we had to leave the hotel. We've been running ever since, escaping everything, heading for nothing."

D sighed. "Before I met Brian and Louis and found my brother, I didn't see nothin' but snow and Stalkers. Tried fiddlin' with a radio I found, but all I heard was static. I tossed it so I'd have room for food, ammo, clothes, and lookin' and feelin' good stuff. I guess I was lucky not to see too many people—most of 'em are crazy now."

Sarah wiped away a strand of dark hair the wind whipped into her eyes. "It's hard to remember mostly everyone used to be normal before all this. Even those creatures were people once, people with families and lives... I was a geologist." She scoffed. "Hardly a useful skill now—unless a natural disaster follows this pandemic. That'd be some rotten luck. What did the rest of you do?"

"I was a psychic," D said. "To tell you the truth, I had no real talent 'cept tellin' people what they wanted to hear. It was fun—kinda like acting."

Cecilia squinted as sunlight beamed into her eyes. "I worked part-time at a coffee shop to pay college tuition. I was majoring in sociology, so D and I bonded over our shared interest in reading people."

"I did all kinds of shitty jobs—and I don't miss *any* of 'em," Antoine said. Grimes snorted and shook her head as if she agreed. "Or laundry and dishes. Takin' out trash, shoppin' for groceries..."

"I don't miss paying rent," Cecilia said. "I don't miss taxes, either. And *nobody* misses Daylight Savings Time."

Brian biked alongside Cecilia, behind D and Antoine and in front of Sarah and Katie. "I never had to do taxes or pay rent. But I don't miss school, summer jobs, or having to live by my parents' rules."

"Wow," Cecilia murmured, "I forget you never even went to college sometimes."

Brian shrugged. "I guess it would've been interesting to go to college, to own a car and hang out with friends, start a career... But wouldn't it have gotten boring? Distracting myself with TV and stuff while I wasted all my money on school and worked a dead-end job just to pay the bills month to month? At least we have freedom now."

"True, but we don't have security," Cecilia said. "There's always a trade-off. I'd take it all back—the chores, traffic, morning classes, the awkwardness of Tinder—just so I knew I had a roof over my head, a bed to sleep in, and food in my stomach."

"I don't miss any of it," Louis said from Cecilia's other side. "I had crappy grades and never went to college, dates were too much effort with too little payoff, I was shit with money, and drivin' pissed me off. Screw the bed and roof—I was always happy with a sleepin' bag and the stars above me."

Sarah's brow furrowed above sharp eyes. "So why not go it alone, be a mountain man or something?"

Louis didn't reply. He glanced at Brian as if it was habitual.

Sarah looked between Brian and Louis. "I guess that's my answer. Did you two meet before or after the outbreak?"

Their eyes darted to each other's, Brian's mouth tightening into a grimace. Louis said nothing, so Brian answered to put an end to the awkward silence. "We grew up together. I was friends with his sister too— the girl we're trying to find. But we drifted apart. When people broke into my grandparents' house, my grandfather took me to their place, and I met up with them again."

"What happened to your families?" Sarah asked.

Louis braked with a screech. "My *mamère* smoked herself to death, I popped my *papère* off with a pistol, started a fire that killed my parents when I was a kid, and I was scared Brian's Vietnam-vet granddaddy would kill me, so I shot him durin' a home invasion and blamed it on the robbers. Oh, and I left my sister behind so Brian and I could escape the same robbers when a pair of two-bit actors conned us into gettin' abducted by 'em. That's all the news that's fit to print."

Sarah's feet fell from her bike pedals. She slowed to a stop and lowered them to the ground. Katie looked around, jerked out of whatever game she'd been playing on Brian's tablet.

Louis stood above his bicycle. The charged air lingered in silence, his chest heaving as his cheeks flushed beet red from a combination of exertion and adrenaline. Brian sometimes struggled to understand what motivated Louis to say and do the things he did; either he was on an honesty kick or trying to scare Sarah and Katie away.

Sarah glanced at each of them before settling on Brian. "If this is true, why do you let this nut travel with you?"

"Fuck *this*." Louis let his bike fall to the ground and stalked off into the woods, kicking away rocks and pebbles in his path. Everyone's eyes followed him. They were all shocked by his impulsive outburst.

Brian got up from his bike, but Cecilia reached over and grasped his arm. "I'll take care of it. I think he knew his past would come up eventually, so he decided to come clean with it; he can't escape it, even if he wants to." She followed Louis into the woods without hesitation. Her confidence and compassion impressed Brian. He envied it, even.

"Listen, Sarah"—D's stern voice sliced the somber silence—"everyone here has done some crazy shit to survive. Shit they woulda never done before the pandemic. Most of us would rather not relive it. I mean, we ain't askin' you where your baby daddy is."

"I'm concerned for my daughter's safety. And mine. That boy frightens me." Sarah's harsh gaze locked on Brian. "You should just take care of him before he becomes a problem. If he did those sorts of things before, he'll do them again."

D snapped her fingers before Brian could stammer out a reply. "What did I say about makin' people relive shit? Let it stay in the past where it belongs, and don't you *dare* bring it up around Louis again unless you *want* his ass to become a problem. You wanna ask us somethin', pull us aside and we might tell you if we feelin' generous. But most of what we been through, baby girl don't need to hear anyway."

Sarah sighed. She reached behind her to pat a curious Katie's knee. "You're right. I just thought it'd be a good way to get to know all of you—you seem to have so much history together. Katie and I have been going it alone so long I guess I've sort of forgotten how to talk to other people."

"You a'ight," Antoine assured her with a cheerful smile. "Just got to find less touchy topics. Ask us about movies—D *loves* 'em."

Branches cracked and leaves rustled at the edge of the woods. They trained their guns—but it was only a sullen Louis being guided by Cecilia. He bent over and jerked up his bike and settled astride it without a word.

Time to move on.

The group's ammo dearth remained a problem. During the chaos, desperate survivors had torn apart most of the shooting ranges and ammo shops. They busted glass cases and stripped their contents, leaving the shops littered with shards of glass and little else.

They were about at their wit's end when they encountered a wooden sign for a gun range. Without many other options, they followed the sign to a dirt road and a barbed-wire fence. Barricades covered the entrances to the gun shop beyond it. The group clipped through the fence with bolt cutters and slunk through the gap. Sarah stayed behind with Grimes and Katie to keep an eye on the hole in the fence and protect her daughter from what might be in the gun store.

An occasional rustle of leaves and footsteps falling on twigs accompanied the constant buzz of grasshoppers. Brian tugged on his windbreaker, his hands moist within a pair of suede gloves. He narrowly avoided crunching bleached bone fragments with his boots.

No way to tell if they're animal or human and no point in wondering.

Antoine and D walked up to the front of the building and pried at the plywood to see how much give it had. Louis swept the rifle around the clearing, searching the fringes of the woods surrounding them. They had a clear shot to the open road and Grimes and the bikes weren't far, but the memory of the bear's gruff roars and dagger-like talons remained fresh in their minds.

Brian spied something in the back of the building: a small window above a dumpster. He summoned Cecilia and Louis while D and Antoine fiddled with the barricades.

Cecilia stood on tiptoe to peer inside. "Why do you think it isn't boarded?"

Louis shoved her away from the window. "Don't get too close. Let us handle it."

"Shouldn't we tell the others?" she whispered, glaring at Louis and brushing her sleeve where he'd shoved her.

Brian nodded. "Tell them to stay put, but let them know what we found. Hurry back."

She returned his nod and jogged away, ponytail swinging.

Brian approached the dumpster and examined the small window. Vague shadows lay beyond it. He exhaled and climbed onto the dumpster, trying to get a grip under the window. The dumpster was sturdy, but the lid was at an incline and made of plastic, and he kept slipping when he tried to use his legs for leverage.

"You're makin' me nervous up there," Louis said. "Get down and let me try."

"I got it." But Brian didn't have it. He furrowed his brow and clenched his jaw, but *someone must've nailed the damn window shut.*

Thunk. He paused, trying to figure out where the noise came from. The plastic beneath his feet vibrated.

He shared a puzzled look with Louis before scrambling to the other side of the dumpster. The lid he'd been standing on popped up like a jack-in-the-box. A pasty figure launched out with a feverish chuckle, its arms straining for him.

Brian slid off the dumpster and skidded to his knees as a bullet burst from the rifle. The Stalker slumped forward onto the dumpster, its head a pile of slick red and white mush.

Louis held out a hand to Brian. He brushed it aside and stood, sweeping dirt off his knees as Cecilia and the Etiennes ran over, summoned by the explosion.

"What happened?" D asked. "You okay?"

Brian nodded, trying to catch his breath. "Stalker was in the dumpster. Louis got it."

D's relieved expression shifted, one eyebrow quirking. "'Course he did."

Louis either couldn't hear her or pretended not to. He walked up to the dumpster and the dead Stalker and lifted the lid on the other side with his muzzle. His nose crinkled at the stench Brian had mistaken for sour garbage. After Louis kicked the Stalker down, he closed the lid to contain the smell and body. He kneeled on top of the dumpster and lifted the window with an ease which frustrated Brian.

"Get down from there." Brian's nerves were still raw. "If something or someone's in there, they sure as shit heard you. I could've gotten it with an arrow, or—"

Louis slid to the ground, tapping his hand against his ear as if trying to knock loose a lingering ring. "*Tuat t'en grosse bueche!*"

"Stop it, you two!" Cecilia said. "I don't even know what Louis said, but what's done is done. The important thing is you're both okay. Right?"

Brian and Louis glared at each other until Brian let it drop.

"What about the barricades?" Brian asked D and Antoine. "Any give?"

Antoine shook his head. "They nailed up there good. Might be we could get 'em down if we keep workin' at 'em, but we gonna have to break 'em, make some noise."

"We've already made enough." Brian's potshot at Louis didn't go unnoticed. "Someone needs to stay on the entrances to make sure nothing comes out. Then we need to find out what's inside."

"Me and D can keep workin' the barricades," Antoine said. "Stay off to the side in case someone tries to pop us through the door."

"Be careful." Brian pointed at Louis. "Try to see what's inside, but don't do anything else until I come back. Cill, come with me." He walked away with her at his heels, not giving Louis a chance to argue.

Several acres of land surrounded the store, but most of it was empty aside from the range in the back. Brian and Cecilia headed for it in silence. Brian didn't want to make more noise, and Cecilia sensed his reticence to speak.

A strange scent drifted into Brian's nose as they approached the range. It still had targets set up beyond the stalls, but they were unlike any Brian had ever seen. At first, he thought they were dummies—but they were bodies in varying stages of decomposition. Some completely skeletal, some with skin still clinging to them in strips, others with gangrenous green and purple masses dripping fluid. Chunks had been gouged from a fresh body like cuts of meat from a pig. They were all tied to posts, arms outstretched in mock-crucifixion. Spent casings littered the range's wooden floor.

Cecilia stooped to her knees and retched. Brian wanted to leave, but something caught his eye: the fingers on one hand of a freshly mutilated body curled into a fist. At first, Brian thought the gusting wind had done it somehow—but wind couldn't make a mouth open and close.

His breath caught in his throat. *It's alive. Someone did this to them. Whoever's inside that building.*

Brian launched an arrow into the forehead of the wretched shrunken face. The open mouth stopped moving.

"What did you do that for?" Cecilia asked under her breath.

He grabbed her by the elbow and turned around. "We need to get back to Louis."

She slid out of his grip but didn't question him. Maybe she'd decided she was better off not knowing the answer to her question.

Louis was there when they returned, to Brian's reluctant relief. Brian hurried over and kneeled next to him below the dumpster, whispering before Cecilia could hear him: "Whoever's in there is using people as targets in the shooting range. One was still alive, had chunks cut out of them. We need to get out of here."

Brian withdrew to examine Louis's expression. His eyebrows arched, but his lips tightened into a grimace. He sighed. "I wouldn't be so quick to leave if I were you."

"What? Why?"

"The window goes to a storeroom. There are shipments of ammo in there, never opened."

Brian rocked back onto his rear and stared at Louis, dumbfounded. "*Fuck.*"

Cecilia kneeled next to them. "What's going on, guys?"

"The solution to our ammo problem is in there, but so is some kinda psychopath." Louis's eyebrows quirked. "Worse than me, apparently."

"Are you sure they're still in there?" Cecilia asked.

"I'm guessin' this window's how they get in and out." Louis shrugged. "Maybe the Stalker in the dumpster was some kinda fucked-up security system. At any rate, they're layin' low and they haven't tried to plug D and Antoine yet, so it's probably just one guy."

"Right. Otherwise, they'd be out here trying to make us into targets too," Brian said. "Well, if there's ammo in there, I guess we should try to get in and take it. Cill, go tell D and Antoine what we saw. Ask them to keep working on the barricade, but tell them to make as much noise as they can and to stay away from the windows. Then I want you to go back to Sarah and Katie and stay with them. If a Stalker or stranger shows up, take Grimes and get out of here."

Her eyes narrowed. "What are you planning, exactly?"

"I'll go in. If someone's there, I'll take care of them." Shock crossed both Louis and Cecilia's faces, but Brian kept talking before they could protest. "I have the bow. It's quiet, ranged. Once my eyes adjust, I'll be able to see. In the meantime, D and Antoine will distract whoever's in there."

"What's your out if shit goes south?" Louis asked.

"Stay here by the dumpster. If I want you to pull me out, I'll throw something to get your attention."

"Brian, I'm not sure you can fit through the window." Cecilia grabbed his arm. "What if you get stuck?"

"If I take my backpack off and Louis hands me my things, I think I can fit."

Cecilia sighed, slipping her hand from his arm. She threw her arms around his neck instead. "Okay. Be careful." She stood, staying away from the dumpster and the open window. "Louis, don't you *dare* let him down." She ran around the building with her silvery ponytail flashing in the sun.

Brian stripped all his gear off and handed it to Louis. His expression reminded Brian of a sulky child. "This is a stupid plan, you know."

He rolled his eyes. "Somehow, I knew you'd say that." He climbed onto the dumpster and exhaled as he gazed into the abyss beyond the window. *I guess I need to go in feet first so I can grab the ledge and lower myself in.*

Brian turned, awash with all the regret in the world as he squeezed through the open window. He used his arms to push himself through until his feet dangled over the ground.

Louis climbed up and grabbed him by the arms. Brian lowered himself until his feet touched cement. He slid his hands free of Louis's and curled his fingers, beckoning for his belongings. Louis obliged. His brow crinkled, and he parted his lips, on the verge of saying something, but he shook his head and retreated beneath the window.

Brian stayed low and felt with his hands for the boxes Louis had seen. He touched several solid cardboard stacks and exhaled, knowing his efforts would be worth it if things played out in his favor.

We need bullets so we can shoot Stalkers, other people with guns, and things like fucking bears. *I hope to God we don't see another cougar.*

Aside from the banging going on out front, Brian couldn't sense anything. He sat still, wedged in a corner behind the boxes while his eyes adjusted to the dim light shining through the tiny window. He steadied his shaking hands and tried to control his breathing.

He watched and listened for movement until he detected a low murmur. Laughter rang out—but words mixed with it. This was a person, or at least something capable of stringing together a sentence. It sounded like they were at the front of the building near D and Antoine, trying to see what they were doing.

Brian scurried up the stairs. The open door allowed him a viewpoint into the range. Rows of display cases lined the walls above floors sprinkled with casings. Slivers of light slipped between boards covering the windows. He memorized the layout of the building: *Up the stairs, perpendicular hallway shaped like an upside-down T, juts off to the right with an entryway. Two windows and double doors, boarded. Outside* and *inside. They must get in and out through the window I came in like Louis said.*

Brian dashed behind a gun case in the center of the hallway, stepping around stray casings which glinted in the sunlight. He kept his bow in his hands and an arrow between his fingers. The stranger moved erratically and kept glancing behind them. Brian couldn't discern their features—only the girth of their body. They'd easily take Brian down with sheer size.

When Brian got closer, he could make out what the person—a man—was saying: "Mine. It's all mine. Too many. Too many, or I'd come out there and kill you all. Eat you if you're clean, dark meat first. Take all your clothes. Fuck the girls. Dead or alive, maybe both."

Brian's stomach soured when he thought of those strung-up, mutilated bodies. Of the chunk of flesh gouged out of a thigh, of a mouth opening and closing soundlessly. Of those things happening to himself or someone he cared about.

This sick bastard's gonna die.

Each time Brian tried to angle around the gun case, the man moved. It was like he could sense someone was in the room with him. When he turned around, Brian hung back and held his breath while the guy scanned the room. As soon as he curved back toward the front doors, distracted by D and Antoine's continuing attempts to break down the wooden barricade, Brian dashed to a different counter. Along the way, he grasped a handful of casings.

Once he was safely behind the second counter, Brian tried to work out an angle in his mind. *If I draw him over to the first counter, I can get a clear shot at him. But if he's looking in this direction, I'm fucked. I need to hide. Once he's got his back to me, I'll take him down.*

Brian calculated his shot and took it. He flung a few of the casings between the door and the first counter. He shoved the rest in his pocket and flattened himself to the ground, waiting for the sound of approaching footsteps.

"Is someone in here?" Heavy weight crunched into the concrete floor. "I'll kill you if you are. But first, I'll have fun with you. Skin you alive. Living flesh tastes best."

When the footsteps stopped, Brian raised himself to his knees and elbows and peered through the glass case at the man's distorted outline. He prowled around the other case, dragging a hand along it with a grating *squeeeeeeak.* In his other hand, he gripped a huge handgun with a longer barrel than Louis's original revolver.

Once the man's back was to him, Brian pressed himself to the edge of the case and lined the shot. *Ready, aim, loose.*

The arrow sailed through the air—and over the man's head as he bent at the perfect moment to avoid it. Brian only had seconds to draw another one before the psycho came looking for him.

Adrenaline stopped him from shaking and slipping. When the stranger whipped around, Brian released the bowstring and sent an arrow into his barrel chest. Brian hurtled below the counter as he yanked the arrow free and let out a rumbling laugh. "I bet you think this hurts, you fuck! Better run, little rabbit, before I rip your skin from you!"

Shit shit shit—stay in here, move in circles, stay in cover?

Go back to the basement, signal Lou, wait for him to pull me out?

What to do what to do—

Brian tossed a few more casings behind him and dashed for cover the instant the freak plodded over to the settling metal shells. *The guy's so big my arrows don't seem to hurt him, but the gun will give me away. But if I put a bullet in his head, he* has *to go down. I still have four chambered. Better make it count.*

Brian took the gamble and swapped the bow for his revolver. He leaned around the display rack obscuring him and steadied his grip with his left hand, centering on his target.

The creep swiveled toward him. Their eyes locked. Brian's finger tightened against the trigger. The man stumbled back, head jerking to the side. Brian fired again, again, again, but the man still stood.

Jesus fuck—I am hitting you in the goddamn head! Go down!

Another shot rang out. Hot pain seared Brian's right thigh. He tossed the empty gun and reached for the bow—but the man finally collapsed, dragging a rack of ammo with him. It spilled out of busted boxes and scattered everywhere.

Smoke misted in the air; the acrid scent made Brian cough. He retreated behind the rack, wincing with the motion of his injured leg. He drew the bowstring and launched another arrow into the fallen man's head for good measure, nearly contemplated hacking it off with a machete.

Brian sank to his knees, trying to catch his breath as his adrenaline plummeted. The buzz in his ears dissipated—in its place, the *tink* of metal rolled over the concrete floor.

This fucking lunatic can't be alive. Are there more?

He withdrew another arrow—his last—and pulled it taut with the bowstring as he stood. When he whipped around the rack, he stared into the abyss of a gun barrel. Louis lingered behind it, cloaked in the darkness of the room.

Louis lowered the rifle. Brian put his bow away and leaned against the rack, forgetting it wasn't as sturdy as the cases. He stumbled a little before righting himself, gritting his teeth when his leg throbbed. "I almost sank an arrow into you," he muttered, trying not to let on how much pain he was in and how exhausted he was. "What're you doing in here?"

Louis's eyes were glued to the hefty man lying amidst his bed of bullets. He approached the body, weapon aimed, and swept the gun from the man's hand with his foot. "I came in when I heard all the gunfire."

Brian narrowed his eyes. "How the hell did you squeeze through the window?"

"I'm more flexible than I look." Louis rolled his right shoulder, wincing. It acted up now and again, probably from the scar tissue. "Or did you forget?"

Warmth soaked into Brian's jeans while he caressed his right thigh. "I haven't forgotten, but I try not to remember." He hissed when he put pressure on his injured leg.

Louis returned to Brian and bent in front of his leg. He reached for it, but Brian backed away. Louis squinted at him, a little irritated. "I'm just tryin' to look at it. Bullet get you?"

Brian nodded. "I'm not sure if it's a graze or if it's in there."

"I can always return the favor."

Brian backed away again. "What?"

Louis rolled his eyes. "Takin' a bullet out of you, *couillon*. Your mind's really not on the pain, is it? Guess that's good."

Brian tried to walk, but his leg seized with agonizing pain. Louis stood and gripped Brian's arms, giving him a patronizing glare more typical of D. "Don't force it. Once we get some light, we'll check it out. We should try to cut off the blood flow for now." He stripped his jacket off, sending a whiff of spice into the air. "Let me help you onto the counter."

Now wasn't the time to be stubborn. Brian lifted his arms with a groan and let Louis heft him up. The relief on his leg was immediate.

Louis smirked when he heard D and Antoine's ongoing attempts to pull off the barricade outside. "Sounds like they're finally makin' headway. Probably think you're dead after all that racket." He gingerly lifted Brian's leg and knotted his jacket above the bloody stain. "It'll be okay. Probably just grazed it."

Brian hovered his hand above the wound, curious about how serious it was. "How do you know?"

"Be a lot more blood if it went deep."

Brian's swaying shins brushed the front of Louis's body. The faint halo of light surrounding Louis's angular face made his expression difficult to interpret. "Don't try any more shit on your own, okay? I'd rather somethin' happen to me than you."

"I'll do what I want, Lou—"

An ear-splitting crack distracted them. Light spilled around the particleboard inside and dust swirled in the air. D and Antoine pressed their faces to the glass door like customers awaiting the opening of a Walmart on Black Friday.

Louis walked over and pushed his hands and face against the glass to mock them before he reached around to unlock the door. Antoine shattered the interior barricade with a swift kick once Louis backed away.

"Baby boy!" D cried when she spied Brian sitting on the counter. She held out her arms and jogged over to him, slowing when she saw the body from the corner of her eye. "Ooh, he don't look right!"

"What happened?" Antoine kicked the lifeless body and sent several bullets rolling along the concrete floor. "Damn—look at all this ammo!"

"I shot him a bunch of times," Brian said. "But he clipped me—"

D gasped and grasped her face. "Oh my goodness—you okay, baby? We need to clean it up and take a look at it! I don't know nothin' 'bout cleanin' no bullet wounds, though."

"Louis can." Brian leaned close to her ear. "But can you come take my mind off it while he works on me?"

D smiled when he leaned back. "You got it. 'Toine, go get Cill and the others, let 'em know it's clear in here and we got bullets and shit to pack up." She slung Brian's arm around her neck and helped him down. "Don't put no weight on it, baby. Let's get you fixed up. Louise, come along."

"*Louise*? D, just fuckin' stick with one nickname, why don't you?" Louis followed them, arguing with D while she led Brian down the stairs to the storeroom. Brian cringed with each step, but when he glanced around at the plethora of loot, he decided it was worth it. Things could have gone a lot worse—his leg hurt like a motherfucker, but he hadn't lost something permanent like a limb.

Yet.

D helped him sit atop the boxes of ammo and set a lantern beside him. Brian snuck a furtive glance at Louis, who leaned against the wall with his arms folded. D snapped her fingers in front of Brian's face. "Sunshine, even if he *does* work miracles with his hands, he can't work on you through your damn pants."

Brian sighed and undid his belt, letting D help him with his jeans. She tossed them into a pile along with Louis's coat and gestured for Louis to come over. "Okay, Louise—take a look. And play nice: I'm watchin' you."

Louis glared at her. "I don't think I'd even manage a half salute with *you* in the room."

D meandered around and inspected the stacks of boxes. "That's the point—or not."

Brian sat with his arms folded, trying to ignore Louis. "What kind of ammo do you see, D?"

She read from the boxes while Louis dug into Brian's backpack for the first-aid kit. He set it beside Brian's injured leg and snapped vinyl gloves onto his hands. While he cleaned the wound, Brian either stared into space or watched D wander, trying and failing to tune out the sensation of a hot hand on his inner thigh and cool liquid on the outside.

"Stop wigglin'." Louis slapped Brian's other thigh. "I can't focus."

Brian stopped kicking, not even realizing he'd been doing it. *Probably nerves.* "Sorry, Doctor."

"Don't turn this into some weird role-play shit. That's not my thing."

D was stooping to tear open a box in the corner, but she sputtered and turned toward Louis. "What *is* yo' thang?"

"Why the fuck you wanna know?"

"Well, Louise, you just an enigma to me, is all. If I can't never know if Bigfoot is real or Atlantis really existed, I'd like to go to my grave solvin' the mystery of what revs your motor."

Louis ignored D and returned to the task at hand. "It's gonna need stitches." He threaded the needle and angled it over Brian's skin, the grasper in his other hand. He glanced at Brian, eyes obscured by the curtains of his bangs. "You can take a prick or two, right?"

Brian glared at D before she could get any ideas. He folded his arms and scowled at Louis. "Don't give her any more ammunition. Just get it over with."

"Punny." Louis cleared his throat and cocked his head to the side. "Here goes." He thrust the tip in. Brian grit his teeth as he tried to ignore the searing pain of the needle threading in and out of his skin. He'd been too embarrassed to inform Louis he had an irrational fear of needles—at least when the sharp end pointed toward him.

Once Louis finished, he unwound a section of gauze, snipped it off, and wrapped it around Brian's thigh. He finished with a square of medical tape and backed away to survey his work. "*Voilà*. You were such a brave boy you deserve a sticker—or maybe a sucker."

Brian glanced at his leg and the white swatch of fabric wrapped around it. "Very funny." He looked at D's quivering lips and held out a finger. "Don't you say anything, D." He flipped his finger around and beckoned to her. "Help me down from here, please."

She obliged both demands and let Brian use her shoulder as leverage while he lowered his feet to the ground. Louis peeled the vinyl gloves from his hands and tossed them. His eyebrows quirked, but he looked away from Brian and said nothing.

"Okay, Louise—let's go upstairs in case one of your kinks is watchin' injured people get dressed." D shooed Louis up the stairs and followed him out, giving Brian privacy while the others rustled around in the store above him. Pulling on jeans proved more challenging than usual. His leg ached a good deal more than he wanted to admit.

He hobbled up the stairs and joined the others in surveying the prizes he'd risked his life for. Antoine kept running over to everyone, showing off the new weapons he'd found. He was particularly enamored of a sword he claimed was a katana from the 1600s used to behead thousands of shoguns.

"Since you're done playin' Bond and you're one of the Seven Samurai now, you can give me my PPK back" was Louis's flat response to Antoine's enthused display.

The others were comfortable with the weapons they already had, so they stuck to ammunition and accessories like stocks, scopes, and mounted flashlights. They found a pair of walkie-talkies, but they were low on batteries. They strapped holsters to their bodies and attached accessories to their weapons, keeping the ammo stored in boxes for safety and organization. They restricted it to .38 special and .357 for the revolvers, .22 hollow-point and .22 LR for the pistols, .308 rifle rounds, shotgun shells, and arrows.

Once they packed what they could carry in their bags, they rolled the excess into a shooting mat from the store so they could strap it to Grimes. Brian hobbled over to the man he'd struggled to kill, still puzzled by the fact he took four rounds to the head before he dropped. D's repulsed exclamation echoed through his mind: *"Ooh, he don't look right!"*

Now he knew why. He bent over and put his hands on his knees, the wind knocked out of him.

Sunlight streamed through the exposed windows, illuminating features once obscured by darkness. A palette of bone, brain matter, and blood stained his pallid flesh. One eye had exploded into a mess of viscous fluid, but the other bloodshot eye stared into space. His nose and half of his mouth had crumbled into pulpy chunks—the remaining half stretched into a taut, toothy smile.

Thoughts of infection crossed Brian's mind, his skin prickling as though invisible bugs were crawling beneath it. *He didn't touch me. And it isn't airborne. The only way anything could've gotten to me was if the bullet was contaminated. He has gloves on, but if his bare fingers touched it, maybe a nail...*

The others wandered over, though Sarah kept Katie away from the body. Louis put his hands on his hips and groaned. "Fuck *me.* This guy's just like that other prick." His eyes went to Brian's leg instantly, and his lips tightened into a grimace. He swallowed but didn't say anything else.

"You got to wonder if the disease makes 'em all crazy or if they already lost so much of their damn minds there's nothin' left *to* lose," Antoine said. The others spoke, but their voices muddled into a cloud of white noise. Brian's stomach curdled, and he stumbled a little, light-headed from blood loss or his own paranoia.

D and Louis reached for him at the same time, but he fell before he knew who caught him.

Brian opened his eyes, but everything was blurry and he didn't know where he was. He grabbed his revolver while he got his bearings.

I'm in a small room behind a counter. In my sleeping bag. The door's shut and posters of tires are on the wall. An auto shop? They must have put me on Grimes when I passed out, kept going and stopped here for the night.

Voices drifted through the door, raised in heated debate. Brian hobbled over and pressed his ear to it, listening for one he recognized.

As if on cue, Cecilia said, "Let's wait for Brian before we decide anything."

Are they talking about my leg? About the possibility I might be sick?

Brian opened the door. The others sat around a table in a waiting room with a drained water cooler, focused on something nestled amidst warped magazines: a radio. A distorted voice played through it.

D caught his gaze and waved him over with a cautious smile. He hobbled to her side and sat on the rigid seat, leaning in to listen to the muffled voices. "Food...power. Safety. North...border of Missouri and Arkansas. Diamond City..."

Some of their faces were hopeful. Others were skeptical. Katie was too young to know what any of it meant and entertained herself by flipping through magazines.

"When did you first hear this?" Brian asked. "Do they say anything else?"

"This is the first time we've heard *anything* on the radio since the outbreak." Sarah tapped short nails against the table's plastic surface. "We must've just gotten into range of it."

"Seems fishy," D said.

"But what if it's for real?" Antoine asked. "What if we miss out on somethin'?"

"What if it's a trap?" D gave her brother a dirty look no one else would dare give him. "You waste so much time on your other muscles you forget your brain?"

"The brain ain't a muscle." Antoine frowned, brawny arms crossed in front of his chest. "You don't think it's worth checkin' out? We goin' north anyway."

"We should see if there's someplace safe to take everyone," Cecilia said, implying they should look for a new area to relocate the group from Evergreen to. They hadn't mentioned the refuge to Sarah yet. Cecilia stared at Brian, silently asking if she should. He shrugged, leaving it up to her. "We have a place to go back to. There are other people there, animals, food, even a well and a tub. But we're looking to move because we don't think it's safe to stay there for much longer. Resources are running low, and people are coming out of hiding since winter's over."

Sarah stood. "Wherever *he's* going won't be safe."

Louis arched his eyebrows, the vein in his neck twitching. "What do you mean by that?"

Katie had been stacking Styrofoam cups next to a defunct coffee maker, but her mother's distressed voice distracted her. "Do I really have to spell it out to you?"

Brian still didn't know which "he" Sarah meant: Louis or himself. The others weren't acting any differently, which either meant they weren't worried about the same thing as him or they were hiding it well. He kept trying to tell himself he was obsessing over it, that he was still woozy from the pain, nothing else.

Sarah switched focus to Brian. "You may only be a kid, but you're putting everyone in danger by letting him come with you."

Brian knew Louis was the "he" in question, and the blur of confusion sharpened into anger. Being called a kid rubbed him the wrong way, for one, but her accusation of his willful ignorance and disregard for his friends' safety made his blood boil.

Katie's cup tower tumbled over. Sarah kneeled beside her and stroked the child's wavy hair; she was on the verge of tears, not understanding what was going on but sensing it wasn't good. "Even if you find this girl, what makes you think you can take her back to these people and live happily ever after? Won't he just try to finish what he started and get rid of her forever?"

Louis's furious eyes shifted from Sarah to Brian, at the limits of his self-control. Brian couldn't decipher whether Louis was asking him if he could handle this, or if he wanted Louis to cool down and step out. Brian jerked his head toward the door; Louis slipped past the others and shoved through it so hard he cracked the glass.

Once Brian articulated a response, he faced Sarah and delivered it, ignoring the pain radiating through his right leg. "You don't know Eva, and you don't know Louis even though you seem to think you do. And you sure as shit don't know me. I'm not a kid. You weren't there during everything I went through—what he and I went through *together*. We have too much history for me to write him off. I knew he was sick, but I guess I am too." He dragged himself to the door and pressed his palm to it. "I'm going to track him down and make sure he stays out of trouble. The rest of you talk some sense into this woman and calm Katie down. Then we'll figure out this radio thing and decide who's going where."

Before anyone could reply or even react, he pushed the door open and tramped into the parking lot, too overcome by adrenaline to feel pain in his leg. Louis was talking to Grimes while he brushed her. She didn't understand, of course, but she seemed to enjoy the attention.

Louis spied Brian from the corner of his eye before Brian could hobble over there. "Brian, why the hell are you puttin' weight on your leg?" He put the brush away and hurried over to sling an arm around Brian's shoulders. "You have to get away from that *putain*?"

Brian wriggled out of Louis's grip. "I'm just tired of people second-guessing me and blaming it on my youth and inexperience, or whatever."

"Like I'm tired of everyone assumin' I wanna murder every goddamn person I see?" Louis scoffed. "All people do is label and assume, anyway. It's been that way for me my whole life. They had to label me with the borderline thing, right? And you got slapped with a big, fat depression."

"I'd like to slap that woman with a big, fat something right now." Brian glared at the auto shop and shook his head. "I mean, I made the call to let her come with us, and she's so goddamn *ungrateful*. I don't need her to praise me, but it's way out of line for her to attack us. I feel bad for Katie. My mom was stubborn, but she wasn't a *bitch*."

Louis stripped a glove off and pressed the back of his hand against Brian's forehead. "You're not runnin' a fever—good." His eyes scanned Brian's face, trying to study it for something. Brian suspected what, but he didn't say anything. "Why don't we take a little ride on Grimes for old times' sake?" Louis scratched the horse's forehead and gave Brian a wolfish grin. "I'll have you back by supper."

"That's a bad idea…"

"Oh, come on—you're young, right?" Louis replaced the glove. "You can blame it on youthful ignorance, impulse and such."

The thought of riding the horse with Louis was far more appealing than returning to a building with Sarah in it. His temper had yet to cool, and he feared he'd say something he'd regret in front of Katie. Of course, he might also regret climbing onto a horse with Louis and riding off without telling anyone.

Against his better judgment, Brian allowed Louis to help him onto Grimes. He hadn't been on her in a while, but he doubted he'd complete the rest of the trip on his bike—at least until his leg healed. Might as well get used to riding her again.

Louis climbed in front of him and kicked her sides. Brian didn't grab onto Louis until Grimes picked up speed and sent him sliding across her saddle. He kept one hand near his revolver, more because he was worried about Stalkers than Louis.

"It's nice gettin' to do this durin' spring," Louis said. "I haven't ridden good ol' Grimes since we left New Orleans, and that was in snow and slush."

Brian surveyed the emerald, chartreuse, and mahogany woods on either side of the road. Sparse grass had flourished into ample strips between asphalt and forest. Before long, nature would overtake the road and every other manmade construct no one managed to upkeep. The forlorn beauty of twisting vines and towering grass would obscure the ugly scars of destruction left on abandoned cities.

"The breeze and sun feel nice on my skin." Unfortunately, this breeze carried the intoxicating scent from Louis's hair and skin to Brian's nose. He fought the urge to lean forward and bury his nose in the back of Louis's neck. "My leg really hurts, though. Is that from the gunshot or the stitches?"

"Both, I'm sure. You got nicked in the muscle. Probably gonna have a scar."

"I'm still a little light-headed." Brian dug his fingers into Louis's side, tugging at the fabric of his shirt. "You know I'm worried, don't you? You're worried about the same thing."

Louis cleared his throat. "The chances are pretty low. There'd have to be some kinda bodily fluid on the bullet for it to infect you, and I doubt he bled on it, spit on it, or jerked off on it. Besides, that shit has to die off once it's outta the body for a while, right?"

"If I was sick, though... Would you take care of it?"

Louis's muscles tightened beneath Brian's hand, easing when he sighed. "I'm not sure I could. I'd probably rather wait it out, take you away from everyone else, and deal with it then. I mean, some of them are still themselves, right?"

"I'd rather not be some monster like them, or like my parents turned into. I don't wanna hurt my friends or lose my mind." He buried his forehead in Louis's back and screwed his eyes shut until he saw stars. "If you couldn't do it, I'd have to."

"If you go down, I'll go down with you." Louis's resolute response convinced Brian he meant every word he said. He reached behind him and squeezed Brian's knee. "But you'll be fine. Don't overthink it. Stay focused on what we're here to do."

Brian considered running away with Louis again if it meant keeping everyone else safe. From himself, from Louis, from their potent, volatile chemistry. But he convinced himself he was jumping the gun, assuming the worst and giving up too easily like his father would have.

Mind over matter. Don't will it into existence.

Louis pulled back on Grimes's reins to slow her. "Stay here a tick." He hopped down and strolled to the side of the road while Brian caressed the revolver and scanned for movement. He kneeled to pluck something from the ground and returned to Brian, holding it out for him to take. "Give this to the kid when we get back."

Brian accepted the item Louis dropped into his hand. "A dandelion? Why do you want me to give this to her?"

"Eva used to love blowin' on those damn things." Louis shook his head, hair whipping into his face when a gust kicked up. "That *putain* got her kid pretty upset in there. This'll take her mind off it. But I don't wanna give it to her—it'll just add fuel to the fire."

Brian twirled the delicate stalk in his fingers; Becky used to enjoy blowing on the fuzzy tufts too. Or trying, anyway. It usually took her a few huffs and puffs before they'd all sail into the air. "It's a nice gesture, but I'm a little surprised you thought of it."

Louis's frown verged on a pout. "That's more than a little insultin'. Besides, just because I don't like kids doesn't mean I don't remember what it was like to *be* one. No kid should have to see what she probably has—"

Something blurry streaked past Brian's field of vision and hit the road beside them with a wet *squish*. Grimes squealed and reared up; Brian scrambled to lean forward and snatch her reins before he tumbled to the ground.

Louis went to inspect the object. He lifted a gray lump with the muzzle of his gun. "What the *fuck*?" A limp squirrel with a raw wound in its side dangled over Louis's pistol. Louis lowered it, crinkling his nose at the coppery scent of blood and exposed innards. "Looks like somethin' bit it."

"All I saw was a blur." Brian arced his arm through the air to demonstrate and made a *whooshing* sound for emphasis. "Like something threw it."

Louis backed away from it and reached for Grimes's saddle horn. "No shit—unless it was a flyin' squirrel that died the instant it hit the pavement. Obviously, it fuckin' wasn't. Could be some nut job like the fuckers who set those mannequins up in the Ozarks—or one of those Stalkers you think is followin' us." He put his foot into the stirrup and pulled himself up, and then whipped the reins to urge Grimes into a gallop. "Let's get the fuck outta here either way and tell the others—except for the kid and her nutcase of a mother."

Unnerved by what they'd seen and what they *hadn't*, Brian tightened his arms around Louis's waist. His mind bounced from worry to worry during the ride back: his aching leg, Sarah's crappy attitude, the message on the radio, Eva's whereabouts, his confusing relationship with Louis, and now more of this weird shit following them. He didn't know what to prioritize.

One thing at a time. We'll keep looking for Eva, stay on track, maybe look into the radio thing—and see if something follows us on the way. I'll talk to Sarah about her attitude, stay civil but reserved with Louis, and let my leg do its thing. I got this.

Everyone was still inside the waiting room when they returned. They leaped to their feet and immediately rushed forward to chastise Brian for running off without saying anything.

"I'm fine—I just needed some space." Brian forced a smile, trying to conceal his worries. He walked over to Katie and kneeled to give her the dandelion. "We found a present for you while we were out, Kat."

Her eyes brightened with joy as she accepted the gift. When she flung her arms around his neck and said, "Thanks, Brian!" Becky seemed to manifest in the present for one excruciating instant. He hugged her back; when he let go, it took every ounce of willpower he had to keep the smile on his face.

Katie brought the dandelion to her lips and blew. The fuzzy white seeds drifted into the air, bringing a quick end to their moment of happiness.

He stood and pulled Sarah to the side while the others entertained Katie. "Listen, I'm still fine with you traveling with us, but this attitude of yours needs to stop. I don't expect you to agree with everything I do, but antagonizing Louis isn't helping things any. He's already touchy enough."

"You've got a lot on your plate for someone so young." Sarah crossed her arms, eyes darting to Katie. "Even us old people make mistakes, fall victim to our erratic emotions. We're at our most desperate when we have something we're scared to lose."

Brian sensed Sarah had something on her mind, so he didn't say anything. She deliberated over it for several minutes, jittery like a caffeine addict going through withdrawal. "Kat's father and I were divorced. When he heard the reports, he came over and tried to take her with him because he thought she'd be safer. He threatened me with a gun. I pretended to let her go, but while he was taking her out to his van, I grabbed my pistol and...and shot him. Kat saw everything, but I told her Daddy went crazy like the rest of them. She's all I have left; I'd do anything for her."

Brian swallowed, intimidated by the conviction in her voice. But it wasn't his place to judge her for what she'd done or the reasons why. "We've all been pushed to our limits, done things we never would've done before the outbreak. To be honest with you, I'm amazed I'm still here." He glanced at the others, at a smiling Cecilia while she watched Katie climb a tire display like a jungle gym, at D and Antoine while they giggled over old gossip magazines, at Louis while he flicked through his old phone using what little battery it might have left. "It's because I have them. Otherwise, I think I would have given up."

Sarah sighed and followed Brian's sight line. "When we were in the quarantine zone, it went okay for a bit. We had rations, thin beds, and company. But when people went hungry, when their bodies started to hurt, when they argued with each other and the military, it became too dangerous. We were stuck between the hell in there and the hell out here. Even if this city from the radio message is real, it'll turn out like the quarantine zone. The more people you get, the more resources they'll eat up. Fights will break out. Personalities will clash. The same thing will happen to the place you came from. You won't be able to protect your loved ones forever—not even from yourself."

She gave him a grim smile and abandoned him for Katie. When she lifted her daughter from the tire display, the haggard, cynical woman softened into a radiant mother. Her daughter truly was the only thing to give her joy, maybe even meaning.

Brian slouched into a chair to ease the weight from his injured leg. He recalled Becky's delighted expression whenever she'd watch silvery dandelion tendrils swirl into the air, remembered his mother and father's tender expressions when they proudly gazed upon their children, Nana's perpetually kind face and Poppa's rare smiles, and the giddy way Eva clapped her hands when he unlocked the door to the skating rink.

He hadn't been able to save any of them.

Radiant Angel

Chapter Eight

What Follows

3/27, Arkansas, dusk

The group moved on from the auto shop and continued to head north along 65. Antoine and Brian swapped transportation, so now Brian rode behind D and Antoine pedaled the bicycle. He didn't seem to mind, but the oxymoron of a huge man on a small bike struck Brian as funny and he'd often muffle his mouth before a snicker could slip out.

By the time the sun painted the sky in pastel streaks, they stopped at one of Arkansas' most plentiful buildings: a church. The scent of dust and ancient paper suffused the dank building. They unfurled their sleeping bags and settled down in the library, where someone had dismantled the shelves and tables to use as barricades. The abandoned books lay strewn on the floor.

Cecilia picked through the piles and created a stack for herself. She carried it to set beside her sleeping bag. She lay back to read, her undone hair cascading around her into a splayed fan of silken straw. D and Antoine pulled out a deck of playing cards from a torn box and set up a game of gin rummy they invited Brian to play with them. Antoine extended the courtesy to Louis; he accepted, so D rolled her eyes and dealt him a begrudging hand.

For a while, Katie entertained herself by reading with Cecilia. But, like most children, her attention wandered. While her mother rested, she bounced over to Brian and the others and plopped down. "Ooh, a game! Can I play?"

"It's a grown-up game, baby girl," D said, though she smiled and patted the space next to her for Katie to sit.

Katie wriggled over and grabbed her feet. "But I'm boooooored. All those books Cecilia is reading are 'bout ugly old guys and donkeys."

Louis sputtered and broke into a crooked grin. "How do you know they're ugly? Are they picture books?"

She slid closer to him and peered at his cards. "No, but all old guys are ugly."

D and Antoine both shook their heads and tried not to laugh. Brian fanned his hand of cards while D deliberated over which one to play. Despite her skill with reading the tarot, she was the most indecisive card player he'd ever known.

Katie plucked at Louis's cards. "You're losing anyways. Let's play a different game."

He tugged his hand free and slapped it onto the floor facedown. "You don't even know what this game *is*, peeshwank."

Brian snuck a glance at Sarah, worried she'd freak out over her daughter interacting with Louis. She'd passed out in her sleeping bag. Cecilia had set her books down and turned her light off.

"You don't have kings and queens, or that jack guy." Katie, on the other hand, still possessed the boundless energy of a child. She leaned back toward D. "She's gonna beat you 'cause she has a buncha them."

"*Girl!*" D pulled her hand to her chest to hide it from Katie's prying eyes. "Will someone get this child the other deck of cards from my bag? I ain't ever gonna play my hand with her blabbin' it out to the whole dang world!"

"She's right—I *am* losin'." Louis shoved his cards into the center of their little circle. He stood and jerked his head for Katie to follow. "Come on—I'll teach you Go Fish. It's easy."

She bounded after him and grabbed his hand. The gesture was innocent enough—she was only a lonely child looking for friendship—but an overprotective mother could read into anything. Once Brian's turn came, he struggled to make a play because he was too focused on making sure Sarah didn't wake up and have a meltdown over her daughter playing Go Fish with "that murderer."

Antoine nudged Brian's arm. "She been goin' all day lookin' after that little girl—the woman's out for a while. Relax. Louis's doin' good with her."

"Cill's been eating, right?" Brian asked after his attention shifted to the petite form bunched up in a purple sleeping bag.

D sighed. "Baby, she's *fine*. We fine, Katie's fine 'cause her momma's ass is asleep, and Louis ain't even been gettin' on my nerves. Well, he been gettin' on 'em, but not the last one yet." She reached out and shook Brian's knee. "I'm more worried about *you*. How's the leg doing?"

Brian dragged his free hand through his hair. "I'm trying not to think about it. When I don't, it doesn't bother me."

Antoine smiled and patted Brian's shoulder. "That's a good philosophy for *all* yo' problems. Why don't you try and get some sleep so you can heal? We all here lookin' after things."

D stood and moved behind Brian before he could argue. She pulled him up by his shoulders, walked him over to his sleeping bag, and practically tucked him into it. This maternal gesture was a dark echo of when his mother used to sit on the edge of his bed and tell him bedtime stories: he missed her comforting touch, her wise advice, and knowing she'd be there if he needed her.

One of his enduring fears was she didn't know how much he appreciated her before she lost her mind.

Another was she'd never lost it at all.

Rumbling thunder disintegrated into a static sizzle. Two voices mingled with the tinny patter of rain on the roof: Antoine's deep baritone and Louis's smoky drawl. Still fading in and out of consciousness, Brian remained adrift in darkness.

"You worried about the kid, ain't you? She remind you of your sister?"

"Kinda. They're equally annoyin'. I don't know how you grew up with D."

The floor quaked with the impact of a lightning strike nearby. A snort punctuated D's steady snores, and Katie whimpered from her mother's side.

Antoine snickered. "Oh, I didn't used to be the amiable fellow everyone knows me as now."

"Really?" Louis feigned surprise. "I never woulda guessed from the riot gear, the katana, and the shotgun."

"Don't be a smartass—I'm tryin' to help you."

Brian peeked at the pair through one foggy eye until his vision adjusted to the dim light cast by a flickering lantern. Louis sat on the ground about two feet from Antoine's side, one arm dangling over a knee. Both of Antoine's legs were extended, his bulk contrasting with Louis's lean form. Their backs were pressed against an empty bookshelf.

Louis sighed and dragged a hand through his bangs. "Go on."

"I was a real hellion as a kid. Got worse as a teenager. Since me and Dee-Dee grown up in a bad neighborhood, we got mixed up with bad kids. Me more than her, 'cause she had more girlfriends than me—didn't know why until later. But you know when boys get together, they don't get up to nothin' but trouble."

Louis had no argument, so Antoine continued.

"Now, boys with nothin' to do and nothin' goin' for 'em got to find power some way. I ended up hangin' with a bad group of guys, got into drug-runnin'. Usin' too. Dee-Dee always told me I was gonna get myself in trouble, but I didn't listen to her. Long story short, I sold to the wrong guy, got arrested by an undercover cop in a sting. They gave me hard time. I didn't feel too bad about it until I saw my parents in court: my *popa* stood there shakin' his head while my *moman* cried her eyes dry. I felt lower than low, like I wasn't worth nothin'. Back then, I had a lot of anger and nothin' to do about it. But Dee-Dee didn't give up on me, came by the prison every weekend. She suggested I spend some time in the prison library readin' about different things I could do. That's how I got into karate. Got into a lotta other things too, like gardenin' and studyin' stuff I didn't pick up in school."

"Prison was your Boy Scouts, huh?"

Deep laughter roared from Antoine, stirring several of their sleeping companions. "Sure was! Besides, you got to learn to protect yourself in prison. They let me out early for good behavior, got to serve the rest of my sentence on probation, went around to schools talkin' to kids about drugs. Then I started teachin' self-defense classes. Musta built some good karma, 'cause I won the Powerball, got my SUV and my house. D had her fallin'-out with our parents and came to live with me, got hooked up with my friend Gus, and there ain't much more to tell."

Louis kept his face angled toward the floor, his eyes obscured by a shadowy fringe of hair. "Everyone enjoys a good old redemption arc, don't they?"

"I grew up a poor black kid in the south—I got so used to the stereotype I played into it. But I learned I could be what I wanted to be, not what everyone else thought I *should* be."

"You tryin' to preach some message to me?"

Antoine's congenial smile tightened into a grimace. "Well, you ain't white, either. You probably got shit for that, didn't you?"

"Oh, yeah. Everyone assumed me and Eva lived on a reservation somewhere and sat in sweat lodges smoking pipes. Assholes used to ask me if my parents worked in a casino too. And all the kids at school gave us hell over our accents. I mean, it's all shit we were born into—we couldn't change it if we tried."

"There's the gay thing too, right?"

Louis didn't respond. The rain picked up, hammering on the roof in a steady rhythm. Finally, he locked onto Antoine with a penetrating stare. "What 'gay thing'?"

Antoine scratched his head, cowed by Louis's intimidating expression. "You and Brian got a pretty intense thing goin'. And you *know* my sister's got a big mouth, so I know what she knows—"

"Whatever 'thing' we have goin' on has only happened with him, and I don't know what it is anymore. All I know is it's impossible for me to ignore." Louis sighed. Brian shut his eyes so Louis wouldn't catch him watching them. "Honestly, it's kinda pathetic. And it pisses me off that I can't change it. You know what I mean?"

"Can't say I do—all my relationships been the short-term kind. I got a lotta regrets 'bout that, but I can't fix things now. *You*, on the other hand, still can."

"But I did bad shit. Shit I can't take back. People don't forget things like that. He won't, and my sister sure as shit won't."

"If I'mma be honest, I think your main problem is impulse control. You gotta have a system to keep that in check. For me, it was a prison sentence, and once I got out, house arrest with my sister as warden. I had someone who cared about me, so I didn't give up on myself. Without D, I wouldn't have stayed clean or won no Powerball—I mighta even ended up dead from an overdose or a bullet." Even with his eyes closed, Brian picked up on the emotions choking Antoine's deep baritone voice. "There are people who don't want to see you fail, cuz. Just stay strong and right your wrongs. But try to get some sleep for now—I'll stay up, a'ight?"

The ongoing downpour pelted the roof and drowned out all other sounds. Brian started drifting off again until a flash of light penetrated his eyelids and a sharp *crack* splintered a tree outside. He opened his eyes, noticed Antoine curled up with a book and all the others buried in their bedrolls—but Louis was looking right back at him. Brian's heart raced, but he offered Louis a woozy smile, assuming the storm was keeping him awake too.

Louis returned the smile and closed his eyes. He wriggled across from Brian in his sleeping bag like they had as kids in their bedrooms. Brian's semiconscious mind dug up buried memories of laughter and playfighting all through the night until the birds chirped and the sun rose outside. Eva was there too, but she usually fell asleep before them. Brian recalled cherishing the hours when it was just him and Louis; sometimes they'd climb into each other's sleeping bag and play cards or snicker while they sneaked peeks at porno mags Louis had filched from his dad.

He drifted back into the kaleidoscopic ether of memories and dreams.

"Wake up, sunshine."

Someone nudged him. Brian groaned and recoiled from their touch.

The nudger persisted. "Baby boy, you gotta get up."

Brian struggled to lift his eyelids. The blurry image of D's face focused into view. He sat slowly and rubbed his eyes. "What's going on?"

She handed him a slip of paper.

Everyone,

Thank you for letting us tag along, but I feel it's best if we go it alone from this point on. We enjoyed your company, but upon further reflection, I decided I couldn't handle the complicated interpersonal dynamics that arise within a large group. We've made it this far, just the two of us, and that's how I want to keep going. Please don't look for us.

Best of luck to you in your travels,

Sarah and Katie

"She said she was takin' Kat to the bathroom," D said. "They never came back. This was tucked under the front door."

Cecilia shook her head, one of those aggravating morning people who woke up completely alert and energetic. "Why would she leave like that?"

Louis shrugged his backpack on. "She just wanted to keep her daughter to herself, couldn't stand to share her with anyone else." He stalked off, cursing under his breath.

Cecilia looked at Brian and the others. "He thinks it's because of him, doesn't he?"

"Boy carries a heavy chip on his shoulder." Antoine finished munching on a stale Pop-Tart from a box they'd found at a Dollar Store. "As he should. But he's right: I think she got used to bein' the only thing Kat had. Didn't want us to get too close to her, take her daughter away from her."

"That don't remind me of nothin' or no one I know at all." D folded her arms. "As much as I love the irony of Louis gettin' a taste of his own nasty medicine, I feel for that little girl—she's gonna be awful lonely. I hope the dumb broad don't get them both killed."

"She said not to look for them, so let's just stick to the original plan." Brian crawled out of his sleeping bag. He rolled it up, his twisted bangs dangling in front of his eyes while he packed. Katie had borrowed his earbuds and accidentally taken them with her. Frustrated by yet another loss he couldn't do anything about, he kicked a pile of books with his good leg. The others stopped gathering their belongings to stare at him, taken aback by his rare outburst.

"What are you all looking at?" he snapped. He tugged his bow, quiver, and backpack over his arms and stormed out, wincing with each step he took. Everyone finished what they were doing and hurried out of the church after him.

Outside, bugs and birds soared through the warm air, and flowers bloomed in colorful mosaics amidst sweeping fields of grass. Despite the uplifting scenery, Sarah and Katie's absence left a noticeable gap like a bulb out in a string of Christmas lights.

They stopped at a creek along the way to clean up. They stripped to their underwear and bathed in groups. Brian hung back to examine his wounded thigh while Antoine and Louis puttered around in the creek and D and Cecilia dressed a short distance away.

He rolled away the gauze and lifted the taped bandage to examine Louis's stitching. It was a little uneven and the loops were long, but he'd brought the skin together so it could heal. Brian's skin was pink around it and it itched like a bitch, but there was no pus or abnormal discoloration.

That's a good sign. Mom's scratches looked way nastier than this.

Antoine strolled over, tall and well-sculpted like a statue carved out of ebony, and leaned over to take a look at Brian's leg. "Don't look too bad. How's it feel?"

"Sore and itchy."

Antoine patted Brian's shoulder and grinned. "You'll live." He straightened up and put his hands on his hips, smile shrinking. "I still can't believe Kat's gone. I know she ain't dead—least I hope so—but it's hittin' your boy pretty hard. I think she reminded him of his sister; maybe he wanted to do right with Kat what he did wrong with Eva."

Brian glanced at Louis. He walked along the water's edge in black boxer-briefs, rummaging for something until he dug up a stick. He cracked it over his knee into a point and waltzed into waist-deep water to spear for fish. *He's definitely trying to distract himself, keep busy. He didn't even want them to come with us, but Katie must've grown on him. She reminded us both of the sisters we failed.*

Cecilia and D joined Brian and Antoine. They sat on top of the hill overlooking the bank of the creek, antsy trigger fingers on their guns.

"It's been a long time since we've seen one," Cecilia said as the chill of dusk crept in. "I wonder if they're dying out?"

D glared at Cecilia. "Baby girl, don't you *dare* jinx things! The less we see of their ugly asses, the better!"

"It's better when you can see 'em; then you know where they at," Antoine said. "I still don't like the thought of 'em followin' us and throwin' stuff. Don't make no damn sense."

"Well, we don't know for sure if they followin' us or not." D crossed her arms and watched Louis, scrunching her nose. "What the hell's he doin'? Ain't he worried 'bout some Stalker chuckin' a rock into his head or somethin'?"

"Gettin' dinner, Dee-Dee." Antoine shoved D's shoulder. "Unless *you* wanna go do it."

D's dismayed expression tightened into a haughty one. She cleared her throat and shrugged. "Nope. I'mma let him earn his keep. One of the few things I trust that boy to do is kill shit."

Cecilia clutched her midriff. "I don't normally eat meat, but my stomach feels like it's eating *itself* these days..."

When he finished, Louis ambled up the hill and dumped a pile of fish in front of them. Cecilia's face blanched: the fish were oozing blood where Louis had impaled them, and some still flopped helplessly. Louis rummaged in his backpack for a rag to dry off with and glanced at Antoine. "I'm gonna get dressed," he said. "Can you clean those, Antoine?"

"Sure can." Antoine stood and scooped the half-writing pile in his arms. He moved over to a tree stump nearby to behead, gut, and descale the fish. Cecilia shuddered. D patted Cecilia's shoulder as Antoine's knife smacked into the wood.

Something splashed in the river. A ripple spread from the spot where something had either jumped out or fallen in. *Maybe an acorn?*

Louis looked over while he tugged on the black turtleneck he favored. He rolled it over his stomach, his hand brushing the gun holstered at his left side.

Brian's gut clenched. *Why'd you have to mention Stalkers, Cecilia?*

He waited for something to happen, but it never did. Antoine kept chopping, oblivious to Brian and Louis's concern. Cecilia and D conversed while Grimes grazed nearby, lifting her head on occasion to survey her surroundings.

The branches on the other side of the creek cracked as if someone was streaking through them. Antoine's chopping and Cecilia and D's chatter ceased. Brian rushed to join Louis.

Silence.

Brian's hand hovered over his revolver. "You heard it too, right, Louis?"

Louis nodded, wet hair clinging to his high cheekbones. He watched the woods intently, jaw clenched.

"We should move," Brian said. "Take the fish and eat them later."

Everyone hurried onto their rides and left the creek behind, the tree stump covered in glistening red, pink, and yellow fish innards. Several dead eyes stared back at Brian. He glanced away, unsettled by the eerie sight.

They kept moving until they reached a small town. A chaotic collection of vehicles and equipment littered the parking lot of a nearby hospital. Ambulances sat in the bay with their doors open, and scattered stretchers and wheelchairs lay turned on their sides as if people had been dragged out of them. The shattered doors to the hospital enshrouded a darkness none of them desired to explore.

An RV park across the road seemed like a cesspool of unsavory surprises, so they continued into town until something caught Louis's eye. He headed away from the group and stopped his bike outside a small brick building with a faded sign reading "Hear Again."

Brian reached around D to pull back on Grimes's reins. He slid off her and hobbled over to Louis before he could move far from the bike. "Where are you going?"

"To get you a new pair of headphones. Katie took yours, right?" Louis started heading toward the ruins of the record store, but Brian snagged his sleeve.

"It's too dangerous; whatever's fucking with us is still doing it. Let's keep moving."

Louis's eyes focused on Brian's with incisive stillness. "I'll catch up with you."

"It's just a pair of headphones, idiot!" Brian snatched Louis by the collar and leaned close to whisper, "You might be able to replace them, but you can't replace Katie—or Eva."

Louis jerked free and marched off despite any protests Brian called after him.

"What the hell is he doin' *now*?" D asked once Brian walked back to her. "What does he want in an old record store?"

"Headphones."

D clicked her tongue. "That boy's always tryin' to get back what you lost." She held her hand out to Brian. "Leave him to it and let's move on— he's probably got some sixth sense for where you at, so he'll find us."

Brian hesitated as he reached for D's outstretched hand. "I don't think he should be alone. Why don't you head for the library a few blocks up? I know you've all been looking for stuff to read, and our walkies reach up to fifty miles away, so we can stay in touch."

D shrugged. "I guess he *should* have someone keep an eye on him... As long as you sure he won't try nothin'. And I ain't worried about him *knockin'* your ass out, if you catch my drift." She snapped her fingers at Antoine. "Give Brian his bike and get up here on Grimes with me; otherwise, he won't have no way to get to us." She looked back at Brian. "It ain't too far to bike; think your leg can manage?"

While Antoine obeyed his sister's command, Brian nodded and grabbed a hold of the bike's handlebars. "Both my leg *and* my ass will be okay. Be safe; I'll call you in a bit."

D quirked a skeptical eyebrow, but she dug her heels into Grimes's sides and told him to be careful. Cecilia pedaled alongside Grimes while she clopped toward the library with the siblings astride her.

Brian let a cursory thought fly by about how low the light was before withdrawing the bow. He shook his head and studied the burned-out record store.

What the hell am I doing? I'm an idiot.

He pursued Louis inside the building. The sweet but oppressive scent of gasoline made his eyes and nose sting. Some sections were scorched and unrecognizable, vinyl and plastic melted into black globs, but others remained intact. Framed records lined the wall, alternating between pristine and damaged. Brian recognized a few artists his parents had listened to.

No surprises on the first floor. Brian propped his bike behind a shelf and ascended a set of wooden stairs. They creaked under each step he took. He had to jump over the broken ones, dreading the settling of his weight into the next step.

"Louis," he called, "you there?"

A shiver ran through Brian when Louis popped up at the top of the stairs instead of replying. He stepped back and lost his footing—but Louis grasped his wrist with characteristic lightning-quick reflexes. "Why'd you follow me in here, *couillon*?"

Brian narrowed his eyes and flicked Louis on the forehead. "*C'est sa couillon.*" He climbed onto the second level. It had been untouched since the outbreak, as if they were back in time. He arched his eyebrows when he brushed past a glaring Louis. "Don't give me that look: *you're* the one who taught me French."

Louis moved toward a wall display where boxes and plastic packages of headphones hung. He rubbed his forehead where Brian had thumped it. "Did it ever occur to you I mighta wanted some privacy?"

Brian surveyed the packages in front of him. "Did it ever occur to you I don't want you running off on your own?" He settled on a pair and sat to slice the packaging open with the knife from his multi-tool. He pried out the headphones and breathed in the pleasing scent of fresh vinyl.

"Where are the others?" The floorboards groaned beneath thin gray carpet as Louis wandered around the shop. Brian glanced up on occasion and watched him flip through rows of CDs in plastic bins.

Brian withdrew his tablet and powered it on. "There's a library a few blocks up. I told them we'd meet them there." He plugged the headphones in and opened his music player.

When Louis got bored with poking through CDs, he kneeled across from Brian and picked at the frayed strands of carpet between them. Brian lifted the headphones from his ears. "Either you followed me in here because you were worried I was up to somethin', or you were just worried about *me*. Which is it?"

Brian powered the tablet off and stuffed it into his backpack along with the over-ear headphones. The contradictions of his behavior—and the motives behind it—were as infuriating to him as they must have been to Louis. He tried to find the words to explain it, but a shrill wail disrupted his thoughts.

Brian held his breath and met Louis's vigilant gaze. *Stalkers don't usually make sounds like that. Was it Cill? Or someone else in trouble?*

They ran over to the window and peered out. A lavender haze enveloped the lifeless town. They had enough light to search, but not much time. Brian brought the walkie to his mouth. "Hey, did you guys make it over there okay? And did you hear that? Over."

Louis leaned his head close to the walkie as Brian held it between them. It crackled to life, making Brian's arm shudder against Louis's. "Yeah, we done made it all in one piece. Heard that freaky scream too. Y'all okay? Over."

Another piercing shriek cut off Brian's reply. His eyes fastened onto Louis's.

Louis snatched Brian's arm. "I know what you're thinkin', but it could be a trap."

"What if it isn't?"

Their gazes remained locked, both challenging the other to back down—until a despairing yowl chilled their bones and made goose bumps ripple along their skin: "Mooooooooommy!"

It can't be Katie—can it? Sarah wouldn't have kept going the same way as us—

Louis took the walkie from Brian. "D, you guys stay put. I got this. Over and out." He handed the walkie back to Brian and pulled the PPK from his holster.

"You're not going on your own." Brian withdrew the bow. "And don't say shit about my leg. Yeah, it hurts, but I'm not crippled. I'll manage."

"I'm not gonna go slow"—Louis double-checked his clip and slapped it back in—"so you better be sure you can take the pain."

"I've had worse." Brian shoved past Louis and rushed down the steps to the first floor of the record store. Louis followed him into the still and silent street of a ghost town. Dark objects flitted across the gloomy sky, maybe bats or small birds, and a light swampy scent saturated the air. The reoccurrence of distressed sobs in the distance set them in motion.

They scurried behind the cover of parked cars and debris until they crossed the street and turned south. Brian spied a ladder near a dumpster and nudged Louis to suggest they climb onto the roof to get a vantage point. They took the ladder with them and used it to cross from roof to roof across the clustered buildings.

The pair followed the intensifying cries until a chorus of muted snickers and muffled sobs joined them. They both spotted movement and flattened themselves to a rooftop, peering through two pairs of binoculars they'd recovered from the gun shop.

Ashen figures were scattered throughout a playground across the street. Some spun on the merry-go-round. Others perched on top of the slide and monkey bars. The chains of old swings creaked, occupied by two drifting figures. Most surrounded a plastic playpen, arms reaching inside an entrance too small for their shoulders to squeeze through. They were all adults.

Brian's breath caught in his throat. He'd never seen them mimic such human activity before. *Is it motor memory, or are they* enjoying *this?*

One by one, they went down. Shells ejected from Louis's PPK and smoke swirled into the air. Brian got himself together and polished off the final few, sending the swinging pair sprawling forward onto their faces. The swings kept squealing.

Once the air cleared, Louis climbed down from the roof. Brian followed, the pain in his leg kept at bay by adrenaline. He jogged after Louis to see what the Stalkers had been straining for inside the playpen. The small figure inside it clung to a dirty stuffed bear.

Katie lifted her head. Thick sniffles clogged her voice as she wailed in relief and reached for Brian and Louis. The bear tumbled to the ground, forgotten.

"Where's your mom?" Brian tried to step forward, but Louis wouldn't let him. He didn't understand why.

"Mommy tuh-turned around... But I ruh-ran away and went buh-back to the church." Her face bunched up, and tears streamed down her cheeks. "Buh-but you were all *gone* and I tried to find you but the scary things chased me and I jus' ran and ran and lost Mommy and they *hurt* me!"

Brian swallowed; now he knew why Louis wouldn't let him near her.

When Katie burst into tears again, Louis turned to Brian and grabbed his shoulders. "Turn around and walk away. Don't look back."

Brian's stomach sank. "Louis, you *can't.*"

"What else can I do?" Louis hissed. "Leave her like this? We can't take her with us and wait for her to turn or infect one of us."

Brian shivered with each sob escaping Katie. The image of her outstretched hand had transported him back to the front door of his house, to his sister's hand slipping free of his, her futile pleas for him to help her.

A shuddering breath escaped him. "You don't have to. I can—"

"It's better if I do it. I know how your mind works—you'll never scrub the image from it. So walk away and don't look back. Wait for me at the record store. I'll do my best to make sure she never knows it's comin'."

Brian nodded, but he stepped past Louis toward a still-sobbing Katie. He made sure his glove was intact before curling his hand around hers. "I-I have to go. The others are worried. I'll tell them we found you. Louis is gonna stay with you, okay?"

Katie nodded. "Wuh-will you luh-look for my....for my mommy?"

Brian forced a smile. "I'll try."

He let go and ran away. A reckless urgency pushed him until he clambered back up the staircase of the record store and collapsed against the wall. He slid to the floor and tried not to imagine what Louis had to do or how he'd do it.

Brian stripped off the glove he'd touched Katie's hand with. He despised himself for treating an innocent child like a leper. He despised her mother even more for caving in to her fear, to her selfishness, and running away from them.

He hoped she was dead. Not because he hated her, but because no mother should live the rest of their life not knowing what happened to their child.

While he awaited Louis's return, he withdrew the walkie from his belt loop with a shaking hand and tried to keep his voice from breaking when he spoke: "D, you there? Over."

"Thank God!" she called back instantly. "I been waitin' to hear from you. What happened? Over."

"We found Katie. She ran away from Sarah, tried to look for us." Brian dragged his other hand through his hair. "A group of them chased her, cornered her. We killed them, but it was too late. She'd already been bitten. Over."

Dead silence followed before D responded, the strength gone from her voice. "Oh, baby, I'm sorry... Are you okay? Over."

"As okay as I can be. Louis is..." His voice cracked. "Louis is taking care of it. Over."

D didn't respond. Brian lowered the walkie to the floor. He switched his lantern on and caressed his revolver with his bare hand; he'd forgotten how cold the metal felt on his skin. His gunshot wound reminded him it existed with a searing throb of pain which ran the entire length of his leg.

It's better if Katie doesn't suffer. But if he kills her, Louis will agonize over the memory the rest of his life.

Can he even do it? He said he couldn't kill me if I turned.

Brian caressed his leg, trying to will away the pain and the thought of spreading infection.

The staircase creaked. Brian lifted his gun—but he lowered it when Louis appeared out of the shadows. He didn't say a word. The pistol he clutched tumbled to the ground, and he collapsed to his knees. His hands raked up his face into his bangs until he bunched his fingers into them, his shoulders shaking.

Brian shoved a shelf of CDs in front of the staircase to block the path up, and then kneeled in front of Louis. He wanted to ask him numerous questions but knew he shouldn't make Louis answer them. "Are you okay?"

Louis lowered his arms from his face and curled them around his knees. His eyebrows knit above glistening eyes. "You cut me open and I can't stop bleedin'."

He buried his face in his knees and sobbed, trying to hide what could no longer be hidden.

Louis cried until he collapsed. He crumpled to the ground in a heap of shaking shoulders and trembling limbs, eyes screwed shut, trying to will away the memories of what he'd done. Brian wanted to curl up with him and comfort him, but he forced himself to maintain distance and give

Louis space. Once Brian was sure Louis was asleep, he unfurled his sleeping bag and draped it over him. He then radioed D to let her know what had happened, that he was staying behind to watch over Louis while he slept, and they'd meet up with them in the morning. He was too drained to even write in his journal; he sat with his back to a wall and stared into the darkness.

Louis woke after a few hours and insisted Brian get some sleep. He drifted off, but it was the lightest sort of sleep where reality wove in and out until he wasn't sure what his dreams were. Once he got enough rest to function, they biked over to the library.

The group shared a short and somber breakfast. No one wanted to broach the subject of Katie's fate, even though Brian witnessed the effect on their faces. Cecilia had dark circles under her eyes once again, and Antoine's cheery smile never appeared. D, who usually had a decent appetite, only picked at a bag of cookies. Louis remained stoic, but the edge returned to his eyes—his attempt to hide his vulnerability from the others.

Even though they didn't feel like it, they returned to the road and headed north.

Eva's still out there. She's the point to all this.

They traveled past ample fields and trees with rustling leaves. Squirrels dashed up the knobby trunks to join nesting birds. Now and again they'd pass through a town frozen in time, each one a different story for Brian to interpret. Mostly, they passed churches. Sometimes an antique store or a car repair shop. Usually some dilapidated farmhouse with a rusted old truck in the yard and an empty doghouse with bowls still outside.

It was obvious Arkansas—or maybe the entire Midwest—hadn't been much of a priority for the military. They had little to no presence throughout it as if they'd decided, "Ah, fuck it—there's nothing here but churches and auto shops. Let it all burn."

If someone somewhere was working on identifying the cause of the disease and curing it, they weren't taking steps to make it known.

They're probably underground somewhere, or maybe some remote base in Alaska. Not anywhere we'll be going anytime soon.

Brian had no grand delusions of making a journey to search for the cure. His primary goal was to survive and protect the people he cared about, but he'd learned time and time again this was something he had little to no control over. Even searching for Eva seemed pointless at times, but when he tried to imagine what he'd be doing instead, he had no satisfying answer.

Existing. Or not.

He kept his ears attuned to the sounds surrounding them: a twig snapping, a whisper in the trees, an animalistic howl. An air of menace clung to them, but they didn't discuss it, like not talking about it meant it wasn't possible. As disconcerting as it was, they pushed on in an attempt to outrun their fear of the unknown and escape the memory of Katie's fate.

Brian's eyes swept across every inch of forest and road. The leaves and trees were too dense for him to see anything, the road a long stretch of asphalt with heat waves rippling over it. But a shiver rippled through him as if a cool breeze had washed over his skin. By the time the sun began its descent, he swore he was in a freezer. His nerves tingled to the point of numbness.

When they set up inside a rustic country store for the night, they could no longer avoid discussing what was escalating from a possibility to a near-certainty.

"Are you sure it's not just animals?" Cecilia asked. She sat on a glass counter alongside an empty register, her short legs dangling above the wood floor. "There are probably more of them coming out since it's warm again."

Brian leaned against the counter beside her. "Sure, but Stalkers are animals too. They called them Stalkers for a reason, right? They used to stalk their prey. But maybe they changed their pattern because they know we're a threat. Learned behavior, like a rabbit that's escaped a hound a few times over."

A curtain of silence enveloped them until Antoine lifted it. "Are they trying to figure out *our* patterns? We don't got a clear schedule: we wake up when we want, sleep when we tired, and stop off and on. Maybe 'cause we throw 'em off, they don't know the best time to attack."

"You might be onto something," Brian said. "Maybe those random events weren't random at all: maybe they were testing us, trying to draw us out or scare us to see if we'd split up."

Antoine crossed his brawny arms. "If they *are* followin' us, how do we find out for sure and how do we get rid of 'em?"

Brian peeled himself from the counter and sat cross-legged in front of D and Antoine. He ignored the twinge in his leg. "I think only a few were following us at first. But what if they found more along the way, like a Pied Piper kind of thing? They'll outnumber us, figure out our patterns, and ambush us. But Stalkers are kind of like monkeys: they may demonstrate learned behavior and even be able to perceive patterns, but they don't know *we* do the same thing. Maybe we need to split up. One group creates a diversion, draws their attention, while the other sets up nearby to watch for them. Then we can lure them out so we know they're there."

"It's a decent plan"—Cecilia plopped down alongside Brian—"but what if they go after whoever's watching them instead?"

Brian eyed the doorway to the other half of the store where Louis had wandered off in search of supplies. "We'd have to stay in each other's sight but far enough apart to throw them off. Maybe you and Lou could go somewhere high with your rifle and his silenced pistol, like a roof or tower. Somewhere difficult for Stalkers to get to. We'd stay low, someplace so easy they couldn't pass up an opportunity to attack or investigate."

Cecilia propped her elbow on her knee and dropped her chin into her hand. "Shouldn't we kill them as soon as we see them?"

"*If* we see them," Brian said. "As soon as you fire, the others will either run or attack us anyway. There's no easy way to take them all out at once. Think of this as a recon mission."

"A'ight." D shrugged and shared a look with Antoine. He nodded. "Cill, you gonna be okay with Louise on your own?"

Cecilia glared at her. "I've been alone with him before; I'll be *fine*. Besides, he's trying to hide it, but he hasn't been himself since what happened with Katie."

D folded her arms over a gauzy yellow blouse. Doubt slackened her typically confident features. "He wants to act all tough, but his skin's about as thick as cellophane—" She stopped talking when Louis poked his head in and tossed something at each of them: sticks of jerky.

D waggled hers and grinned. "Beef! Thank God—I was tired of this turkey junk."

Cecilia grimaced. "Ugh..."

"Stop bein' picky and eat it, Cecilia. Damn cow's already dead. You gonna let it go to waste?" Louis's question was rhetorical; he retreated into the other side of the store before she could answer.

Cecilia sighed to herself. "I guess not." She peeled back the plastic wrap and snapped into the stick along with the rest of them.

While the others nipped at the smoked meat, Brian tried to distract himself from the pain in his leg by meandering around the store. Pictures of folks dressed in rustic attire like plaid shirts, overalls, and straw hats hung on the walls. Customers, maybe. "Danger: Will Lick" was scrawled over a photo on the door of a droopy dog. A large space was worn into a dog bed by the register.

Ambient chatter drifted in the air while the others enjoyed their beef jerky. Brian moseyed into the area next door and opened a freezer door. Rotten food had spilled out, creating a bizarre ecosystem within the moist, enclosed space. The unpleasant scent of mold wafted out, so Brian quickly shut the door and moved on.

The floorboards behind him creaked. He turned, still on edge—but it was only Louis. He leaned against a barren shelf and offered Brian a weary smile. "There's not much in here. I checked."

Brian nipped at his half-eaten beef stick. "I know. But sometimes I like to imagine what these places were like before...you know."

"You've always had your head in the clouds." The buttons of Louis's shirt strained as he rested his elbows on an empty shelf behind him. His sleeves were rolled to his elbows, displaying the muscular clefts of his forearms. "Back when we were kids, you always thought up these scenarios, dreamed up characters for us to play. Like, we'd be in some fantasy world and Eva was the princess we had to rescue. Knights and dragons, shit like that. I bet you woulda tried to talk me into *Dungeons and Dragons* if we'd been friends in high school."

Brian leaned against the freezer across from Louis and fiddled with his flashlight. "We might be able to start a game. Antoine would totally be into it. You know how much he loves that sword." Louis's eyes dipped and dimmed as if his mind was returning to dark places, so Brian dug into his jeans and withdrew Jacque's good-luck token. He flipped it along his fingers and grinned. "Here's the treasure we're all seeking."

Louis snatched it from Brian's fingers so he could study it. He practically snorted when he glimpsed the image etched in the burnished coin. "And why are we tryin' to find this particular treasure?"

"It's for luck. Dark Wizard Jacque hid it in the swamps of *le Quartier Français*."

They both knew this conversation only existed to keep others from occurring, but they kept it going anyway.

"Well, we could all use some luck." Louis slapped the coin back into Brian's hand. "But what happens once we find it? Doesn't the game end?"

Brian considered his answer; the coin might as well be a stand-in for Eva and the game itself the journey to find her. He rubbed his thumb along the warm metal ridges. "We just set a new goal and keep going. Usually you level up, keep the same characters."

Louis smiled softly and tweaked Brian's nose. "Dork."

"That's not a character class." Brian's snarky comment made Louis snicker. "I'd probably be the Dungeon Master."

"I don't know what the fuck a Dungeon Master is, but it sounds too intense for you."

"It's the person who runs the game. They come up with scenarios and make sure people follow the rules." Brian jammed the coin back into his pocket. "And frankly, I'm a little insulted you think I'm some vanilla dork."

"There's nothin' wrong with vanilla—it's sweet and reliable." Louis stepped past Brian and squeezed his shoulder. "But maybe one day you can be the Dungeon Master, teach me all the rules—we could both surprise each other."

Brian went against his better instincts by dipping his toes back into the shallow end of the pool. "I'm versatile: I've got a good balance of creativity and discipline."

Louis's lips and eyebrows quirked into an intrigued, slightly dazed expression. "You're *already* surprisin' me." He headed for the doorway and paused, one foot still in the darkness, the other surrounded by the sunlight streaming through the windows of the adjacent room. "Thanks for givin' me somethin' to dream about. Fantasy's always better than reality, anyway."

He slipped out of the shadows. Brian exhaled and slumped back against the shelf, lingering in the world of fantasies before he forced himself to join Louis and the others in reality.

They selected a rock quarry across from an empty field for their stakeout. Woods surrounded the fields for the Stalkers to hide in, and Brian, D, and Antoine could dash across the road if they needed to. Louis and

Cecilia isolated themselves on the neck of a bulldozer to use it as a vantage point. Brian left a walkie with them and kept the other clipped to his belt. They'd inserted fresh batteries Louis had scrounged from the record store.

"Are we gonna frolic in the field?" Antoine asked while they walked to it. Although no one led her, Grimes followed. She wanted the grass. The quarry had no spoils for her to enjoy.

D laughed. "I'm picturin' *Hair* or somethin'—you know, when they all run around singin' 'bout the dawn of Aquarius."

"Forget all that hippie shit"—Antoine put his hands on his hips as he surveyed the field—"I'm gonna swing my sword, pretend I'm in a Kurosawa flick."

"We all gon' be too busy laughin' at you to watch out for Stalkers!"

"Go on and laugh then—I got no shame in my game." Antoine stepped away a few paces and withdrew the sword. Sunlight rippled in waves along the edge of the deadly blade as it sliced through the air, creating mosaic-like reflections. There was indeed no shame in his game, and Brian thought he'd make a fine Fighter if they ever got around to that game of *Dungeons and Dragons*.

D elbowed Brian. "When he learned karate, he used to twirl those magic staffs like Gandalf, do kicks and stuff while he played '90s dance music. That shit was *legit*! Too legit to quit."

Brian glanced out at the woods. Their surroundings were deceptively calm and clear: a picture-perfect sunny day with a brisk breeze and chirping birds. Butterflies flitted from flower to flower, ranging from purple thistles to something with small orange petals. A sweet scent lingered in the air. "D, is *Lord of the Rings* your favorite movie series or something?"

D sat cross-legged and wiggled her knees. "Baby, I'm almost twice as old as you—I only reference it 'cause you wouldn't know most of the things *I* do. The MC Hammer one flew right over your cherubic little head."

Brian sat beside her, torn between the comfort of the company and setting and a fear of the unknown. His hand hovered over the walkie. He fought the urge to bring it to his mouth and call to ask what they saw.

"What're some of your favorite movies?" he asked, trying to distract himself. "I know you like scary movies—and *Lord of the Rings*—but what else?"

"Ooh, boy, don't you get me started!" D was either distracted or hiding her own concerns well. "Antoine used to make me watch a buncha Bruce Lee movies. Jackie Chan too. Used to hate 'em 'cause they dubbed 'em and the mouths didn't match the words, but I got used to seein' all those sweaty, shirtless men. And I like me some comedies—"

The walkie crackled. Brian brought it to his mouth. "This is Brian. Over."

"Hey." Static distorted Cecilia's pleasant voice. "Louis says he sees something to the left of where you're facing. He's got a bead on it, but keep an eye out. Over and out."

"Thanks, Cill. Over and out."

D tried not to turn her head toward the location Cecilia pointed out. "Should we get 'Toine?"

Brian shook his head. "We have to relax; otherwise, they'll sense our fear." He grinned and nudged her with an elbow. "Hey, since you're so old, I bet you played *Dungeons and Dragons* with 'Toine."

D gave him a playful shove. "I'm allowed to call myself old; *you* ain't." She primped her hair and shot a feisty look in his direction. "But yes, I've played a game or two in my many years on this earth. Mostly so I could spend time with 'Toine's hot buddies. I was a Druid—I think?"

"It'd be fun to play some time. We're always so bored when we're on the road, and there's five of us—"

"You shouldn't play games with him, baby. I know you feel bad for him 'cause of what he had to do to that poor little girl, but don't give him false hope 'cause you feel vulnerable and think he does too."

Brian stared into D's eyes and shook his head. "He's not faking it, D."

D alternated between watching Antoine and the edge of the woods. Her hand remained close to her shotgun. "I know how much you love him, even after what he done. Don't mean I like it or think it's healthy, but I also know how much I miss Gus, and I'd forgive him for anything long as it meant he was still around." Her lavender nails tapped along the varnished wood of the gun. "I guess what I'm tryin' to say is don't do anything before you're ready, and don't make him *think* you're ready for somethin' you ain't. You need to give it time, see what happens if we find his sister. Then we'll *all* see what he's fakin' and what he ain't."

"But what if I don't *have* time? What if we never find her, and—"

D pressed a finger to his lips. "Baby, yo' melodramatic ass ain't infected. You just lookin' for an excuse to jump off the cliff again—or sail away on a boat in your case. But I ain't gonna let you do it. We are gonna *find* this girl. If she's anything like her damn brother, she ain't dead."

The conviction of her words reassured Brian, as usual. He embraced her, squeezing until she wheezed and a bone cracked somewhere in her back.

"Ooh! Felt like you was tryin' to Heimlich a shrimp out my throat!" D pressed a hand to her chest while she tried to catch her breath. "I didn't know you was *that* strong!"

Brian reached for her hand and squeezed. "Only because you're here. You're my best friend in the entire world, D. No—the entire *universe*."

D smiled often, but he'd only seen her cry once: during the first Cleansing they attended at Evergreen. Her golden-brown eyes gleamed in the sunlight until a tear rolled over her rouged cheek. She wiped it with a finger and tilted her head back to look at the sky. "There's a whole lotta universe out there. I guess I'm pretty lucky some alien didn't swoop in and beam you up first." She thrust a finger toward the sky. "Don't you get any ideas, aliens—he's *my* best friend."

Brian laughed until his stomach hurt. D sputtered until she cracked up too, and they just sat there giggling like a couple of idiots. Antoine stopped swinging his sword to stare at them, but he smiled and resumed his exercise when he realized they weren't in any danger.

Pale rays of sunlight rippled along swaying blades of grass, and the wind spread the sweet scent of flowers. Songbirds chirped from within rustling tree leaves. The beauty of this ephemeral moment reinforced the transience of a seemingly infinite life.

The sonic wave of a gunshot roused Brian from his daydream. A white pile slumped into the grass along the edge of the woods, its skull hollowed into a bowl of red porridge.

He jumped to his feet and raised the walkie to his mouth. "What the fuck is going on? Talk to me, Cill. Over."

"One of them got too nosy, so Louis put it down. He says there's more and he doesn't want to risk it, so get out of there. Over and out."

Brian clipped the walkie back to his belt and withdrew the revolver. Antoine and D stood at his side, armed with their sword and shotgun. Grimes trotted over to them, her glossy chestnut coat shimmering. Strands of grass still stuck out of her mouth.

A Stalker sprung out of the tall grass, one pale hand clawing for her leg. Brian took aim—but Antoine leaped forward and swung down, his sword glinting in the sunlight like a crescent moon. A head rolled toward them, bloodshot eyes going glassy, the grotesque grin reminding Brian of Henry's mauled "family" and the disembodied head smiling at him from bloodstained snow.

Antoine flicked the blade toward the ground, sending a spray of blood into the jade grass. He sheathed it and leaped onto Grimes, taking hold of her reins and angling her toward Brian and D. Brian helped D on first. After she pulled him up, they took off at a gallop that nearly sent them all sliding.

Grimes skidded into the quarry within a red-hot minute. Louis and Cecilia were already down waiting for them with their guns aimed at the field. Brian slid to the ground and bent to inspect Grimes's leg, fearing Antoine had been too late.

He exhaled. *It didn't get her. Thank God.*

When he stood, he swore his leg was trapped in an inferno of blue flames, but he clenched his jaw and turned to survey the field. His breath caught in his throat: at least a dozen pale bodies kneeled in the sea of grass. *They're just staring at us.*

Cecilia lifted her rifle and fired, making Brian's ears ring and sending a shudder through his spine. Smoke swirled into the air, the acidic taste sinking into his tongue. One Stalker fell; the others scattered into the woods.

D helped Brian back onto Grimes. He dug his feet into her haunches and pushed on despite the pain in his leg, his revolver aimed at the empty field. The Stalkers were gone for now. Out of sight, but never out of mind.

Chapter Nine

Disarmed

4/07, Lead Hill, Arkansas, 4:55 p.m.

The group spent the night near a town called Lead Hill. Frightened by the awareness of what followed them, they neither slept well nor long. Even Grimes was hesitant to drift off; she wandered around the office building they'd secured, startling herself and everyone else when she bumped into the cluttered furniture.

Not long after they left, signs popped up for Diamond City (north) and Bull Shoals Lake (east). They stopped at a gas station several hours later for loot and rest, but the sweet and sour stench of a decaying body swiftly forced them outside. Based on the location and position, Brian suspected it had been a lingering Stalker that had curled up and starved to death.

He leaned against the front window and pulled out his wind-up radio to give it a few spins. Before long, he found the station with the repeating message, now clearer: "We have food, water, and power. Safety and shelter guaranteed. Come to Diamond City, near the Missouri-Arkansas border. Surrender your guns and submit to an inspection; if you are not infected, you are welcome."

Shelter and safety had never been more appealing—the constant fear of being followed by Stalkers was worse than the occasional shot of adrenaline when one jumped out at them. But Brian dwelled on the conditions: turning over the guns which had kept them alive this long was no easy proposition. And what if everyone else was fine but *he* wasn't?

"Seems kinda dumb to send a message like that." D slid off one of the parking bollards and wriggled to redistribute her weight. "It's like askin' for someone to come take your stuff—and they straight-up askin' to take *ours*."

"Or they just nice people like at Evergreen, want to help others but got to be cautious." Antoine's fingers drummed the top of the empty ice chest beside him. "They gotta be armed or they wouldn't play that shit out, you know? Might be they could protect us better than we can protect ourselves."

"They must have power or else they wouldn't be able to keep sending the message." Cecilia swung her feet while she sat on the hood of an old Cadillac. "If there *are* good people there, we'd be able to rest, talk to them, dig up information. Sleep in beds, maybe even take a real shower…"

Everyone let out a wistful sigh. Brian flashed back to the shower in the RV, a brief taste of bliss he yearned to experience again. Among others.

"We're getting close." Brian snuck a glance at Louis, studying the cigarette trapped between his lips. He'd found a pack inside the gas station, and although Brian recalled Louis mentioning he used to smoke and drink, he still didn't like seeing him do it. "We need to be careful. Maybe move off the main roads."

"You wanna go in the woods?" Antoine asked. "Them fields ain't gonna offer no cover."

"Stalkers are still following us," D said. "I saw one overnight. Came right up to the window and pressed its face to it, tryin' to look through the slits in the boards. All I saw was one cloudy eye and a sliver of that nasty-ass grin. Nearly gave my ass a heart attack!"

"*What*?" Cecilia's eyebrows arched as high as they could go. She brought a hand to her mouth and glanced at the woods to the west. "Oh, Good God—that's so creepy! Why didn't you tell us?"

"I told 'Toine. The rest of y'all were asleep—figured we'd wake you if the asshole tried somethin', but it just slunk back to the woods. Maybe they take turns keepin' watch too."

"We can't travel much longer with Stalkers on our trail," Brian said. "We need to take a chance on this city—even if Eva isn't there, Antoine's right: it might protect us while we figure out what to do. We could tell the people there about what happened, see if they've noticed any changes in their behavior. And maybe they can help us take them out."

Louis blew out a cloud of smoke. "Out of one hole, into another."

Brian narrowed his eyes and waved away the vaporous sting. "This isn't an easy call, Louis. We either lead a bunch of Stalkers back to

Missouri or try to take them out on our own—and it doesn't matter how much ammo we have if we're outnumbered and they end up flanking us and decide to attack."

Louis tapped the crumbling ash from his cigarette. "We're already flanked, *boug*."

Brian plucked the cigarette from Louis's lips, flicked it to the ground, and crushed it beneath his boot. "I know you're out of gum, but isn't there something else you can stick in your mouth? I'm trying to discuss something important, not choke on your smoke."

Louis stared at Brian for a moment, his expression wavering between irritated and shocked. "You've never had a problem with chokin' before, but fuck it." He stuffed his hand into his jean pocket and withdrew the pack of cigarettes. "I got news for you—there's plenty more in here."

The cloud of cigarette smoke had been replaced by a cloud of resentment and humiliation. D and Antoine glanced at each other with saucer-sized eyes but kept their mouths shut. Cecilia looked between Brian and Louis, her lips stretched into a grimace.

We have to make a crucial decision, and he's still not used to anyone but him making them. The shit with Katie made things worse, reminded him he has no control over anything. He's always hated feeling helpless. The cigarettes are an escape, and I don't like what it says about where his head's at.

Brian screwed his eyes shut and rubbed the bridge of his nose, willing his anger away. "I'll go check out this city. I don't want to put D and Cecilia in danger—I'll never forget the fucked-up way that asshole and his gang treated women—and you and Antoine are both kind of intimidating. I straddle the line between scaring people and making them want to kidnap me. Or at least I hope so."

"You just as pretty as Cill," D said. "And you *way* prettier than me. Just let Louis do it—he wants to see if his sister's there, and if somethin' happens to him, I won't exactly be heartbroken over it."

Louis nodded. "I don't agree with her often, but D's right on all counts."

Brian gave Louis a tight smile and arched both eyebrows. "I'm going, end of discussion. But you and Antoine can lead the Stalkers away from the rest of us. They'll follow the smaller group, like when a pride of lions goes after the straggler in the herd. The only reason they followed me, D, and 'Toine into the field instead of Lou and Cill is because we pretended to let our guards down, and they couldn't pass up the opportunity. And since we killed a few of them, I think they'll be too wary to try anything. That'll give me the opportunity to sneak up to the city without a bunch of Stalkers on my ass."

Louis groaned and slapped a hand over his hip. "*Fine.* Whip out your map and show us where you want us to go."

Pleased with his victory, Brian shrugged his backpack off and withdrew his crinkled map and a pencil. He gestured for the others to huddle close to him. "Louis and Antoine will take their bikes and go east of this route"—he dragged his pencil along it—"until they're sure the Stalkers are following them, not us. Once we know we're in the clear, D, Cill, and I will take the western path and split off outside the city. They'll be my backup, stay close by while I keep a low profile and scope out the perimeter with the binoculars. I'll keep a walkie; Louis can take the other one. Once I reach the city, I'll radio and tell him where he can meet up with Cill and D. Antoine, you keep those Stalkers on top of you as long as you can so Louis can sneak past them. That way he can get the radio to Cill and D in case I need them to provide cover fire or another distraction, and he can come help me if he's so inclined."

D's lips rippled in an exaggerated raspberry. "Oh, he's inclined. But if you get into the city on your own, what do the rest of us do? Do we go get my brother? If we out there too long, those things might wait us out, surround whatever building we camp out in."

Brian folded the map and tucked it in his backpack. "If I make it into the city and everything's okay, take Grimes and get 'Toine, then meet me where I tell you to. If you don't hear from me—"

"I'll go after Brian if we don't hear from him," Louis said. "You two take Antoine and get outta there. Go back to Evergreen if shit hits the fan. This was never your problem to begin with."

"You mean you woulda rather had him come up here all on his lonesome?" D crossed her arms and gave Louis a stern look. "Boy, please—*he's* the reason we're here, and we ain't gonna leave him. You ain't the only thing in the world he's got, not anymore, never again. Get over it."

"I just don't wanna drag you into a pile of shit you don't need to stick your foot in," Louis snapped, taking a step toward D, "so try and keep your sassmouth shut for once."

D dropped her arms to her sides. One hand curled into a fist and her eyebrows arched as she pursed her lips. Brian wedged himself between them, facing D, and gripped her arms. "D, please listen to him. I don't want anything to happen to you guys. If you don't hear from me, run."

"I'll be okay on my own for a bit." Antoine stepped up behind his sister and wrapped a hand around her shoulder. "I'll play fetch with 'em, throw some firecrackers and shit to keep 'em curious. Me and Louis'll find a building, block it off, and I'll sneak out while they distracted if push comes to shove. It ain't no thing. I mean, I'm the big buff dude with the riot gear and the samurai sword—what's gonna fuck with me?"

D's tensed muscles relaxed at her brother's urging. She dragged a hand down her face and exhaled. "I got this. I'm cool." She craned her head around Brian to glare at Louis. "Don't fuck this up. Let my brother or Brian down and I *will* come back and take care of your ass myself, you dig?"

She backed away, apparently satisfied with whatever face or gesture Louis made in response. Then she whipped around to give her brother a hug that made him cry out in surprise or pain. "You better take care of yo'self—you ain't an army all on your own."

"Sis, wasn't I fine last time you came lookin' for me?" He withdrew and patted her shoulders. "Look after Cill and Grimes and let those boys do their thing. They made it on their own before they met you, didn't they?"

D's resigned grimace meant she knew he was right. She gestured between her eyes and Louis with two fingers, but Brian didn't know how she planned to watch him when they'd be several miles apart. Binoculars and psychic sense?

Cecilia stood on her tiptoes and wrapped her arms around Louis. He patted her back as if she was some breakable object made of china or porcelain. She let go and spun to hug Antoine, but she couldn't reach his neck even on tiptoe and settled for his shoulders.

"Be careful, Antoine." Brian had less trouble reaching Antoine for a hug. "And thanks for going with him."

"No prob." Antoine glanced at Brian's leg when they parted. "You gonna be okay? I know you said it's healin' up, but it's gonna hurt if you leave D and Cill, go on foot."

Brian smiled. "I'll live."

Antoine ruffled Brian's hair; for an instant, he felt like a kid with his dad again. A bashful smile accompanied a swat of his hand against Antoine's arm. "Aw, your hair already looked a mess before I touched it. Why you think I ain't got any?"

Brian snickered as Antoine climbed onto his bike. Cecilia straddled hers; she'd helped D onto Grimes while Antoine and Brian said goodbye. Louis sat on his bike and fiddled with his equipment, but Brian knew he wasn't *really* paying attention to it—he was just trying to pretend he hadn't been watching Brian.

Brian deliberated with himself for a moment, but they'd already drawn this out long enough and needed to get a move on. He stepped up to Louis and kicked his foot, arms crossed. "Hey, watch yourself out there, okay?"

Louis stopped fidgeting and fixed his gaze on Brian. "I shouldn't have said what I said. I'm sorry."

"Yeah, well, I started shit when I snatched your cigarette away like you were a disobedient kid." Brian glanced at Cecilia and D. They both looked away like something interesting had appeared in the opposite direction. "You're not on probation anymore, okay? I shouldn't have been a condescending prick. I'm putting my trust in you, so don't make me look like an idiot again."

Louis stood and leaned forward. He picked at locks of Brian's hair, trying to rearrange and untangle the mess Antoine had created. When Louis plopped back onto his bike seat and smirked, Brian let out a breath. "There—now you don't look like an idiot."

"I'll call you soon." Brian backed away, one hand jammed into his jean pocket and the other clinging to the strap of his backpack. "You have to trust me too, okay?"

Louis nodded. He pawed at the walkie clipped to his belt and pushed off with Antoine hot on his heels. Brian watched them for a moment before he forced himself to turn and take D's hand. He stuck his foot in Grimes's stirrup and slung his injured leg over her with a wince.

"We have to wait for them to make some headway, but we can't go into that stank-ass store," D said. Brian couldn't see her, but he knew she'd crinkled her nose. "Let's just ride up a ways, see what we can find."

Brian and Cecilia agreed. They secured a nearby house and relaxed for a few moments, trying to give Louis and Antoine time to attract their followers. Minutes felt like hours to Brian; he wanted to get this over with, know once and for all whether they were heading into a trap or into the sanctuary Sarah swore didn't exist.

And ditch these Stalkers or take them out. Find Eva. Deal with this shit between me and Louis. Know for sure I'm not sick—

Brian shuddered when the walkie finally went off. "*Bonjour*, boug— we just passed a truck shop with your name. Now we're at a church. Big surprise, right? Antoine stayed out, made a bunch of noise, and swung his sword all over the damn place. Anyone saw him, they'd think he was schizo and leave his crazy ass alone. I went up on the roof and scoped the surroundin's, saw a few of our friends watchin' him. I counted ten, all scattered in the woods around us. Over."

Brian stopped picking at the material of his jeans; he'd been trying in vain to reach his hot, itching skin. "Just stay there for now. I'll call you once D and Cill are settled somewhere safe. Over and out."

"Copy that. Be careful. Over and out."

They left the house and traveled up the road until signs revealed they were ten miles away from Diamond City. At this point, they climbed off their transportation and entered the woods west of the road. They moved at a meticulous pace over rocks, dirt, and grass, the occasional stick cracking under feet and hooves.

The emerging leaves of surrounding trees offered coveted shade. Small animals like squirrels or chipmunks sometimes streaked across the shadow-dappled ground and disappeared up trees or behind felled logs. On occasion, a gust of wind rippled through the canopy of trees, mimicking the sound of ocean waves rolling against the shore.

As a child, Brian had found visits to scenic parks boring. He'd never appreciated the serenity. Now it frightened him.

A country club with rolling fields of turf grass loomed beyond the woods. After consulting with the map, they confirmed they were heading in the right direction and continued. The group cut across the course and over a paved road until they reached the truck shop Louis had mentioned.

"Ain't seen nobody yet," D whispered from behind the shop, "but we definitely near the city now. This where you want us to wait for Louise?"

Brian nodded. "Let's check it out, make sure you're safe before I call him." He slapped Grimes's haunch to send her away. One close call was enough—he didn't know if he could stand to lose her after all this time.

She's been with me longer than D. God, that's fucking insane.

He strung an arrow and pushed the door open. Something scuttled into the bowels of the building. D pumped her shotgun and stepped in, her back to a wall. Cecilia slipped in after D with a pistol clutched in both hands. Brian swung the door shut and surveyed the small building. *Waiting room, garage, bathroom, service desk. Door to the garage is blocked, so it didn't go there—*

A high-pitched screech drew Brian's attention. He swiveled in the direction of the harsh noise, spotted a black-and-gray object in the corner behind a withered potted plant, and released the bow string when the thing hissed and came at him with claws outstretched.

Brian stepped closer and glimpsed raw wounds in the ragged fur. "This raccoon looks sick. Let's toss it and check the bathroom before I head out."

Cecilia winced, but she dragged the poor creature outside while D and Brian inspected the bathroom. They recoiled from the stench of festering bodily fluids and slammed the door shut. No other signs of life inhabited the truck shop. They went outside to summon Grimes and let her into the waiting room. She tried to eat the dead plant and clearly regretted this bold undertaking.

Brian called Louis while D and Cecilia set their bags down and rested for a moment. "Hey, Lou, you guys still doing okay? I'm about to leave Cill and D. They're at my truck shop. Over."

Mere seconds passed before Louis's already throaty voice rasped over the walkie. "Antoine's still givin' the performance of a lifetime. Those Stalkers are probably so confused they can't keep their eyes off him. None of 'em have budged; they just sit there in the woods starin'. It'd almost be funny if it wasn't so goddamn creepy." He scoffed regardless. "He's actually a better actor than those gangster wannabes. Mighta missed his callin'. Anyway, I should be able to slip out. I'm gonna go on foot since they'll notice a bike for sure. Tell the girls I'll see them in about fifteen. I'll buzz you once I've made it to them. Over."

"If I don't answer, don't freak out. Just give me a couple of minutes in case I didn't hear you or it's too risky to talk. Over and out."

"Copy that. Don't push yourself. Over and out."

Brian sensed the hesitation in Louis's voice, like he wanted to say more, but he figured they were both saving a lot of things they wanted to say for later conversations—ones taking place after they determined Eva's fate and needed to decide what to do about their own.

"All right, D. Cill. Time for me to go. Lou's on the way." Brian leaned in to hug both women, cherishing the strength of D's embrace and the warmth of Cecilia's. "He's bringing his walkie, so if you need to talk to me, just let him know—or grab it from him. If he doesn't show up for some reason, go to Antoine."

"He'll show." Cecilia smiled. "I have faith in him. So do you."

D's expression made it obvious she didn't attend the church of Louis, but Brian didn't expect her to. He couldn't blame her. Their constant state of peril helped keep his own judgment at bay and reminded him of the times Louis had been there for him. Now he needed to take Cecilia's lessons to heart and remember there was more out there than just this, and love—in whatever form it might take—did heal most wounds.

Even if they still left mental and physical scars.

Brian kissed Grimes's nose and slipped through the door with his gear. D and Cecilia watched him through the window, waving as if he was leaving their house after a weekend visit. Grimes joined them, her breath steaming against the glass.

As he crept through the fringes of the city, he kept his eyes open for familiar triggers: the glint of taut wire, a suspicious pile of leaves or logs, ropes and snares mingling with scattered debris and underbrush, or anything that could make noise such as tin and aluminum cans or glass bottles. So much wreckage had been left behind in the chaos of the pandemic's aftermath it was hard to discern what was "natural" rubbish.

He tested anything he felt uncertain about by staying back and lobbing whatever he could throw without making too much noise. Deeper within the city, he slipped between buildings and encountered bear traps half-hidden in decaying leaves and broken gravel.

Either there are still people here or there were not too long ago. Did they set these traps for Stalkers? It doesn't make sense to leave traps if you're advertising safety in your city.

They probably expected people to travel using the road, not creep through on foot like me. And it probably is smart to trap anyone who might try to sneak up on them.

While Brian picked his way around the scattered traps, Louis called him to let him know he'd made it to Cill and D—he even let them say hello, so Brian knew he was telling the truth. This erased one fear from his mind.

He kept going until he reached a fence. When he poked it with his finger, he was shocked—literally *and* figuratively. *Someone had time and resources to build this. Military?*

Either the electric jolt lingered or the prospect of running water, power, and civilization sent a surge of excitement through him. He dashed to the nearest building—a gas station—and lifted the lid of a dumpster to inspect its contents before he climbed onto it. He leaned around the corner of the building with the binoculars pressed to his eyes. *There's a gate. Locked, no doubt. There have to be eyes on it, but where?*

Brian scanned along the fence until something glinted in his field of vision: a rifle scope. He retreated behind the wall and caught his breath before lifting the walkie to his mouth. "Louis, I found a fence. There's a gate, but someone's guarding the perimeter. The area outside the fence is littered with traps, but none of them were set off. Over."

An agonizing silence followed until the walkie crackled with startling clarity. "You want me to come to you? Over."

In situations like these, Louis was Brian's safety net. He hated himself for it, but he knew he'd feel more confident if Louis was nearby. "It wouldn't be a bad idea. But tell Cill and D to hang back if you think Antoine will be okay for a bit. Over."

The walkie remained silent while Louis presumably relayed Brian's instructions. "I'll head your way. Stay put until I get to you, but let me know if you see anythin' else." An elongated silence followed this, but Brian waited since Louis hadn't indicated the transmission was over. "If somethin' happens to you, I'll kill every last person in there. Over and out."

A gratified smile spread across Brian's face. He clipped the walkie to his belt and took in a slow, steady breath before whipping around the corner to peer through the binoculars. He aimed for the last place he'd seen the flash and searched for the person holding the scoped weapon. *Post office, laundromat, houses—*

A *buzz* spooked him into darting behind the wall. The metallic rattling of the gate made his skin crawl. After a moment, a voice carried through the air, distorted by an electronic filter. Maybe a speaker. "Come out where we can see you. We don't want to hurt you—we want to help you."

He didn't dare peek through his binoculars now. He kept his back to the brick wall, wincing at the mysterious stains next to him. He withdrew an arrow from his quiver and strung it but didn't pull tension.

"Blondie with the binoculars—we know you saw us. You're the one who snuck up on *us*, so can you blame us for being wary?"

Whoever that is sounds pretty chipper. Is it a girl? Guess they saw my hair... Makes me kinda miss all my winter hoodies.

"Hey, we expect people to come here—it's why we send the message out. Just walk down the road with your hands up... Yeah, I know it sounds pretty dicey, but we're being straight with you, I swear." The other voice definitely belonged to a man, but the speaker warped both voices beyond recognition. They could be recordings for all he knew. Except the "blondie with binoculars" thing was pretty spot-on.

"Listen, don't make us come out there. We'll actually have to earn our pay." The woman giggled as if she found this funny. "There's power here. Food. Beds. Showers! You know you want it..."

"Hot meals, hot showers, hot folks—what more could you want?" The man's vocal cadence reminded Brian of a fairground barker. "Come one, come all," that sort of thing. "Geez, you came all this way... Don't be scared. We don't bite—or scratch. Or eat people. Listen, we'll come out to meet you. Isn't that nice of us? We'll introduce ourselves, you introduce *your*self, and we'll figure this thing out, all right? For starters, my name's Craig."

Brian's breath caught in his throat, forming a painful lump. *No way.*

"And I'm the light of his life, the fire of his loins, the sin of his soul—well, okay, I'm not Lolita. *My* name's Billie."

It was them: Billie and Craig, formerly known as Parker and Spike. Their voices clicked for him now, half performance, half authentic. Clearly, they hadn't transitioned out of the roles completely.

But why are they here? I guess it is *on the border of Missouri. Not crazy far from Joplin.*

More importantly, can I trust them? Fool me once...

"I'll tell you what," Billie called, "I have a craving for sugar cookies."

His heart fluttered. *They know it's me.*

"Yeah, but all the Cajun left a bad aftertaste..." Craig called. "Oh, come on, kid—you know you missed us. Let's catch up! No booze or betrayal this time, pinky promise."

Then, the line which sealed his fate, delivered in Billie's dulcet tone: "If you're looking for her, she's here."

He didn't know where Louis was, but he worried Louis might reach them before he did—and he'd do exactly what he promised the actors the night they fled the park: *"If I ever see either of you again, I'll put a bullet in both your brains."*

Brian scrambled down from the dumpster and stepped out into the road. He kept an arrow pulled tight. Two figures in protective padding approached with their guns trained on him. His pulse throbbed in his neck and wrists, but he held his ground as he called out to the approaching pair, "You better not fuck me over again, or I swear to God—"

"Brian Jameson! What a sight for sore eyes!" Billie dropped her gun and ran to him. He had to lower his arrow or she would've impaled herself on it when she flung her arms around him. The momentum of her collision sent her twirling through the air, spinning him until he nearly stumbled. He clenched her narrow waist to recover his balance. "Oh, darling, we did so wish to see you again!"

Although she retained the flair of her prior persona, Billie's hair fell to her shoulders and her plucked eyebrows had filled in. She no longer wore dramatic mascara, but her eyes were still a startling emerald green. Her blush-pink lips spread into a broad smile instead of a rouged Cupid's bow.

"Your hands are a little *too* low, kid." Craig grinned and angled his shotgun toward the ground. Instead of a tipped fedora, a helmet covered his tousled waves. Tan skin complemented his electric-blue eyes, and his lips lifted into a familiar roguish grin. "But I'll let it pass as long as you give me a hug too. Put your hands a *little* higher, though."

Billie let go so Craig's strong arms could encircle Brian. When Brian inhaled a whiff of enchanting aftershave merging with Billie's lingering honeysuckle aroma, his knees went weak. Despite their slight physical changes, the duo retained a magnetic dynamism amplified by each other's presence.

Craig withdrew and grasped Brian's shoulders. "You look good, kiddo. Cleaner, happier, healthier, hotter. Your guess whether I mean sweaty or attractive. You alone? Figured your pal Louis wouldn't let you out of his sight."

Brian shook his head, swimming in a daze. He glanced at the buildings around him, worried other people might be hiding within them. "You're not still working for him, are you? Tell me this isn't part of some con because your sister and niece got captured again."

Billie and Craig's ebullient faces drooped with shame. Craig curled an arm around Billie's shoulders. "I can't blame you for thinking the worst. But if you have a shred of trust in us, believe me when I tell you it's different this time. Everything you heard in the message is true."

Billie nodded. "We work shifts as guards along the fence here. When Red—one of our coworkers—saw your little blond head poke out, I tried to tell myself it was wishful thinking. But then I thought you might've come looking for Eva, so I convinced him to let us talk to you..." She leaned close to Brian and whispered, "Do you know what Louis did? Eva told us. We can protect you."

"I know." Brian sensed the charge of electricity in the air. He withdrew from Billie and turned to block the pair. "But *you're* the ones who need protection. Louis, I don't know where you are, but I know you can hear me—don't do anything rash. Let's hear them out."

"Let's do this." Craig lowered his shotgun to the ground and lifted his hands. Billie did the same, though both remained close to Brian. "See? We're unarmed. We trust your friend. And we saved your sister—the one you left. If you wanna see her again, get the story straight from her mouth, then come out. Though you kinda already did when you ran away with Brian..." He looked at his lover. "Was that not funny, sweetheart?"

Billie shook her head, frowning.

Although Brian was looking at Billie and Craig instead of watching for Louis, he knew exactly when Louis emerged: the warmth disappeared from Billie and Craig's eyes. Billie didn't smile, but Craig's lips lifted into a grin which didn't meet his pointed gaze.

"I'd say it's good to see you, but even *I'm* not that talented an actor."

Brian's skin prickled when Louis appeared next to him. "You're a shitty goddamn actor. And you're fuckin' lucky he's here or I'd make good on my promise." Louis tightened his hand around the PPK aimed at Craig until the vein in his temple throbbed. "Take me to her."

"Easy there, tiger," Billie stammered. Craig maintained an air of confidence, but all of hers had flown out of the window. "It's not that simple. We're just a couple of guards. We don't have enough clout to get you in without an exam, still armed, to see a sister who probably doesn't want to see *you*."

Louis winced from the sting of her words. "Fine. I don't trust you and you don't trust me. Now what?"

Craig kept his hands in the air, but he stepped up next to Brian and edged Billie behind him. "We both have one thing in common: we trust Brian. Obviously, he's a forgiving kid, too nice for his own good—that's how he got mixed up with a buncha no-gooders like us, am I right?"

"What are you gettin' at?" Louis had crossed into an extremely impatient mood, perhaps worried about Antoine and the girls, but more likely eager to see if they were telling the truth about Eva.

"You give your weapons up, but we'll let him keep his. Normally, we'd have to take them, and we'll probably get into trouble for doing this, but it's better than the alternative... I mean, I won't lie; there are other guns trained on you two right now and I could give the signal to shoot, but we both know I'd be dead before that." Craig laughed, but this time a bit of his confidence faltered. Honestly, it startled Brian how much they feared Louis.

Have I forgotten how dangerous he can be?

"Fine." Louis thrust his PPK out—and flipped it so Craig could grab the grip. "As long as it gets us into your city." He proceeded to pat himself down for every other weapon he'd strapped to himself or shoved into a pocket somewhere, producing the pocketknife, a set of brass knuckles he'd never used, a smaller handgun in his boot, and a stun gun he got from somewhere *Brian* didn't even remember. "Don't tell me you need to frisk me."

Craig sighed and tucked the PPK into a holster on his belt. "Well, we'd rather not do it either..."

"You trust me, right?" Brian just wanted to get it over with, ease the tension between Louis and their gateway into the city—and Eva. Craig nodded, so Brian turned and gave Louis a long, searching look, trying to tell him not to misbehave or else he'd fuck everything up with everyone.

Louis nodded, quick and shallow. Brian patted along the length of Louis's torso, but his tight turtleneck didn't leave much room to hide anything except the toned muscles beneath it. Brian wished he was doing this under drastically different circumstances—not outside a fence with Billie and Craig watching and Louis still fuming mad. Louis's strained muscles betrayed the rage boiling within him.

Brian sighed and rolled up Louis's sleeves and the bottom of his shirt. He fought the urge to sweep out a hand like some game show assistant and say, "Look here: you've won a set of lovely weapon-free abs and forearms!" Instead, he stepped back and considered the engraved belt buckle (a wolf) and tight jeans facing him.

This is so goddamn awkward. Just pretend he's a statue or something.

This time, Brian's sigh went longer and deeper. Even though Louis stared dead ahead into the distance, Brian avoided looking at his face. He patted along sultry loins and firm ass cheeks—and as if that wasn't awkward enough, he had to kneel to finish out from knees to feet, even taking Louis's boots off and shaking them out. No surprises awaited Brian or the actors.

Relieved Louis was too distracted to enjoy this pat-down, Brian wiped his hands together and smiled at Billie and Craig as if to say, "Job well done, right?"

Craig gave him a sharp nod, but Billie's chest heaved as if she was trying to let out a heavy breath in silence. Maybe she'd been holding it.

"Come with us if you want to live," Craig said, imitating Arnold Schwarzenegger's accent. Brian scoffed and followed him past the gate, strolling between Billie and Louis. The gate hurtled shut behind them with a startling crash.

Craig turned to face them. "Before we go any farther, you'll have to submit to a work-up by our resident doc. Got to check you for any bites and cuts, you know. Hope you're not into any rough stuff."

Billie caught Louis's irritated glare and cleared her throat. "Don't look so sour: you *could* go into quarantine for two weeks to make sure you don't act weird. Or weirder than normal in your case. But since the virus isn't airborne, all Felicia needs to do is look for suspicious marks and plop some kind of liquid she engineered onto them. It goes all fizzy if it touches a wound infected with the Stalker disease. Pretty nifty."

Brian tensed up. He scratched his thigh and glanced at Louis. For an instant, Louis's features relaxed, and he brushed Brian's arm with his hand as if trying to tell him he'd be okay. Brian exhaled and nodded, tried to give Louis a tight smile. *I'm just paranoid. If I was sick, I'd know by now.*

They arrived at a modest gray building with a faded wooden sign for North Arkansas Regional Medical Center. It barely passed for a clinic, but from what Brian had seen of the city during their brief trek, it didn't seem very impressive for something named after the most valuable gem on Earth. It resembled a coastal resort town, a little run-down but peaceful and quaint. He had yet to see people aside from Billie and Craig.

That changed when Billie and Craig led them into the medical center. A bored woman glanced up from a counter protected by a glass partition. "Oh, hi, Craig. Billie." Her lips spread into a welcoming smile. Obviously, Billie and Craig had gained some affinity with her and were going by their real names here. *That's promising.*

"Val, does Felicia have time to check these two out?" Craig asked. "We want to take them to meet the mayor ASAP. They're here looking for Eva."

Val narrowed her eyes when they focused on Louis. She adjusted her glinting glasses. "He *does* look an awful lot like her. You her brother?"

"Don't poke the snake, Val. This one's plum full of venom." Billie settled into a cushioned maroon chair and crossed her legs. She lifted an old magazine to her lap. "Just be a dear and go tell Felicia she's got patients."

Brian examined the room while Val retreated from her post and headed into the back of the building. Louis remained where he was, watching and waiting. Craig sat next to Billie and stretched his legs out. "It'll be fine, kids. Felicia's a sharp cookie: you'll be outta here in no time."

Brian had seen a few ransacked waiting rooms during his travels, but none this pristine. The rows of empty chairs, the table with old magazines, and the pair of potted plants in opposite corners were a reassuring return to normalcy. Usually, he wore his headphones and fiddled with his tablet, bored out of his mind, but the placid environment now soothed him.

Val opened the door into the waiting room, a clipboard under her arm. "You can follow me, boys."

"We'll wait out here." Craig shot them a thumbs-up. "Good luck!"

Brian knew they wanted as much space from Louis as possible. It still puzzled him how they were scared of someone he'd come to know more intimately than anyone else in his life—and vice versa. Oddly enough, he was more scared *for* Louis at this point.

Brian and Louis wandered after Val through austere white halls past open doors and empty rooms. Medical supplies and examination tables covered in layers of protective paper filled most of them. Val stopped outside one and adjusted her curly blonde ponytail. "Right in here." She held out her arm.

Louis groaned and glanced at Brian from the side of his eyes. "I hate doctors..."

Brian quirked his eyebrows in reply. They walked past Val into the office. She followed them in and shut the door. She directed them to sit while she ran through a series of questions about their names, ages, and medical histories, and then something more tailored for signs of the disease: shifting appetites, irritability, memory loss, and changes in appearance such as greasy hair and dry skin. Both Louis and Brian were able to answer "no" to all of those. Louis didn't appreciate Brian's attempt at a joke when he told Val Louis was *always* irritable.

When a knock thudded against the door, Val opened it. A woman slipped in without a greeting or smile and took the clipboard with Val's notes. "Thank you, Val. You can go."

Val offered them a slight smile before ducking out of the room. The doctor, Felicia, was youthful and attractive, yet her almond eyes were sharp and hard, with a glint implying she could hold her own. Those eyes scanned Val's notes as Felicia clicked her tongue.

"That girl needs to work on her handwriting; you'd think *she* was the doctor." She continued to read while she paced the room and snatched items from the dresser and the containers on the wall. A white coat flapped as she walked in modest flats. When she finished assembling her tools, she slid the clipboard into a plastic container mounted to the wall and sat on a stool. She leaned forward and studied Louis and Brian in silence, her elbows on her knees and her chin in her hands. The intensity of her stare disturbed Brian a little; her eyes were nearly as dark and piercing as Louis's.

"Okay," she said eventually, "the two of you need to strip."

Louis scoffed. "Some kinda bedside manner *you've* got."

"I need to examine you for injuries and signs of illness." Felicia pressed her lips into a neutral line: she didn't find her inquiry as amusing or befuddling as Louis did.

Louis stood and tugged his shirt over his head. "You need me to take it all off?"

She nodded but didn't look at him, busy penciling something onto her clipboard.

Louis narrowed his eyes and jerked his belt loose. "What, you think some Stalker snapped into my dick like a beef stick? You wanna tell me how the hell someone would get attacked *there*?"

"You'd be surprised. Many people let their guards down when they're relieving themselves." Felicia stood and swapped her clipboard for a blood pressure cuff. "I've seen dozens of naked bodies; yours is no different. If you're embarrassed, your friend can step out—"

"There's nothin' here he hasn't seen." Louis rolled his jeans over his boots and flopped onto the examination table. He snatched the modesty paper Felicia handed him. She zipped around Louis, looking up his nose, into his ears and mouth, and listening to his heartbeat through his chest and back. When he stood so she could inspect his body, he gave Brian a weary look. Brian returned it with a sympathetic smile, his arms crossed over his chest while he tried to keep his eyes high and his tensions low.

"You're in excellent shape, all things considered," she declared to Louis once she finished. "Get dressed. You're free to go."

Louis gathered his clothes and thanked her with feigned gratitude.

While Louis dressed, Brian stood and unbuttoned his shirt. Felicia disinfected her tools. When she glanced over at Brian, she snapped her fingers. "I have other appointments today, young man. Do you have arthritis in your fingers from overdoing it with that bow?"

Intimidated, Brian increased his pace.

"You want me to go?" Louis asked.

Brian shook his head and wriggled out of his jeans, exposing the bandage.

Louis jerked his shirt over his head, making his hair stick out at odd angles, and flopped onto one of the padded chairs. He tried not to look at Brian, correctly assuming it would make him feel more uncomfortable than he already did.

Brian finished undressing and sat, allowing Felicia to proceed with her examination. She had him go "ah" and stuck the tongue depressor in. "How do you two know each other? Did you meet on the road?"

Of course, he couldn't answer with a wooden stick in his mouth, so Louis answered for him. "We grew up together in Kansas."

She stuck the cold tip of the flashlight into Brian's ear. "Funny: you've got such a distinct Cajun accent, and Lavellé is a French name." Felicia withdrew the instrument from Brian's ear and fixed him with her penetrating stare. "Jameson... Kansas. Was your family involved in the attack by Jim Sullivan?"

Her excitement took him aback. "H-how did you know?"

"I worked for the CDC in Atlanta."

"Like *The Walking Dead?*"

She didn't laugh. "I was around for the beginning of this pandemic. We were aware of the incident where Jim Sullivan attacked his family, but it was isolated. An anomaly, not a sign of an impending outbreak. It turns out the virus didn't spread because he killed all his victims—until your mother. That's when things started to spiral out of control and we had to take action."

"By quarantining my family's bodies?"

She knocked on his knees with a little rubber mallet, not rattled in the least by the pain in his voice. "I'm sorry you weren't able to say a proper farewell, but many weren't in those times." Her condolences were robotic, like something she knew she should say but didn't mean.

Louis glared at her back, practically seething, but Brian gestured for him to keep his mouth shut.

"Can you explain how this disease works?" Brian asked, suspecting she would appreciate the opportunity to share her knowledge.

"Bacterium spread by bodily fluids such as blood, saliva, and sexual excretions attack the anterior insular cortex. It's similar to *kuru*, a neurodegenerative disorder transmitted by cannibalizing a body already afflicted by it—particularly the brain, where the most infectious prions are concentrated. Ultimately, kuru culminates with the infected losing the ability to speak despite maintaining consciousness."

Brian's heart fluttered. Since her stethoscope was pressed against his chest, she noticed this and placed a gloved hand on his forearm. "There's no way to know if this disease travels the same path as kuru. It may be some sort of evolutionary tangent. We can hope even if Stalkers are aware of themselves as a unique life-form, they've forgotten all memories of their past lives."

But the tightening of her eyes betrayed her fear: she suspected their consciousness remained. Their sense of self and the memories of the life they had lived before their infection.

Which meant Mom and Dad knew what they were doing but couldn't control it.

Felicia sighed and let the stethoscope fall against her chest. "We did our best to engineer a vaccine, but it achieved nothing. The quarantine couldn't contain the rapid spread. We went underground to keep working, but paranoia took over. A coworker with a grudge against me convinced the others I'd been infected and I was hiding it. They even went as far as to injure me to make it look as if I'd been scratched. My word against theirs. Apparently, I lost the popularity contest. They threatened to kill me if I didn't leave, so I left. At least I'm appreciated here."

She gestured for him to stand. While she inspected his torso, he asked, "Will there ever be a cure?"

Her sharp laugh startled him. "Even if I could figure one out, I wouldn't have the tools to engineer it. My hands are full enough since I'm the only doctor in town. With any luck, the Stalkers will degrade, starve, and die—they don't reproduce, so we will outlive them and rebuild." She stripped the bandage from his thigh. "Where did you get this wound?"

He deliberated over whether he wanted to reveal the man's condition, but he decided it might influence her opinion. "Some crazy guy inside an ammo store shot me. It was only a graze. Louis cleaned and stitched it."

"How long ago?"

"A week and a half, I think."

She backed away. "Sit. We're going to take the stitches out."

Brian sat. Felicia dug inside several drawers, objects rattling around while she searched. She returned to him with a small pair of scissors and clipped the stitches threaded in his skin. When she finished, she examined the wound, poured several liquids over it, and swabbed it with a Q-Tip.

"No frothing. Doesn't seem to be infected. Your friend did a good job cleaning it out."

All the tension in Brian's muscles escaped with his sigh. He flashed Louis a relieved smile, which Louis returned.

Felicia's lips quirked so briefly Brian thought he'd imagined it. "Something tells me you're the one who took care of the bullet in your friend's shoulder. Where did you learn how to dig out a bullet and do such intricate stitch-work?"

"My grandfather taught me. He was in the Army. Vietnam."

Felicia leaned against the dresser and folded her arms. "My great-grandfather fought on the other side. Don't worry; he survived." Her eyes flashed to the door. "You're not exhibiting any symptoms, and the rate of healing corresponds with the timeline you gave me. You're free to return to your friends."

"Thanks." His clipped response failed to express the relief flooding throughout him. He rushed to retrieve his clothing while Felicia meandered around putting her instruments away.

"If you're having any concerns about this place, don't," Felicia said. "I arrived here before they even had power. The people here care about each other. It may not be perfect, but it's the closest thing to safety I've known since I left the bunker."

After Brian finished buttoning his jeans and shirt, Felicia led them out into the waiting room and flashed a cordial smile at Billie and Craig. "Clean bill of health for both. Send them over to Mayor Halloran."

Craig grinned and lifted his hand. "Stick it here, kid!"

Brian slapped his palm since it would be rude to leave him hanging. Felicia retreated into the hall, her long black ponytail swaying above rolling hips. Brian and the others returned outside into the startling brightness and clear air.

He'd grown accustomed to wandering deserted towns, but the sight of people walking around the streets and filing in and out of buildings startled him. They seemed at ease, clean, happy, like the people at Evergreen. Diamond City had the atmosphere of a town where everyone had known everyone by name before. Going from the backwoods of Arkansas to a fully powered, populated town threw Brian for a loop. He pinched himself, relieved by the pain pricking his nerves.

I hope the others are okay. But we need to meet this mayor before I give them the okay. Fingers crossed.

Just past the post office, they entered another building with "City Hall" emblazoned on the door. They jogged up a set of stairs past photos of smiling men in suits and entered a confined hallway. Two armed men blocked a nearby door, but they lowered their weapons a hair and nodded when they saw Billie and Craig.

"Hey, fellas," Billie said. "Got some new recruits to see the mayor. Felicia gave them the go-ahead. I know the kid's got a bow and all, but look at him: he's too cute to be dangerous, right?"

The Men in Black remained unconvinced by Brian's inoffensive cuteness.

"Oh, come on"—Craig stepped in to assist Billie—"I know it's against the rules, but we know them from before, and I trust the kid. Kinda owe him one, in fact, which is why we let him keep the weapons to begin with. We took them from the scary guy. Can you at least let Mayor Halloran know the sitch? We don't have to go in—"

"Let them in," a lilting female voice called from within the room. The accent sounded Irish or Scottish. Brian often confused the two.

The guards stepped aside. One opened the door into the room, exposing the image of a woman sitting behind a desk, her auburn hair pulled back in a harsh ponytail. A placard in front of her was engraved with the name Gloria Halloran. He immediately thought of Marie.

I hope they're doing okay. If this pans out, they'll have a place to go.

The mayor stood, dressed in a sensible business suit, and extended her hand. "What's your name, young man?"

Brian stepped into the room and took her hand, surprised by her firm grip. "Brian Jameson. I'm from Kansas, originally, but Billie, Craig, and I go back a ways. How long have you, uh, run this town?"

"Long before the pandemic." She sat back behind her desk and glanced at Louis. "Your companion can come in too."

Louis leaned against the doorframe. "I'm good here, thanks."

Mayor Halloran's lips tightened into a neutral line. Faint wrinkles appeared on her fair skin. "Very well. And what's *your* name?"

"Louis Lavellé."

Her thickly lined eyes widened. "I assume you're the brother who abandoned Eva, then."

Louis burst into the room, but Brian snatched his wrist before he could approach the mayor. He snaked his hand down to Louis's and squeezed it, silently warning him to exercise some restraint before they both got kicked out and lost any chance to reunite with Eva.

Louis slipped his trembling hand free of Brian's. "Is she really here?"

Mayor Halloran nodded, maintaining a calm mien. "Billie and Craig arrived here with her, Cassandra, and Bailey after they escaped the so-called King."

"You know about him?" Brian asked. "We heard your radio message while we were searching for Eva, but the last place we saw her was Joplin. That's where we met Billie and Craig—and him."

"He defected from our group," Mayor Halloran said. "After the outbreak, the military raised this fence and used our town as an outpost; they wouldn't let us go south to the bigger towns. Once things got worse, military presence decreased. All but two of their men left the town—one of whom remains to this day. Fernando Garcia lived here before the military put the fence up. He was a smooth talker, tall, good-looking. But he tried to start a mutiny and kick me out of office. We exiled him, but I suppose my mercy's coming back to bite me: Billie and Craig told me although he's infected, his mind's still intact. It's a crueler punishment than even he deserves."

"I wouldn't say that." Brian turned to Billie and Craig, who'd silently slipped in after Louis and lingered near the closed door. "What even happened to him? How'd you find Eva?"

Craig cleared his throat and stepped past Brian and Louis to settle into one of the chairs at the mayor's desk. "We figured something happened to Eva because Bill didn't find her at the arcade when she went to help her. But Louis's cagey demeanor helped us put two and two together, so after you two ran off, I decided to go back and look for her. We couldn't leave her to the same fate Bill's sister suffered. Billie took her family to Caldone's, but I waited around, kept an eye on the fairground. They were scurrying around like ants because of the grenade you two tossed in. I pulled my mask back on and blended in, another face in the crowd. Went into the arcade where Billie told Eva to meet her. I didn't see her, but I *did* see a cabinet in front of the electrical closet that wasn't there before, so I knew someone had put it there recently. I pushed it aside, and guess what? I saw Sleeping Beauty curled up on the floor inside.

"I woke her up, made sure she was okay. She was pretty out of it, but when she came to, she wanted to know where her brother was. I told her you two were long gone, but I'd help get her out. Asked her to wait there for me and went into the storeroom to see if I could find something to dress her in. I found a dead body on the ground, so I took his mask and clothes and brought them back to her. She wasn't excited about it. We marched out of there and disappeared into the darkness, hoofed it all the way back to Caldone's while their base burned behind us. A real epic movie moment."

"How did we miss you?" Brian asked. "We went to Caldone's after we left."

Billie took the empty seat beside her partner. "When you came in, we were hiding in the kitchen. We thought you were the King's men. I poked my head out to see who it was, but when I saw Louis, I decided not to say anything since I had to protect my sister and niece. He was in a rush and you seemed pretty out of it, just clung to his hand and followed him everywhere. I guess you didn't notice us. By the time Craig and Eva made it, you were long gone."

"Yes, Eva told me all about your little escapade," Mayor Halloran said to Louis, though she kept her tone and expression restrained. "You're here to make amends, I hope."

"I'm not sure there's anythin' *to* mend, but at least I know she's alive." Louis rubbed his temples and exhaled slowly. "She deserves the chance to lay into me for what I did. That's what I came here to do, so all I ask is you let me do it. I don't care what you do after that: kick me out, lock me up, whatever you want."

Mayor Halloran leaned forward onto the desk and laced her fingers together. Her nails were short and unpainted. "I don't have some insidious agenda or some grand aspiration to rebuild society: for now, all I care about is *this* town and its people. Eva is one of those people now, and while I fear she won't react well to the news of your reappearance, I agree she deserves the right to whatever closure you can offer her." Her keen eyes swept to Brian. "And what are you here for? Do you want to see Eva as well?"

"I do." Brian considered whether he wanted to mention Evergreen yet, but he decided to test the waters first. "Also, we traveled here with three others: a brother and sister, and another girl. Could you put them up for a day or two while we figure things out?"

Mayor Halloran stood and placed her palms against the desktop. "We have a policy about weapons here: you can have blades less than six inches long, but we keep all guns locked up. Our guards check theirs out when they go on patrol. Your bow straddles the line, but since it's not a crossbow, I'll allow it. I understand you might have been skeptical about our city, but you'll have to surrender the rest of your weapons—which Billie and Craig openly defied me by allowing you to keep." She extended her hand to Brian. "As long as your friends do the same and receive a clean bill of health, you may inform them they're welcome and meet them at the gate. I'll call ahead and set up some lodging."

Brian glanced at Billie and Craig as he stepped between them to approach the mayor. They both nodded, attempting to assure him this wouldn't blow up in his face, to trust everything they'd said was the truth this time. He fought the urge to look back at Louis for approval: this was the end of the line, everything they'd been looking for wrapped up in one neat little bow. No more searching, no more escaping, no more questioning. All their answers were here.

He sighed and took Mayor Halloran's hand. "Thank you, Mayor. I'll be honest: I've been betrayed by several people I trusted—all of whom are in this room. But people are driven by complex motivations, and deep down, I still want to believe in them, same as I think you do."

Mayor Halloran's warm smile reinforced her resemblance to Brian's mother. She seemed to regard him with similar affection, perhaps a mother to her own children. "I think all of us experience betrayal at varying levels within our lives. Sometimes we even betray ourselves. But what I believe in, as you say, is the ability to learn from our mistakes and mature, and I am happy to encourage this chance at every opportunity." After a tight shake, she released his hand and nodded at Billie and Craig. "Go ahead and disarm your friend."

The pair patted Brian down with light movements on either side. Their eyes kept flitting to Louis, who watched them with the same keen stare as a predator studying its prey. Thoughts of prowling predators and skittering prey reminded Brian of what followed them to the city.

"Madam Mayor," Brian said as she returned to her seat, "a large group of Stalkers followed us here. I don't know why. Other groups attacked us during our travels—or maybe the *same* group. They did some strange things, like throwing things at us and watching us. Maybe even barricading a bear in a rest-stop bathroom, but that one's a stretch. Have you noticed any change in their behavior?"

Mayor Halloran folded her arms and leaned forward onto the desk. "We haven't had a problem with Stalkers lately. Any time they try to sneak in, the fence or my guards take care of them. Eventually, they stopped trying the fence, and we've seen less and less of them. Now isn't the time to worry about it, though; I lead a mandatory meeting each week. The next one is in two days. This gives you time to collect your friends and settle in, and you can sort things out with Eva. If all goes well, feel free to stay, get a taste of what life's like here, and you can speak your piece during the meeting. If those Stalkers rear their heads in the meantime, we'll take care of them."

Brian managed a tense smile, a little perturbed by her dismissive attitude toward what he perceived to be a pressing issue. "Thank you, Madam Mayor." He wrestled with himself and erred on the side of boldness. "But I wouldn't have such a cavalier attitude about this. I'm guessing you do pretty well here, don't have too many issues. Maybe you feel safe because you never knew what it was like outside your fence. But I've lived out there for months, traveled through the Midwest down into Louisiana, and I've seen some things I wish I could unsee. Stalkers aren't stupid sacks of flesh. There's more humanity left in them than I thought, which makes them more dangerous—and unpredictable. I'm saying this with all due respect, but I don't want you to underestimate this just because you've gotten comfortable here. The same goes for the guy calling himself the King; I doubt you've seen the last of him, especially if you exiled him from your city. You should make sure you're ready for the day he decides to come back and try to take your town again. And the Stalkers you want to wait on are right outside your fence."

Although the mayor remained silent, a stoic smile spread across her pale face. Billie and Craig withdrew from Brian and grinned like proud parents. Louis's arched eyebrows accompanied a slight shake of his head and the tiniest hint of a smile. The swell of pride fluttering through Brian deflated when the mayor finally spoke.

"You're a bold speaker, Brian Jameson. And wise beyond your years. But make sure not to overstep your boundaries and remember to respect your elders. I've run this town since you were probably still in middle school, and I'll continue to run it during the duration of your stay here— possibly beyond it. I'll see you at the meeting; until then, I'll keep what you said in mind. Good day."

Louis opened his mouth, but Brian snagged his arm and pulled him out of the mayor's office. "We'll walk you back to the gate so you can meet your friends," Craig called. "Wait for us outside, okay? We'll be there in a jiff."

While this jiff stretched into what felt like *for-fucking-ever*, Brian and Louis loitered outside the building. Brian finally placed his finger on what made the town seem so different: the absence of wreckage and destruction. No boarded doors and windows, no bodies, no graffiti, no cars with shattered windows and missing tires, no overgrown vegetation. Diamond City was preserved in the pre-pandemic era like a living time capsule.

Brian unclipped his walkie to call D and Cecilia. He snapped his fingers in front of Louis's vacant eyes. "You good with this?"

Louis came to life. "I don't have a choice. I made the bed I gotta lie in."

"It'll be nice to actually lay in a bed again." Brian's attempt to lighten the mood only ended up exacerbating the tension. He cleared his throat and spoke into the walkie: "Hey, D, Cill. We're inside the city. The mayor says you're good to come in, as long as you surrender your weapons and submit to a medical checkup. We're both okay, by the way. Get Antoine and take the main road, come meet us at the gate. It's kinda funny, but we actually met up with some old friends of mine, and they said Eva's here. We'll see how it goes. Over and out."

Louis gave Brian a harsh look, probably because he'd referred to Billie and Craig as "friends." He withdrew the pack of cigarettes and a lighter from his jeans, smacked out a cigarette, and lit it before sticking it between his lips. The smoke puffed out, but Louis angled it away from Brian this time.

Brian watched him and tried to suppress his disapproval until the walkie buzzed to life and took a year off his. "Thank the Good God you okay, Sunshine! We okay too, just bored and worried as hell. We'll take ol' girl and go get 'Toine. Long as all goes well, we'll see you at this gate, meet yo' friends. Over and out."

Billie and Craig burst through the door just as Brian clipped the walkie to his belt. Craig spotted Louis's cigarette, his eyes alighting on it like a cat spying a shiny toy. "You got any more of those I can bum?"

Louis responded by blowing smoke in his face.

Craig swatted it away. "Shoulda known better than to ask." He curled an arm around Brian's shoulders and steered him onto the road with Billie at his other side. "You boys are gonna have fun here, I can tell. I can't wait to meet these friends of yours."

Brian fought the urge to shrug Craig's arm off, but he *did* shrug off his residual anger and doubts. *Eva's okay. They saved her. If I can live with what Louis did, I can live with what they did too. Shades of gray— and not the shitty bondage kind.*

"How'd you even find this place?"

"Well, Eva was steaming mad, wanted to confront Louis and tear into him good"—Craig drummed his fingers along Brian's shoulder—"so we headed south to get some space from the King and his men, then look for you. Close to the border, we bumped into this affable redheaded lunk who said he was out searching for supplies for his city—Red, the guy I told you we work with. We picked up on his Texas twang, so we disarmed him with some flights of fancy about our time in Texas and he offered to take us in. He's actually the one who spotted you, let us decide how to handle things. He's a good guy."

"Did they have power when you got here?" Brian asked.

Craig shook his head. "They had a bunch of solar-powered stuff around—some of it's still there. When they got enough people, they went on expeditions to the hydroelectric dam at Bull Shoals. Took about a month to get it up and running, and another month to get power going on the grid. Barry, this funny Hispanic fellow, used to be an engineer; things sped up once he got here. More and more people showed up once the snow stopped falling and started to melt, and soon we got the town up and running."

The familiar sight of small brick churches and decrepit bait-and-tackle shops trailed them as they neared the gate. Brian caught movement in several windows: Diamond City's watch guards, apparently. The inoffensive buildings were an inconspicuous location for them to camp out in.

They stepped up to the gate and awaited the others. Billie and Craig remained with them. Brian glanced at Louis, studying him for signs of apprehension or any emotion triggered by his impending confrontation with Eva. But Louis remained unreadable, his cool eyes scanning the town beyond them, smoke trailing into the air and ash crumbling to the ground.

Although the pair of actors enjoyed needling others, they knew better than to push Louis while whatever might be going through his mind preoccupied him. They prodded Brian for details about D, Antoine, and Cecilia instead. Brian obliged them, overwhelmed by these different aspects of his life colliding—not to mention the prospect of meeting the townspeople, of enjoying a return to electricity, and of dealing with the Stalkers pursuing them.

Reuniting with Eva was the bitter cherry on top of the sundae.

Billie's excited squeal signified the appearance of the others. She hopped up and down, tugging on Brian's arm. "You didn't say you had a *horse!*"

The fond, gentle way Craig smiled at her resembled those little looks Louis had once given Brian when he'd thought Brian wouldn't notice. *What did D say? "You the only thing that make those dead eyes of his light up."*

Those shark-black eyes were lost at sea once more.

When Craig buzzed the group in, Brian's mood brightened. He introduced Billie and Craig to everyone. Grimes enjoyed the attention and Cecilia and Antoine were friendly, but D seemed to sense some of Brian's anxiety despite his attempts to hide it. She was polite but restrained, trying to feel out the situation and Billie and Craig's character.

Billie and Craig led them to a parcel of land on a corner of the street. A chain-link fence pinned with a "Beware of Dog" sign protected a trailer and a shed enclosed by another barbed-wire fence. Craig lifted a tin windchime next to a handwritten sign: "Jingle my bells for service." A deafening bark soon overtook the delicate chimes, and a large German Shepard ran over to the gate and leaped and pawed at it. The metal rattled while Brian winced from the intensity of the dog's furious barking.

Louis kicked the gate. "Shut it, mutt!" But the dog nipped at his foot through the fence, and Louis didn't kick it again.

The trailer door opened. A lean but wiry man barreled out of it and yelled at the dog to quiet down. It backed away and lowered its ears, tail swishing. The difference in demeanor astounded Brian. No pretense of aggression, only submission.

Billie and Craig introduced the man as Rod, an ex-military man in charge of all the guns, ammunition, bladed weapons longer than six inches, and explosives in town. D, Antoine, and Cecilia surrendered their weapons but weren't in a hurry to leave the dog, named LD, behind. He'd flopped onto his back, begging them all to rub his belly.

While the others were distracted by the friendly dog, Craig ruffled Brian's hair. "This is where we part ways. You can take it from here, get your friends to the clinic so Felicia can give Mayor Halloran the okay. I have faith in you, young Padawan."

Billie grabbed Brian's shoulders and spun him, pointing. "Once you're all done, just head north, take a right onto Skyline, and turn left onto 7. Keep following it until you reach the treehouse resort. You'll be staying across from there in the *lakeside* resort. Or at least that's what the mayor told us to tell you after she smacked our wrists for letting you keep your weapons."

"Lakeside, not treehouse. Got it. And thanks."

"No worries." Craig flashed Brian a jaunty wink. "We'll come by and see you soon about Eva, okay? Probably sometime tomorrow. Until then, settle in, relax, and behave yourself." He cleared his throat to distract the others from the dog and shook the hands of everyone except for Louis. "Charmed to meet all of you lovely people—and your horse too."

Billie wrapped her arms around Grimes's neck. The horse reached around to nose at her, which made her giggle in a way that reminded Brian more of a little girl than a seductive vamp. "My family had a horse when I was growing up in Texas. I never knew how good I had it until I didn't have it anymore… I should've been happy with what I had, but that's life, right?" When Craig hooked an arm through hers and gently tugged her away from Grimes, her smile remained but the happiness left it.

The pair walked in the opposite direction, Billie's head tipped against Craig's shoulder, until they disappeared. Brian couldn't quite put his finger on the reason he liked them so much, aside from finding them charming and attractive. Maybe it was their unshakable loyalty to one another he envied, a loyalty his parents once shared until his father betrayed it.

Brian didn't know how long the couple had been together—he doubted it was over twenty years like his parents—but he yearned to know more about them: how they met, what history they'd built, who they truly were. Billie and Craig seemed to share an identity like the ruthless yet devoted couple they'd emulated, but he wanted to know who they'd been before they'd met. Had they felt lost, their lives lacking meaning, until they found each other and the revelation hit them like a ray of sun: *we were meant to be together and nothing can part us.*

He shook the thoughts from his mind and led the others to the doctor's office, where he waited in silence with Louis while his friends underwent their examinations. All three popped out within the hour, exclaiming they were healthy—and that Antoine found Felicia more beautiful than any woman he'd ever seen. D asked Brian: "Why don't you shoot *me* with one of your arrows, Cupid?"

Outside, the clouds swelled with moisture, threatening to dump buckets of rain on them. They followed Billie's directions to the resort. "Lakeside" was a bit misleading: the complex resembled a small trailer park with no lake in sight. There were four buildings: a large pink one, a long yellow one with an ice bin outside, and two bluish-green buildings of moderate size.

"You must be the newbies!" a cheery voice greeted. A heavyset woman approached them, brown hair done up in a perm and dressed in a floral-patterned muumuu dress. "I'm Andi. I run the resort. Mayor Halloran called over to set y'all up with rooms. Ain't she a peach?"

Brian sighed inwardly; he'd forgotten how exhausting social interaction could be. "I'm Brian. This is Dionne, her brother Antoine, Cecilia, and Louis. Our horse is named Grimes."

"Glad to know ya!" Andi spun and pointed to the pink house and a small cabin with wooden furniture on the porch. "Got a nautical and a hideaway ready. Nautical's got two beds and a foldout couch, a full-sized kitchen and a dinin' table, and the hideaway's got a queen-sized bed and a kitchenette."

D raised her hand. "I want the full-sized kitchen! I love me a big breakfast—need room to cook it!"

"Guess I'm goin' with D in the pink house." Antoine sighed. "I'll take the couch if one of you wants a bed—D gon' want the other one."

Cecilia looked between Brian and Louis. "I don't mind sharing the hideaway with either of you—"

"You deserve a bed to yourself," Brian said. "I'm used to sharing with Louis, anyway."

Confusion commandeered Louis's indifference. "I'm not sure that's a great idea—"

"I'd rather let Cill have her own bed than make her share one with either of us or sleep on a couch, and I'm sure there's a couch in the hideaway I can sleep on—right, Andi?"

D gave Brian a perplexed look and shook her head, trying to ask what the hell he was doing. Cecilia kept her hands linked behind her back and rocked on her heels. Antoine crossed his arms and studied the darkening sky, muttering to himself about the imminent storm. Louis glared at Brian until his lips tightened into a thin line of defeat.

Andi smiled, oblivious to the complicated dynamics fluctuating around her. "Well, there *is* a couch, but it doesn't fold out—but I'm sure y'all are used to sleepin' bags and such. At any rate, here are the keys." She dipped into her purse and dropped garish plastic key chains shaped like palm trees and flip-flops into their hands. "I don't know what to do 'bout the horse, though... We could take her to the farm, I guess. She'd have shelter there, keep her outta the rain. The lake's down a ways—well, up, 'cause it's north. You can get there direct by taking 7, but I can show you the way if you need to get your bearings. I got me a little golf cart I can putter y'all around in."

Louis eyed Andi up and down in a blatantly rude way which gave Brian secondhand embarrassment. "It'd be a tight squeeze. I'll pass."

D slugged him so hard in the bicep he lost his footing. He glared at her while she jingled her palm tree and ignored him, flashing Andi a broad smile. "That's awful generous of you, Miss Andi—my brother and I would love a tour!"

"I'll take Grimes and follow you." Cecilia patted the horse's sturdy neck and smiled at Brian. "You've been all over the place. You probably need some rest, right? Why don't you stay with Louis and get oriented?"

She's picked up on his shitty mood too. And she knows I'm the only one who can keep it from getting worse.

Brian rubbed his forehead, attempting to ward off an emerging headache. "Sounds like a good idea, Cill. Thanks for looking out for us." He stepped forward to help her onto Grimes since she had difficulty reaching the stirrups. Antoine was talking with Andi, but D broke away to pull Brian aside.

"You sure 'bout all this? Seems nice—*too* nice. You trust these actors who already fucked you over? They could be lying 'bout Eva—"

"D," Brian sighed, "I'm tired of suspecting everyone and everything—and I'm just plain tired. Can't we let our guards down a little and rest?"

"What about Louis?"

Brian glanced at him. He'd already unlocked the cabin door to stow their belongings inside and was currently busy rolling their bikes up onto the porch. "What about him?"

D sighed and curled a hand around her hip. "You know that tingly feelin' you get when you around someone you like?"

Brian nodded. He knew it all too well.

"That's all the common sense leavin' yo' body."

Brian's brow furrowed. "Give me a break, D: we've been alone before and everything was fine. It's not like I'm going to jump his bones just because there's a bed."

D's arched eyebrows were the inverse of Brian's. "I doubt you got the self-control to stay as celibate as a damn monk. You think I'm blind to *your* roamin' eyes? You can't quit it if you still wanna hit it."

Brian grabbed D's shoulders. "You're very witty, but I'm more concerned with his mind than his body right now. He's nervous about seeing Eva tomorrow. He probably won't even *sleep*. I don't want him to run away from this, slip out in the night or something." Brian squeezed D's shoulders before he let go of her. "Try to enjoy yourself and stop worrying about me, okay? I'm fine, especially since I'm not worried about my stupid leg anymore."

D put a hand on her hip. "Sure, Jan." Brian didn't quite catch the reference, but he knew it meant she didn't buy what he was trying to sell.

She strolled over to join Antoine and Andi. Brian climbed onto the porch and watched the others disappear much like he'd watched Billie and Craig. *When everyone else is gone, it's always me and him.*

He slipped into the cabin and shut the door behind him, making sure to lock it. When he turned to survey the cabin, he cringed. "This is…"

"Small? *Yeah.*" Louis stood in a kitchenette to the right of the entry hall, surrounded by the not-long-forgotten technology of a stove, fridge, microwave, and sink. "Look at this, though." He lifted the handle above the sink's faucet: water gushed out in a magical stream.

Brian laughed, amused by the ironic wonder caused by something so simple, once so guaranteed. "Holy shit—running water. Toilets you can flush…" He poked his head into the bathroom directly across from the kitchen. "This tub is tiny, but the shower has a detachable showerhead." He withdrew and wriggled his eyebrows at Louis. "The last time we had a hot shower was on the boat. What if we could do that every *day*?"

Louis filled an empty glass with the running water, a slight smile fading from his face. He stepped into the hallway across from Brian and drained half the glass before offering the rest to Brian. "Maybe, but I doubt you still wanna share. We *should* conserve water, though, it still bein' the apocalypse and all."

Brian did a shitty job of conserving water by nearly spitting his out. He wiped his mouth and squeezed past Louis to return the empty glass to the kitchen sink. "Not gonna happen."

"I'm gonna go enjoy all that hot, steamy water by myself then, since you don't care about the environment." Louis plucked at the buttons of his shirt, face obscured by a cascade of jet-black hair. His faux cockiness escaped in the form of a deep sigh. "You wanna tell me why you even decided to share a cabin with me?"

Brian stepped into the kitchen entryway—it couldn't be considered a doorway, he thought, without a door—and leaned against the sky-blue wall. "Is that really the predominant thing on your mind?"

"You wouldn't wanna know what's runnin' through it at this immediate moment…" Louis slipped his shirt off and made quick work of his jeans. He left both in a puddle on the ground. "But I'd rather think about your discipline and creativity than my goddamn sister." He turned toward the bathroom door and started pulling the door shut, but Brian stepped forward and snatched the knob.

"I'm here so you can talk to me instead of trying to suppress or ignore this shit."

Louis's hand lingered on the knob from the other side of the door. "I'm used to suppressin' and ignorin' shit—how else do you think I made it this long without tryin' to rip your clothes off?" He tried to jerk the door shut, but Brian tugged it back. "Come *on*, Brian—let go already. You're drivin' me crazier than I already *am*."

"Listen to me, Lou." Brian arched his eyebrows and searched Louis's eyes, making sure he was actually paying attention. "I'm sure it's obvious I'm still unreasonably, infuriatingly attracted to you, but I have to be careful after what happened. My head's not on straight when it comes to you."

"Funny—I know exactly what you mean." Louis released the knob and curled his hand around the edge of the door. He tipped his head onto it and exhaled. "Either I'm stuck wishin' things between us could be like they used to, or I have this giant storm cloud of Eva hangin' over my head—and I've got no one to blame for it but my own goddamn self."

Brian slipped his hand free of the doorknob to cover Louis's white-knuckled hand. "Even though you did some terrible things and hid them from me, that doesn't mean I forgot all the shit you held my hand through. The bad doesn't undo the good."

Louis snaked his hand out from underneath Brian's. "The good doesn't undo the bad either."

He spied a sheen of moisture glazing Louis's eyes before he abruptly shut the door in Brian's face. Brian lingered outside the door, a little confused by what had just happened.

Before long, the sound of streaming water hissed into the hall. Brian envied Louis, picturing him luxuriating in the warm spray as the room swelled with steam. The pulse of frustration plagued him until another sound undercut the steady torrent of water: erratic, muffled sobs.

The revelation of Louis's self-loathing struck Brian like a knife straight to the heart. He clutched his chest and tipped his forehead against the door, fighting the urge to burst into the bathroom, to hold Louis while he cried and tell him he'd never known how broken he was, how deeply he ached and mourned and pretended, that everything would be forgiven and he was loved despite his grievous faults.

Brian felt everything Louis felt, as if some witch had cursed them to be joined by an invisible, inseverable thread. But he knew Louis needed to embrace the pain, so Brian let him suffer, no matter how much it twisted the knife in his own bleeding heart.

Chapter Ten

Diamond City Blues

4/08, Diamond City, Arkansas, Lakeside Resort, 9:26 a.m.

Louis wasn't in the cabin when Brian climbed out of bed. He opened the front door, still dressed in the shorts he'd gone to sleep in, and found Louis sitting on the porch with a cigarette between his fingers. His knees kept bouncing.

Brian sat in the other rocking chair, frowning when he glimpsed the ashtray filled with cigarette butts. "Have you been out here all night doing this?" He plucked the cigarette from Louis's fingers and crushed it into the tray. "It won't help your nerves, I can tell you that much."

Louis tried to give Brian a dirty look, but he couldn't maintain it. He sighed and flopped back against the chair cushion. "I didn't sleep a wink."

"I can tell." Brian crinkled his nose at the smoky stench of ash. "Why didn't you talk to me, then?"

Louis jammed both hands into his bangs and rustled them with a frustrated groan. "You don't know my sister as well as I do. She was all sugar and sunshine around you, but she's got a nasty streak just like me. If she reacts half as bad as she did when I told her I set the fire, I'm in for it."

Brian's eyes widened. "She knew?"

"She knew, and she never forgave me for it. She'd go back and forth between sayin' I used my 'borderline thing' as some excuse, same as my grandparents used to, and tryin' to look it up so she could make sense of why I did it. I tried tellin' her there *was* no sense in it, it was another one of my fuck-ups, somethin' I did on impulse, but it drove her nuts she couldn't figure me out. I guess maybe she thought she could fix me if she knew what was wrong with me, get her 'old' brother back. But there's no fixin' this."

Brian reached over and curled a hand around Louis's knee. "At least you're here. You didn't run away from her again."

Humid air swirled around them. Puddles lingered in the yard from the storm which had rolled through overnight. The erratic thunderclaps had contributed to Brian's inability to sleep throughout the night, in addition to his nerves over seeing Eva and his fears about Louis's mental state.

Louis squeezed Brian's hand. "Whatever she does will hurt. And it should because I hurt *her*. But it doesn't mean I'm not scared." He let go of Brian's hand, eyes fixed in front of him. "Fuck *me*—it's those goddamn two-bit actors."

Brian glimpsed the pair strolling up to the cabin. Sunglasses covered their eyes, protecting them from the relentless sun shining in the wake of the cleared storm clouds. Instead of their retro thrift-store attire or guard uniforms, Billie had dressed down in a tapered sundress while Craig wore khaki shorts and a buttoned shirt. They still looked effortlessly glamorous.

"Morning, boys!" Billie waved with a pageant queen's practiced elegance. "What a nasty night! Did you all bring this storm with you?"

"We have the day off," Craig said, "so we came to tell you we talked to Eva last night." Louis said nothing, just swallowed, so Craig continued. "She was... Well, she was more dramatic than Bill, and that's saying something. Threw a buncha things, punched the wall, screamed curses in Cajun she probably didn't think I'd know... But she agreed to see you."

"Fan-fuckin'-tastic." Louis stood and paced along the porch. "When? Where?"

"We can take you to her now if you're ready." Billie put her hands on her hips, but her expression was difficult to discern through her gigantic glasses. "She's staying in a room at one of the strip motels here. Sometimes she works at the farm to pay her dues, but she doesn't go in until the afternoon."

Louis spun and snatched Brian's hand, frantic eyes scanning Brian's. "Come with me. Please. I don't know if I can do it alone."

"Well, *we'd* be there," Craig started to say, but Louis cut him off.

"You don't fuckin' count. I need *him*."

"Obviously." Billie fanned her face. "He can come, of course." She lowered her glasses and studied Brian. "You might wanna put a shirt on though, handsome. Could give the scene a strange vibe with you flashing everyone those fledgling abs of yours."

Louis let go of Brian and followed him into the cabin. He jammed a finger between his lips and gnawed on his nail, which Brian had never seen him do. *Is he scared of her, or just of what she'll say to him?*

Brian tugged on a polo shirt and slipped on flip-flops. Because they usually wore boots and clothes which covered their limbs, he still felt exposed.

Louis withdrew his finger from his mouth and groaned again. He walked over to Brian and buried his face between Brian's neck and shoulder. "This won't go well. If she doesn't kill me, I'll still have to leave before she *can*. Or they'll kick me out, lock me up—I know I told them they could and I didn't care, but I *do*."

Brian's hands hovered above Louis's back while he blinked, flustered and unsure of what to do. Louis dug his fingers into Brian's fresh shirt, yanking at the material. This wasn't sexual—Louis was seeking comfort, an emotional connection, and Brian allowed himself to embrace him.

He tipped his head against Louis's. "This is what you came here to do. You'll have to do it eventually; may as well get it over with now." His hesitant back pat evolved into a more assured rub. "If this is all it's cracked up to be, we'll go back to Evergreen to tell them about this place. But we should stay a while to make sure, try to take care of these Stalkers that have been following us so they don't follow us right back to Evergreen. Besides, they won't let her kill you. *I* certainly won't."

Louis lifted his head from Brian's shoulder and broke free of his embrace. "I thought you said she'd earned the right to kill me?"

Air fluttered through Brian's lips as he recalled his harsh words to Louis. "Well, I only meant if *anyone* should kill you, it'd be her. But it doesn't mean I'm hoping for that. I was pretty mad back then—"

Louis grabbed Brian's shoulders, expression switching from anxious to hopeful. "So you want us to work things out?"

"Of course!" Brian crossed his arms and shrugged off Louis's hands. "I want you both to find closure and heal, and I want this to be a safe place for Evergreen and all of us—"

"Okay. I can do this. Let's go." Louis whipped around and rushed through the front door. He ambled down the steps past Billie and Craig, who'd gotten bored with waiting and plopped into the rocking chairs. They got to their feet in a hurry when Louis yelled at them to get off their asses. Brian couldn't pinpoint what he'd said to make Louis turn the corner from troubled to determined, but it helped ease *some* of his concerns.

Brian's flip-flops clung to the moist earth and made plasticky squeaks as they abandoned limestone and grass for pavement. It took them about twenty minutes and several blocks before Billie and Craig stepped into the empty parking lot of a single-story strip motel with twenty rooms and window A/C units. A steady stream of water leaked from one of the gutters.

"She's here," Craig said. "Room three. We should send Brian in first to soften the blow."

The quartet drifted into silence, aware of how momentous this occasion was.

Brian had been fine on the walk, but now they were so close to Eva, his nerves twisted into bundles of knife tips. He folded his arms and rubbed them. "Okay. Uh, should I go by myself, or—?"

Billie wound her arm through his. "I'll take you." She rubbed his arm with her free hand. "It'll be okay, darling. Remember: every moment becomes a memory. Nothing lasts forever, even if it might feel like it."

Once he stood in front of room three, Brian's blood chilled. He took in a shaky breath and exhaled slowly through his mouth. Billie rapped on the door. "Eva, it's Bill. You in there?"

"Hold on a moment." Even though the door muffled it, Eva's distinctive accent still sent shivers down Brian's spine. *She's really here. Shit.*

The door opened to a familiar pair of chestnut eyes and freckled cheeks. Those eyes widened, and her lips parted—but she didn't say anything for what felt like an eternity. When she did, her eyes narrowed and hardened. "*He*'s here too, isn't he?"

Brian hadn't known what to expect, but this dashed his hopes for a joyous reunion. "Eva, we should talk before—"

She shoved past him, past Billie, and stepped out onto the sidewalk. Eva stared into the parking lot, homing in on her target with laser-like concentration. She clenched her fists and pressed her lips together until both trembled.

Brian glanced at Billie, but not for long. He returned his attention to Eva, scared to let her out of his sight. Louis was too far away to read, about fifteen feet from the room. Neither twin budged.

Brian swallowed, his gaze sweeping between them, waiting for one of them to make the first move.

Louis took a step forward. "Eva—"

She dashed toward him, swiping a glinting object through the air. Brian closed the distance between them and snatched Eva around the waist to jerk her back from Louis—but a knife clattered to the asphalt, the tip slick with blood.

"Fuck you!" she yowled as Louis clutched his face, blood streaming between his fingers. *"You're my brother! You were supposed to look out for me!"* She elbowed Brian. "Let go of me, *bon de rien*! He left me for *you*, some fuckin' kid we forgot about for nine years until you waltzed back into our lives and destroyed *mine*!"

Her words tore through him like a barrage of bullets. He loosened his grip on her and glanced past her at Louis. Half of Louis's face gleamed with a slick crimson ooze. Brian didn't know where she'd sliced him; he feared she'd taken an eye out.

Eva spun and slapped Brian hard in the face, nearly knocking him off-balance. "Go to him!" Her flushed cheeks shone with tears. "You ran away with him before—do it again! I don't fuckin' care! I don't need either of you sorry *pédés*!"

Brian retreated from her, his cheek throbbing with heat. Billie ran to Eva and pulled her close as she burst into frustrated sobs.

Craig grabbed Brian's shoulder. "Let me and Bill calm her down, tell the mayor what happened. We'll come by and see you later. Keep your shirt on, kid—she's just going through a lot. Give her time to think it over."

Brian wanted to assure Eva it was okay to feel what she felt, that he understood, and he'd been angry at Louis too. But anything he said right now would only make things worse. He turned away from her and walked over to Louis. He tried to pull Louis's hand from his bleeding face, but Louis twisted his face away and stalked back toward the road. Brian didn't push it; they made the trip to the cabin in silence.

Louis shoved past Brian and opened the door. He retreated into the bathroom and turned the sink on, probably to wash the blood off his face, maybe to mask a stream of tears. Brian sank into the couch and squeezed his aching head with both hands until Louis emerged from the bathroom several minutes later. He held a blood-soaked washcloth to his damp, flushed face.

Brian stayed put, trying not to step on Louis's toes. Louis lingered in the doorway, sniffing, eyes flitting everywhere to avoid Brian's. *He knows he'll break down as soon as he looks at me. He's wounded in more ways than one.*

"Why don't you let me take a look?" Brian patted the couch cushion beside him. Louis settled down and lowered the washcloth. He'd washed away the mess of blood from earlier, leaving a diagonal gash from the right edge of his nose to the outline of his jaw. It cut longer and deeper than the nick Brian had left all those years ago.

Brian moved to his backpack and kneeled to dig for the remnants of his first-aid kit. He set it onto the end table beside the couch, returned to his seat between the table and Louis, and reached over to turn the lamp on. "It's gonna need stitches, but you already knew that." He thought back to when Louis mended his bullet wound and sought to offer a similar distraction. "You can take a prick or two, right?"

Louis finally looked at him, though he refused to turn his head, only exposing the right profile of his damaged face to Brian. He didn't speak—Brian assumed this would stretch the torn skin and hurt horribly—but he grabbed Brian's knee and squeezed.

Guess that's the go-ahead.

Brian applied disinfectant to the wound with a sterile cloth, making Louis shudder and hiss. He threaded the eye of the needle and angled it over the gaping slit in Louis's cheek. "I'll go slow. Let me know if the pain is too much for you." He jabbed the needle into Louis's skin and stitched across the dark-crimson gash, wincing each time the tip penetrated Louis's skin.

Louis shut his eyes, his breathing fast and light. He tried to hold back, but his eyes twitched every time Brian pulled another stitch through. He pressed his dry lips together into a grimace, and his fingertips burrowed into Brian's knee.

Brian snipped the thread and knotted it. Louis's skin rippled with goose bumps when Brian pasted liquid adhesive over the stitches. He started to pack everything back into the bag, but a light weight bumped against his back—he realized it was Louis's head and stopped what he was doing.

"Thank you." Louis's voice was so quiet and raspy Brian had to strain to understand him. "For always fixin' me."

He carefully angled toward Louis, trying to avoid brushing his fresh stitches. Louis buried his face in Brian's shoulder and flung his arms around him, shivering with sobs.

Brian rubbed Louis's shaking back with one hand and stroked his damp hair with the other. His chest ached a little. "I'll stay with you for a bit, but D and the others will want to know how it went. I should talk to them, then go tell the mayor what happened. I don't know how their justice system works here, but—"

"Don't punish her," Louis muttered thickly against Brian's neck. "She's had enough."

Brian didn't reply. He let Louis cry until the tears ran dry and his back stopped heaving. "You should get some rest. Come on." He withdrew from Louis and stood, offering him a hand. Louis took it and followed Brian to the bed. He slumped onto it as though it took every remaining ounce of his energy. Brian pulled the cover over him and smoothed it, eyeing the stitches he'd made in Eva's deep cut. Somewhere in there was an allegory for the complicated relationship the three of them shared, but Brian didn't like the implications he arrived at.

Why do I want to take care of him when he's *the one who hurt us?*

He turned and marched through the door. He popped by the nautical cabin so he could explain everything to the others. Cecilia reacted with a tight frown and Antoine shook his head, but D sputtered into bitter laughter and said Louis deserved it. Brian didn't disagree with her, but he didn't enjoy seeing either twin suffer.

When he spoke with Mayor Halloran, she informed him Billie and Craig had just left with Eva, and she'd already requested they take all of Eva's weapons for the time being. She agreed not to punish Eva beyond that—especially since Louis himself requested this—and they'd give Louis time to recharge before they decided what to do about *him.*

Brian suspected everything with Eva wouldn't be as easily stitched as Louis's wound.

When Brian returned to the resort, he found Eva sitting on the porch with Cecilia. A dusky orange glow illuminated Eva, reminding Brian of how effervescent she'd once been. Of her enthusiastic kiss when he had agreed to go into the skating rink, and the light press of her lips to his in the fireworks warehouse. Guilt and regret pulsated within him in overpowering unison.

"Eva"—he stuffed his hands in his pockets and approached her—"are you okay?"

"Better now." She stood and walked down the steps, her eyes meeting Brian's. Her irises were darker than he remembered. "Sorry to show up like this; Bill and Craig told me where the mayor set you up. Don't worry—they took all my weapons. You mind if we go somewhere and talk?"

"Um, sure." Eva's stern gaze flustered Brian. "We could go watch the sunset at the lake, maybe."

Brian waved at Cecilia to thank her for entertaining Eva and to let her know he'd be okay. She nodded with a smile and disappeared into the cabin.

He cleared his throat as they walked away from the resort. "Do you like it here?"

"Beats the alternative," Eva said, hands jammed in her pockets. "I wasn't sure how I felt about Bill and Craig at first, but when I saw her sister and niece again, I forgave them in a heartbeat. My family was all I had too—even if I didn't always like them, I still loved them."

Silence drifted between them while they walked up the road. Fading light blanketed the buildings surrounding them, ushering the town into evening repose. When they arrived at the dock, they sat on the edge and dangled their legs into the water. Rays of sunlight shimmered along the ripples left by a pair of coasting ducks.

"Cecilia said she talked to him. She thinks he regrets what he did, but I still don't know *why* he did it." Eva leaned back on her arms and looked at the tree limbs stretching above them. "She said you made it to the island. I thought it sounded too good to be true, but I still wanted to go with you. Then my brother snaked an arm around my neck and whispered into my ear, 'You'll be better off without me, Eva. Just go to sleep; when you wake up, pretend it was all a bad dream.' I don't know what the fuck he thought I'd wake up *to*—Craig found me, but he said Louis blocked the door to keep me in or keep others out."

Brian wanted to reach for her hand, to squeeze it and tell her everything, but he restrained himself. "I left the island once he told me what he'd done..."

Eva latched onto his hesitation, took the opportunity to dig deeper. "It wasn't one of those masked freaks who shot your granddaddy, was it?"

Brian shook his head.

"And our papère wasn't infected."

Brian didn't reply, not sure if this was his answer to give.

Eva's bitter laugh stunned him. "He's even crazier than I fuckin' *thought*. But here he is, still with you even after he told you the truth, even after you fuckin' left him sittin' on an island like Robinson Crusoe. I woulda killed him right then and there—and I woulda plunged that knife into his heart instead of slicin' up his face if I wasn't worried about bein' exiled." The lack of hesitation in her voice and her unwavering gaze made Brian swallow. "You coulda done it. He wouldn't have expected it from you. Why wouldn't you? Weren't you angry about what he did? All of it?"

The truth hurt, but she deserved to hear it. "He told me he fell in love with me, and I fell in love with him. I don't know if I could *ever* kill him."

Eva's derision shifted into astonishment. Her brows knit above wide, searching eyes, and her lips parted into a stunned scoff. "Are you fuckin' kiddin' me? Cecilia kept beatin' around the bush, hintin' at it, but I had no idea it was like that." She dragged her hands through her hair, which now flipped over her ears and neck in jagged spikes. She'd done away with the feather earring she used to wear. "No wonder you were so awkward when I kissed you. I made a damn fool of myself. I mean, I guess it makes sense for you, but my brother—" Her eyes brightened with a revelation. "God, he left me because he was *jealous*. He had a new toy he thought I wanted to play with, and he didn't wanna share."

Her shoulders shuddered with scornful laughter. A gentle gust shook the leaves of the trees across the lake. Sand drifted across the pier, catching in the swirls of the wood.

Eva offered Brian a smile both mocking and pitying. "He'll just throw you away once he breaks you, you know. Like he threw me away. He probably just wanted to keep you around longer 'cause he can fuck you."

Brian dragged his fingertips through the sandy grooves in the wood, trying not to let her contempt get to him. Sympathy and resentment fluctuated within him in a seesaw of emotion. "I don't know why he left you, Eva. Maybe he wanted to abandon his past, the last tether to a life he wanted to leave behind. Maybe I was as much of an escape for him as the island. Either way, he left you and I left him, but he came back for us both. So now what?"

Eva reached for his hand, closing the agonizing gap between them. "He doesn't deserve to be here. He doesn't deserve *us*. And what he *does* deserve hasn't happened to him yet."

Brian searched her eyes and then glanced at her glistening lips, at her tan skin and the modest curves of her lithe figure. For a moment, a brief suggestion of what might've been bounced around in his mind. *An ordinary relationship with an average girl. Pleasant but boring like the life I would've led before the outbreak.*

His hand wriggled out from beneath hers. "Ultimately, it's the mayor's city, and she gets to decide what happens to him. He came back to make things right with us—that opportunity is what he deserves. I don't care if you think I'm an idiot for giving it to him."

Eva's eyebrows arched and furrowed, alternating in a pattern of confusion and dismay until she seemed to conclude something. She scooped a rock from the pier, stood, and tossed it into the lake. It splashed into the water and disrupted the still surface with receding ripples.

"Why don't you save us some trouble by goin' back to that fuckin' island with him? You can keep on pretendin' he loves you, and I can keep on pretendin' both of you never existed." She spun on her heel and walked away. The stone sank beneath the surface of the lake.

After she left, Brian finished watching the bright-orange sun descend beneath the banded horizon. Stars sparkled in the midnight-blue sky, reflected in the glassy surface of the lake. *Some of them are probably dying or already dead.*

Tormented by the ironic beauty of something so ghastly, he fled from the vista of flickering stars and returned to his cabin.

Louis remained dead to the world, a bundle of black trying to retreat into the bottomless void of sleep. Brian leaned over to tuck a stray lock of hair behind his ear. "It's only a temporary escape, *chéri.*"

He retreated to the couch and tossed and turned, troubled by his conversation with Eva. Trapped between her rage and Louis's misery, Brian sought the same momentary respite as Louis. He faded in and out of a fitful slumber until several knocks on the door roused him.

"You alive in there? We was tryin' to let you rest, but it's time for the mayor's meetin'. We all gotta go—even Boo-Boo Lou-Lou."

Brian rubbed his eyes and frowned. "Isn't the meeting tomorrow, D?"

"Uh, Sunshine, it's in half an hour. How long you been asleep?"

He bolted up from the couch and opened his eyes. They immediately searched for Louis and found him curled up in bed where he'd left him. Even D's knocking and yelling hadn't yanked him out of the abyss.

"We'll meet you at your place in a few minutes, D," Brian called. He dragged himself over to Louis and curled a hand around his shoulder to shake him awake. "Lou, time to get up. You've been in bed for nearly *twenty hours*. We have to go to the meeting."

"Don't wanna," Louis grumbled. He turned away and tugged the blanket over his head.

Brian groaned, ironically even *more* exhausted by his protracted rest. "Well, you have to." He thought of what his sister used to do when he refused to get out of bed. "Or I'll jump on the bed until you get up."

A blanket muffled Louis's response: "Go for it. We can both stay in this bed forever."

Brian knew this was a depression thing, not a sex thing. He'd been there. But other people had been there to pull him out of it—like Louis. And Brian was determined to return the favor. "Don't make me tickle you."

Louis flung the blanket off and glared at Brian. "Don't you dare." His threshold for tickling, which hadn't changed since childhood, was extremely low. "Fuck it—I'm up."

"I don't want to go either"—Brian helped Louis to his feet and tried to circumspectly examine his healing injury—"but everyone else is already waiting on us."

Louis pouted and butted his head against Brian's. "My sister will be there."

Brian grabbed Louis's shoulders and steered him toward the bathroom. "I don't really wanna see her, either. She chewed me out while you were asleep. I don't know what I did—or didn't do—but she thinks I'm an idiot and wants us both to leave the city. But I'm not eager to leave with all those Stalkers still out there, and it's up to the mayor anyway. Now hurry up and take a shower so I can get one too."

Louis stepped into the bathroom and held his hand out. "Just come in with me; I don't wanna be alone with my thoughts." His voice was a groggy whine, quite unusual for him, and he could barely keep his eyes open.

"Nice try." Brian crossed his arms and arched his eyebrows. "I can just take one at D's while you're in there. But hurry up."

Louis let out a dissatisfied grumble, but he turned the water on and started undressing. Brian wandered outside; D, 'Toine, and Cill were all sitting on the porch enjoying a sunset which Brian found extremely disorienting. He jogged up the steps and waved his hand at them. "I know, I know—I slept forever. But I'm fine. Louis is taking a shower, and I need to take one too. Mind if I use yours?"

D gave him a funny look, like she suspected they'd both been up to some strenuous activity requiring immediate showers (in which case he would've just joined Louis), but Cecilia smiled and spoke over her: "Not a problem. We're all ready to go anyway." While he scurried past, he overheard her whisper, "Eva came over and asked to speak to him last night. I think he and Louis are both emotionally exhausted after dealing with her. They must be dreading the meeting."

Right on all counts, Cill.

He rushed through a shower but realized on the way out he'd forgotten to bring a change of clothes, so he knotted a towel around his waist and jogged out past his friends' baffled faces, then streaked into his cabin and startled a half-dressed Louis.

Louis's lips quirked into a knowing smile. "Ah—you forgot a change of clothes."

"I'm all over the place." Flustered, Brian yanked open the dresser drawers and rummaged for clean clothing. "Sleeping so long threw me off, and I'm rushing so we aren't late for that meeting." He kept one hand firmly clenched around his towel so it wouldn't fall, but he didn't know why he cared when they'd just seen each other stark naked during a medical exam—and numerous times before *that*. "How are you doing?"

"Better," Louis said, his "-er"s sounding like "-uh"s as always. "It still smarts, but I imagine it will for a while. Could be worse." He threaded the buttons through his shirt, wet hair clinging to his forehead and cheeks. "What do we do after all this?"

Brian let the towel fall and then turned and tugged on his underwear, in too much of a hurry to care whether Louis saw. "This meeting will probably define where we go from here. Eva, the Stalkers, you, me—all of it. Why else do you think I'm so nervous?"

While Brian was in the middle of trying to button his shirt—and realizing he'd lined it up all wrong—Louis crossed over to him and shooed his hands away. He slipped the buttons through for Brian and made shushing noises. "Calm down. We got this, okay? It's gonna suck, but we've already made it this far." He stepped back and straightened Brian's collar. "At least I'm not breakin' your buttons anymore, right?"

Brian bit his lip and studied Louis's bashful smile—more of a smirk, really, but Louis's smiles were *always* crooked.

"Eva said you were lying. That you weren't really in love with me, you were just playing with me or something." Brian paid close attention to the slight changes in Louis's countenance, his swelling chest, the furrow in his brow, the bob of his Adam's apple, the way his eyes never shifted from Brian's. "But I don't believe her."

Louis's chest collapsed, driving a gasp of air through his lips. "I have never loved you more than I do in this moment. And if things weren't so weird between us, I'd show you exactly how much."

For some reason, this undid the tangled knot of Brian's nerves. His lips eased into a smile. "I believe you." He stepped forward and snagged Louis's hand to drag him out onto the porch. They joined up with the others (after D huffed out an exaggerated *"Finally!"*) and ambled down the road until they reached City Hall.

The swarm of people trickling around the lobby put Louis on edge, especially when he glimpsed Eva. She gave Cecilia a cordial nod but didn't even bother looking at Brian or Louis. Brian tried to get a head count of the attendees, but he lost track at around forty.

A pair of slick wooden doors opened into the auditorium, where the Men in Black herded the sheep into rows of drab gray seats. Louis ducked into the first empty aisle and took the end seat. Brian sat next to him with Cecilia, D, and Antoine filing in after him. Eva's head poked up from a row ahead of them on the opposite side of the aisle. When Louis's eyes flitted to his sister, his jaw clenched and strained the stitches of his fresh wound.

Eventually, the doors clicked shut, and the Men in Black moved to block them. Mayor Halloran entered from a door at the opposite end of the hall and approached a podium on stage while Felicia, Rod, and Barry sat in chairs behind her. The mayor grabbed the microphone in front of her and tapped it until a hollow *thump* silenced the chorus of murmurs.

"Thank you all for attending. By now, you will have noticed a few new faces among you." Mayor Halloran scanned for Brian and the others. "Why don't you introduce yourselves so everyone can put a name to your face?"

Brian wanted to sink into his seat. His groan synchronized with Louis's, but Cecilia elbowed him like his mom had the few times they'd gone to church with Nana and Poppa.

D popped up like a whack-a-mole. "I'm Dionne Etienne, but you can call me D. I'm from New Orleans, used to be a psychic. Anyone wants their palm read or their tarot spread, I'm your girl. I'm a big fan of scary movies—might be why I made it this far!"

A polite chorus of greetings followed. Antoine stood with a shy smile on his face and scratched the back of his gleaming head. "I'm her brother, Antoine, but folks call me 'Toine. I'm from NOLA too, actually won the Powerball before everything went to hell. I enjoy karate, cookin', and gardenin'. Nice to meet y'all."

Brian caught Louis rubbing the bridge of his nose; he had a headache coming on. Cecilia cleared her throat and stood, her hands joined behind her back. "I'm Cecilia Moss. I'm from Baton Rouge, but I originally lived in Minnesota. I was studying sociology and working in a coffee shop when the outbreak happened. I enjoy reading, sewing, and baking. Thank you for having us!"

Mayor Halloran's eyes landed on Brian, so he stood with a nervous smile. "I'm Brian Jameson, from Kansas. I don't really know what to say other than I'd just graduated high school when all this happened, so I never got to go to college and figure out what I wanted from life. I guess life had other ideas for me. I used to read and write a lot, and I played lots of video games and stuff. I guess I'm kind of a dork, really. I lost my family, but I'm lucky to have met people like D, Antoine, and Cecilia...and I reunited with my childhood friends, Louis and Eva—"

"I wish you hadn't," Eva snapped over him. She stood and gestured toward her seated brother. "That's my piece of shit brother, Louis. He's a psychopath who set fire to our house and killed our parents, then lied about our granddaddy bein' infected so he could kill him. Oh, and then he choked me out and stuffed me in a closet so he wouldn't have to deal with me anymore and he could run away with Brian to an island and live happily ever after. Except they didn't, because it turns out he killed *Brian's* granddaddy too. And his dog. So I guess his hobbies include killin' things, lyin', and honeydickin'."

Louis's face reddened as he slumped into his seat and shaded his eyes with his hand, but he kept his cool while the assembly erupted into stunned gasps. Brian sank beside him and glared at Eva until a victorious smirk curled her lips and she spun away from him.

Mayor Halloran waved her hands to silence the stirring crowd. "All of us have done things we regret to survive in this new world. We've been pushed to our limits, forced to fight in order to protect what we're most frightened to lose. With regards to the situation between Eva and Louis, I don't feel it's our place to discipline him for mistakes he made prior to arriving here. Were we to do this, we'd have to go back and punish everyone here for past transgressions—"

Antoine raised his hand, but he didn't speak until the mayor nodded at him. "I killed people before. While I was waitin' on D in New Orleans, people tried to come up in my grill so they could steal my shit. I shoved a shotgun in their face, fired if they didn't turn around. Your mind goes someplace dark, primal, when yo' life or something you care about is threatened. Ain't we all been there? Push comes to shove, even saints become sinners."

Cecilia stood, drawing numerous pairs of eyes to her. "As the Good Book says, 'Judge not lest ye be judged.' When I first met Louis, we didn't exactly see eye to eye, but I believe he has gained perspective since then. Brian put his trust in Louis by giving him the opportunity to travel with us, and I don't think that trust has been betrayed. Trying aspects of his personality and room for growth remain, but I've seen marked improvement. I wouldn't abandon such potential for redemption, nor should any child of God."

Eva's narrowed eyes swept between Cecilia and her brother. "Don't tell me he screwed *you* too. Why else would anyone give a damn about someone with a fucked-up personality like his?"

Cecilia folded her arms, pale-blue eyes locked on Eva's. "Damaged people need even more affection than most. You and I may not know each other well, but I must implore you—along with everyone else in this room—to allow the fact people make mistakes and *we* must forgive them for it. How else will we grow? How else will we help *them* grow? Hatred is so stifling, Eva. Don't harbor it." She fell back to her seat with a little huff. Brian patted her arm, thanking her for having the courage to stand up and say what he couldn't—not when faced with Eva's scorn again.

"Fuck it." Eva pushed past Billie and Craig and stomped into the aisle. "Go ahead and throw my brother a goddamn welcome party if you want, but I'm not gonna stand here while everyone defends him instead of punishin' him for what he did." She charged out of the room, shoving through the doors when the mayor gave the signal for her guards to part from them. For the first time since Brian had known Eva, he'd witnessed the same anger erupt from her as smoldered within Louis.

"I think it's time we adjourn this meeting," Mayor Halloran said to the murmuring crowd. "Please return to your homes or shifts for the evening, and thank you for attending." She turned and said something to her council members.

Rod jogged through the sea of people swarming out of their seats, out of breath by the time he reached Brian's row. They were still sitting while they waited for the mob to thin. "The mayor wants to speak with you. All of you, come sit in the front row." He swatted the back of Craig's seat. "You and Bill too. All my folks are stayin'."

Brian's friends shared baffled looks, but he figured it had something to do with the Stalkers he'd told the mayor about since she didn't seem eager to share the news with her townsfolk. Once everyone else left, Brian and the others swapped seats as Rod requested. The remaining group filled in the front two rows on either side.

Mayor Halloran sat on the edge of the stage, which struck Brian as rather informal—but maybe it was part of her managerial style, lowering herself to the masses to make her relatable. "I've spoken to my council about what you told me, Brian. Rod advised his guards to keep an extra eye out for Stalkers. Rod, tell them what you saw."

Rod plopped beside the mayor. "They're out there. Hard to spot with the naked eye, but easy enough with infrared. Just sittin' and watchin'. They swap around like they're rotatin' shifts. We tried to shoot some, but they keep to buildings—and when they'd pop their heads up from behind a window and catch a glint of scope or bowstring, they'd duck down before we could catch 'em. Clever bastards. Clever but curious." Rod laced his fingers over his knees and shook his head. "You wanna know what's real strange? Red clipped one, and I thought for sure the others would tear it apart. But I'll be damned if they didn't go help the thing drag itself back to cover, wounded leg and all."

Felicia sat at the mayor's other side and wrapped her hands around her knees. Antoine's eyes went straight to her, but she remained oblivious to his attention while she spoke. "We all know the saying: curiosity killed the cat. In this case, it might be a combination of compassion and curiosity. We need to lure them out and keep them in one spot long enough for us to kill them. If we capture one, they might be drawn to its struggles and try to free it."

Cecilia looked to the others, aghast. "Good God—does that mean the people they were are still in there somewhere?"

"It means they're learning there's safety in numbers, just like Neanderthals learned thousands of years ago." Felicia finally caught Antoine's gaze and offered him a small smile. "Especially since our population outnumbers theirs—at least in regard to our city and the group that followed you here. It's entirely possible they might draw others in to try and match our numbers—in which case, it's imperative we make a preemptive attack."

Barry yawned since this conversation had little to do with his area of expertise. Mayor Halloran looked at Brian. "It seems fitting since you led them here, you help us get rid of them. Think of it as a way to pay rent for the nights you and your friends have spent here."

He nodded. "We've taken care of our share of Stalkers. Catching one might be a little tricky, but I can do it—"

"I'll help him." Louis's tone gave no room for argument. "No need to drag anyone else into it. But even if we catch and use this Stalker as bait, it doesn't guarantee the rest will all come out at once."

"Mayor"—Billie raised her hand, ever the dutiful student—"we *could* throw that welcome party—except we'll use it to welcome this group of Stalkers. We'll use the speaker system the military set up, blast some tunes. They'll come investigate, see their squirming compatriot and try to free it—then *bam!* We rain bullets on them, posse-style."

"It certainly seems more efficient than going out to hunt them down or waiting for them to launch their own attack." Mayor Halloran looked at her three council members in turn. They all offered solemn nods. "Very well. Brian, Louis, meet Rod at his trailer tomorrow morning. He'll work out the specifics with you. Now, is there anything else?"

"You've gotta stop sleeping on the King," Craig said. "You might've known him as a person, but he's a monster now. Even though he still thinks like a human, he's the same as the Stalkers. Worse."

"You've seen what he did to my sister—she barely leaves her room. I don't know how my niece made it out intact." Billie shook her head, her hair brushing her shoulders. "If he took this place over, we'd all be doomed to similar fates—or worse. So why not track him down before he can try?"

"We haven't seen hide or hair of him since the boys torched his fairground," Craig said. "I'm not sure if he lost his men, but if he has, he's probably recruited more by now. He's got to be hunkering down, planning something. The asshole holds a grudge—as you oughta know, Madam Mayor."

"Do we have any idea where he might be?" she asked. "Any sightings? We can't blindly search for him. It wastes time, manpower, puts us at risk by exposing the people we send out and leaving us vulnerable with fewer eyes to guard us. For now, we focus on one problem. Unless anyone has any other pressing concerns, we'll adjourn. I'm sure you're all ready to eat dinner." Her gaze lingered on Louis when she stood. "Be on your best behavior, Mister Lavellé—you're lucky your friends and I believe in second chances. You'll have to forgive me for requesting Rod not lend you anything capable of firing projectiles, but Brian can take whatever he wants. Good evening, everyone, and good luck tomorrow."

The mayor and her guards filed out. Barry followed with a yawn, and Rod clicked his tongue and made finger guns at Brian as he and his squad passed by. Antoine jumped out of his seat and sidled up to Felicia. He pulled her aside while D rolled her eyes and groaned.

Brian smiled, but Billie and Craig weren't in jovial moods for once. They stared into the distance with sullen expressions, arms crossed and feet tapping. He found their shared body language fascinating, but he also understood why they were upset.

"We'll talk to her about the King again after we deal with these Stalkers," he said. He stood and stuck his hands into his pockets, trying to think of a way to get their minds off the subject. "Hey, what're we supposed to do about dinner? We're running low on food, but I passed some restaurants here. Can we eat at them, or is there another way to buy food? And how do we pay?"

Louis remained distracted by his thoughts, but D and Cecilia looked at Billie and Craig expectantly. D's stomach rumbled to punctuate Brian's inquiry, and she smiled sheepishly.

"We go out on excursions to capture animals," Craig said. "Bill grew up on a farm, so she's pretty good at it. We wrangle escaped sheep, cows, horses, pigs, and chickens if we find them. Once we bring them back, we keep them in a quarantine zone for two weeks. If they're healthy, they go to the farm. There are crops of rice, corn, wheat, and assorted vegetables and dried goods we keep in a storehouse there. Most folks work at the farm and dam. The rest work in restaurants or other local businesses, or maintenance and security—like us."

"Furthering Brian's question: how do you keep track of services rendered and goods received?" Cecilia asked. "Where I'm from, it was like a commune: everyone contributed for access to food, shelter, and amenities such as an outhouse and bathtub. But we didn't have power. Contributing meant growing plants, tilling the land, taking care of the animals, building fences, and repairing things. Others went out to search for supplies and to take back the Turned—Stalkers, that is—for a Cleansing ceremony. We ran on an honor system and didn't keep track of who came and left."

The smile Billie gave Cecilia reminded Brian of a teacher's: tolerant but a little patronizing. "Well, sweetcakes, everyone in town gets a punch card with their name written on it. Each time we complete a service, our supervisor punches in one column for each hour, depending on the difficulty of the work—riskier and more labor-intensive jobs like ours get two punches per hour. They punch the column next to that whenever labor punches are redeemed. For example, one meal costs one punch. Goods like food, clothing, and toiletries are labeled with prices like 'one punch' or 'a punch and a half.' When your punches in both columns equal out, you're broke."

"So how do they charge for, like, utilities or rent?" Brian leaned against the mayor's podium and crossed his feet. "And do they keep track of people, have a guest book or something so they know who's who and what their schedules should be?"

"No rent, but power usage is monitored like it used to be in the pre-pandemic days. It's paid for with the same currency as everything else." When Craig spoke, he punctuated his words with animated gestures. "The mayor and her council assign jobs, but supervisors monitor shifts using a sign-in sheet. Ours is Rod, if you haven't figured it out. He's a nice fellow. I saw him whip out the ol' finger guns on you." Craig mimicked him with a *pew-pew*!

Brian snickered, but his good mood diminished when he spied Louis's head drooping against the back of his seat, eyes closed. He'd gone somewhere else, retreated inside himself. He should've been relieved about staying in the city—like Brian was—but Brian knew Eva's outburst had put a damper on his happiness.

"What else is around here?" D asked, oblivious or indifferent to Louis's mood. "Restaurants, a grocery store, clothin' shops, this farm, and the dam... There's gotta be more for people to do. Got a brochure or somethin'?"

Craig smiled. "No brochure, sorry. There's a library, a coffee shop, and the lakeside park. There's also a movie theater, but the films are limited to a few old-fashioned prints—not even good ones, if you ask me. You should come by, watch a few from our private collection. It beats the trash at the theater."

Excited by their shared interest in movies, D sidled over to the free seat next to Craig and started to pick his ear.

Billie rolled her eyes and slunk over to Cecilia's side. "We also hold get-togethers here at City Hall where people bring food and socialize. Those happen every Sunday at dusk. Tomorrow's Sunday, in case you've lost track of time out on the road, so I suppose we'll be having the party instead of the potluck." Her charming smile took on a devious affect. "You sew, right? I have a dress that would look *fantastic* on you if we adjusted it a bit. All the boys would be drooling at your cute little feet." She cast a surreptitious glance at Brian and Louis. "With a couple of obvious exceptions."

Cecilia tossed her hair over her shoulder and giggled, a bashful flush rising in her cheeks. "Oh, that's sweet of you, but I don't think I'll be in the mood to make boys drool even if I *could*. I'll be thinking of those Stalkers the whole time..."

"Oh, phoo. Let's not dwell on things like that." Billie flicked Cecilia's nose and then stood, wrapped in a dress which *had* no doubt made many men drool over time. "You're all so young and beautiful—enjoy life while it's in the palm of your hands, darlings!" She held out a hand to Craig. "My love, why don't *we* adjourn for dinner and dessert?"

Her rouged smile implied dessert wasn't going to be food. Craig took her hand and stood. He slipped an arm around her waist. "Looks like your brother already stepped out for dinner, D. I gotta hand it to him: Felicia's a tough nut to crack." He kicked Louis's leg on the way out, forcing his eyes to flutter open so they could glare after Craig.

D flung her hands onto her hips. "My asshole brother didn't even say nothin'! Just snuck out like a damn alley cat so he could rub up on that doctor." She sighed and headed for the aisle. "I forgot how he was with women. Not one of his finer qualities..."

Cecilia jogged after her while Brian helped a groggy Louis out of his seat. "D, what are *we* doing for dinner? We don't have those punch cards yet..."

Brian wanted to join their conversation, but he felt obligated to stay close to Louis after the tongue-lashing his sister had given him in front of 95 percent of the town. His normally tan complexion was wan, and his strut slowed to a lethargic shuffle.

"Are you gonna be okay tomorrow?" Brian whispered. They stepped out onto the sidewalk behind D and Cecilia, who were giggling about something. "You seem pretty out of it."

Louis stuffed his hands into his pockets and trudged along. "I'm just tired, I guess."

Brian nudged him. "How the hell are you tired? You were in bed for almost twenty hours!" Part of him suspected Louis had been subsisting on cigarettes instead of food for the past couple of days and this lack of energy was from his poor diet. The dark circles under his eyes reminded Brian of Cecilia's when she'd been depressed by the children's deaths in the schoolhouse inferno.

Another part of him suspected Louis simply didn't want to *exist* at the moment.

D and Cecilia slowed so they could walk in step with Brian and Louis. Cecilia clutched Louis's arm and craned around to examine his face. "How are you doing, Louis? You don't look well."

D clicked her tongue. "Come have dinner with us before you waste away—you already skinny enough, can't afford to lose no muscle."

Too exhausted to combat D's determination, Louis shrugged indifferent assent. Cecilia lingered beside him and rubbed his back while D complained to anyone who would listen—even the cawing crows— about Antoine running out on them.

Chirping crickets and twinkling string lights surrounded them during their stroll. Dusk had settled over the town, but lights still glowed behind several windows. The skeletons of shops and houses contained the beating hearts of people once again.

It almost feels like home.

"I like this place," D piped up, "but it's kinda weird, like some '50s sitcom world come to life. You remember that movie where it was black and white but turned color in the end? People was livin' in a fantasy world, but it was all bigoted and uppity. For some reason, when they started gettin' freaky and expressin' themselves, it all went up in flames. The world *needs* color if you ask me."

Cecilia giggled. "You're so funny, D. But I agree. I think we should stay here for a little while to see if this city would be a good fit for Evergreen, but I have a good feeling about things."

"Oh, if they ain't got no problem with Louise stayin', they sure as heck won't have no problem with our church pals comin' over." D looked at Louis, awaiting a snide response or glare, but he didn't offer either. "I'd like to ditch those robes though. Look a little culty like the KKK, and I can't dig that."

They stepped into the parking lot of the resort. D turned to Louis and put her hands on her hips. "Your *manman* teach you to cook Cajun or Creole cuisine, Louise?"

Louis finally snapped out of his trance. "My *what*?"

"Guess you don't know much Creole. Don't matter anyway—you cook or not?"

"No 'manman' taught me, but yeah. I know my way around a kitchen."

D turned and swooped an arm, gesturing for him to follow. "Come help me, then. We got rice still, and Andi gave us some crawdads and spices to work with. I think there's even a jar of stock, but I ain't been brave enough to taste it. You can be my guinea pig."

Louis gave Brian a beleaguered look. Uncertain if he was asking for assistance or approval, Brian cleared his throat. "D, do you want Cill and me to help too?"

"Nope. Just chill out on the porch, watch the sunset. I'm puttin' Scarface to work."

Louis's shoulders slumped in defeat. He trudged up the stairs after her while Brian and Cecilia plopped into the rocking chairs and enjoyed the cooling air.

Cecilia smiled at Brian and reached over to squeeze his hand. "I'm proud of you, Bri. You've done so well with him. I'm proud of him too, for doing so well with all of us. I mean, he's in there cooking with D, of all things. I guess I'm proud of *her* for asking him. We can all see how much his sister's attitude troubles him."

"I don't think there's any point in trying to talk to her." Brian's chair creaked as he rocked, reminding him of Poppa and Nana's rustic porch. "She straight-up said she wished we'd both go back to the island so she could pretend we didn't exist and I could keep pretending he loved me. But he's not pretending. I don't think he's pretending with *anyone*. His reflexes are fast enough to have seen her pull out that knife, to snatch her wrist before it made it to his face, but he gave her a moment of satisfaction—and Eva *still* told me she would've killed him if she wasn't worried about being exiled. She refuses to see past his mistakes, to give him a chance to show her he's capable of learning from them..."

Cecilia released Brian's hand but gave it a reassuring pat. "I don't think you made a mistake by letting him come with us. And one day, Eva may appreciate the fact she was able to confront him. I think it upsets her you're sympathetic to both of them, not just her, and that everyone else isn't crying for him to be hung or something—but you already freed him from a prison of his own making."

The thin walls of the cabin barely muffled some old-timey folk music warbling through a speaker. D barked out instructions over it, but Brian didn't catch any of Louis's replies. The scent of whatever they were making was a bit fishy, but his roiling stomach yearned to be filled.

Cecilia curled a hand between her chin and shoulder, smiling at him in a wily way that reminded him of Billie. "I know you offered to share a cabin with him because you wanted to support him, but in the back of your mind, you're hoping to reconcile, aren't you?"

"That's a super complicated way to ask me if I plan on sleeping with him again, Cill. Just be like D and blurt it out." Brian scoffed and shook his head, glad to switch topics from Eva and to keep his mind off their Stalker-trapping mission in the morning. "I mean, I'd be lying if I said I didn't want to. But that's like reopening an old wound, you know? The blood just starts flowing and it gets messy..."

Cecilia winced. "What kinda stuff are you guys *into*?"

"I don't mean it *literally*—" He recognized she was being facetious and lightly shoved her shoulder. "Listen, I'm already trying my damnedest to not think about that stuff, and you're not helping. If things go well, maybe. Probably. I can't see myself being with anyone else. I like how he smells. I like his snaggle-toothed smirk. I like his thick accent and the slang he uses, and the smoky quality of his voice. The 'edgy' ear piercing he got when he was fifteen and the kanji he got tattooed on his left hip. His wry sense of humor, his skill at everything he puts his mind to, how he only dresses in dark clothing and refuses to change his outdated hairstyle because he *knows* it looks stupidly good on him. I never had a type before him... Now it's just *him*."

Cecilia's wistful sigh made Brian want to reach over and hug her. "In my experience, it's all in how someone holds you. You feel secure in their embrace and know they won't let you go unless you ask them to. Your head fits in the crevice between their neck and shoulder perfectly, like it's molded to you."

"It's always nice to have someone who'll wrap their arms around you when you need to cry," Brian said. "When we were on the island, everything had a chance to sink in because I was finally done running and fighting to survive. It hit me that my family was really gone, and if I went back to my house, I'd find nothing but an empty shell. Looters probably took everything, so all I'd see would be the walls and floors that used to surround us while we'd play games, watch TV, eat, talk, and laugh... And when I thought about that, I'd go to a dark place even though it was sunny and gorgeous outside. The only thing capable of pulling me out of it was him—the only thing that *got* me to that point was him. And the few times it got really bad, he'd curl up in bed with me and stroke my hair while I cried. That's the side of him Eva never saw, and I don't think anyone else ever sees, and *that's* how I know he isn't faking it."

A gentle breeze sent tufts of silvery hair flying around Cecilia's heart-shaped face while she considered Brian with a thoughtful expression. He realized his eyes were welling with tears at the mere conjuration of these memories and from his frustration with the situation with Eva. "You're a lot like me, Brian: we both want to see the best in people. It's a hazardous trait in a time like this where everyone is frightened and desperate, but I think we recognize the difference between a bad person and someone who needs guidance. In that respect, Eva's a lot like her brother. The funny thing is, I don't think she knows how alike they are. I suppose the difference between them is he has us now, and she thinks she has no one."

"I'm going to give her space for now." Brian curled his hands around the arms of the rocking chair. His nails picked at the wooden knots. "I'm one of the last people she needs around her, anyway. Maybe you can spend some time with her—"

D poked her head out of the front door. "Soup's on, kiddos. If you wanna see Louise in a KISS THE COOK apron, you better hurry on in."

Cecilia and Brian followed D inside, sharing a smile when they spied Louis beside the dining room table (sans apron; both Brian and Cecilia were disappointed). Steam misted above a serving dish filled with white rice and bright-crimson crawfish covered with some sort of sauce.

D swept out a hand with a little flourish. "Budget étouffée, y'all." She grinned, pleased by Brian and Cecilia's enthusiastic "ooh"s, and patted Louis's shoulder. "He makes for a fine sous chef, I have to say. Kinda surprised me."

Louis dragged out a pair of chairs for Cecilia and Brian. "You guys want drinks? They got water, sweet tea, and lemonade in the fridge."

"Woah, I'm not used to those kinda options..." Brian propped his elbows on the table and curled his hands around his chin, inhaling a mouthwatering whiff of the étouffée. "Where did the sugar come from?"

"Sugarcane plants," Louis said with a straight face.

Brian flung a cloth napkin at him. "I'll take a tea without a wedge of smartass, *s'il vous plaît.*"

Cecilia asked for a lemonade. D sat at the table and smiled at Brian and Cecilia while Louis fulfilled these drink orders. Frank Sinatra crooned about a sunshine place through the speakers of an old boombox.

Once Louis took his seat, they joined hands so Cecilia could lead them in saying grace, D on Brian's left and Louis on his right. When Louis slipped his fingers between Brian's and his thumb started stroking the back of Brian's hand, a warm sensation gushed from Brian's chest and flowed to the tips of his fingers and toes.

This feels good. This feels right.

Frank assured them the best was yet to come, and Brian believed him.

Old Scars, Fresh Wounds

Chapter Eleven

Full Circle

4/10, Diamond City, Arkansas, Lakeside Resort, 10:00 a.m.

Brian and Louis headed to Rod's after they ate breakfast with their companions. When Rod emerged from his trailer and strolled over to unlock the gate, LD burst out barking and leaped against Brian with such strength he nearly knocked him back.

Brian laughed and kneeled to pet the slobbering dog. "It's okay. My grandfather had a dog. I'm used to them."

Rod grabbed LD by a jingling collar, trying to stop him from licking Brian's face. "LD's an ol' mutt who wandered up to the fence looking for food. After the quarantine, the mayor let me keep him. With a bark like that, he makes for a good guard dog."

Louis's eyes softened with affection when Brian glanced at him, but his strained smile hinted at lingering regrets about what had happened with Rocky. Brian swallowed a bitter taste in the back of his throat and forced himself to smile back, refusing to dwell on the past like Eva.

"You were in the military, right?" Brian stood, but LD sat on his feet to keep him captive. He scratched the dog's ears while Rod nodded. "My grandfather was too. He fought in Vietnam. He was there during the My Lai massacre."

"Shit." Rod's amiable visage drooped. Brian placed him in his late forties because of the wrinkles creasing his tanned skin and the thick whiskers prickling avround his thin lips. His close-cropped hair was mostly pepper with a sprinkling of salt. "You think about it though, we *all* survived a massacre." Rod glanced at Louis, keeping his expression indifferent. "Your sister blurted out some nonsense about you killing this grandfather of his. This kid's your friend, right? So tell me how all that happened."

Louis's eyebrows alternated between arching and furrowing while he tried to work out an answer. "I mean, it's complicated... Basically, our granddaddies fought in the war together. Mine was a drunk who used to beat me and beat my père when *he* was a kid, so I wasn't real fond of him. He told Brian and his granddaddy they could come stay with us after shit went bad, but he pulled me aside and tried to rope me into some plan to tie them up and take their stuff—he was always paranoid, but the outbreak made him even worse. Anyway, I didn't wanna do that, so when a Stalker broke in and attacked my sister, I took advantage of the opportunity—I snuck into my granddaddy's room that night, thought about tyin' *him* up, but the hate got a hold of me when I saw his face and remembered all the times he hurt me. I shoved a pillow over it and shot him, told Eva and Brian's granddaddy he got infected so they wouldn't freak out, but I could tell Brian's granddaddy didn't buy it. I saw the same edginess in his face, the paranoia and ruthlessness, and it scared me. I thought he'd just take my granddaddy's place and kill me... So I killed him first."

Rod broke the solemn silence drifting between Louis and Brian. "It's a hard thing to say, but you probably made the right call on both counts. His granddaddy mighta killed you, and yours mighta killed *them*. That mercilessness gets burned into you when you're out there on the field, the motivation to survive at all costs. You two probably know what I mean, right? You didn't make it this far by bein' nice."

"My grandfather used to say all that brotherhood stuff was bullshit," Brian said, "and the only time someone saved your skin was when it helped them save their own. I was the only family he had left, but even though he trained and protected me, it felt more like duty than love. The moment he slit a woman's throat right in front of me, I struggled between surviving for survival's sake like him or choosing to trust people and surviving because my friends gave me a reason to. I think I made the right call."

Rod studied Brian's self-possessed expression, surprised by the conviction of his response. "I can see how much they all like you, and how much you like them." He clicked his tongue. "I bet you *really* like that pretty blonde girl."

Brian let out a nervous laugh, amused by Rod's drastic misconception and a little perturbed by his interest in Cecilia. "I like her a lot, but let's just say my interests lie elsewhere and leave it at that."

Rod crossed his arms and looked between Brian and Louis for a moment, studying them with keen eyes until his tight lips slackened. "Ah. Don't ask, don't tell, I guess. I don't mind; means you two are outta the runnin' when the need to repopulate rolls around."

"You won't be repopulatin' with Cecilia, I can tell you that much." Louis's defensive, puffed-up posture deflated into impatience. "Now can we go get our stuff?"

"I'm glad your buddy gets the gun, not you," Rod said with an arch of his eyebrow, but he headed toward the shed and signaled for them to follow. He punched in a code on a keypad next to the door and pulled it open, revealing meticulously organized gear stacked on the floor and shelves against all three walls.

"I change the code every day." Rod smirked when he caught Louis's kid-in-a-candy-store expression. "I wish I could say it's all mine, but most of it belongs to the townsfolk. A lot of it goes to the guards or out on loan to hunters. But I have a few special things squirreled away someplace else in case of an emergency." Rod stepped into the shed and swept out his arm. "Well, boys: pick your poison."

In addition to his typical gear, Brian grabbed a thermal rifle, a box of ammo for it, and all sorts of fun protective equipment. Velcro straps dug into the crooks of his elbow and knees, and he kept fighting the urge to pick at them while Louis grabbed what he wanted. All the layers made an instant trickle of sweat roll down his brow.

Louis spotted Antoine's sword and snatched it since it was longer and sharper than a machete. After strapping on similar accessories to Brian, he shoved some wire, bells, rope, and firecrackers into his backpack, then stuffed a bear trap in after it and snagged a flare gun.

Brian gave him a funny look. "What are you gonna do with all that?"

"Firecrackers will draw their attention, the wire and bells will create a perimeter alarm, and the bear trap should be obvious. Lure it out, ensnare it, disarm it, tie it up, and drag it back." Louis wiped his gloved hands together. "We've done this before—should be a cinch, right?"

"If we manage to isolate one from the rest—or they even show up." Brian glanced at Rod while he locked the shed up. "How do you wanna do all this? Have me take a vantage point and cover you while you set it all up?"

"Pretty much." Louis snapped his fingers and pointed at Rod when he approached them. "If we need your guards to bail us out, I'll fire the flare gun. Got it?"

Rod nodded; if Louis's authoritativeness bothered him, it didn't show. He led them down the road toward the gate and gave the signal for a guard to unlock it. It rattled open, revealing a world Brian wasn't eager to revisit. Once they stepped past the gate, it clattered behind them, cutting them off from a safety they might never return to.

Brian crept to the nearest building and climbed up a fire ladder. Louis followed and kneeled beside Brian while he surveyed their surroundings through the rifle scope. "You see anythin'?"

"Nothing yet. Guess they're feeling shy today."

Louis unzipped his backpack and dug out what he needed, motivated by being back in his element. "Once I start movin' around and makin' noise, they'll come. You see more than one, let me know and I'll head back."

Brian exhaled quietly so Louis wouldn't hear. His willingness to let Brian cover him while he worked meant he had complete faith in him—no small confidence to uphold. "All right. Set up my perimeter before you go; I'll keep an eye out for you."

Louis went around the rooftop, stringing the bells onto the wire and tying it to jagged cracks in the brick walls. If anything tried to climb up, a tinny ring would alert Brian while he focused on covering Louis.

He slipped his backpack on and descended the ladder. Brian followed Louis through the scope while he fixed the wire around the borders of Brian's building and the adjacent building, creating a square around the two with a narrow gap of alleyway between them. He worked with quick but deliberate movements, keeping his back to the brick walls.

Louis kneeled and set the bear trap in the alley about two feet from the wire perimeter. A thick expanse of shady forest stretched in front of Louis, the only area where a Stalker—or anything else—could approach from. Unless they tried to climb into the alley from one of the two rooftops, but Brian had that covered. He hoped.

After Louis lit and tossed the sizzling firecrackers near the fringe of the woods, he paced the alley and toyed with Antoine's sword, examining the subtle pattern inlaid on the polished metal. The way he swung it made Brian more nervous than waiting for a damn Stalker to appear. Sweat created a sticky barrier between his skin and clothing, and the sun kept glinting in his scope when he moved it.

Oh, winter, how I miss you.

Within the next fifteen minutes, Brian noticed movement in the vegetation. A hand curled around the gnarled bark of a tree, reddened by the scope.

His breath caught in his throat. *It's a kid.*

It watched Louis dawdle with harmless curiosity. When Louis happened to glance up in Brian's direction, Brian signaled toward the woods to indicate something was there. Louis stopped in place and tried to spot it, but the kid stayed hidden.

Brian held his breath and watched the child. Impatient as always, Louis yanked Brian's pocketknife from his boot and lofted it into the bushes in an attempt to draw the creature out.

It worked. The Stalker lunged for the knife and picked it up. It studied the way the metal caught the light. The chime-like tinkling of childish laughter filled the otherwise silent air.

Brian glimpsed Louis's perplexed expression through the scope. *He wasn't with us when we rescued Antoine from the schoolhouse or when that kid followed me, so he's never seen one of the infected kids. After what happened with Katie, this must be fucking rough for him—*

The child threw the knife back at Louis, who stepped aside and stared at it, dumbfounded.

It's playing. It wanted him to catch it.

Protected by the dual barrier of wire and bear trap, Louis lingered in place. He stooped to pick up the knife and tossed it into the waiting hands of the child. It emerged from the thicket, lured by this fun new game.

Or old. If it remembers.

Tattered clothing clung to the emaciated body. Mere wisps of hair remained, and its cracked skin had raw wounds in it. The gaping smile bared a mouthful of tiny teeth. Its gender remained mercifully ambiguous.

Aware of the wire, the kid stepped over it and threw the knife again. It clattered to the ground at Louis's feet. He backed toward the wall, trying to lure the Stalker into the trap and to avoid scaring it away.

The Stalker crouched like the kid who'd kept calling to Brian, ready to pounce, to attack or flee. After a moment, a voice chirped: "Throw!"

Louis stepped back and sank to his heels, mirroring the child's posture. The weight of understanding had crushed him like an anvil. Brian knew Louis was remembering Katie, wondering if he could've saved her, could've saved *himself* from having to shoot her. Brian's chest tightened and his finger tensed against the trigger, sights lined on the gleaming dome of the child's pale head.

Neither the kid nor Louis budged. Louis's hands moved to his face, fingers steepled over his nose and mouth. *This is too much for him. I have to get down there.*

Brian strapped the rifle around his torso and scurried down the ladder. He crept up behind Louis, taking measured steps to avoid startling the Stalker. When it spotted him, it got to its feet and tilted its head, intrigued.

Louis stood slowly and stepped back parallel to Brian. His right hand clung to Brian's sleeve, trying to keep him in place. "It's fuckin' *playin'* with me, Brian."

"Good—that means it's interested. We just have to get it to come closer." Brian stepped in front of Louis, leaving only the bear trap between himself and the kid. He withdrew a wrapped turkey stick from his pocket and peeled back the plastic. "You want this? You hungry?"

The Stalker's nose wriggled as it latched onto the savory scent. It stepped forward. Tiny hands reached toward Brian, clawing for the food. "Give!"

Brian jerked his hand back like he used to when he was teasing Becky with something she wanted. The child lunged forward—and the bear trap clamped around its foot with a sickening *crack*. A shrill cry like a panther's yowl pierced the air, thick with pain. Louis cursed under his breath.

The kid squealed and bent over to grab its clamped leg. When the prone creature attempted to pry its leg out, the skin tore and blood trickled down its foot. The child peered up at Brian, bloody tears rolling down its round cheeks, but he resisted the urge to put it out of its misery.

"Let's end this," he said to Louis. "We have to neutralize it and tie it up so we can drag it back to the gate."

"It's just a kid..." Louis's brow bunched as he winced, affected by the child's pained wails. "Jesus, that's fucked *up*." He rummaged for the rope and handed it over. But he clung to the sword and hesitated, eyes flitting to the diminutive figure trapped in the metal teeth. "I don't know if I can do this. I already had to kill one fuckin' kid..."

"We're not killing it." Brian shuddered when an earsplitting wail erupted from the agonized creature. "And it's already in pain. There's no point in not finishing what we started. If you can't do it, I understand— just give me the sword. I'm sure I can figure out how to use it."

Louis held it out to Brian. The weight of the sword felt heavy in his hands although the blade was quite light. It sliced through air and flesh with equivalent ease, separating hands from wrists and staining the ground with virulent blood.

Brian's stomach lurched, but he handed Louis the sword so he could clean it and stepped behind the frantic child to strap one of LD's muzzles around its mouth. *It's not human anymore. There's no way to save it.*

Louis helped him tie the rope around their quarry and stayed with it while Brian took a quick trip back onto the roof to sweep for any Stalkers that might've been drawn by the noise. Wary or unaware, none appeared. They hauled their pitiful bundle to the gate undisturbed by anything except the horror of what they'd done.

Brian propped the pale figure up like a living mannequin. It whimpered and reached for its leg with gory stumps. Blood pooled along the rims of its eyes, which retained an innocence that reminded Brian of how long ago he'd lost his.

Someone approached the gate, drawn by the spectacle: a portly redheaded man wielding a rifle. Brian suspected this was the infamous Red. "Holy *shee*-yit—that a fuckin' kid?"

"It's a Stalker." Brian's eyes swept to Red's. "Can you let us in, please?"

Red kept babbling under his breath while he signaled for a coworker, too stunned for words. The gate buzzed and rattled open. Louis and Brian slipped through, safely within the city limits. The gate slammed shut in front of the captive Stalker.

"H-help," it stammered, eyes fixed on Red.

Brian thought of the parrot once more, of the child cheerily calling, "Hello!" *Do they repeat what they hear people say? Maybe they're just sponges, absorbing the world around them.*

"They *talk*?" Red's thick drawl trailed into a squeak. He held his hands to his mouth while his eyes shifted between the child and the men who'd caught it. "Oh, man. Dang. Guess y'all was right: they're changin' up their patterns after all."

"They're *all* children," Brian murmured. Louis lingered near him but had to look away from the sobbing child. "They repeat what they see and hear, emulate other people or Stalkers. The laughter, the way they hide like it's a game... They just want to play with us before they eat us."

He turned his back on the child's pleas.

The entire population of the town gathered at City Hall after dusk, apart from the guards. Everywhere Brian walked, he bumped into a body. When Louis glimpsed Eva—unavoidable, since attendance at this gathering was mandatory, even for Billie's reclusive sister—he hung behind Brian for cover.

Cecilia steered Eva off with a friendly smile while D and Antoine mixed with the townsfolk. Brian approached a refreshment table in the foyer and ladled himself a drink he prayed was alcoholic from a punch bowl into a red plastic cup.

"That booze?" Louis asked, obviously hoping for the same thing.

Brian swallowed; his throat burned. The wince on his face answered Louis's question, so Louis filled a cup and chugged it in one go and then filled another.

A sultry female voice slithered in amidst the chatter: "Easy there, tiger: we're gonna have to pick you up off the floor before the party gets going!" Billie leaned against the wall while Craig spooned a drink for them both and handed hers to her. She sipped it delicately, leaving a light-red froth across her upper lip. "Not much of a party guy are you, Lou-Lou?"

Louis crinkled his cup. "If you saw the shit we saw today, you'd be tryin' to drink yourself into a coma too."

Craig wiped his mouth with the back of his hand. He flashed broad but disingenuous smiles at people who walked by and greeted him. "Red told us. I went and took a look. Regretted it instantly, wouldn't let Bill near it."

Billie nodded. A crimson-red halter dress clung to her, revealing a flattering amount of décolletage. "I didn't argue with him for once. I'm the sort of person who can't wipe an image from my mind. Sometimes they resurface out of the blue."

"My mind works the same way." Brian pictured the body splattered on the street in the French Quarter. The pleading gazes of his sister, Katie, and the infected child flashed through his mind immediately after.

Billie set her cup down and embraced Brian, a delightful perfume drifting from her. "Sweetheart, it's nasty business, but it's business. And now your work is done, so it's time to play."

Craig's firm body clasped Brian from behind, his oaky cologne mingling with Billie's perfume. The two scents combined into something beguiling and soothing, meant to go together. "We're here for you if you need us. But just so you know, I think you're pretty brave—braver than either of us."

Brian's empty drink cup stuck out from this smothering encirclement. Louis plucked it from Brian's hand and pried the pair away from him. "He might be brave, but he'll suffocate if he keeps inhalin' the shit you spray on yourselves."

Billie sighed, her thick eyelashes fluttering as she curled up against Craig. Her fingers toyed with his low shirt collar while she regarded Louis. "Oh, right—you're suffering too. Poor you. Well, I don't know if it's that new scar of yours or the bad-boy attitude, but plenty of girls are giving you more than a passing glance. That's a good way to blow off some steam—"

"Bill"—Brian narrowed his eyes at Billie—"stop fucking with him."

She blinked and pursed her lips. "My, my, what language. I guess that's what happens when you teach a puppy to bark." She rippled her lips in a rude noise and rolled her eyes. "*Relax*—I'm just trying to loosen you two up."

Craig flashed them a wily grin. "You know, Bill and I firmly believe everyone should have a 'fuck it' moment—just throw caution to the wind and go for whatever it is you want. You two have one of those yet?"

"Your preoccupation with our personal lives is fuckin' weird." Louis went to refill the cups he clutched in each hand. "Why don't you two go have a 'fuck off' moment?"

The loudspeaker crackled to life with Mayor Halloran's distinctive accent, defusing any imminent explosions: "Good evening, everyone, and thank you for attending. Tonight, we're here to celebrate the arrival of our new guests and the enduring success of our fine city. Please assemble in the auditorium for music and dancing. Eat, drink, and be merry—or Shirley, or anyone you want!"

Of course, Brian and his friends knew the *real* reason the mayor was throwing this generous party. But she didn't want to frighten the townsfolk with stories of bogeymen—she just wanted to wipe the bogeymen out and never have to tell the story again.

The herd stampeded through the double doors, dragging Brian and the others with them. They dispersed to sit at circular tables surrounded by metal chairs with sad excuses for cushions. Candles encased by glass vases cast light onto a bed of sparkling confetti and dusty white tablecloths while a warbly speaker system blared "Safety Dance" at them. Brian felt like he was in some sad museum display labeled: *Dad's Boring Work Party, circa Brian's Memory, Age Eight.*

D, Antoine, and Cecilia were out dancing on the floor, but Brian made a beeline for an empty table. Louis sat across from him, toying with the confetti and muttering curses he suspected related to Billie and Craig. Neither of them was in the mood to dance—or any good at it even if they *were.*

The punchy beginning of that damn Britney Spears song (*hit me baby something something*) startled Brian into nearly knocking his cup over. Louis snickered at him, but his smile shrank when his eyes flitted to something behind Brian. Brian turned his head and spotted Eva at a table with Billie and Craig; she gave Louis a death glare resembling some of the ones Brian had seen Louis himself give.

Brian looked at Louis and cringed. Louis downed the rest of his drink and avoided looking in his sister's direction. He didn't seem to know where to look, so his eyes darted around the room, never lingering on one area for long. Brian followed his example and watched the crowd mingle and writhe, his eyes adjusting as the lights dimmed and colorful orbs swirled on the floor and ceiling.

When their gazes met, neither of them knew what to say. This silence wasn't the same void which had pushed Brian to speak back in the suicidal woman's house; this silence was filled to the brim, threatening to overflow—until a giddy D wandered over with a drink in her hand, holding it high so it didn't bump into any of the twisting bodies.

"Feels like a real party, don't it?" Her eyes narrowed when they fell on Louis's stressed expression. "You don't know the meanin' of the word fun, do you?"

Louis blew air through his lips and leaned back in his chair. "I'd rather be anywhere else than here right now. I hate parties. Kinda hard to enjoy myself anyway with my sister tryin' to murder me with her eyes."

D shook her head and slumped into a seat. "Why don't you find something to be happy about instead of focusin' on what makes you miserable? For example, you sittin' here with *l'amour de ta vie*—I wish *I* could still do that."

Louis narrowed his eyes beneath furrowed brows, hiding the rest of his face behind his cup. After a moment, he set his drink onto the table. "I'm sorry you had to put him down. That took a lot more strength than I got, I can tell you. Then to keep goin' after..." He streaked his hand through his hair and glanced into the crowd. "You're right, D. I've got no excuse to be miserable."

D gave Louis the closest thing to a genuine smile she'd ever given him. But Cecilia emerged from the crowd behind D and leaned down to whisper something into her ear. D's expression changed drastically within a minute: first confusion, then curiosity, and finally exhilaration.

Cecilia sat between Brian and D. She leaned toward D with a smile while Brian and Louis exchanged a perplexed glance. "Here he comes!"

When Louis sputtered, Brian strained to see what he was looking at. *Oh, it's Red. Why does he think that's so funny?*

Louis scooted his chair closer to Brian and whispered, "I guess Colonel Sanders likes dark meat."

Brian shoved Louis's shoulder and gave him a dirty look, but try as he might, he couldn't fight back a grin. The punch was starting to sink in.

Sure enough, Red walked up to D (while she pretended not to notice him) and tapped her shoulder. "Hello there, pretty lady. I saw you at the meetin'. Dionne, isn't it? I'm Al, but everyone calls me Big Red." He scratched his close-cropped red hair and then cleared his throat and tugged at the white coat draped over the swell of his belly. "I'd be honored if you'd dance with me."

D's fingers brushed the upper swell of her chest, and she fluttered her eyelashes, affecting a demure demeanor—quite unusual for her. "Little ol' me? Why I'm flattered! I never say no to a dance, Red. Folks call you that 'cause of your hair, your bow tie, or do you just like the gum that much?"

Brian snuck a look at Louis, who *did* like the gum, but Louis was too entertained by the interplay between D and Red to notice. *At least he's in a better mood. We both are. It's kind of impossible to be in a bad mood around D.*

"Honestly, I never thought to ask." Red's shoulders bounced with a good-natured chuckle. "Probably the hair or my cheeks. You can probably see where they got the 'Big' from."

"Oh, can I now?" D stuck her hand out and eyed Red up and down. Cecilia hid a smile beneath her hand and looked at Brian and Louis, amused by D's not-at-all-subtle innuendo.

"I like the cut of your jib, Miss Dionne." Red curled his large hand around D's. He pulled her up and led her out to the dancefloor. D looked back at her tablemates and flashed them a broad grin, waggling her fingers over her shoulder.

And as quickly as their fairy godmother had appeared, she was gone.

Louis glanced between Cecilia and Brian, smirking. "Should we start a countdown to the weddin'?"

Brian snorted, but Cecilia made a "tsk" sound. "Don't be rude, Lou. Do you know how lonely she's been? Or care? D's pretended to be something she's not for most of her life; it's a hard habit to break. It's nice to see her having fun!"

"Do you think people will even *get* married now?" Brian asked. "I don't see a point."

"It's to show commitment before the eyes of the Good God." Cecilia tucked her hair behind her ear. "Or to celebrate a bond between two people. I think people will still get married, at least symbolically."

Louis leaned an elbow onto the table and cradled his chin with his hand. "Rod seemed pretty interested if you're lookin' to get hitched."

Cecilia glanced askance at Louis. "Gross—he's my *dad's* age." She stretched her arms across the table and buried her face in them. "I miss my family. My parents, my brother, even my weird uncle and my aunt who barely spoke English. I miss my family at Evergreen too. Deep down, I want to think we'll get rid of the Stalkers, that this masked gang has dispersed and won't return, that this town will flourish and Evergreen can join them. But this pandemic made me question the existence of God or whatever benevolent being might've created us. Before all this, I led a comfortable life driven by blind faith—but now my eyes have been opened to the possibility all I believed in was a series of fables no more real than a book of Greek mythology."

Brian wanted to say something to comfort her, to assure her he'd struggled to find meaning in his own life—but Louis scooted out of his seat and held his hand out to her. She looked at him, blinking away the glint of tears. "What?"

Louis glanced at the crowd and sighed. "The least we can do is stop sittin' here bein' miserable. Let's go pretend to be happy like everyone else. What did Billie say? We're young and beautiful so we might as well enjoy life. Well, I'm young, anyway—these scars I keep gettin' are chippin' away my good looks pretty quick."

Cecilia's distress shifted into confusion and eventually acceptance as she curled her small hand around Louis's. Brian smiled at her, but a sour taste lingered in his throat. Louis led her out into the crowd, a shadowy figure contrasting with a golden-haired angel in white.

While Brian sat alone at the table, all the couples danced around him: Billie and Craig pressed together, D laughing with Red, Antoine impressing Felicia with his smooth moves, and Louis and Cecilia locked in some deep conversation. The sight inflamed a jealousy he'd never experienced before, filling his body with a scorching ache from throbbing head to tightened toes.

I'm being stupid. I should just be happy for everyone. There's no reason for any of us to be miserable, like D said.

Someone tapped his shoulder. He turned, shivering when he met Eva's apathetic gaze. "Eva, hi..."

Eva smiled with the same practiced graciousness as Mayor Halloran. "You're all alone too. Guess we should dance."

"I'm not any good."

"I'm not askin' you to do anythin' except stand and sway with me. Think you can manage that?" Eva's defiant tone stunned him into nodding. He followed her out onto the dance floor and placed his hands on her hips while she dangled hers over his shoulders.

"It's all fake," Eva murmured, studying the swirling, glittering lights above them. "Like this is some production in a theater and we're all actors, not just Billie and Craig."

"What do you mean?"

"This entire town. The party. It's all make-believe, a ruse to keep us from remembering the ugliness outside. I almost forgot about it until you and my brother came back into my life."

He couldn't bring himself to look at her. His eyes swept across the room until the sea of people surrounding them blurred into a kaleidoscope of color.

Eva snatched his jaw with one hand and forced his eyes to meet hers. "You came here lookin' for me: here I am. Now what?"

Brian searched her eyes. They were so different from how he remembered them. Colder, darker. Emptier. "I don't know. I just wanted you to be okay."

They swayed amidst the winsome refrain of "Linger." "I can't stand to look at myself anymore because I just see my brother. I'm sure you see him when you look at me too, and it makes you wish I was him instead."

Brian didn't have a response for her; she was right. The song played on.

Eva dug her fingers into his shoulders. "After all the things he did, he's sittin' there at a table laughin' with y'all like you're family. He doesn't deserve it. Cecilia says he felt unloved his whole life, but it's because he makes it so hard for anyone to love him—I *tried*. How do you do it, huh? How can you love a monster?"

Her eyes softened with the glint of welling tears. When she blinked, they rolled down sanguine cheeks over a splash of freckles. She buried her face in his chest and sobbed, bringing them to a dead stop while the crowd swirled on around them.

A girl was in his arms, a girl who cared for him. A girl who'd been wronged, abandoned, and betrayed. Yet he wished he was holding the person who'd hurt her, who'd hurt them both, and he hated himself for it.

Brian lowered his chin onto her head and exhaled. "He's not a monster. He was just scared of being hurt, of feeling unwanted—just like you. But you're not, you know."

Eva withdrew from him. In that instant, she resembled a beautiful yet fragile porcelain doll. She stood on tiptoe and pressed her lips to his while the music pulsed around them, bodies writhing in a mass of heat. The curves of her warm body pressed against him, her hands locked behind his neck and velvet lips trapping his. His body agreed: *This is nice. You're supposed to like this.* But his mind screamed at him, *We don't fit. This feels wrong—*

Eva withdrew and grinned at him like a child withholding a naughty secret. "You're sick too. And there's no cure for what you're infected with."

She disappeared into the crowd. Brian fled into the bathroom to escape from the suffocating press of bodies. He splashed water onto his face and glanced at his reflection, sparing an idle thought to how the low lighting gave his skin and hair a bluish tint.

A peppy song played outside, at odds with the turmoil churning Brian's gut. A woman's voice chirped over a familiar electronic beat. The lyrics circled back to the prior song like someone was trying to mash the two. *Love me, fool me, I'm such a fool for you.*

The doors opened, letting in a swell of air and removing the buffer from the music. When the person holding it open slipped in, Brian exhaled. *Of course it's you. It's always you.*

"Did you follow me in here?"

Louis walked over to the sink next to Brian and splashed water onto his flushed face, then flicked water from his fingertips onto his hair and smoothed it. "It'd be a remarkable coincidence if I didn't. You okay?"

"I feel a little light-headed." Brian leaned onto the counter. The chemical aroma of bleach and toilet bowl cleaner clung to the stark bathroom. "I always hated crowds."

"Me too." Louis spun and pressed his rear against the edge of the counter. "I think I got Cill outta her funk, at least. Antoine's got Felicia tucked into a corner; I can tell he's tryin' to put the moves on her. Far as I can tell, it's workin'. And D's havin' a gay ol' time with the Colonel."

Brian snickered. "Thanks for the synopsis. What's on next?"

Louis curled his hands around the edge of the counter and tucked his head into his shoulder. "You tell me, Dungeon Master. This is *your* game."

The door opened. A random man staggered in, smiled at the pair, and strolled over to a urinal. He must have thought it was terribly strange how Brian and Louis stood there in silence while he pissed, washed his hands, and exited. Hopefully, he was drunk and would forget the whole thing.

Brian leaned close to Louis and lowered his voice to a dramatic tone. "A wild ogre interrupted the heroes' respite; when he left, the room smelled of piss. In desperate need of fresh air, the pair elected to exit and search for more rations to fill their empty stomachs."

Louis arched his eyebrows and laughed. "Wow, you really *are* a dork." He parted from the counter and jerked his head toward the door. "Rations it is. But first we have to, what, pass a stealth check or some shit? Make sure no one sees us."

Floating on the cloud of a strong buzz, Brian was unbothered by his typical self-consciousness. He grabbed the rolled sleeve of Louis's shirt and tugged him through the crowd. "As long as we avoid the Druid, Fighter, and Cleric, we'll be fine. Oh, and the Bard and the Warlock—they're out to steal the Dark Wizard's magic coin." The erratic strobe lights made it hard to identify anyone, and he couldn't hear anything above the pulsing bass of the music. "Hey, it's that 'chica cherry cola' song. You remember it from the skating rink?"

Louis stayed close to Brian, a light trace of alcohol lingering on his breath. "I still don't know what the fuck 'chica cherry cola' *is*—but I'm dyin' to find out. Get it? 'Cause he sings it—"

"Now *you're* the one being a dork."

They sprinted out of the auditorium, unable to escape the music but comforted by the diminished volume and the freedom from the crowd. Both exhaled at once, cracking into matching grins as soon as their eyes met. Their shared sense of mischief mimicked their childhood experiences of exploring a world they thought belonged to them.

"Oh, no—" Brian flung an arm in front of Louis's chest to keep him in place. "Those dastardly goblins have absconded with most of our rations. Quick, let's take what potions we can." They approached the table with the punch bowl and ladled whatever they could into fresh Solo cups. The food had been reduced to a few crackers and pieces of fruit and cheese, but they stuffed them into their mouths anyway.

"Be honest," Louis whispered after he swallowed, "how drunk *are* you?"

Brian pinched his fingers. "*Un peu.*"

Louis laughed. "*Très bon.*" He undid the top buttons of his shirt and plucked at it to air his chest out. "I'm feelin' pretty good, but I'm not drunk enough to blurt out any confessions this time."

Brian poked Louis's chest. "You better not have anything left *to* confess."

Louis wiped away the crumbs clinging to his lips and held up three fingers. "Scout's Honor—there's no more to tell. Or should I say somethin' like, 'I swear fealty to you, Lord Brian. I'd lay down my sword for you—or would I pick *up* a sword for you?'"

Brian gave Louis a playful shove. "No more swords for you. That's 'Toine's thing. But I don't mind being a Lord. You can keep calling me that."

"I dunno if I can do it with a straight face—" Louis's smile shrank. He snatched Brian's collar and dragged him into the hallway and then poked his head around the wall. "Fuck—isn't that the Bard and the Warlock?"

Brian spied Billie and Craig by the refreshment table, spooning more punch into their cups. The pair looked around; when they thought they were alone, Craig swept Billie into a passionate clinch. One of the drinks tumbled to the floor, leaking red liquid all over the carpet while the couple kissed. Riveted by the sight, Brian forgot to pull his head back when they broke apart—but Louis jerked him into the hall in the nick of time. They sat on the floor, on the verge of laughter. It spilled out as soon as they looked at each other.

"What was *that*?" Louis whispered. "Was he puttin' a spell on her or somethin'?"

"He was siphoning the life from her, far as I could tell." Brian froze when a pair of shadows towered over the pair, who remained huddled on the floor.

Billie and Craig looked down at them, utterly befuddled. Craig shook his head and smirked, but Billie leaned down with her hands on her knees, exposing the window of her ample cleavage. "What on *earth* are you two doing sitting on the floor grinning like a couple of idiots?"

Louis scrambled to his feet and grabbed Brian's hand. "Run before they try to use their charisma on us!"

Brian stumbled up the stairs behind Louis, snickering the entire way. They emerged into the upstairs hallway leading to the mayor's office. Still clinging to Louis's hand, he kept his voice to a whisper: "After narrowly escaping the murderous Warlock and his Bard, the Rogue and his Lord stood in a dark hallway. Without a torch to guide them, they could encounter dangerous spiders with dripping fangs or slithering, venomous snakes—but if they continue to explore, they might find insurmountable amounts of treasure."

"I'm all about the treasure." Louis rummaged in his pocket for something. He produced a wind-up flashlight. "And I always come prepared."

Brian elbowed him. "Boy Scout."

Louis cleared his throat and led the way forward. "I don't know what this 'Boy Scout' you speak of is, my Lord. I thought I was a Rogue."

The pair tried to open each door they found until they literally stumbled into some sort of equipment closet with cameras, tripods, and lamps. The door closed behind them with a *click*, shielding them from everything except the faintest throb of music.

"What *is* all this strange machinery?" Brian muttered as he plucked objects from the shelves and examined them.

Louis fiddled with a handheld camera until a green light blinked on. "Uh-oh—I seem to have triggered a device of some kind."

Brian withdrew something which expanded like a windshield screen, startling them both. They laughed when they realized it was a greenscreen. "I guess this is a cloak of invisibility." He sputtered and tried to contort the wiry thing back into a circle. "What're you doing with that camera—er, I mean that soul-capturing orb?"

Louis pulled it to his face. "I guess it *is* capturin' you pretty well—"

"Are you recording me? Oh, God—turn it off!" Brian dropped the greenscreen and fumbled for the lens, trying to cover it with his hands. He tripped over the legs of a tripod and stumbled into a laughing Louis.

Louis set the camera onto the shelf and tried to help Brian right himself. "All right, all right—your soul is safe now. You happy?"

Brian clung to Louis's shirt, glaring and pouting. "You displease your Lord."

"Do I now? Well, how do I please him?" Louis's hands lingered on Brian's hips before he slid them up the back of his shirt. Brian plucked at the buttons of Louis's shirt, skin itchy, burning all over. His forehead bumped against Louis's, alcohol and cranberry clinging to their breath.

"It seems you've cast some sort of spell on me..." He refused to meet Louis's eyes, knowing it would tip him over the edge. "What sort of treachery do you have up your sleeve, Rogue?"

Louis slid his thumb beneath Brian's chin and tipped it up. Brian's vision swam as Louis searched his eyes. The heat of their bodies fused until he could scarcely remember where he ended and Louis began. "No treachery. I swear it on my life. All I want is to serve you for as long as you'll have me."

The wooden floorboards outside the room creaked.

"*Fuck.*" Louis grabbed the flashlight and turned it off. He fumbled for Brian's hand; Brian took it and dragged him into the back of the room, both tripping over the filming equipment and muffling laughter. They huddled in the corner behind the abandoned greenscreen and duffel bags filled with electronics. The threat of discovery sent a surge of adrenaline through Brian like they were errant children about to be discovered by a teacher. *Or a Lord and his Rogue about to be discovered by a Warlock...*

Louis's side pressed against Brian's in the darkness, sending another tingle rippling along his spine. The door creaked open and allowed a sliver of light into the room along with a dreamlike wave of music.

"I thought they went in here." A shadowy figure poked its head into the room. "Hey, look, babe—cameras. Those could be fun."

Craig, you scoundrel. Why the heck did you guys follow us?

"Darling, I'm sure they're fine—I know it's unusual to see that prick laugh, but Brian seemed okay and that's all I care about. They're probably both just shitfaced after what they had to do this morning." Billie picked her way over the scattered equipment. A phone cast bright light but didn't reach the back of the room where Brian and Louis were huddled. "I'm going to break an ankle if I keep tiptoeing over this crap. Let's sneak in later and rummage through everything."

"I can't wait to get you outta that dress." Craig slipped in behind Billie and wrapped his arms around her torso, making her giggle with delight. "But we should probably get back and check on your sister and Bails. I really wish Gloria would listen to us about that sick motherfucker—it's gonna bite her in the ass one day, I know it. Probably the rest of us too."

Billie turned and pushed Craig, trying to ease him out of the cramped room. "Nothing we can do about it now; let's just try to enjoy ourselves and hope the kids are up to something fun too."

The pair slipped back through the door and pulled it shut, cloaking the room with total darkness.

Louis turned the flashlight on. It cast a dim glow along the outlines of their bodies. "We should try to pick our way out of this weird fort we've built ourselves and get back before the Warlock blabs to the Druid and they send a search party after us."

Brian grinned at him. "You're *totally* into role-playing. Don't even lie."

Louis ruffled his hair. A slight flush darkened both scarred cheeks. "I got a little carried away. Sorry."

The alcohol swirling in Brian's system eradicated his inhibitions. He twisted his hand underneath Louis's and laced their fingers together. "Don't be. I had fun for the first time in a while. I needed it."

"Yeah. Me too."

Brian leaned his head against Louis's shoulder. A satisfied sigh slipped out of him. He preferred this coziness to the tension, the distance, the pleasurable but unbearable agony.

"I'm having one of those moments," he whispered.

Louis's head tilted against Brian's. "The one the Warlock was talkin' about earlier?"

"Yeah." Brian withdrew from Louis and cupped his hand around the scar he'd left all those years ago. Their eyes searched one another's, debating whether they should reopen the wound.

Brian said, "Fuck it," and drew blood.

4/11

The party was memorable, but it wasn't a success.

No Stalkers took the bait. There aren't any signs of them around the city. Maybe the music had the opposite effect and scared them away—or they knew what we were trying to do. Our efforts weren't in vain, at least: Felicia took the child we trapped, but I don't want to know what sort of tests she's running.

The mayor asked us to stay around a few days in case they come back. We agreed. I'm cautiously optimistic about things for once.

4/29

Mayor Halloran offered us jobs, so we accepted. No one wants to leave the comforts of power and running water. I work in the library. It's so dull and comfortable it's almost boring. Louis goes out to hunt for supplies and set traps for animals, Cill's a barista at the coffee shop, and D's a server in one of the diners. Antoine runs the projector in the theater and lets us watch movies for free during his evening shifts.

I work and go home, then Louis cooks or we go to dinner at D's diner. It's nice to take regular showers and watch TV or play video games. Sometimes we go out for coffee at Cill's place or play volleyball at the lake. We started a Dungeons and Dragons game with D, Antoine, and Cill. They all picked the classes I thought they would, and I get to be the DM, which is hilarious because I make shit up on the fly and piss everyone off when they get attacked by monsters instead of finding treasure. Cecilia and Antoine know how to play as a character, but Louis and D make the same decisions they would in real life—and argue just as much.

D still goes out with Big Red (she likes to say, "If you don't like Big Red, then fuck you!" I think it's a quote from some dumb movie). 'Toine pursued Felicia with varying degrees of success, and Cill made a new group of friends. I asked around to see if anyone had seen or heard of Sarah, but no dice. I have a sneaking suspicion she killed herself after she realized she'd lost her daughter.

I visit with Billie and Craig sometimes. I learn a little more about them each time. Before he was an actor, Craig was an insurance salesman. Bill did some modeling—she really got a kick out of showing me some of her lingerie pics. She scared me when she asked me to watch something with her one day. I half thought it would be a sex tape because I remembered overhearing them while Lou and I were hiding. But when her red nail hit play on the camera she stole from City Hall, I heard my voice. I tried to stop it, but Bill wrestled with me and laughed until she cried. She quoted everything we said word for word until I slurred "fuck it." Lou and I didn't go too far, mostly because we were worried about someone else looking for us, but also because there wasn't much room on the floor and we kept getting poked in strange places by things that weren't us. So all Bill (and Craig, I guess) heard was about fifteen minutes of groaning and stuff like, "Fuck, I missed this," "I can't keep my hands off you," and "I want you so bad," etc. I swore them to secrecy because I don't want to risk it getting out to Eva. I'm not embarrassed (if I get screwed over again, it's my own damn fault), but I don't want to rub salt in her wounds.

Oh, Eva. Eva, Eva, Eva. Her name rolls off my tongue pleasantly but leaves a bitter taste. She loathes Louis and gives off this scornful air around me because she thinks I'm just as crazy as he is and I abandoned her too. If I've learned anything, it's that you can't force your feelings to go one way or another. I was destined (or doomed) to fall for Louis, and I've accepted that. I also have to accept Eva might be just as helpless when it comes to her feelings for us.

Lou says I should go see her, but I don't want to confront the ruins of our friendship. Let it linger, like the song we danced to, and we'll never hammer the final nail in the coffin. Knowing she's safe will have to be enough.

It's ironic: I wanted to escape Louis and find Eva, but he found me and I lost her.

Chapter Twelve

Fluctuations

4/29, Diamond City, Arkansas, Bull Shoals Lake, 4:46 p.m.

Brian tucked his weathered journal into his beach bag. He'd gone out with the others to enjoy a day by the lake, but they'd all returned home except Louis. While he swam, Brian stretched out on the dock, content to absorb the enchanting atmosphere around him. Studying the sky reminded him of the unquantifiable size of the universe and its mysteries, of what Cecilia said about there being something more out there.

The wood beside Brian creaked. A dark shadow leaned into his vision and blocked the sun. Beads of water plopped onto him, making his skin prickle. "Ugh! *Louis*, you're dripping water all over me!"

Louis grinned and shook his hair out like a wet dog, spraying Brian with a mist of water. He stretched beside Brian on the dock and leaned on his elbow, his right hand curled beside his mostly healed wound. "Don't wipe it off: the way the sunlight's hittin' your skin right now makes the water look like diamonds." He dragged a finger down Brian's chest, his eyes glittering with the reflection of these gemlike droplets. "Gorgeous..."

The serene convalescence of twittering birds and rustling leaves relaxed Brian. Sun saturated his skin, and the buttery scent of suntan lotion transported him to days by the lake with his family. *Was my entire life before this a dream, or is* this *the dream?*

"We should go soon. Back to Evergreen."

Louis stopped tracing invisible patterns on Brian's dewy skin. "Sounds like you don't wanna go."

"I do. They helped us so much, and I want to do it for Cill..." Brian stared at the unblemished azure expanse above him. His cheeks tightened with heat, maybe from an emerging sunburn. "But it's a pipe dream, isn't it? To have one big, happy family all come together to replace the one I lost? You can't fill the spaces people leave."

He sat and stared into Louis's searching eyes, which no longer seemed so dark and blank. Subtle flecks of mahogany danced in the light, brightening his irises as his pupils dilated. Brian glanced around to make sure no one was around and then reached out to grasp Louis's hand. "When I'm next to you at night and you're asleep, I think about how one day, all of this will be gone. You'll be gone—*I'll* be gone. This panicky feeling swirls in my stomach, and I have to reach out and touch you to make it go away."

"As long as I'm around, you're not goin' anywhere. Tooth, nail, bullet—I won't let a single one touch you. I still kick myself for lettin' you go in the gun shop alone; if that bullet *had* been infected..." A gust of wind whipped Louis's bangs into his face. He swiped them away and lowered his gaze to the sand-covered dock. "I'm glad you're here. And I'm glad I'm with you."

A warm, gooey sensation spread within Brian while he swirled his thumb atop Louis's smooth hand. "I guess we're like magnets—we keep coming back together. I've made peace with that, but there's no way Eva will. Should we leave and give her space? Or should we be honest with her—"

"Bri," Louis scoffed and shook his head, "you don't know my sister half as well as you know me. Shovin' this shit in her face'll only piss her off more. Listen—I'll tell you a story. When we were about six, we got this pet rabbit. Eva named it Bugs, wanted it to be her best friend, but it wouldn't give her the time of day. Funny thing was, it cottoned to me. The damn thing even chased me around the yard; I couldn't shake it off. I tried to pretend it annoyed me, but the day after Eva caught me pettin' that rabbit, Mère found it dead on our porch. That fluffy black body was covered in bloody gashes, convinced Mère and Père some coyote or dog got hold of it. But I knew better. For one, why would a coyote leave the damn thing on our porch? Eva stabbed it to death, tried to make it look like tooth and claw marks. Of course, they never even entertained the thought since she was such a perfect child—I'm lucky they didn't blame *me*."

Brian released Louis's hand. "Was she ever diagnosed with anything?"

"Dunno. Crazy just runs in the family." Louis stood and put his hands on his hips. "If she finds out we've stoked the embers, one or both of us might end up like poor ol' Bugs."

Brian followed Louis back to their bikes and gathered his belongings. He surveyed the area for Eva like she was some Stalker hiding behind a tree or in the bushes and then slid sunglasses over his eyes. "Lou, if you're bullshitting me with that rabbit story, I'll never forgive you."

Louis climbed onto his bike and lowered his own glasses over his eyes. "*Bebe*, you've forgiven me for a lot worse. But no, I'm not bullshittin' you. Let's stay on our toes and work out a plan to go back to Evergreen, get some space from her. Two birds, one stone. Those Stalkers seem to have moved on, so we'll just have to deal with the usual bullshit."

They whipped out from the beach onto the pavement. "Hey, Lou, I'm kinda craving ice cream. Can we go see D?"

The sun hovered at the edge of the horizon, blanketing the town with a warm golden glow. People milled about, biking or walking home from their day shifts or out to their night shifts. The absence of car engines accentuated the chirps of crickets and croaks of frogs. A brisk breeze thrashed wet hair around their faces.

Louis's turn around Diamond Boulevard indicated his answer: as usual, agreeing to whatever Brian wanted. Brian smiled and shifted his concerns to the back of his mind. His predominant thought was his craving for cool sugary ice cream and salty, crisp fries. Maybe a fresh burger on home-baked buns. No pickles.

Brian and Louis leaned their bikes against the rack, not bothering to lock them since crime wasn't an issue in Diamond City, and ducked into a corner booth inside The Cove. Brian pressed the buttons on the tabletop jukebox, recalling the diner he'd eaten in alone—but this time the song changed and someone was across from him. An oldie called "The Wanderer" played while people sat in booths nearby, chatting over steaming platters of food provided by the farm.

Louis slunk back against the red vinyl cushion and lifted a laminated menu. The options were limited, but they were fortunate to sit in a restaurant with a menu they could order from. "You gonna share that ice cream?"

"If you want. I was gonna get a burger and fries too."

Louis dug into his bag and slapped his punch card onto the table. "How much you got? I'm down to a third. We gotta figure out how to budget for the rest of the week."

"I could work out a spreadsheet on my tablet, but since we might leave soon…"

Someone rapped on the table. Brian met his waitress's honey-hued eyes. "You two gonna elope?"

Brian grinned at D. A tray with glasses of water pushed against a nametag with "Dionne" written on it. She'd drawn a heart over the "I" instead of a dot. "Ha-ha, no. We were thinking of heading back to Evergreen, actually."

Louis slid his punch card toward her. "I'll cover both. Can you get me a beer? Whatever's cheapest."

"I'll stick with water, thanks." Brian handed his menu to her with a smile. "And a cheeseburger, no pickles, with a side of fries. And vanilla ice cream after."

"Louise?"

Louis shoved the menu at D. "We'll share all that. Just double up on the fries."

D grabbed it from him. "Y'all back to sharin'? That's cute. Better dial back the body language though—I can see you kickin' each other's feet under the table."

Louis flung his balled straw wrapper at D. "Not a word to anyone, you hear me? Or I'll stitch your mouth shut."

D pointed her pen at Louis. "I known you two long enough to see the signs—they about as ubiquitous as that damn Ace of Base song. I don't care what you do in the privacy of your cabin, but you ain't gonna fool anyone for long. So tell me why I gotta zip my lips."

Brian folded his straw wrapper into a neat square. "Eva."

D sighed and lowered her voice. "Cill's been workin' on her. Tryin', anyway. She's a sulky little thing—takes after her brother. That why y'all leavin'? Think givin' her some space might help her get over this shit?"

Brian blew bubbles into his water. "It can't hurt."

The lights flared and dimmed before going out completely. A collective gasp from the startled patrons mingled with the *whoom* of dying power and rockabilly music. Brian barely made out the contours of Louis or D's faces in the last bit of sunlight. The dam sometimes experienced power fluctuations while Barry tweaked things for efficiency, so Brian expected the power would turn back on eventually.

"God damn it," Louis muttered. "I was actually lookin' forward to that greasy-ass food. When's the power gonna kick back in, D?"

She slapped a flickering flashlight she'd withdrawn, accustomed to these brief outages. "Usually only lasts five minutes, max. I'll go in back, check in with the walkie."

D strolled behind the counter and through the swinging red door into the kitchen. A few squares turned on in the booths: people's mobile phones, now only useful for offline games, music, and flashlights.

Brian shivered when Louis's foot snaked its way up to his thigh. He snatched it and hissed, "Don't."

"Why not?" Louis hissed back. "I can't see anythin'. Neither can anyone else. Their eyes are all glued to their phones anyway."

Brian shut his eyes and let go, allowing Louis to entertain them while they waited for D to return with news or for the power to turn back on.

When D's flashlight signaled her imminent arrival, Louis's foot abandoned Brian. She squeezed into the booth next to Brian, her face glowing in the light. "We don't know what happened. Walkies still work, so we got in touch with a few other places 'round town. They got the generator goin' at City Hall for the fence, but power's out everywhere else. We won't know why or how long until someone from the dam gets back to the mayor. Those solar-powered lights are still goin', so you better hustle back home before they go out too."

Louis sighed. "So much for a hot dinner and dessert." He scooted out of the booth. D and Brian followed.

D patted Brian's shoulder. "Be careful, baby. Go home and lock yourselves in, keep your knives handy."

"You too." Brian smiled at her, but Louis was already through the door.

D glanced at Louis and back at Brian. "You playin' with fire. Don't get burned again." She pressed a finger to his lips. "I know what you gonna say—I ain't worried 'bout him. You tamed that tiger. Like y'all said, it's his sister I'm worried about. She ain't gonna take this shit well. In fact, she probably already knows you done reignited the flame. I know you probably sick of all my puns, but don't let this escalate into no towerin' inferno."

Brian jerked his head toward the door. "I'd better get going before he starts banging on the window or something. I'll check on Cill and 'Toine on my way home."

"Thanks, baby. I'll make my way there soon. Got to help 'em shut down in here."

Brian hugged D and followed Louis outside. The streetlights had gone out, but several strings of solar lights were wound around the trees and dangled from their limbs. A few businesses had spotlights aimed at their signs. These guided them home even though they remained enshrouded in the final throes of dusk.

After they checked in on Antoine and Cecilia, they went home and blocked the front door with the couch, moved bookcases in front of the windows, and gathered lanterns, flashlights, candles, matches, and batteries. Their lantern illuminated most of the combination bedroom/living area, and candles covered the kitchenette and bathroom counters.

Once they finished, Brian was at a loss for what to do. "Wanna play a board game or something?"

"Not now." Louis sat on the bed and crossed his arms.

Brian sank onto the mattress beside him. "Why're you so grouchy all of a sudden?"

Louis sighed. "Don't you get it? It's over."

"It's just a power outage." Brian's attempt to reassure Louis was also an attempt to reassure himself. He wasn't sure either of them bought it. "Those happened before the pandemic too."

Louis ran his hands through his hair and exhaled. "I wanna believe you, but I got a gut feelin' about this. And you know my gut's usually right."

"There's nothing more we can do about it right now. It's in the mayor's hands. She'll call a meeting once she finds out what caused it. Probably not until tomorrow, though." Brian wandered over to the alarm clock and the iPod docked in it. He cued up his music, preferring it to silence.

Louis glanced at him, his concerned expression easing slightly. "You gonna take my mind off it with your girly music?"

"Shut up—you know you like it."

"I like *some* of it. Half of it's in languages I don't speak 'cause—I said it before and I'll say it again—you're a little hipster."

"Whatever, edgelord. It's better than all your Tool, Disturbed, and Nine Inch Nails." Brian moved into the kitchen and opened the refrigerator to withdraw two cold beers before the fridge warmed up. They didn't keep much in there; most of their food came from the farm and ended up cooked and eaten before it needed refrigerating. The beers were from a lucrative haul at a boarded brewery about fifteen miles east.

Brian handed Louis a beer and sat next to him. "One more beer won't dull your edge, *mon loulou*. Come on."

The caps popped off with a little sizzle, metal tinkling as they clattered onto the floor. Brian held his breath, despising the yeasty scent of beer. But he needed to calm his nerves, so he chugged the foamy beverage and set the empty bottle on the ground.

Louis trapped his bottle between his knees and dug underneath his fingernails with his other hand. His knees started bouncing. Brian put a hand on one, instantly halting it.

"I didn't want this to end," Louis said in a rushed breath, as if he wanted to get it out while he had the chance. "But I knew it would."

Brian squeezed his knee. "We're okay. Everyone else is okay. There are armed guards patrolling the town, keeping an eye on the fence, and it still has power. This is just a hiccup."

Louis looked at Brian, dim incandescence highlighting the angular contours of his face. "What if it isn't?"

"If everything ended tonight, I don't think you'd have anything to regret. You went back for Eva, and even if you didn't fix things with her, you tried. You're friends with Cill and 'Toine, and D may get mad at you during *Dungeons and Dragons*, but she doesn't mind you now. Bill and Craig aren't even scared of you anymore."

Louis's eyes fell from Brian's. "What about you? Do you stay with me because you're scared of what I'd do if you didn't?"

"I'm not scared of you, either." Brian tipped Louis's chin up with his thumb, forcing Louis to meet his gaze. "But I know how scared *you* are to lose everything we have here."

Louis startled Brian by grabbing his thigh and leaning in close. His suppliant eyes searched Brian's while he bit his lip, fighting with the words on the tip of his tongue. "I want you to tie me up and blindfold me. I wanna be completely at your mercy while you have your way with me."

Simultaneously taken aback and titillated by Louis's admission, Brian froze. Although he didn't move a muscle, his mind burst into erratic thoughts, unable to stop envisaging what Louis asked for. *He wants me to punish him, to know I can control him. Christ, I don't know if that turns me on or just makes me feel bad... Maybe both?*

Louis had just tipped the scales in Brian's favor, giving him all the power in whatever the relationship between them was. He thought of D's comment about the tame tiger and knew exactly how someone must feel when a force of nature that could easily kill them trusted them above all others.

Brian withdrew from Louis and stood, deliberating with himself at length before he committed to obliging Louis's request. He kept his back to Louis and worked his shirt buttons loose. "I know you want to hear me say it, so I forgive you." He tossed his shirt to the floor and turned. "But if you can't forgive yourself until I punish you, so be it."

Louis tossed his empty beer bottle to the floor. It rolled across the floor with a hollow *tink*. He reached for his shirt to unbutton it, but Brian snatched his arm.

"Don't move a muscle unless I tell you to." Brian channeled his residual anger toward Louis into assertiveness; the shocked but satisfied look on Louis's face fueled Brian's performance.

He jerked his belt out of his jeans and rolled them down his legs, vaguely aware of the song playing and of the sporadic hiss of the lantern beside the bed. He told himself they were only playing at danger, both inside and outside the cabin, that everything would go back to normal after the power returned.

But deep down, he knew Louis was right: *It's over. But over doesn't mean the end. It means the beginning of something new.*

Brian tore Louis's shirt off, sending his buttons clattering to the ground like he'd promised he would back at Evergreen. Tit for tat, button for button. Louis watched them bounce onto the ground before his eyes returned to Brian, riveted like a kid seeing fireworks for the first time. Brian twisted Louis around and pushed him into the bed face-first, tugging his hands behind his back. He knotted his belt around them, flashing back to the time he'd tied Louis's wrists on the island.

There it is. The anger, the resentment. Use it, embrace it, then let it go.

"Is this what you want?" Brian flipped Louis over and hooked his fingers over Louis's belt. "If I keep going, I won't be able to stop."

"Go all night if you want." Louis wriggled beneath Brian, testing the tightness of the belt. "Even if I wanted to break free, I couldn't. You're too good at tyin' me up."

Brian undid Louis's belt and tugged it through the loops in one deft motion. He leaned down and coiled it around Louis's eyes, tight and efficient. His lips ghosted over Louis's, tickled by the moist heat of his breath. He traced his fingers along the scar he'd left on Louis's cheek, inhaled the scent of Louis's hair and skin, high on lust and power.

"Can you see me?" he whispered.

"Only darkness. But I smell you, that salty sunscreen ocean scent—it's like we're adrift in the boat cabin again."

Brian grazed Louis's dry lips with the tip of his tongue, caught the lower one between his teeth until he tasted blood. Louis hissed in pain, but his body arched toward Brian, craving more contact.

But Brian withdrew. He buried his face in Louis's neck, lips close to his ear, and murmured, "Eternity is a fallacy. This moment is everything, the whole of existence. And then this moment becomes a memory, so we create a new moment, a new memory, because it's all we have."

"I've never been turned on by philosophy until now." Louis's voice lowered into a throaty growl. "You're right: you *are* creative."

"I'm just getting started." Brian's nose brushed Louis's hair. He caressed the cheek Eva had sliced open, then rubbed his thumb along the blood welling on Louis's lower lip. "I still have to discipline you too."

"I can take it. Bare your fangs, *mon petit monstre*."

Eager to accept the challenge, Brian sank his teeth into Louis's neck. A sharp intake of breath shuddered through Louis's lips, but it soon eased into a moan Brian smothered with his mouth.

He ravaged Louis until they were both breathless and shaking. They'd now bared the most monstrous parts of themselves to each other—and embraced them.

A knock woke them: Louis answered the door to one of the mayor's guards informing them they were required to attend an emergency meeting. When Brian reached over to inspect the iPod, he realized it had been playing all night and drained the battery. The power was still out.

Aside from the force guarding the perimeter, the entire town filed into the mandatory meeting. Some dragged their feet and had dark circles underneath their eyes. Felicia, Rod, and Barry sat behind Mayor Halloran with their hands folded in their laps and solemn expressions on their faces.

Once the doors clicked shut, the mayor cleared her throat and tapped the microphone. "Good morning, everyone. I'm sure you're concerned by our loss of power last night. I wish I had better news for you this morning. Obviously, it's still out. What little we have is running on a backup generator. When I tried to get in touch with the supervisors at the dam, no one answered. For lack of a better term, I'm in the dark with the rest of you. Barry will get things working again if he can, but I don't want to send him until I know it's safe. Therefore, I need a number of you to go with Rod and investigate the dam."

Craig stood immediately. "It's *him*, Mayor. We kept telling you he'd come back. Now it's time to take him out. Bill and I will go. We still owe him for what he did to Cass and Bailey."

Impressed by Craig's bravery, Brian took in a deep breath and followed his lead. "I'll go with them. You've been good to us, and we want to bring our friends from Louisiana here. And if it *is* the King, I don't want him to be a problem for us anymore."

Louis rose beside him. "I go where he goes. Count me in."

"I'll go too, Madam Mayor." Eva's offer visibly startled Louis. Brian tried to keep his expression neutral, but it surprised him too. "I've been feelin' a little stir-crazy, and I used to go huntin' with my père. I can track as good as any of 'em."

"I appreciate your spirit," the mayor said before anyone else could jump up and volunteer, "but some of you need to stay here in case someone or something takes advantage of our power outage. Antoine, Felicia tells me you're an excellent martial artist and a natural leader: I'd like you to stay here and help Red since Rod will be absent." She continued to announce a list of other names, delegating who she preferred to remain behind. Brian and the others sat, awaiting further plans.

What the hell did I just do? Whatever's going on out there can't be good.

I must still be running off fumes from last night. Acting all "large and in charge" like Mom used to say about Dad when he was in a good mood.

"For this excursion, you may take as many weapons as you need," Mayor Halloran announced. "But I'd prefer a group of you go separately from Rod's. After the meeting is over, I'll summon you to my office for further details."

She finished the meeting with a politician's assurance of a return to normalcy. Mayor Halloran descended from the stage, her council and bodyguards following while she mingled with the dispersing crowd. As expected, Brian, Louis, Eva, Craig, and Billie were tagged to meet with her in her office.

They headed upstairs and dawdled in the hallway while they waited for the mayor. Billie and Craig leaned against the wall, but Eva folded her arms and glared at her brother.

"You better not try to pull any shit on me this time, Lou."

Louis narrowed his eyes but quickly relaxed them. "Eva, I ain't gonna try anythin' like that ever again. But I guess I could tell you I'm sorry until the day I die and I'd still go to my grave with you hatin' me."

"You guessed right." Her gaze lowered to the hand he kept on his hip. "You sure you should go, the way you're carryin' on?"

"I just banged it on a table last night. Nothin' to worry about."

Eva narrowed her eyes. "You clumsy all of a sudden?"

"It was dark. A little thing called a power outage happened, remember?"

"Did you bump your neck too? That's a nasty bruise."

"Enough already." Brian stepped between them. "We have to work together. This is too important to let petty differences get in the way."

"*Petty*?" Eva scoffed. "That's what you've reduced this to? One of Louis's little fuck-ups? Sure. Leavin' his sister behind to be raped or sold by criminals is nothin' big."

"You can't dwell on it forever, Eva." Brian stood his ground against her scornful glare. "It'll eat at you for the rest of your life. Just let go and move on so you can be happy—unless you enjoy being miserable."

She shook her head, her contemptuous smile shrinking. "You're one to talk. I've got a few guesses about why *you're* so damn relaxed now. You know, I used to think you were smart, but you're just a naïve little—"

Louis shoved past Brian and stood toe to toe with his diminutive sister. "*Le bon Dieu*, Eva! Just stick a knife in me now if it'll end this for you, but leave him outta it! He wanted to come back for you, and he left *me* to do it. I'm the clingy asshole who followed him; it's not like he asked me to come. He wanted to give you the chance to confront me, so he let me. After we deal with this shit, I'll leave, okay?"

Eva's hardened features relaxed until her eyes shimmered and twitched. She sniffed, her brow furrowing as she frowned. Her fists strained at her sides, but she didn't reach for the switchblade she kept in the back of her jeans. "Gettin' rid of the knife doesn't heal the wound it cuts in you. You oughta understand that, Lou."

Louis stepped back. His fingertips ghosted the scar she'd left him; he seldom touched the one Brian had left all those years ago.

The ground beneath them creaked under heavy footfall. Eva wiped her eyes and pulled herself together, attempting to erase all traces of her anguish. Brian wanted to offer her his sympathy, but it meant nothing to her anymore.

Neither did he.

The mayor approached with her guards and council. She unlocked the door to her office and entered without a word and then settled into her seat behind the desk. Brian and the others followed. The guards shut the door and stepped outside to make sure no one overheard what they were about to discuss.

Felicia and Barry took a seat while Rod and the others dispersed throughout the cramped room. Louis kept his back to a wall, his eyes flitting to and from Eva with a combination of wariness and resignation. Eva stayed close to Billie and Craig. Brian stood off to the side, not wanting to be near Louis while Eva was in the room.

"Thank you for meeting me," Mayor Halloran began, "and for offering your services. Obviously, this supersedes any duties you have until we discover what happened at the dam. Barry got in touch with Sylvio, his second-in-command, but their correspondence ended abruptly and Barry hasn't heard from Sylvio since. Rod's job is to get everyone in there and escort the employees to safety. Your job is to scope out the area first and give Rod a read on how many heads are in there. If your hypothesis about Fernando is right, it won't be as simple as a sweep and snipe."

"You want the five of us to do this?" Craig gestured to the people in question. "I'm good with me, Bill, and Brian, but the situation with the twins is a bit...spicy."

Louis folded his arms. "If Brian's goin', I'm goin'. End of discussion."

"I'm not a goddamned liability." A heat wave of indignation radiated from Eva. Her unwavering gaze met the mayor's. "Don't I deserve the chance to strike back for once? I mean, this fucker wanted to keep me like some personal pet—or worse. I wanna put a bullet in his head."

Everyone's silence implied assent, regardless of whether they had any reservations. Alienating someone who already felt isolated seemed like an even worse idea than letting her come with them—and it didn't seem fair to give Louis a chance and not Eva.

"If it's him, the five of you know what Fernando has become. This 'King' he's made himself into. You survived the situation at the fairground—you can do this again." Mayor Halloran looked at Rod. "Rod, you're our last line of defense: I can't send you in first. Follow Craig's group in the van, but stay back until they give you the go-ahead."

Craig's eyes lit up. "Ooh, we get a car?"

Mayor Halloran gave him a tolerant smile. "Of course. You need to get there as quickly and safely as possible. Granted, you can't drive right up to the dam or you'll draw attention."

"Once I'm able to fix whatever's wrong at the dam, it won't take long for power to return," Barry said. He had a tawny complexion, a wispy combover, and a bushy black mustache. Somehow, he looked older than Rod even though he was likely younger. "We need to get information from you, first of all: if there are people or Stalkers inside, how many of our people you see, and what knocked the power out."

"How are we supposed to know?" Rod asked. "I got some training, but I'm handier with guns and explosives than tech stuff. What do we need to look for, Barry?"

"It's doubtful anything happened to the reservoir unless someone blocked the intake or messed with the turbine. But that would take a lot of effort," Barry said. "The problem is probably inside the powerhouse, maybe one of the generators or the conduits along the spillway gates. Maybe even the power lines. My guess is someone cut the power to the generators."

"Must've been a distraction," Rod said. "Means someone took their security out."

"Try not to engage if you can help it," Mayor Halloran said. "Leave that to Rod and his men." She unlocked a drawer in her desk and withdrew two sets of keys. She dropped one into Rod's hand and the other into Craig's. "The van is fully gassed, Rod. Craig, you get the—"

"Tesla! Sweet!" Craig curled his hand around the keys, grinning. "Hope that puppy's all charged up."

Mayor Halloran quirked an eyebrow. "Yes, it's charged. You can make it about three hundred miles on a full charge, so you should have more than enough power to get there and back. Please be careful with it: it's my personal vehicle."

Craig pressed his hand to his forehead in a salute. "Aye, aye, Captain. Not a scratch on her."

"Okay." Mayor Halloran sighed. "I need to get in touch with Red and the others, check the ins and outs of the town while you're on your mission to the dam. Rod, take everyone to your trailer and outfit as many as you can. Make sure you bring a walkie and give one to Craig. If you have spares, give their group two in case they need to split up and check the dam from different angles."

Mayor Halloran stood and went to shake everyone's hand. She had a firm, two-handed handshake and maintained eye contact with a reserved smile. A politician through and through.

Everyone aside from the mayor and her guards stepped into the hall. They exchanged weary looks until a collective sigh seemed to escape them.

This is it. The end of the dream.

Felicia and Barry broke off from the group once they left City Hall, but Craig and the others followed Rod to his trailer. He unlocked the shed and allowed everyone to reclaim their weapons and ammo, loaning them as much tactical gear as he could. For Billie and Craig, this was probably just another pair of roles, another scene to act out.

Once they were all decked out, Rod handed them two walkies and told them to go on ahead to the Tesla. He revealed the location—the mayor's house to the southeast—and shook hands with them, wishing them luck and assuring them they'd keep in touch.

The once lively Diamond City was a ghost town. Everyone stayed home, afraid of the unknown. The roads were empty. Aside from the occasional bird flitting overhead or a squirrel scampering nearby, all was still and silent. Lifeless. It reminded Brian of the world outside—a world he'd hoped to leave behind forever.

I said it myself—eternity is a fallacy.

When they arrived at the mayor's house, two little faces peered out at them through the windows. Craig clicked the button for the garage, revealing a silver Tesla in pristine condition. Billie and Craig waved at the kids, but they recoiled behind the curtains, frightened by the sight of people in tactical gear wielding guns. Brian didn't know who or where their father was; he'd never heard anything about him. He'd seen Rod give Mayor Halloran a few less-than-professional once-overs, but he was kind of a perv to begin with.

"Shotgun!" Billie called, lifting her free hand. With the other, she cradled her tommy gun to her chest. She and Craig jogged up to the front doors of the car and piled in like a couple of eager teens about to go on a joyride.

Eva slipped in behind Billie while Louis opened the door behind Craig. Brian climbed into the cramped backseat before Louis, buffering the feuding twins once more. They were like grenades with pins waiting to be pulled.

Craig pressed a button, making the car hum with a low buzz. Music blared out of the speakers: "*You belong with meeeee—*"

"Ugh! Turn it off!" Louis winced and covered his ears.

Billie craned her head to study the backseat passengers while Craig skipped the track. "Guess you're more of a Beyoncé fan, huh? Makes sense: 'Crazy in Love' is practically your theme song."

"Why the fuck would I listen to Beyoncé?" Louis muttered, his head flopping back onto the leather seat cushion. "That's more D's thing."

Brian studied Eva for a reaction, but she stared through her window like she hadn't even been listening. The car reversed with a slick, nearly undetectable motion. Billie aimed the garage key at the door and lowered it to keep the mayor's home and family protected.

The faint chemical scent of new car lingered. Brian inhaled, briefly transported to a time when his family's old truck had been new—that same truck where he'd waited for his father to return with news of Becky's fate. To him, vehicles were a death trap.

Craig coasted through town until they passed through the gate. Once the fence shrank into a faint glint in the rearview, he accelerated to a speed that pressed the backs of their heads to the seats. Brian leaned forward, straining to read the dashboard meters.

Ninety? Christ!

"Can you control this thing going this fast?" he asked. "What if something runs out in front of us?"

"Then it's gonna get hit." Craig whipped around a stationary car, barely turning the wheel. "We gotta go fast. People's lives could be at stake."

"Yes, but—" Brian stuttered as Craig shifted the car, maneuvering to bypass a pile of cars in the right lane. They rumbled over the grass, the wheels squeaking when they hit asphalt again. "*Our* lives'll be at stake if you wreck this thing! Not a scratch on her, my ass!"

Craig's lips quirked into a grin, but he kept his eyes on the road. Aside from a few cars pulled over onto the side, a clear stretch lay ahead of them.

Eva and Louis remained unusually silent. Probably because they were crammed together in a car when they'd barely been in the same room since they reunited. Eva kept one hand on her rifle and cradled her chin with the other, staring through the window at the line of blurry trees. Louis's eyes were shut, and his chest swelled with deep, slow breaths like he was meditating. He kept one hand wedged between his thigh and Brian's, the tip of his thumb stroking Brian's jeans.

The featherlight motion eased the regret and anxiety pumping through Brian. He took in a deep breath and glanced past Louis, watching the trees drift by like Eva. He couldn't get a read on her mood or motivations.

He conjured an image of a bloodied black rabbit on a weathered porch. The slight body sitting next to him didn't seem capable of such violence. But her dimpled smile no longer reached her eyes; a void now lurked behind them.

The ride to the dam was longer than Brian expected. He glanced at the screen, looking for a GPS route—but all the satellite information was down. *Duh.* Craig was navigating old-school, using a folded map Billie had spread in her hands.

"How much longer?" Brian asked her.

She looked at him, her eyebrows lifting slightly. "Another half hour. Tired of your backseat buddies already, or do you need a bathroom break?"

Brian gave her an irritated look and retreated into the backseat. Before long, the mayor's monotonous mix CD and the chartreuse streak of trees coaxed his eyelids to fall. He drifted into the transition where bits of his surroundings blurred with his imagination, the confusion of reality blending with dreams.

Gentle Giant

Chapter Thirteen

Curtain Fall

4/30, Middle of nowhere, Arkansas

The click of a seat belt and a slamming door woke Brian. He withdrew his head from a warm, rigid object: the shoulder he'd leaned on both metaphorically and literally.

Louis offered him a light smile as he reached to undo his seat belt. *"Beaux rêves?"*

"Non." Brian rubbed his eyes, trying his best to stretch in the confines of the car. Eva exited without a word, lugging her gear with her. Billie and Craig were already standing outside.

Brian stepped into the open air. The weather was pleasant: sunny and warm with a brisk breeze. The Tesla sat neatly in a space at a park with amenities like restrooms and covered areas for grilling. Statuesque trees shaded several picnic benches with verdant branches. Craig spoke into the walkie with Rod while the others arranged their equipment.

Craig attached his walkie to his belt and handed the other to Brian. "Rod's about fifteen minutes out. He says to go ahead; he's going to park somewhere else so we aren't all lumped together in one convenient spot. We'll radio him once we've scouted the location."

"Where *is* it?" Brian slid the uncomfortable goggles over his eyes. Light body armor protected him—knee, shoulder, and chest pads—but it was nowhere near as extensive as Antoine's riot gear.

"West," Craig answered. "There's a road that takes you straight in, but we'll want to stick to cover. Try the trees. Barry made us a map." He snapped his fingers at Billie, signaling for her to retrieve the map.

Billie withdrew it from her backpack with a little glare. She unfolded the piece of white letter paper, which had a crude map sketched on it in chemical-scented Sharpie. Brian and the twins leaned in to examine it, crowding around Billie's shoulders.

The park was east of the main road leading into the dam. A thicket of trees filled the area slightly northwest of their location and directly south of the powerhouse. Admin sat east of the powerhouse, and a river cut across the dam north of both buildings.

"The generators are in the powerhouse." Craig pointed the area out on Barry's chicken-scratch map. "Everyone's probably hiding here in admin. First things first, we'll head for the thicket south of the powerhouse, avoid the roads. But we need to scope them out along the way, see if they're blocked by someone or something that might give Rod a problem."

"Should we stay together or split up?" Eva asked. She kept her rifle in front of her while she took in her surroundings.

"Well, it's never good to keep all your eggs in one basket..." Craig glanced at Billie. She nodded, her lips pressed into a slight grimace. "We'll check out the powerhouse. You scope the roads. We'll meet near admin. Radio if you don't hear from us or you get into trouble, okay?"

Brian nodded and stuck out his hand. "Good luck."

Craig shook it, a lopsided grin flattering his ruggedly handsome face. Billie wrapped Brian in a tight hug once Craig let go of him. "Whether this is that prick's handiwork or not, he needs to pay for what he's done. We all owe our dues." She pressed a kiss to his cheek and withdrew. "Be careful, sweetie."

Brian watched the duo disappear into the thicket of trees to the west. *I hope this isn't the last time I see you.*

"Let's head south." He sighed as he turned back toward the twins. It threw him to see them geared up together outside the city again. He'd stepped into a memory within a sideways world where Eva was the loose cannon, not Louis, and Louis submitted to Brian instead of trying to boss him around.

Have they changed that much? Have I?

The twins shadowed him through the park until they reached the rim of the road. Louis crawled atop an embankment and peered through his rifle to get a vantage point of the road leading into the dam. A serene field of shaded grass and vibrant flowers surrounded Brian, yet a sense of unease trickled through him, making his skin prickle like an Arctic wind had blown past it.

Brian turned away from the rocky ridge to ask Eva if she noticed anything—but she'd vanished. His hands tightened around his rifle, and he pressed his back against the wall.

"*Louis,*" he hissed through his teeth, hoping Louis could hear him.

A silver light flashed from the woods beyond him, followed by an earsplitting explosion. Brian held his breath and lifted the rifle scope to his eye. Enclosed by a field of darkness and overlapped by the red line of his reticle, Eva reloaded her rifle and kept the smoking barrel aimed in Brian's direction.

She shot him.

Brian fired out of instinct, maybe anger. Eva flinched and dashed through the grove of lush trees. He wanted to chase after her, but he couldn't abandon Louis.

He slung the rifle over his shoulder and scrambled up the mound of rocks. Shaky breaths trembled through his dry lips when he glimpsed blood-matted hair on the back of Louis's head.

Fuck fuck fuck, *he's not moving—*

Brian sank to his knees and pressed his fingers to Louis's neck, trying to detect a pulse over his own rapid heartbeat. Several agonizing seconds passed before he registered a weak but steady throb. He exhaled and swept the bloody fringe of Louis's hair up from where the shorter hairs tapered into his neck: a red-and-white horizontal gash striped the lower third of his scalp. It went fairly deep, like half of the bullet had skidded through the skin just over his skull. But it was superficial. She'd either hesitated, calculated her shot incorrectly, or Louis had turned his head at the last second.

Nausea swirled in Brian's stomach. *Eva ruined our cover. Whatever's out here will be on high alert now—Christ, I hope Bill and Craig are okay.*

He brought the walkie to his mouth with a shaky hand. "Craig. You there? Over."

No answer.

Brian stripped his backpack off and rummaged for the first-aid kit. He poured iodine into Louis's wound and then worked on a quick stitch. *She planned to shoot him. It wasn't some impulse, an opportunity she took. Once she knew he was going, she volunteered, asked to split up, get Bill and Craig out of the way.*

Was she about to shoot me too?

The image of the bloodied rabbit flashed through Brian's mind.

He snipped the thread and knotted it before taping gauze to the back of Louis's head. Brian dropped the roll of medical tape into his kit and withdrew the walkie, switching channels to call Rod.

"Rod, I can't get a hold of Craig and Bill. I'm gonna go after them. But Eva shot Louis and ran off—I need you to get over here, make sure she doesn't come back for him. He's up on the ridge south of the park and east of the dam, just next to the road. I took care of the wound already. Over and out."

He swapped between watching Louis and scanning his surroundings for movement while he awaited Rod's reply.

"I was about to call you when I heard those shots, but I didn't want to set your walkie off in case you were in a precarious situation. I never woulda guessed it was *Eva*. Now it makes sense why she was so gung-ho to go. I can be at your location within five minutes—just hold out until we get there. Over and out."

Brian smoothed a lank strand of hair out of Louis's eyes, paying attention to the depth and frequency of his breaths. *Steady and slow. He'll be out for a while.*

Those five minutes felt like five *hours*. Brian needed to find Billie and Craig. But even if they'd lost the element of surprise, a pair of gunshots didn't betray the fact they'd sent an entire squad of people out, or even that they'd sent *one* out—for all anyone or anything knew, it was just a straggler shooting a Stalker or an animal.

This was why he resolved to finish the job on his own. Plus, it was personal. Billie and Craig were his friends, and the King was their shared enemy.

While Rod's subordinates checked Louis over, Brian relayed his intent to Rod. Rod was hesitant to let Brian go alone, but he recognized and respected his determination.

"We'll take him back to the van, keep a couple of people with him in case she follows. It's too risky to split up and waste time trackin' her down—if she tries to come back to the city, she ain't gettin' in. But she might come after you. Can you handle her on your own? I can send someone with you, or you can go wait with him in the van—"

"I'm sick of waiting while other people do the dirty work." Brian thought of the winter evening he would never forget, of the cruel cheer of the Christmas song, of his breath fogging in the truck while he watched his father disappear. He grabbed Rod's arm. "You're the last line of defense, remember? Even if someone heard those gunshots, they don't know who fired or why. Let's keep it that way, not send everyone into a trap. Let me go in alone." He squeezed. "Don't let anything happen to him—give me your word."

Rod clapped his hand over Brian's. "You got it. I know how hard it is to leave behind a brother-in-arms."

He's so much more. And it's harder than you could ever know. But Brian let go, cast one last look at Louis while a pair of men lifted his lank form, and then ran for the cover of the embankment and didn't look back.

The road leading to the dam appeared suspiciously clear, a drab stretch of asphalt surrounded by foliage struggling to return to life. Nothing stirred within the trees, no Stalkers or hostiles ready to ambush whoever might brazenly stroll along the road. A rudimentary gate remained closed at the edge of the bridge parallel to the dam; the only ways around it were to brave the rushing river or to slide down a steep ridge from the thicket. But a simple fence surrounded the powerhouse, easily breached with the right tools.

They had guards here. If they're dead, where are the bodies?

Brian stayed low and scurried across the road toward the grove Billie and Craig had entered. It remained picture-perfect aside from a few twigs shattered by the weight of someone's feet settling onto them.

Brian followed the trail of broken sticks and drag marks left in the wet dirt. It led him to the edge of the fence, which had a neat hole in it—possibly from a set of bolt cutters. It transported him back to that freezing cold night, to his sense of shock when he'd thought they'd lost Eva, to the sense of urgency Louis had instilled in him to keep moving.

Taking care to avoid snagging his clothing on the sheared metal links, Brian squeezed through the gap in the fence. He glimpsed a van parked behind the building north of the powerhouse. He assumed it transported the dam's guards to and from Diamond City, but it wasn't going anywhere any time soon: all four tires were flattened to the ground.

Would a Stalker have thought to do that? He didn't know what to expect from them anymore. What they were capable of, what they *were*.

Water rushed from the dam, creating a soothing hum which enveloped the area. A light spray misted and moistened the air against the scant areas of his exposed skin.

Maybe they didn't *hear us shooting. Maybe Craig couldn't even hear me calling over this.*

Brian debated between going to the powerhouse or admin building first. He settled on admin since the people inside might be able to tell him what was interfering with the power. He knew jack-all about how dams worked and would waste too much time staring at things he didn't understand.

He scurried past the powerhouse and pressed himself to the side of the useless van. The entrance to the administrative building was directly east of the parking lot, so close he could see what remained of the door: someone had shattered it into dozens of glittering slivers.

I don't see another way in. But the door's a landmine: I'm gonna have to break all those jagged pieces or they'll slice me up.

Brian dashed to the door, avoiding the glass on the ground, and tried the handle. Locked. He turned his rifle and tapped out the jutting shards, trying to minimize what noise he made. They drifted to the ground in elegant shimmers like snowflakes.

He slunk through the busted door. Most of the building remained saturated with shadows except for the few diffused rays cast through several office windows. But it wasn't enough.

Brian swapped to the night-vision scope and peered through it, suspecting if a Stalker had heard him break the last of the glass, it would've already come at him. As he thought, the hallway was empty.

If I block the door, I might block my only way out, and Rod and his people wouldn't be able to get to me. Guess I'll leave it.

After double-checking his walkie to make sure the volume was turned down, Brian plunged into the depths of the building, staying low and staring through the rifle scope. Several doors branched off on either side of the hall. A startling collection of smudges and puddles stained the dull gray carpet as if a group of people had been assembled and dispatched. Whether by gunshots or Stalkers, Brian couldn't tell. He didn't see any bodies.

He took the methodical approach and went from door to door, starting with the first parallel pair. The left one hung open, displaying a cramped office with a desk and a chair lying on its side. A resplendent plant sat on the windowsill alongside a framed poster offering futile inspiration.

There's light from the window. I need to swap to my bow; the rifle won't be great in close quarters. I'm not fucking Louis with his miraculous reflexes and aim.

Brian swept around to the back of the desk, bowstring taut—nothing.

He scurried across the hall to the opposite door. A red smudge on the doorknob sent a wary jolt through him. When he opened it, a gun barrel glinted in the rays of sunlight shining through the window. A frazzled face loomed behind it, blood smudging their cheek.

"I'm here to help," Brian whispered, although he kept his arrow strung and taut. "I'm from Diamond City. Maybe you remember me from the weekly meetings—"

"Yeah. You're the kid with the crazy friend." The bloody man lowered the gun, giving up the fight much earlier than Brian expected. "Gun's empty anyway. There's only one way you can save me." The man brought a finger to his forehead. "Hit here. One of 'em got me on the arm. I know it takes a couple of weeks, but I don't want to be there when my family finds out or have that bitch doctor experiment on me."

Brian crept inside and closed the door behind him. "I'll take care of it. But first, tell me what happened. If there are other survivors here, I need to help them. And I need to know what went wrong with the power so Barry can fix it."

"The turbines are still running, so I think they took out the generators. I never made it out to look. All I know is everything went dark all at once. Then I heard something shatter. Probably the door. A group of people shoved those shit guards inside. Some tall guy whistled, and a bunch of Stalkers came running in like a pack of dogs. Tore the guards to shreds. Most of us locked ourselves in our offices, blockaded the doors with desks, and waited. While the Stalkers were busy, the other guys busted the doors and shot us—they got me in the kneecaps so I couldn't walk. I think the sickos did it on purpose, left us alive for the Stalkers to play with. The bastards left, but the freaks didn't. Those fuckers must've smelled the blood, came into the offices. I wouldn't go looking through the rest if I was you."

"Where'd you get the gun?"

The man's lips curved into a bitter smile. "You wanna know what's really fucked up? When they smashed in the doors and shot us up, they tossed 'em to us. But mine only had one bullet in it. Guess it was supposed to be the fool's dilemma: use the bullet on yourself or one Stalker of many. I wasted mine on the fucker who threw me the gun, didn't think ahead. So when a Stalker broke into my office, I had to bash its head in with a paperweight. It got a hold of my arm, dug into it with those nasty nails—and that's all she wrote."

Brian scanned the room, spotted the blood splatter and gore where the man had smashed the Stalker's head in, but not the Stalker itself. "Where's the body?"

"I dragged it outside when things went quiet. Guess if you didn't see it out there, they got to it. They're like fucking vultures." The man spat to the side. "Disgusting. That's why I can't be one of them. I told you all I know; now do it."

Brian stood and angled an arrow at the man's forehead. "One more thing: did you see a man and a woman at any point? Dressed like me, in camo gear?"

"Can't say I did. But I heard gunfire out in the lobby not too long ago. It's a good bet whoever it was headed to the monitor room in the back of the building—if they survived." The man exhaled, strands of greasy black hair flopping over his tanned, creased forehead. "Put it here, kid. End it before it starts."

"Tell me your name." Brian pulled back the bowstring, which he'd let slacken slightly as the man spoke. "If I make it out of here, I'll let your family know what happened."

"Vinny Costas. I live in the house with the red door on Sherwood. My wife's Maria, and I got two kids, Dot and Benny. Tell 'em I love 'em. Tell 'em I'm sorry. And tell that asshole Barry to stay away from my wife."

"Got it." The arrow sailed into Vinny's forehead with a *crack*. Blood trickled down as the light dimmed in his eyes. Brian moved on.

He continued from office to office past evidence supporting Vinny's version of events. In most cases, he considered himself lucky the light was dim. A few Stalker corpses mingled with the remnants of the dam's employees. Shells and casings gleamed in the scope. A fallen walkie revealed why Craig hadn't answered Brian. He pressed on, more determined than ever to find them.

Shadows obscured the rear of the building, but a sporadic thumping persisted in sync with an underlying chortle. Brian swapped the bow for the rifle and brought the scope to his eye: at least a dozen white bodies were huddled in front of the door to the monitor room. Some were beating on the door. Others twisted the knob.

They're waiting them out.

His options were limited. The walkway offered no vantage points, no furniture to climb. Moving anything out from the offices would make too much noise.

He crept into one of the offices close by. After shutting the door and dragging the desk in front of it, he crawled on top and angled the rifle butt at the window next to the door. He bashed it out and quickly swiveled the scope back to his eye. The crowd of Stalkers seemed to turn at once, dozens of glittering eyes now focused on him. They froze, attempting to assess the situation.

Predator or prey?

Brian blew out the back of the closest one's head. The rifle was a semiauto, so he aimed and fired again. Again, again. The Stalkers scattered, torn between running for their prey and away from the predator slaughtering their kin. Brian took them out until the trigger clicked.

Shit.

By his count, only one or two remained. He slid down from the desk and put his back to a wall, keeping an eye on the broken window. He fumbled for the flashlight strapped to his side, turned it on, and scrambled to swap the rifle for his revolver.

A head popped up in the window. Fingers curled around the shattered glass, ignorant or indifferent to pain. Curious eyes stared back at Brian, choked laughter slipping through the stretched smile. It forced moist hisses through its teeth.

"Wha... Ooo..."

It's talking. Why? What is it trying to say?

Brian aimed his gun as the fetid creature slithered through the window—but another explosion erupted. The figure hunched over the window, front half dangling inside the office. Blood and gore seeped out of an entrance wound too large to be caused by anything except a shotgun.

Another face appeared in the window. "Nice going, kid—you got the rest of 'em."

Brian's heart fluttered. He lowered the handgun and moved the desk away from the door, avoiding the Stalker's corpse. He reached for Craig's arm, but Craig backed away. Billie wasn't alongside him.

"What happened to you guys?" The flutter in Brian's chest tightened.

"We got in here, managed to find a few stragglers—but these fuckers all came outta the woodwork and chased us. I don't know what the hell triggered them. The employees directed us here, so we ran for it, mowed a few Stalkers down, and blocked ourselves in."

Eva triggered them.

Brian exhaled and swept his sticky bangs out of his forehead. "You scared the shit outta me. I thought you were goners."

Craig offered him a halfhearted smile and gripped his shoulder. "Well, it's not all for naught. We have some survivors in there. And since you went all Rambo on those Stalkers, we can get them outta here. Radio for Rod."

"No sign of the King or his men? Are we sure it was even them?"

Craig nodded as he led Brian into the monitor room. "From what the survivors told me, he didn't ditch the masks. Guess he can't bear for anyone to see how hideous his mug is—that, or he thinks it's some kinda fucking trademark now. But that shit is played out, don't you think?"

They entered the spacious room. A group of disheveled, frightened people huddled in front of two pairs of curved desks and large LCD monitors mounted to the walls. Brian glimpsed Billie among them, her arms curled around her knees. She looked up when they entered, managing a smile as feeble as Craig's had been.

Brian lifted his walkie to his mouth as Craig shut the door. "Rod, I found Bill and Craig, and I have eight additional survivors. I haven't made it to the powerhouse yet, but one of them said it's probably the generators. It's all clear, though—no hostiles left. Over."

The walkie crackled to life with Rod's heavily accented voice. "No hostiles *left*? You take care of 'em? Over."

"Yeah. My hand was forced. I'm fine, though—no injuries." He exhaled. "How's Louis? Over."

"Still out. Not sure if the force of the shot bounced his brain around, gave him a concussion. But his breathing is fine. How about the folks with you? Any injuries? Over."

Billie and Craig shared a glance. It stirred Brian's already mounting concerns. Craig walked over to Brian and took the walkie from him. "Hey, Rod, it's Craig. Just about everyone in here has some kinda battle scar. Mostly their knees. A few in the arms. Far as I can tell, they're all bullet wounds or scrapes, but you'll need to send them all to Felicia, and I'd handle them with kid gloves. Over and out."

"Good to hear your voice, Craig. You and Bill better go keep an eye on things outside. Tell Brian to stay in there with the others. See you in about five to ten. Over and out."

Billie rose and joined Craig, overhearing Rod's request. Craig handed Brian's walkie back to him, but Billie gave him a strange look as she passed him: forlorn and weary. Defeated.

The couple exited in silence. Brian watched their silhouettes disappear into the shadows, though the lone beam of a flashlight lit the path ahead of them. He shut the door and pressed his back against it.

"We had to leave them," a heavyset woman wearing glasses said. She clutched her bloody left arm with her right hand. "They were going to die anyway, and we needed something to distract the Stalkers." She sniffled. "We're horrible people..."

The dream's over for everyone.

Brian didn't reply. Someone kept spinning in an office chair. The creak of a ball bearing was the only sound within the room until a knock on the door vibrated into his head.

He spun, hands tightening around the rifle. "Who is it?"

"Rod Miller, at your service."

Brian opened the door. Rod's brigade swarmed into the room so they could offer aid to the wounded. Brian escaped into the hall and broke into a jog, in desperate need of fresh air.

Once outside, he inhaled until he was forced to exhale. Billie and Craig sat on the hood of the van. They'd stripped off all their protective gear and looked remarkably small and plain in T-shirts and jeans. Craig's hand clung to Billie's knee, fingers digging into the fabric of her pants.

Brian approached them. "There's something you're not telling me. What is it?"

Craig curled an arm around Billie's shoulders. "You know why we wanted to be actors, Brian? Because people remember them. Even when they die, they live on screen forever—even outside of it, sometimes." He scoffed. "You know Marilyn Monroe had a Twitter account? Crazy isn't it, how someone who's been dead for over fifty years can shill makeup? That's the lamest form of immortality I could ever dream of."

"Why the hell are you talking about Twitter and Marilyn Monroe?" Brian narrowed his eyes. "No one gives a shit about any of that stupid social media crap anymore."

"No. But people remember it. People remember *her.*" Billie lifted her head from Craig's shoulder and sniffed. "When you die, all your memories rot with your brain—everything that ever made you who you were disappears as if you never even existed to begin with. You don't remember anything; it's all forgotten. So what's the point if no one remembers *you?*"

Brian swallowed, his pulse a steady throb in his ears. "I don't think anyone who's ever met you could forget you, Bill. I never would."

Billie's lips twitched into a drawn smile. "That's sweet of you, Brian—exactly what I'd expect you to say." She lifted her leg, rolled up the cuff of her jeans, and dragged a finger along a slight red mark above her sock. "One cut my leg when we were running. Pulled my boot off, got me to the floor. Craig took it out, but it was too late. One slice of the nail—that's all it takes. It's in me now." Her eyebrows and lips started quivering. "But I don't want to play this role, Brian." She shook her head and burst into tears, covering her face with both hands.

Brian's head lightened. He stumbled back, on the verge of fainting.

It barely registered for him when Rod approached. He could've been standing there for a minute or an hour. "You tell him?"

Craig nodded. Billie kept wailing.

Rod frowned, sighed. "You sure you don't wanna come back, let Felicia look at it?"

Craig shook his head. "She won't dredge up a cure in two weeks. And Bill would rather go out on her own terms, not be a lab rat or a monster."

"What about you?" Rod asked.

Craig tipped his head against Billie's as her cries turned into frantic gasps for air. "I can't leave her."

Heavy breaths puffed out of Brian's nose while he clutched his queasy stomach.

Rod saluted the pair and walked away without a word, but Brian's feet remained rooted to the ground.

"What happened to Louis and Eva?" The torrent of a waterfall nearly overwhelmed Craig's cracking voice. "I overheard what you said to Rod on the walkie…"

"She shot him." Although it had only happened an hour ago, it felt like another lifetime. Brian wasn't even sure he was awake right now. "I shot her back, but she ran away. I don't know if either of them will be okay."

Craig's brilliant blue eyes shone in the late-afternoon sun. Billie buried her face in his chest, her shoulders shaking with silent sobs. "I know this is all hard on you, kid, but don't go numb to dull the pain. Part of me regrets that I pretended to be different people for half my life; it was *my* way of dulling it. Long story short, I was given up for adoption and passed from house to house—I never really found a home until I met Bill. She made me feel wanted, *loved*, for the first time. It didn't take long for me to realize I couldn't go back to a life without her in it."

Billie withdrew from Craig's chest and rubbed her face. When she let her hands fall to her lap, her red, raw face shocked Brian. Her bleary eyes found his while Craig wiped the mess from her face. "We can't pretend anymore, Brian. This is the end of the line for us." She dragged an arm across her face and forced a defiant expression. "I want to go out with a bang, not a whimper. I want to have a memorable death, to share it with the man I love, for us to hold hands and stare into each other's eyes until it hits us all at once—but I don't want to know when it's coming. I want my last thought to be that I loved and was loved, and that I'm not alone and never will be." Tears started streaming down her cheeks again. "I *know* you understand, Brian. If our situations were reversed, you'd ask the same of me—and Louis would sit in the seat right next to you."

Brian flexed his fingers, trying to return the feeling to them. "*What* seat? What are you even asking me?"

Billie slid down from the van and snatched her Chicago Typewriter from the ground. She thrust it into Brian's chest until he grabbed it and then gestured to the van. "We're going to sit in there, enjoy this lovely view together, and wait for you to climb onto the rooftop. Once you're up there, just—just unload that thing. We'll go full method, die as we lived."

Brian stared at the instrument of death clutched in his hands, trying to picture himself doing as she asked. He shook his head and looked back at her, wanting to tell her she was crazy. He'd never be able to do it, and if he did, he'd wish he hadn't—but her expression had shifted into one of such desperation he couldn't find it in himself to deny her.

"If it's really what you want, I'll try..." He looked at Craig, who hadn't been injured or infected like his partner. "Are you sure about this, Craig?"

Craig exhaled. Tears rolled down his ruddy cheeks even though he smiled. "I'm fucking terrified, kid—but I'd rather go wherever the hell she's going than go anywhere without her." He smiled at Billie and smoothed her frazzled hair. "Love defies explanation. Who we love, why we love them the way we do. Your identities get twisted like strands of DNA. Without her, I don't exist. If she died and I survived, I'd practically be a zombie anyway—alive but not living, if that makes sense."

He hopped down from the van and pulled Brian into a tight hug, cramming the gun which would be his undoing between them. "I know we gave you a lot of shit about Louis, but part of the reason I couldn't stand him was he reminded me too much of myself. The false bravado, the insecurity, the desperate need to be with the person we live for. And don't kid yourself: you're just like Bill. Drama reminds you you're really *alive*, not just sleepwalking through existence." Craig backed away and smoothed Brian's bangs out of his eyes. "I know this can't be easy for you, but it's the best parting gift you could give us. The gun makes a lot of noise, but so does this damn waterfall. Put us down, toss it, and get the hell out of here." He rummaged through his pocket and dropped the key into Brian's hand. "Here's the key to the Tesla. Don't push it to ninety like I did."

Billie blew Brian a kiss and gave him a shaky smile. She climbed into the van as if she was going on a trip somewhere, not to await her imminent death. "Please tell my sister and niece that I love them. Live long and love well, my sweet—we'll see you in another life."

Craig retreated inside the van and turned it on. Brian didn't dwell on the logic of where he got the key from; the entire situation remained too surreal for him to question. He almost thought he was still asleep inside the Tesla, trapped between Eva and Louis while Taylor Swift crooned over the speakers.

Instead, delicate harp strings swelled into an apex of brass instruments nearly smothered by the waterfall beside them. Craig leaned his head out of the open door and smiled, his cheeks shining with tears. "'Waltz of the Flowers' by Tchaikovsky. There's a sort of mournful beauty to it, isn't there? The perfect accompaniment."

Craig sank into the seat. When the door slammed shut, Billie faced him and smiled. The orchestral instrumentation blended with the backdrop of rushing water while Brian climbed the ladder of the admin building. He flattened himself against the rooftop and aimed the gun at the windshield, finger twitching against the trigger.

He screwed his eyes shut and pulled. A barrage of bullets shattered the glass, orchestrating a violent symphony in time with the waltzing flowers. He released a primal yell as he tried not to picture their bullet-peppered bodies bouncing inside the van, splattering blood onto what remained of the glass.

Click. He clung to the empty gun and opened his eyes. His ears rang so much he could no longer hear the music or water. His throat was raw. The smoke-filled air made him cough into his arm, and the residual vibration of firing the gun lingered in his muscles. The clearing miasma revealed the gruesome image of Billie's gore-spattered head drooping against Craig's shoulder. His mutilated face was pressed against the shattered driver's side window, blue eyes wide open but seeing nothing. Brian tossed the machine gun to the ground, sick to his stomach.

A dark shape popped over the edge of the rooftop. Brian withdrew his revolver and aimed it, unable to decipher the object obscured by his hazy vision. Something rose above the buzzing in his ears—a voice saying something he couldn't make out. The figure closed in on him until the blurred outline sharpened. Brian dropped his revolver and slipped from the tightrope.

"They asked me to, Lou—but I didn't want to do it. Oh, God, I didn't *want* to!" He flung his arms around Louis's neck and buried his face in his shoulder, screaming, crying, trying to bury the image of Billie and Craig's bullet-riddled bodies. The stirring waltz and gushing waterfall couldn't drown out his gasping sobs, wouldn't silence the persisting ringing in his ears, didn't ease the lingering *ratta ratta* of gunfire in his trembling body.

Louis held him tight and stroked his hair until the sweeping strings built to a brash and abrupt end.

Chapter Fourteen

Playing with Fire

4/30, Middle of nowhere, Arkansas

A car, again. The patter of raindrops on a metal roof. Blurred scenery through the window. The scent of aftershave, of vanilla. Of a smoky musk. Night drive loneliness.

The Tesla hummed on. Louis drove. He'd turned the music on. *Can't you see? You belong with me.*

It seemed like a lifetime ago, but it had been only hours since Billie had sat in this seat. Since Craig had pushed the car to ninety and whipped around the wreckage. Brian rewound his memories like a distorted videotape.

A hand reached to stroke his hair, squeeze his shoulder, his knee. That husky accent, coarse, somehow eloquent, asked if he was okay.

"I'm not here," Brian answered. He rewound to his grandfather's death, Rocky, Nana, his father, sister, mother. Back to the locker room floor of the Topeka mall. Foaming mouth, outstretched hand, empty bottle. The beginning of the end.

The cabin at Diamond City. Songs about doomed love. Scars beneath his lips. The taste of cranberry. D's laughter, Antoine's smile, Cecilia's angelic face. Grimes nickering, Jonesy trilling. Marie, Jacque, the flock of white-robed shepherds. A passionate kiss against a wall, a storm dying into a soothing drizzle. Connection, uncertainty, anxiety, animosity. Fond but murky memories. Eva and Louis, laughing, playing, a Nerf gun and a fateful cut. Rewind, rewind, stop.

The tape whirred to life. "Where's Eva?"

Louis stared ahead, focused on the road. "I don't know. I woke up with a splitting headache in a van surrounded by strangers who told me I'd been shot by my sister. Next thing I knew, I heard a bunch of gunfire, sounded like that tommy gun, so I ran toward it and saw you on top of a roof. I won't say what else I saw—but you know."

The car might as well have been a bubble drifting underwater. Everything was murky and muted. *Dull.*

Lifeless eyes and bodies filled with dark holes flashed through Brian's mind. "They talked me into doing it. They said I understood, that if our situations were reversed, they'd do the same for me and you'd be in the seat right next to me."

"Yeah, well, here I am." Dual headlights lit the road ahead of them with surreal perpetuity. Dark shapes surrounded them beneath a murky gray sky. Raindrops rolled down the windows. "I thought about drivin' this car until the juice ran out, about takin' you as far away from here as I could. But I realized it would just be the island all over again. The best thing I can do is bring you back to your friends."

Brian rubbed his heavy eyes and focused on Louis. His eyes darted to the rearview mirrors on occasion, and he clutched the steering wheel so tight his knuckles were white. When he caught Brian studying him, an anxious little laugh slipped out. "I always hated drivin'. Now you know another one of my weaknesses."

The bubble finally popped for Brian. "You're worried about them, aren't you?"

"I don't want you to lose anyone else."

Brian didn't reply. He raised the volume of the radio instead, letting the music fill the void. He placed his hand on Louis's thigh and left it there while the night streaked by.

True to Louis's word, their headlights soon bathed the gate to Diamond City. Louis rolled the window down when one of the armored guards jogged over to them. Several guns were trained on them.

"Mayor Halloran said to expect you." The guard looked around, searching for things Brian couldn't see. "You'd better hurry in. She said you should head for the basement in City Hall—she's got most of the town gathered there. Felicia's checking people out, and she'll need to check you for wounds too."

"Let us the fuck through, then." Louis shifted gears before the guard could reply. The gate whirred open at the guard's signal just in time for Louis to accelerate through it. He whipped into an empty parking lot near City Hall and shut the car off. He stepped outside along with Brian. The ground felt foreign beneath Brian's feet, like it might give way beneath him and crumble into an abyss.

The familiar sight of the Men in Black posted outside City Hall gave Brian minuscule relief. When they approached, one withdrew an ID card from his jacket pocket and jerked his head. "Mister Jameson, Mister Lavellé: please follow me." He led them into City Hall, through the lobby, and down the stairs in the rear of the building. When he slid his ID card through a reader beside a locked door, it beeped and displayed a green light.

They descended into the basement. The bulk of the town's populace were stuffed in the cramped room, not unlike the shelters Cecilia described from the pandemic: families huddled together, couples embraced, and friends held their frightened companions' hands. The stagnant air and chaotic noise made it hard to think.

"Sunshine! Louis!" D forced her way through the crowd until she reached the base of the stairs. She pulled Brian into her warm arms and squeezed, the fruity scent of her perfume overpowering the stench of mingling body odors. Brian squeezed back, hands digging into her back, clinging to her.

"What the fuck happened?" Louis asked. "Antoine and Cill okay?"

D withdrew from Brian. "'Toine's fine, thank the Good God, but some asshole with a gun plugged Cill in the arm. It was like a gotdamn Wild West shootout. A bunch of Stalkers dressed in riot gear tried to climb the fence, but most of 'em got zapped. Our people shot the rest. But they was just a distraction: a group of regular people tried to sneak in from the water. We took most of 'em out before they got into the city—the rest turned tail, ran away." D squinted as she regarded a stunned Louis. "You both look like you need a day's worth of sleep! What happened to your head—and where's Eva? Billie and Craig?"

"Tell you later. Take us to Cill and 'Toine." Louis grabbed her arm and leaned in to say something while they walked. Brian followed in silence. He wanted to find a bed, any bed, and sleep forever.

D guided them inside a storeroom packed with a makeshift medical tent and supplies. While the mayor flitted around the room speaking to people, Felicia summoned Brian and Louis for their physicals. They stripped and let her do them behind the "privacy" of a curtain, too exhausted for modesty. Both passed. She offered to fix Louis's injury, but he flatly told her he'd come back later and wanted to see Cecilia.

Cecilia tried to sit up from a gurney when they approached her, but Antoine nudged her back. He stood and gave both boys one of his crushing hugs. "Glad you two okay. Shoulda known all this was goin' too smooth. I bet D told you all 'bout what happened—think it's this King motherfucker's work?"

Brian sat on the edge of Cecilia's gurney; the presence of his friends helped wake him from his trance. "I'm positive. But I can't figure out why he's got Stalkers with him dressed in armor, or why they wouldn't attack him and his people—or why they'd act on his command."

Louis grabbed his arm, fingers digging in so deep it hurt. "That fuckin' King is infected too. Maybe they can sense it."

Brian gave Louis an incredulous look, but the gears in his head spun wildly. Maybe Louis's suggestion wasn't as crazy as he thought.

"Where's yo' sister at?" Antoine asked as he returned to his seat. "You two been through some crazy shit too—I can tell. Got that shell-shocked look on your faces."

Louis leaned back against the side of Cecilia's gurney. "Eva shot me, knocked me out cold. Brian clipped her, but she ran away. We lost her."

Cecilia lifted her groggy eyes to Louis's. "I tried to warn her. She clung to her anger, her resentment, and it ate away at her. It'll be even worse now."

Louis didn't have a response for her. The muscles in his jaw flexed as he grit his teeth.

Brian tugged at the stray threads sticking out from the knees of his jeans. "A Stalker scratched Bill. Craig wanted to stay with her. They asked me to...to take them out together."

"He wasn't scratched or nothin'?" Antoine asked.

"They were two halves of a whole," Brian murmured. "Without her, he would've been incomplete."

Ambient chatter cloaked the group's reflective silence. No matter who died or how many, life went on for everyone else.

"I'll tell the mayor what happened." Antoine smiled and curled a hand around Brian's arm and then gave Louis a pat on the back. "You boys just get some rest. If I need help, I got D."

Antoine approached the mayor while Louis leaned in and whispered something to Cecilia. He walked by Brian and grazed his side with his hand. "I'm gonna let Felicia fix me up. Not that I don't appreciate what you did, but if I got a professional at my disposal, I may as well use her."

Brian resisted the compulsion to snatch Louis by the sleeve. When he walked away, Brian buried his face in his hands to hide the trembling from Cecilia. She remained silent, waiting for him to speak.

He couldn't bring himself to say anything about Billie and Craig, or even Eva. He dragged his hands down his face and exhaled. "How are you feeling, Cill?"

Cecilia followed Brian's gaze to her arm. "Oh, this is nothing. I thought after my experiences traveling with you all, I'd improved enough not to be an impediment. I guessed wrong. If it wasn't for Antoine, they would've put another one in me. He's a born protector. Felicia's a lucky woman."

Brian spied Louis between the folds of the flimsy privacy curtain. He kept wincing while Felicia worked with his injury. He'd been hiding how much it hurt—or he'd tried to suppress the pain like he'd done his entire life.

When Brian noticed Cassandra and Bailey in the crowd, his own pain resurfaced.

Cecilia gripped his hand. "Cassandra had a panic attack when she saw one of those masks, but they're fine. The mayor will tell them about Billie and Craig. She's used to delivering bad news. I'm sorry, by the way. They seemed like nice people. And they helped us find our place here." She sighed. "It's a shame Eva couldn't. I think she expected everyone here to hate Louis, to throw him out like he was Frankenstein's monster or something. Their acceptance of him was another rejection to her."

Brian withdrew his hand from Cecilia's. "I don't know if I want to go looking for her this time—she might be lost forever."

"Don't blame yourself, Brian." Cecilia's eyelids fluttered shut. Her modest bosom swelled with the effort of a heavy breath. "Your happiness has no bearing on another's misery. You forgave him; she didn't."

Brian smoothed Cecilia's bangs out of her face to kiss her forehead. Her pale lips lifted into a slight smile as she drifted off, somehow able to tune out the pandemonium around her. Perhaps she'd been administered some of the "feelin' good stuff," as D called it.

An agonized wail pierced the chaotic veil. Brian's eyes swept to the source: Cassandra. The mayor grabbed her shaking shoulders while Bailey clung to her mother's legs, too young to fully understand the cause of her mother's misery.

Unable to bear reliving the image of Billie and Craig's bloody bodies in the van, Brian pushed through the crowd and rushed up the stairs. Someone called after him, but he didn't care. He cycled through the pain of Billie and Craig's loss, his anger toward Eva for contributing to it and nearly killing Louis, and his disappointment in himself for being unable to break through to her. Maybe he hadn't tried hard enough. Maybe he'd given up too easily. Maybe he hadn't cared enough, or maybe he'd been too focused on dealing with his complex feelings for Louis to help Eva deal with hers.

Brian emerged into the empty night-darkened streets. Wind whipped his sticky bangs away from his face as he ran, staring ahead into the Cimmerian shade. The streetlights were all out, the moon reduced to a dim crescent obscured by distant trees.

A thin line of light shone onto Brian. "Brian Jameson, that you?" Rod jogged up to intercept him, a headlamp strapped to him. "You shouldn't be out here. We still got to clean this mess up. Try to relax—you've been through hell and back today."

"I can't stay there, Rod." Brian bent over and grabbed his knees, huffing. "Billie...Craig. Eva. I can't. I can't deal with it right now."

Rod hefted something onto a pile amassed on a pushcart. "Son, you already lost so many folks, you should be used to this by now. Give yourself some time, but you need to pull yourself up by your bootstraps."

"I tried to tell the mayor—so did Bill and Craig. It's him. We know he has people and Stalkers, somehow. Can we track him down?"

"He probably don't have a base." Rod wiped his gloved hands and leaned against the handle of the cart. "From what Craig told me durin' our shifts together, the grenade y'all lobbed destroyed the bulk of his stockpile. The man won't make that mistake again. He'll keep his group separated, but he won't go far. He'll watch us, try to plan another attack. We took out a good bit of his resources, but we're vulnerable to retaliation." Rod spat onto the street. "Give the mayor time to settle everyone down, shake hands, and kiss babies. Then we'll talk some sense into her."

Rod paused and looked around before he walked over to Brian. "You and your group been here a while now. Proved you got good heads on your shoulders, loyal to one another and to our town. It may not be right for me to be the one to tell you, but you got a right to know: that Fernando Garcia fellow, the one you call the King, is Mayor Halloran's husband."

Brian stared at Rod, his mouth opening to utter words that didn't come.

Rod nodded and stepped back. "Yep. That's why she doesn't wanna go after him. Part of her feels bad for him, thinks she drove him to this.

He got real jealous, tired of sharin' her with the city. He wanted her at home with him and their kids. That's why he tried to get her ousted. She evicted him from the town instead. Guess that's when he got infected, and now he's got a real bee in his bonnet about gettin' back at her."

"How do you know all this?"

"He was still here when I got stationed, just a salesman with nothin' to sell no more. Felicia knows too, and a few others. But you know what they say: outta sight, outta mind."

Brian couldn't picture this monster being married to a strong-willed woman like Mayor Halloran. But it made sense: he wanted to own his wife like he wanted to own everything else.

Before he could ask Rod more, Rod cleared his throat and nodded at someone behind Brian. Brian turned to Louis as he jogged up with a flashlight clutched in his hand.

"You okay?" Louis scanned Brian's face, which must've still looked stunned from Rod's revelation. "I didn't even see you leave 'cause Felicia was pokin' and proddin' at my head. D said you ran out. I had a hell of a time findin' you."

Brian's lips opened and closed. He wanted to protect the information Rod had shared with him, but he had a difficult time keeping things from Louis.

Rod smacked a hand to his arm. "If you trust him, tell him." He resumed his duties, pushing the cart. Brian squinted to discern what he'd piled atop it. His eyes widened: *bodies in riot gear.*

Louis nudged Brian's arm. "Tell me what?"

Brian shook his head. "Not here. Somewhere private."

Louis withdrew something from his jean pocket. He dangled a gleaming object in front of Brian's face: a key. "Halloran keeps a spare of every key in this place. This goes to Eva's room."

"She keeps a lot more than that..." Brian muttered, still absorbing everything Rod had told him.

Louis cocked his head and narrowed his eyes, confused by this ambiguous statement. He curled an arm around Brian's shoulders and guided him in the direction of the motel. "Technically, we're not supposed to be out here, but D and I make quite the persuasive pair. She cares about you a lot, you know. They all do."

Brian glanced at Louis through the sides of his eyes. "I don't know why, but that's a weird thing to hear you say." His feet sent something clattering as they entered the motel parking lot. Spent casings, he suspected.

Louis parted from Brian and approached room three. "Told you I might surprise you. You've certainly surprised me, but in a very good way." He plunged the key into the lock and twisted the door handle.

Brian stepped into the room. The door clicked shut behind him as he surveyed the cramped room: an unmade bed underneath a tacky painting of flowers; a small, smudged flat-screen TV on a dresser; a bedside table with a lamp, book, and the TV remote; a window A/C unit; a closet with dirty clothes piled on the floor and clean dresses hanging from the rod; and a bathroom filled with perfumes, makeup, and travel-sized soaps and shampoos.

Everything Eva had was here. Now she had nothing but a vendetta and a rifle with several boxes of ammunition.

Louis plucked a book from the bedside table and sank onto the bed to read from it. Brian sat beside him, straining to read the messy handwriting the Lavellés shared.

4/29

Dear Diary,

I wish my fucking brother had never come back. I wish he'd died after he abandoned me, then I'd at least be able to feel something besides this anger.

I doubt Brian even missed me. He wanted to find me for some peace of mind, maybe to reassure himself Louis didn't actually kill me and lie about it. And I don't know WHY the fuck Louis bothered coming back for me. Probably because of Brian. But I'm not sure if my brother's even capable of love, so it doesn't make any goddamn SENSE.

I never suspected a damn thing. For one, we were too busy trying to fucking SURVIVE—and I thought Brian was nervous around Lou because Lou intimidates EVERYONE. When Brian showed up at Papere's, I was happy to see him. I was lonely, and he was cute and safe. I guess I misread his kindness as interest, made a fool out of myself trying to kiss him while he was probably wishing it was Louis. So fucked up, right?

Let's be honest here: I don't want my brother's sloppy seconds. Maybe I even dodged a bullet. But why even bother coming back for me if you're gonna avoid me like I don't exist?

And now you're all shacked up in that "lakeside" cabin playing house. How the hell can you do it, Brian? How do you live with what he did? How do you let him touch you? Why do you WANT him to? I can barely stand to look at him. To look at either of you. Not quite an angel and not quite a demon.

I try to think of other things, distract myself, but my mind always circles back to this. I wish I could take Lou's toy from him, but he'd fucking murder me for sure if I tried. So the only way to fix it is to take him out, then either let Brian suffer without him or put him out of his misery.

Lord help me—am I just as insane as the rest of my batshit family?

Louis flung the diary to the floor. "I told you my sister was better at hidin' her crazy than me." He stood and slammed his fist into the wall; plaster cracked and crumbled onto the floor. "*Fuck.* I knew she'd never forgive me. I didn't expect her to. But now she's out there with a rifle, and we've got targets on our heads."

Brian walked over to the window beside Louis. He leaned a hand against the wall and stared into the void of the darkened parking lot. "The King is the mayor's husband, you know. Rod told me. She probably felt betrayed when he tried to get her thrown out of office and regretted being forced to throw *him* out of the city. I can't imagine how she feels now, if she wishes she'd taken him out before he became a problem, if she's angry at herself for not listening to Bill and Craig. She couldn't bring herself to hunt him down because she still loved him despite everything— but he's crossed a line now."

Louis studied Brian's face in silence, lips shut tight and brow knit over darkening eyes. When he spoke, his voice broke. "I...I thought Eva hated me, would be half-glad to be rid of me. I didn't mean to hurt her, to hurt you... I just wanted to leave my old life behind and start a new one with you." He screwed his eyes shut and slumped against the cracked wall. "Fuck—I'm not as bad as *him*, am I?"

While Louis clutched his chest for emphasis, Brian reached out and squeezed his hand. "I wasn't trying to compare him to you. I was trying to decide what to do about Eva. Reading that entry, I understand how she feels. And I can't blame her for it, even if I'm pissed she shot you. But do we go out there and find her before she becomes a problem, or do we forgive her and let her go?"

Louis sighed and skirted Brian's eyes—but when he finally met Brian's gaze, menace and resolve hardened his eyes. "I'd let her go, but she wrote about doin' somethin' to you, and I don't plan to let her carry her intent through."

Brian swallowed, more frightened of what Louis might do—and *undo*—than Eva. "Do you really think she would? She probably wrote that in a moment of anger—"

"You read the same thing I did, Bri: she was *constantly* angry. At me, at you. I know her—and after what she tried to do to me, I think you saw she's capable of the same things as me. I don't care that she shot me, but I told you I wouldn't let anythin' hurt you again and I meant it."

Louis's passion was a potent force, as deadly as any weapon. People like D and Craig had realized this long before Brian himself. In this moment, it occurred to him *he* was the hand wrapped around Louis with a finger tight against the trigger—and he needed to switch targets.

Brian grasped Louis's shirt collar and wrenched his fingers into the coarse fabric. "Mon loulou." This pet name, loosely translated to "my wolf," disarmed Louis instantly. "Don't go looking for her and do something else you'll regret." His forehead collapsed against Louis's. "If she shows up and tries to shoot us again, we'll shoot back. But right now, we have bigger problems to deal with. My friends are dead—and even though I pulled the trigger, I have to tell myself *he* killed them." He withdrew from Louis and grabbed his face in both hands, looking deep into Louis's eyes. "I want him *dead*, Lou."

"Then we'll finish the job Halloran couldn't, wipe this scumfuck from the earth." The rage coursing through Brian saturated Louis. *Everything I feel is everything you feel.* "We're not runnin' away this time, *mon précieux.*"

Brian rewarded and redeemed Louis with a zealous kiss, breathing in his essence like oxygen, clinging to the one thing keeping him rooted to the ground even when the rug was pulled from beneath his feet.

When they parted, coppery blood swirled into Brian's mouth from the nick left by Louis's incisor. Louis tried to wipe it away and apologize, but Brian took him by the hand and dragged him out into the night, underneath the stars, once again tethered by gravity instead of adrift within the universe.

Several hours later, someone knocked on their cabin door. Louis tugged on his jeans and grabbed a kitchen knife. When he called out to the visitor at the door, D answered, "It's Santa Claus comin' to drop some coal on your ass!"

Louis opened it. A flashlight beamed from D's silhouetted side. Her face was unreadable, but as usual, her voice conveyed her mood without issue. "The mayor finally let everyone go home; thought I'd check on you special cinnamon rolls since she done let you go early."

Louis stepped aside to let her in. D stumbled over a guitar plugged into the PS3. "You can tell a coupla boys live here—y'all awful at pickin' your shit up!" She disentangled herself from the strap and flopped onto the couch with a huff. "Queen Elsa's over at our place. 'Toine thinks I'm tryin' to give him private time, but I just can't stand her frigid ass."

Brian remained on the bed with his legs crossed underneath the blanket. D winced, noticing his prone state in the incandescent light cast by their lantern. "Sorry to bust in on you like this; I just wanted to make sure you were okay." She didn't voice the obvious: "*After you shot Billie, Craig, and Eva.*"

Louis flashed her a glare to warn her away from the topic, still leaning against the door.

"I'm not great, but I'm okay," Brian assured them. "Actually, D, I need to tell you something."

Her face fell. "Oh, shit. What now?"

"You know the guy we told you about, the one we think is behind the attacks on the dam and the town? Rod said he's the mayor's husband—and the father of her kids."

"*What?*" D's stunned outburst resembled an irate parrot's squawk.

Louis crossed his arms and tapped a foot. "Husband or not, he's a fuckin' prick, and she has a town to take care of. Those Evergreen hippies need a safer place to set up, and we need to swat this mosquito before he draws any more blood. You get me?"

"Of all the things you are, Louis, stupid's never been one of them." D shook her head, a strained expression on her face. "I agree 100 percent. She's put this off long enough. We got to set this shit straight if we wanna get back to Evergreen, help them travel here. They probably think we all dead. I shouldn't give 'Toine so much shit—I been lost in la-la land with Red. I done forgot about my Jonesy, the one thing that kept me goin' after I lost Gus." D shut her eyes, head slumping back against the couch cushion. "*Shit.* The sicko attacked the city where his *kids* live. If I had kids, I'd go murder his sorry ass, husband or not!"

Brian fumbled for his boxers underneath the blanket and wriggled into them. "We shouldn't go behind her back. We owe it to her to be up-front about this. But it wouldn't hurt to bring a little extra ammunition. If we can convince her council this is the right thing to do, she'll be more likely to offer her support. Since Felicia is next door, let's start with her."

D made a *yech* sound while Brian yanked the top sheet off and swiveled his legs over the side of the bed. "Well, I guess her little fling with 'Toine won't hurt matters none. My brother knows how to sweet talk a lady, I'll give him that much."

Brian pulled on jeans and a T-shirt. He jutted his head toward the crumpled pile on the floor, indicating for Louis to throw on his shirt. "She let Cill go home?"

"Yeah. She's sleepin' in her room, on bed rest. The other reason Elsa's freezin' our place up—and another good reason to find this asshole and put a bullet in his brain." D stood and put her hands on her hips. "Hurry up and blow out your candles, boys. The more I think about it, the more I wanna kill this prick—and I ain't even *met* his ratchet ass!"

Brian and Louis put all the candles out and snagged the lantern before hurrying out after D. They followed her into her cabin and strode straight into the living room. Felicia and Antoine stood from the couch to greet them.

Felicia's full lips lifted into a slight smile. "Hello, Mister Jameson and Monsieur Lavellé. I assume you're here to check on your friend?"

Brian stepped toward Felicia. "Actually, we're here to talk to you." Her eyes remained glued to his, brows quirking with curiosity. "Felicia, you'd know better than anyone: is it possible someone who was infected but still in control of themselves could also control other Stalkers? Sort of like a pack Alpha?"

"I'm a doctor, Brian, not a psychologist." She sighed when he folded his arms and frowned, awaiting a more informative answer. "Physiologically speaking, yes. They retain enough rudimentary control and instinct to respond to command. It's possible if their appetite is neutralized, they wouldn't attack each other—or another similar to them. In fact, it could be a form of reward: perhaps they're fed for performing as requested."

"You think he's buildin' an army of those things?" Antoine asked. "They'd make for some stealthy soldiers."

"Easier to keep happy too. No morale to worry about." Louis crossed his arms and leaned against the bar connecting the kitchen to the living room. "And when they fall, it's easier to replace them."

Felicia's sharp eyes flashed to Brian. "Did you talk to Rod about this yet?"

Brian nodded.

"He told you then. Who this 'King' is."

"Why do you think we're talkin' to you?" Louis asked. "You're smart enough to know this shouldn't have been a problem to begin with. She shoulda taken his ass out ages ago, but she felt guilty, wanted to forget he existed instead."

"Because of him, Bill and Craig are gone." Brian forced away the image of Billie's tear-stained cheeks and Craig's sad smile. "And Cill and several others were shot. If this wasn't a wake-up call for Mayor Halloran, I don't know what *could* be. She listens to you guys, right? So help us talk to her—please."

Felicia's indifferent gaze softened. "You're right. Rod's been wanting to take care of this ever since Billie and Craig brought it up. He'll support you. Barry's upset about what happened to his employees and the dam, which will make him easy to persuade. And I find the prospect of these Stalker soldiers intriguing—as well as frightening."

Antoine grinned at her. "I feel like I won the lottery again meetin' this gorgeous, intelligent woman."

Felicia returned his smile, ivory cheeks flushing. "No need for the compliments, even if they *are* appreciated."

Brian cleared his throat. "We should get some sleep. It's been a long day. Will you talk to Rod and Barry tomorrow, or should we find them?"

"I'll take care of it." Felicia's face returned to her neutral, all-business expression. "Mayor Halloran won't expect anyone to return to their duties yet. She'll call an assembly, go over what happened and what she'll do about it. I'll speak with Rod and Barry beforehand—the rest of you can bring your case to her after the meeting."

Brian stuck his hand out. "Thanks, Felicia."

Her hand wrapped around his, small but strong. "Life here was close to the lives we lived before—so close we lost sight of the dangers outside our walls. Since we've been reminded of them, it won't take much convincing to get anyone to help you. Even the mayor will come around."

She smiled at him as Antoine escorted her out onto the porch, a muscular arm wrapped around her slender shoulders.

D sighed, a begrudging smile slipping away as they disappeared behind the door. "I ain't gonna lie; it's nice to see my brother smilin'. I been smilin' a lot more too. That goober I been seein' knows just how to tickle my funny bone." She ensnared Louis and Brian through their arms and led them through the front door. "I'll admit, I used to think y'all was a toxic combination, but these past few weeks, you been happier than I ever seen you—just a couple of kids foolin' around and havin' fun. It's kinda strange, but I guess I got used to it... And I don't want any of us to lose what we found here."

She released their arms when they reached their porch. Louis smirked at D, the lantern dangling in his hand. "That your seal of approval, D?"

"As close to one as you gonna get." D folded her arms over her silk bathrobe. It glinted rich purple in the light. "But if you ever, *ever* fuck over Brian or anyone else I love again, I'll make sure you get thrown outta here onto your tight little ass." She reached for the bandage on the back of his head. "You deserved the cut your sister gave you, but I can't believe she tried to *kill* you."

Louis flinched away from D's hand. "I can't be mad at her. I had it comin'. But I'm worried about her bein' out there on her own with this freak—and if she's still angry, she might be another problem to worry about. If she comes after me, that's one thing, but I don't want her to hurt anyone else."

D patted his shoulder. "I'm more worried about that sick goon than your skinny little sister." She leaned in and hugged Brian. "Keep your clothes on and get some sleep—you both need it."

She retreated to her cabin draped in indigo moonlight. Brian and Louis collapsed into bed and followed her advice.

The mayor called an afternoon meeting as Felicia surmised. Everyone attended—including Vinny Costas's family. Brian pulled Maria aside to deliver his message and was rewarded with a tight hug and teary-eyed appreciation. It reinforced to him that a population of individuals lived here who had lost people they loved and were scared to lose the ones they had left. Yet another reason to eliminate any threats to their safety.

Diamond City's denizens filled the auditorium, distributed across the metal chairs with the subtle drone of their conversation carrying through the stale air. The persisting lack of power contributed to the unsettled atmosphere swirling around the townsfolk.

Brian and the others slipped into a row together. Flashbacks of meetings where he'd sat behind Craig, Billie, and Eva amplified their absence. Cecilia cradled her injured arm, which rested in a sling given to her by Felicia. Antoine and D were as resilient as ever, but the humor that usually danced in their eyes had disappeared in lieu of steely focus. When the mayor and her council appeared on the stage, Louis reached over to squeeze Brian's thigh—a silent "we got this."

"Thank you all for coming," Mayor Halloran said. Her typically confident voice warbled with static feedback over a battery-powered microphone. "What happened yesterday was unspeakably terrifying for all of us—"

A stocky man stood. "Billie and Craig used to say this man was coming for us, but you didn't listen. Well, he came for us, and now they're *dead*. Those folks at the dam suffered horrible deaths, and we're lucky no one here got more than a bullet wound!"

Brian winced. This had to dig into the mayor like the tip of a knife twisting inside her.

A charged silence followed until she finally spoke. "You're right. I was complacent. I had too much faith in myself and underestimated the threats outside my town. *Our* town." She exhaled so heavily it reverberated throughout the room. "I owe the truth to those of you who haven't been here since the beginning. Fernando Garcia, the man who calls himself the King, who attacked our dam and our city, is my husband."

A stunned hush descended upon the room. No one even let a surprised swear slip underneath their breaths.

"I wanted to forget about him"—Mayor Halloran sat on the edge of the stage—"to ignore him. When it came down to it, I felt I'd done enough to punish him. I was foolish to think he'd forgotten about *me*. To think he wouldn't want to hurt me and those I love—which includes all of you. I'm just as responsible for the losses we suffered as he is. And I'm not certain I deserve to be up here speaking to you, that I deserve to remain the mayor of this fine town."

The townsfolk retained enough respect for her to allow her a contemplative silence, to keep their agreements or rebuttals to themselves.

A shaky sigh warbled through the microphone as Mayor Halloran pinched the bridge of her nose. "The inaction which condemned us to this will not be a mistake I repeat—I promise you this. We'll gather ourselves and strike back. My council has already spoken to me about a potential plan. I'll work out the details with the pertinent parties after this meeting disperses, and we will personally approach each of you at your homes to inform you of our decision and whether you can contribute. For now, I'd like you to stay home, regroup, and enjoy the company of your loved ones. Barry and his crew will restore the power once we work out the details. Beyond that, I can only offer my apologies and ask for the chance to make things up to you. Please return home—our guards are hard at work maintaining the perimeter and patrolling the streets, and our generator has enough gas to keep the fence going overnight."

She lowered the microphone and returned to her council. The perfunctory yet enthusiastic applause of her typical assemblies didn't follow this speech, but the townsfolk didn't leave with disapproving stares or jeers. They mumbled to each other or themselves as they left, eyes cast to the ground or searching around anxiously.

Once the crowd cleared, Brian scooted out of the aisle and climbed onto the stage with his friends. Mayor Halloran turned to greet him with eyes and cheeks nearly as red as her hair. "Brian, I can't apologize to you enough for what you had to go through... Especially since I could have prevented it. I'll send someone to collect Craig and Billie, and we'll hold a memorial—"

"You have to do something about your husband first or more people will die." The wound was still raw and she'd thrown salt into it. Brian didn't care if his words stung her. "If you're finally ready to get rid of him, we're willing to help you. To be honest, I plan on doing it whether you want me to or not."

Rod chuckled from his seat. Barry seemed preoccupied, no doubt with anxieties about fixing the problems at the dam without further attacks from the King. Felicia maintained a stoic façade, her hands clasped between her knees. Her cool gaze momentarily thawed when it darted to Antoine.

"You've got a lot of heart, Brian." Mayor Halloran sighed. "And a better head on your shoulders than me. I've been foolish. I've been blind. In my mind, Fernando remained the man I married eleven years ago, the father of my children. I hadn't accepted him as a monster, this 'king' of his own making. I even forgave him for trying to remove me from office. Maybe I pitied him."

"He attacked your city with your children still in it." Brian stuffed his hands into his jean pockets and toed the polished wood beneath his feet. He kept his eyes focused on the mayor's shimmering gray gaze. "Whatever was left of him is gone now. What does he want? To take you from the city or to take the city from *you*?"

"He wants me to see what he's become," the mayor said. "To see what he thinks *I've* turned him into. For all his charm, he was always a dreadfully insecure man—a man who wanted to make something out of himself because he lacked self-worth. He thinks my love or death will give him whatever he's missing, but I can't fix him. But I couldn't kill him, either, or I'd kill the good left in him, my memories of our marriage and our children. Tell me, were you me, would *you* have been able to?"

Her stone-cold stare froze Brian in place as if she were Medusa herself. He withdrew his hands from his pockets and dug underneath his nails, eyes flitting from hers while he considered his answer.

Brian swallowed and met the mayor's gaze once more. "No. I'd have left the city behind to protect it, to give him what he wanted."

Mayor Halloran's eyebrows furrowed. "Are you suggesting I walk out there and offer myself to him?"

"Sort of. If you called for him to propose a truce, to talk terms, he'd answer. He'd bring whatever forces he has with him—but so would you. But both of you would be smart enough to leave some behind as an out."

Mayor Halloran crossed her arms over a shirt with yellow flowers printed on the fabric. It reminded Brian of his mother's nightgown the night she'd been attacked. "How would we counter his men? Their guns? These Stalkers he's trained? Why not bolster our forces here and defend against him?"

"If you want this city to expand," Barry spoke up, "you need to eliminate anything that threatens it. Especially a vindictive *pendejo* with an army of Stalkers. Once he's gone, you don't have to worry about him coming back for us. We can extend the fence, repair the dam, expand our search for more resources."

"I agree with Barry." Rod stood and stepped toward the mayor. "We gotta get out there to hunt, to search for more ammo, more food, more supplies. And I don't exactly wanna waste all my time worryin' about dealin' with his ass while I'm out there already worryin' about Stalkers. I don't wanna stress my people out at the fence by makin' 'em worry he's gonna pop up on their watch, launch another attack."

"And we need medicine for the sick and wounded," Felicia said. "I need more materials. More tools. Eliminating him eliminates the impediment for the search. With a healthy population, I can focus on research—potentially, a cure. I find it fascinating how he's infected but completely cognizant; however, I allow he may be too dangerous to bring in alive. But these other Stalkers, the ones who plan, who speak, will allow me a viewpoint I have yet to explore."

"Yes, but is this personal for you? For any of you?" The cool gray of Mayor Halloran's eyes flared with flame matching her copper hair. "You're asking me to kill my husband, the father of my children!"

"It's personal for Cassandra and Bailey." Brian drew the mayor's furious gaze back to him. "For me. We lost Billie and Craig. Maria Costas lost her husband—her kids lost their father. Others died in that dam, were injured in your town. You're the mayor of the city where all these people live—you nurture them, protect them, and they *trust* you. Haven't you jeopardized them enough already by refusing to do anything?"

"Let me put it this way," Louis said, "with or without you, we're gonna take this guy down. I don't care if you kick me outta the city, but I've got a bone to pick with your asshole ex. Brian and I have history with him, and if we're the ones who led these Stalkers here somehow, we owe it to your people to take them out. Plus, my sister's out there, and I don't want him gettin' a hold of her again."

D moved beside Brian and crossed her arms. "Me and Red got a good thing goin', and I ain't gonna lose another man to this mess. I'll help in any way I can. Then I wanna get back to my cat, bring him home with me."

"I'm with Dee-Dee." Antoine joined his sister. "When you love people, you got somethin' to protect—and somethin' you scared to lose. I got my sister, my friends, and Felicia. Maybe your man actin' out 'cause he ain't got nothin' to protect no more. But you do."

Cecilia forced her way in front of everyone, too short to be seen behind them. "Madam Mayor, *please*—you've been so good to us. You care so much, and that's why you can't let him go. But he's already gone. Let us bring him peace and peace of mind to you and the city. Once this threat is gone, our group from Evergreen can come here and you can combine resources. Imagine everything we can build here—*beyond* here. This isn't an ending: it's the beginning of something better."

The mayor's stunned gaze swept over them. She sank to her knees and brought her hands to her mouth.

"He might be able to control Stalkers, Gloria"—Felicia kneeled beside the mayor—"but not all at once. If we separate him from his reserve forces, Barry can help me engineer traps to catch them. Their armor can't protect them from everything."

"And I can take out the rest." Rod flopped down on Halloran's other side. "Men, Stalkers, whatever. Me and my folks got this covered."

"You know what'll sweeten the deal?" Louis's eyebrows quirked. "Me and Brian. He'll remember us from the fairground: the *other* ones who got away. With the two of us standin' next to you, he won't be payin' attention to nothin' else. You get D, 'Toine, your council—whoever the fuck else wants to help—we can set 'em up in the trees, snipe and lure the Stalkers toward Barry and Felicia while Rod does his thing."

"Won't that put you at risk?" the mayor finally said. "Make you sitting ducks for your sister?"

"No risk, no reward," Brian said. "Besides, even if she *is* angry enough to try to take us out there and then, I still think she's too smart to give herself away so quickly. She'll bide her time, watch and wait. The others will keep an eye out for her. And we'll help protect you along with your bodyguards."

Mayor Halloran rubbed her eyes, exhausted. A prolonged sigh escaped her. "Okay."

Brian's fingers tightened into his folded arms. "Okay?"

Mayor Halloran looked at the group and nodded. "Get a map. We'll start marking out a plan. My people can't live in fear, and I can't keep living in the past."

Excitement bordering on giddiness surged through Brian. He glanced at his friends and smiled, felt Louis squeeze his side. But they'd only won a battle.

Now they had to win the war.

Godless Girl

Chapter Fifteen

No Sanctuary

5/1, Diamond City, Arkansas, 6:30 p.m.

After they worked out a plan, the involved parties split up and went door to door to speak with the civilians of Diamond City. They didn't reveal the details in case someone was spying for the King; instead, they instructed the citizens to go about their business as normal and assured them the King would answer for his actions. Some wanted to help—people like Cassandra, whose vendetta against the King and his men had only intensified. Rod made the call of who got to come with them. Cecilia remained behind to help watch the kids and the elderly, but D and Antoine wanted to be out there with their friends and lovers.

Once they prepared the town and its citizens, the mayor made an announcement through the loudspeaker: "Fernando, this is Gloria. Let's meet on neutral ground to discuss a truce. I'll bring my personal guards and a pair you might remember from a Missouri fairground; I expect you'll bring insurance as well. I'll await you at the First Baptist Church within the hour."

But this announcement had been prerecorded. The mayor and her party were *already* at the church. They'd done this to avoid crossing paths with the King and allowing him to attack them while they traveled. While they waited, they prepared and radioed to their allies via a line Barry had secured for them.

Rod's group snuck out ahead of time to rig various traps utilizing pits, nets, and the remaining bear traps. Barry engineered remote radios that would receive a signal from the transmitter back at Diamond City, all battery-powered. Several civilians volunteered to make distressed cries which might lure the innately curious Stalkers to the traps. They arranged a failsafe for those who didn't fall for the ruse. As Rod said with a far-too-gleeful grin, "Fire burns through everything."

The mayor's group huddled inside the church, positioned around the windows so they could peer through with binoculars for any sign of the King. The highway split south of the building, running west and east of the church, but trees offered thick cover around all directions but the south. They anticipated the King would show up armed, armored, and backed by several lackeys. Their lookouts would radio as soon as they saw him and direct them to the direction of his approach.

The thought of seeing that featureless mask and the indifferent eyes behind it intimidated Brian. He felt like the ignorant boy who'd entered the fairground, not the hardened survivor who'd emerged from the island. Although Rod had lent them his best gear, Brian's hands trembled.

He kneeled in front of the eastern window, which looked out to the church Louis and Antoine had waited at so long ago. "You're sure you have enough people protecting the city, right, Mayor? If he doesn't come here, he'll go there—"

"He'll come." Mayor Halloran sat at the pulpit of the church with her fingers laced in mock prayer. "He can't pass up the opportunity to see me in the flesh. To gloat about his 'victory' in the dam and his penetration of my city. He won't traipse over without thinking about all the angles. But even if he brings a hidden force to counter ours, we have additional numbers out there ready to neutralize them. We'll watch him carefully, stop him if he tries to radio, whistle, or make any sort of signal to trigger his men—or what's left of them."

"I can't help but worry about everyone out there." Brian glanced through his binoculars, startled by the motion of a bird flitting out of a bed of tree leaves. "He's not stupid—"

"But he's desperate, Bri," Louis said from the window adjacent to Brian. "The mayor's right: he wants her more than anythin' else. I hate to compare myself to that putain, but I get where he's comin' from. And he's opportunistic enough to organize whatever he's got left to go after *her*, not the city that already sent him scamperin' with his tail between his legs. He doesn't care if he dies as long as he takes her down with him."

The mayor's walkie crackled to life. She lifted it to her lips, thin slits of light curving across her face. "This is Halloran. Speak. Over."

"Three bogeys at your four, about fifty feet out. Over and out."

"Copy that. Over and out." She lowered the walkie and clutched her stomach. "I haven't seen him like you have. Wearing this mask. The thought of it frightens me."

Brian tucked his binoculars into his backpack. "He's not the same person you married. Don't lower your guard if he pretends he *is*—just remember he tried to take everything from you: your city, your children, and your people. And don't forget the people he already took."

Mayor Halloran stepped next to Brian while he withdrew a revolver from his holster. Louis swapped the binoculars for a rifle scope to watch the King's approach. The mayor's stoic and silent guards did the same from the southern doors and eastern window.

"I see him," Louis said. "He's covered in riot gear. Gonna be hard to get around that. But he's tall, broad-shouldered, has a mask on behind the helmet. Soon as we hear his voice, we'll know if it's a decoy. I assume not."

"What's he got with him?" Mayor Halloran asked.

"Two men, armed. No Stalkers in sight, ma'am," Ethan answered.

"Great." Louis sighed. "Means they're *outta* sight."

Mayor Halloran raised the walkie to her lips. "Rod, Barry, did you hear Chip radio? Over."

The brief silence after her words didn't *seem* brief. "Copy that, Mayor. Everything's on track. We'll signal you when we're ready. Over and out."

Rod's voice instilled Brian with confidence. They had reliable, intelligent people on their side. If the worst *did* come to pass, their failsafe would still reduce the King's numbers substantially.

"He's here, ma'am." Allen lowered his rifle. "How do you want to approach this?"

"Lou and I will go out first," Brian said. "It'll throw him off, stop anything he might have planned. When the mayor walks out, it'll excite him to know he's got three people who've eluded him in the palm of his hand. You two back her up, keep her protected. We'll talk to him, draw it out as long as possible so Rod and the others can cut his numbers down."

The mayor arched her eyebrows, her mouth gaping as if she'd been put off by Brian's assertiveness. But her lips pressed together into a smile, and her brow relaxed. "We'll follow your lead, Brian. You may know him better than me now."

Brian rolled his shoulders and exhaled through his tight lips, low and slow. *This is it. No going back.*

He pushed the front doors open with Louis at his heels. The setting sun made him squint behind the glare of his goggles, and a red bandana swelled in and out with his heavy breaths. Three dark figures hovered like shadows before the meeting horizon of sky and road. The one at the rear towered over the others, resembling the figure Brian anticipated.

The deep voice booming across the air confirmed the King's identity. "You weren't the pair I expected. Last I remember, you were a trio."

Brian didn't know if the King—*no, Fernando*—had seen Billie and Craig before he left the dam or if he even knew they'd lived in the city. "Did we pass your gauntlet?"

"With flying colors." Fernando stepped forward between his men. They wore similar gear to their leader's. "Did you know they planned to double-cross me? Were you a part of it the entire time?"

"Nope." Louis kept his gun trained in Fernando's direction. Their surroundings remained motionless apart from a light draft rustling the grass and leaves. "They blackmailed us into helpin' them take you out, then handed us over. Didn't have much of a choice—they took our guns."

"Did they throw the grenade that took my supply out, or was that you?"

Brian spoke before Louis had a chance to gloat: "I *wish* we'd thought to do it. We barely had time to get out of there."

"Yet you left something quite important behind. Unless, of course, she's tucked away within the city." Fernando took a step forward. His men followed at his heels, as obedient as LD was to Rod. "Any idea what happened to Parker and Spike?"

"You don't know?" Brian submerged the pain of their loss that briefly surfaced. He didn't want Fernando to have the satisfaction of Craig and Billie's deaths.

"I'm afraid not. They escaped with a woman and a little girl I suspect were dearly important to them." Brian didn't notice a weapon in Fernando's bare hands. The latent infection beneath his nails was weapon enough. "Do *you* know?"

"No." Brian shook his head. "We couldn't find Eva. Did you?"

"I didn't find her amongst the rubble, sadly." The glare of Fernando's visor obscured his eyes and his gravelly voice neither elevated with agitation nor dropped in anger. "Funny the two of you would find your way here, yet Parker, Spike, and Eva wouldn't. Stranger still that you'd abandon Eva and not bother going back for her."

"That was my fault." Louis kept his voice as indifferent as Fernando's. "I was in a hurry to get Brian out. I let him think she was dead so we wouldn't have to go back for her."

"You valued a friend over your own sister?" Fernando's tone finally changed, conveying mild amusement. "And you're still together despite all this? Or is this the first you've heard of it, Brian?"

God, I hope Eva isn't near enough to hear any of this.

"I knew."

"Yet you don't care?"

"Of course I care. I left him once, but he found his way back to me. Just like you're here going after your wife."

Fernando curled a hand into a fist at his side. "Is that why you're here protecting her? You bonded over your shared attraction to monsters?"

"We heard the radio signal. She took us in. We were there when you attacked the dam—a lot of good people died there." Brian's hand tightened around the revolver's grip. "You did a lot of horrible things: abducting people and selling them, letting them use a woman like she wasn't even human, forcing people to run a gauntlet, killing and eating my goddamn cows... But mass murder is the worst thing you've done yet."

"That grenade robbed me of my power. Many of my men left me because they perceived a weakness in me. Or should I say, they *tried* to leave me." Fernando held a hand in front of his face, scrutinizing his nails. "Destruction lies beneath these nails. Invisible to the eye. I find it fascinating." He moved both hands to his guards' visors. When he lifted them, clouded eyes stared back at Brian.

Brian's stomach constricted into an acidic knot. *He infected them. He infected them so he could control them. And somehow, he got the others to follow him. The ones outside Diamond City—the ones following us.*

"How do you... How do you make them follow you?"

"They're pack animals, like people." Fernando lowered their visors. "And I'm their Alpha. The one who demonstrates strength, rewards them for their obedience. All I have to do is snap my fingers and they'll shoot."

"How the fuck can they shoot?" Louis asked. "I've seen a lotta those things, even heard 'em talk, but never seen 'em hold a gun or attack with anythin' other than their hands and teeth."

"Not all of them have this capability. Just like some can speak and others can't. The infection varies in potency. Some retain the ability to plan, to follow, to make decisions, to understand what's around them—

even what they are. Some speak. Others are silent, not as amused by nature's joke on them as the rest. Much of it depends on age. The younger the mind, the more resilient it is. I've seen the children play, even carry on a conversation. They learn more quickly."

Brian swallowed. "You have *children*?"

"They think it's a game. I keep them entertained."

Brian thought back to the child that had followed him, who called "Hello!" over and over until he'd sunk an arrow into its skull. About the schoolhouse full of the delusional woman's children she'd gathered. About the child he'd mutilated and left to suffer in front of Diamond City's front gate.

He couldn't read Louis's face, but he sensed the change in the electrical field his body gave off. Regret and doubt washed over him. Brian wanted to reach for him, but he couldn't shift his attention from the former King.

"They followed me," Fernando said. "I didn't know it at first, but they started doing things to test me: throwing objects, making noises, trying to scare me into their waiting arms. When I decided to test them back by approaching them and taking my mask off, they openly followed me. At first, I disciplined them when they tried to go for my men. But I realized people are unreliable, vulnerable—so I turned my men, quashed the power struggle between man and Stalker, and created an army I could control; dogs I could teach new tricks. I rewarded them by feeding them the men who failed me—like the ones who ran from Diamond City."

Fernando's muffled scoff accompanied the horrified expressions on Brian and Louis's faces. "As fun as it's been to catch up, boys, it wasn't you I came here to meet. Where is Gloria? If this has all been a ruse, I warn you, I won't find it amusing—"

"I'm here, Fernando." Mayor Halloran emerged from the cover of the building with her guards at her heels. Fernando had to envy her: people followed her out of respect while he only commanded obedience from shells of human beings with a restricted ability to choose.

"Gloria..." The neutral quality to Fernando's voice faltered. Brian likened it to the moment he'd turned the corner of the slaughterhouse and seen Louis bathed in golden light. Despite the control he'd struggled to maintain, he'd lost himself for an instant. Fernando must've realized he'd suffered this same loss and quickly corrected it. "What compelled you to seek me out after all this time? The last time I saw you, you stood behind the gate with a look on your face as if you pitied me. Then you turned your back on me and broke me."

"You tried to manipulate everyone, Fernando. To force me out of the position I still love to this day—and now you're trying to destroy everything I love because you think I don't love *you* anymore." Mayor Halloran stepped up behind Brian and Louis. She placed trembling hands on their arms. "Even though I was angry, I thought I understood you. But the things you've done make it hard to love you: stealing from people, stealing *people*, enslaving them, selling them, letting your men rape and murder... Oh, Fernando, it's unforgivable. Even for me. Perhaps you were frightened to show me your face after all this time, but you've *always* worn a mask."

Her hand tightened around Brian's arm before it fell.

"I don't want your city, Gloria." Fernando stepped forward. "I just want you. I've been so lonely. You can come with me and end all this. I won't attack this place ever again."

Mayor Halloran inhaled sharply, perhaps because this mirrored Brian's earlier answer to her so closely. *But is that a sacrifice she'd be willing to make? He's gone too far. She may still love him, but she can't live with him. And he won't get on his knees and beg for forgiveness. He won't try to change. He's changed too much already.*

"The man I married is gone, Fer. You attacked the city our children live in. Would you have me abandon them so you can have me to yourself?"

"You're the only one, Gloria—the only one who ever loved me. *Really* loved me. Who accepted me. I stood by you, supported you... And what did you do? You threw me out. You threw me out and *this* happened."

In an instant, he stripped the helmet and mask from his face. The mayor gasped, wobbling as her knees buckled. Her men caught her by the elbows while Brian and Louis stepped in front of her.

He's vulnerable. We could shoot him now. End this.

Fernando held up his hand as if he was about to snap his fingers. "Do it and my guards come after you. And I don't mean the two behind me— I mean the dozen positioned behind me in the bushes."

We expected that, asshole. That's why we have people where you can't see them. Even if the Stalkers do, they won't act without your command now.

"You'd be dead before you could even snap your fingers," Louis said.

Fernando laughed. "Have you never seen a dog trained to help its owner when they have a seizure? If they see me fall, you *all* go down."

"It doesn't have to be this way, Fernando!" Mayor Halloran cried in a quavering voice. She covered her face, nails raking the thin skin beneath watering eyes.

"What other way can it be?" Fernando's grotesque face looked worse than Brian recalled: skin covered in raw, oozing patches; more teeth and gums exposed by his stretched smile; the bloody tracks leaking from his eyes even thicker. The ripe stench of rot emanated from him. "This ends here. Either you come with me or I *make* you come with me."

"Don't hurt anyone else, Fernando. Please." Gloria's voice broke from the strain of trying to keep tears at bay. "I-if I came with you, what would we do?"

"You'd never leave me again—Fernando's voice lowered to a menacing growl—"because I know how to command obedience now."

A plume of smoke streaked across the sunset behind Fernando. *Rod's signal flare.*

Fernando reached for Mayor Halloran. She gasped and stepped back. Brian and Louis moved to block her, guns trained on him, his guards' guns trained on *them. Pop pop pop.* One guard went down, then two. A dark circle appeared in the base of Fernando's skull as a shot sent him sprawling to the ground. The mayor's bodyguards dragged her back toward the church while more fireworks cracked the air, halting the black figures breaking out of the bushes.

Fucking seizure dogs was the absurd thought going through Brian's mind as he and Louis ran for it, trying to escape the open battleground for a protected vantage point.

Louis shoved him into the building behind the mayor's guards. He followed Brian in and slammed the doors shut. Their feet skidded on the wooden floor when the Stalkers started pushing against them. Brian shoved a bookshelf in front of the entrance while the mayor's men moved to the windows, bashing out the glass so they could snipe through the slits between the boards. Mayor Halloran sank to her knees in the aisle.

After Louis caught his breath, he looked between Brian and the mayor. "I knew he couldn't live without her. Takin' that helmet off was like a suicide bomb meant to take as many of us down with him as possible. I just wish I knew who the fuck shot him."

Eva said she wanted to put a bullet in his head; maybe she wanted to trigger all those Stalkers too.

The shelf shuddered against the door. Brian hurried to the window to see how many Stalkers were trying to push their way in. Several fell as he watched, taken out by snipers from the trees. Small white blurs clambered up the trunks—children. Most toppled before they could make it as far as the snipers.

Brian knocked out a chunk of window and fired through it, mowing down the rest of the Stalkers pounding at the doors. The floorboards shook beneath his feet with each shot. His ears buzzed. By the time the last Stalker fell, he couldn't even tell if the gunfire ceased. The traumatic memory of being on the powerhouse rooftop with the tommy gun made his muscles seize, but he forced himself to move.

Mayor Halloran said something into the radio. She headed for the doors with her guards beside her. Brian and Louis followed. Brian knocked on his ears in a futile attempt to clear the lingering rings.

People climbed down from the trees and ran to the mayor. Brian glimpsed Red and Cassandra among them. Cassandra gestured to Fernando and mimed the pull of a trigger before collapsing to her knees and erupting into tears.

She *shot him. Jesus.*

Louis jogged over to Red. They exchanged dialogue before Red clapped a hand to Louis's shoulder. Brian's thoughts wandered to D and Antoine, who were with Rod and the others. To the city, to Cill, to Evergreen. To Eva.

When his hearing cleared enough to understand speech, it still sounded like he was underwater. He joined the mayor while she inspected her squadron. "Mayor, did you get a hold of Rod?"

"Felicia got what she needed. The traps worked. They took out what they could and rushed back once they heard gunshots from our end. Apparently, they triggered a group of Stalkers hiding outside the city. Rod corralled most with a bonfire and caught the rest."

Brian grabbed the mayor's shaking arms, noticing the thickening smoke within the woods to the north. "We're going back. We've got to help them take out whatever's left. I don't think—"

A painful force shoved him to the ground an instant before a sonic boom erupted in the clearing air. The mayor's guards grabbed her and ran for cover. Somebody yelled, "Sniper!" Everyone scrambled to get away while someone dragged Brian behind the pickup truck parked in front of the church's double doors. Louis slumped next to him, smudging blood against the oxidized paint.

Brian kept his head low, examining Louis to see where the blood was coming from. A single shot had ripped through the vest protecting his chest, leaving an entry wound below his ribs and an exit wound to the left of his spine.

The cold chill of panic froze Brian, but adrenaline helped him break free. He jerked his rifle loose and angled it around the truck. He fired to frighten the sniper, still unsure of their identity and target. *Was it me? Did Louis shove me out of the way, take the bullet?*

Brian didn't want to think it, but Eva was the first person to cross his mind. He grabbed a nearby log and stuck it out past the edge of the truck, trying to goad the sniper. No shots fired. *Now or never.*

"Lou"—he placed a hand on Louis's wan cheek—"I have to find whoever did this."

Louis covered Brian's hand with his, eyelids fighting to stay up. "There are a lotta things...I wanted to do with you. Like take a walk in town...once the leaves changed...and the air got cool and crisp. Like when we used to go...trick-or-treatin'..."

"Stop fucking talking like this is the end—you can't die, you hear me? You *won't*." Brian spun around and pounded against the church doors. "Mayor! I'll go after the sniper. Get Louis in your Tesla and take him to Felicia. Whatever it takes, *do it*." He left before he heard a confirmation, propelled by blinding rage and the urge to escape frustrated tears fighting to surface.

I told him to leave her alone. I tried to give her a chance. And she fucking shot him again. *Well, I'll shoot back, Eva—and this time I'll aim better.*

Someone called after him, but he ignored them and climbed onto the bike he'd propped against the side of the building. He didn't care if a shot took him out and knocked him from the bike. He didn't care if a Stalker flew out of the woods and tried to pull him off. He didn't care that he was heading into the fire consuming the woods outside the city. All he saw was Eva. All he wanted was to knot this last dangling thread—or snip it off.

Brian whipped past the blur of emerald and olive trees. The sandy road beneath him dissolved into an endless streak. "I know it was you, Eva! You heard the gunshots, didn't you? Figured you'd take the opportunity while we let our guards down." He pedaled with all his energy, sweat trickling down his skin. "That potshot you took at Louis triggered the Stalkers at the dam, you know; one of them got Billie. Craig asked me to shoot them both, take them out on their terms. How's that for poetic? Your petty bullshit ended up killing the people who saved you!"

He'd gain on her. She was on foot. But she wasn't stupid enough to run out in the open, to leave tracks behind. She'd be in the woods, watching, waiting, listening to his furious tirade.

Brian pulled back on the brake and let the bike fall to the ground in a cloud of dust. Nothing moved, so he entered the woods and kept talking. "I shot you out of instinct, you know. I wish I could say I was sorry, but you tried to kill him—and me, for all I know."

A blur of black leaped for him. He lifted his revolver and put a casual end to it, too high on adrenaline to feel fear. "Maybe it's our fault. We should've left. I say 'we' because there's no way either of us can exist without the other at this point. I bet you think that's pathetic, but you should be happy you've never felt so incomplete you needed someone else to survive. Codependence is what *we're* infected with—what's your excuse? What made you stab Bugs Bunny to death?"

Twigs snapped to his right. He spun his head toward the source and caught the residual motion of swinging branches in the bushes. Smoke misted into the air, spreading the acrid scent of charred wood. *She's heading into it for cover.*

"Careful, Eva—you'll pass out if the smoke gets too thick." Brian swapped the revolver for his bow. The wood felt reassuring in his hands—familiar. It transported him to those first days of training with Poppa, to a time when he was a victim who preferred to escape his reality.

Reliving those days with Poppa, with Louis and Eva, eased him back to a more sentimental state. Regret swirled within his rage.

"You could shoot me now, but you haven't." Brian put his back to a tree trunk, listening for snapping twigs as she moved within the brush. "You couldn't do it, could you? You hesitated with Louis. But you were angry I didn't hesitate with *you*. You wanted to hurt me, to hurt him, but it shook you when he took that shot for me, so you ran." Brian dashed to the cover of another tree, muffling a cough as the air thickened with soot. "Do you still feel guilty you told your parents I cut him? Do you think you're to blame for him setting the fire that killed them? Eva, nothing you did made him do anything *he* did. We're responsible for our own happiness—and our own misery."

Something cracked about fifteen feet to the northeast. Brian whipped around the cover of the tree with an arrow pulled tight. Nothing. Maybe wood popping in the heat. His clothes clung to his skin. Breathing took effort. If Eva headed deeper into the woods hoping the smoke would chase him out, she'd faint. The flames would consume her.

Does she want *to die?*

"Eva, for fuck's sake!" Brian brought his sleeve to his nose, trying to block the smoke. "Just show yourself! I'm not going to kill you, but I can't let you go—you'll have to come back to Diamond City and face what you've done. Your brother might *die*."

"You were lost in your own little world." Her voice sent a jolt of electricity through Brian. She coughed, voice choking on smoke or tears. "Even when we were kids, I was never really part of it. I just tagged along and you tolerated me. I never did anythin' to you like he did, but you fuckin' shot *me*, not *him*!"

Brian let her simmer for a moment. "The barrel of a gun was aimed in my direction after you'd already fired it; did you just expect me to take it? Did you wanna kill me? Did you wanna kill *him*?"

"I just wanted him to feel helpless, for you both to hurt like I did..."

He wasn't sure if Eva was crying for herself or her brother. Frustration tightened his voice, made him yearn to shut her up. His stinging eyes watered. "I'm not gonna say he changed, Eva—but he *evolved*. Why wouldn't you give him a chance?"

"Oh, I gave him a shot." Eva's reedy voice sounded closer. When Brian leaned around to search for her, he glimpsed her right shoulder and the profile of her face peeking around a tree trunk about ten feet to the northeast. "How did it come to this? We used to be kids rollin' on skates, runnin' around with sparklers, and tryin' to catch fireflies..."

"The world changed, Eva." Brian struggled to speak through the suffocating heat swirling around them. The foliage to the north sizzled. "We had to grow up."

"If he dies, you'll kill me." She lifted her right hand. Something glinted in it: the blade of her Bowie knife.

Brian angled around the tree trunk and pulled the bowstring tight, aiming an arrow at Eva. "I don't want either of you to die, but this has to end."

The arrow plunged through her hand, knocking away the knife she'd angled against her throat. He dashed over and snatched it and then dragged her out from behind the tree. Eva burst into choked sobs and grabbed her bloodied right hand while he disarmed her. She'd torn off strips of fabric and knotted them around a bullet wound in her left shoulder.

Brian's head lightened. He pinned Eva's hands behind her back and tied them together with his belt, absurdly reminded of Louis's willing submission. When she buckled at her knees, he jerked her up by the elbow and led her out of the stifling smoke. The raging fire cast golden warmth over the lavender dusk. He didn't speak, trying to preserve his breath until they reached clear air.

No Stalkers struck from the shadows on their way out of the woods. *They must've fled to escape the smoke. Then Rod and the others took them out or captured them.*

Eva cried until her sobs dwindled into dry gasps for air. The arrow slowed the blood streaming from her right hand, preventing her from losing too much. Felicia would snip it off and take both it and the bullet out, no problem. Eva would be fine.

Louis is tough. Strong-bodied and strong-willed. And Felicia's a gifted doctor. As long as the vest slowed the bullet, as long as the caliber wasn't too strong, as long as it didn't puncture a vital organ or artery, as long as they got him there in time...

There were too many variables to complete the equation. Louis's survival remained a question mark hovering in Brian's mind.

Irritated by Eva's whimpers and his inability to help Louis, Brian wrung her arm until she moaned in pain. He marched her out of the forest, onto the road past his abandoned bike, and up to the gate. The sight of the city, placid and pristine, reassured Brian. *If anything happened here, they had it well under control.*

He stripped the fogging goggles from his eyes and lowered his bandana, smoke clinging to the fabric. To the fabric of *all* his clothes, probably. One of the guards ran over within the minute, out of breath, gun in hand. "You're Brian, right? The mayor said to keep an eye out for you. You're the only one still out here."

Relief softened Brian's grip on Eva's arm. "The others made it back? Good."

The guard buzzed Brian and Eva in, eyes glued to Eva. "Hey, isn't that...uh...Eva?"

Brian ignored the question. "Is the mayor at City Hall?"

"Yeah, she's holding a debriefing—"

Brian broke away from the guard and dragged Eva to City Hall. He hustled into the building with Eva shuffling beside him. The mayor's unshakeable Secret Service remained posted outside the auditorium doors. Their composure crumbled for an instant when they glimpsed the smoke-singed pair standing in front of them.

"Woah. She said to expect you... But—"

Brian shoved past them and strolled into the aisle between the rows of seats occupied by the citizens of Diamond City. The mayor froze mid-speech. D shot up from her seat and ran to Brian, followed by Antoine.

As soon as he saw them, his front crumbled. He burst into tears and released Eva before sinking to his knees. He lost track of her, buried his face in his arms, and sobbed while D kneeled in front of him and wrapped him in a tight hug. Antoine circled behind him and squeezed his shoulders. Though they spoke, no words sank through the pressure building in Brian's head. He tightened his eyelids until green patterns spun beneath his eyelids and the world tilted around him.

D wrenched his face from his arms, forcing him to open his eyes and meet hers. "Sunshine, you gonna be okay. Now, you can't just stroll up in here in the middle of the mayor's speech with Eva on your arm, both of y'all covered in soot, and break down without tellin' us what the hell happened."

"It's okay." Mayor Halloran's voice echoed from the microphone. "Let's ease one burden from his mind at a time. Take him to the clinic, please."

Antoine and D lifted him to his feet. If they let go, he'd wobble right back to the floor. Neither of them did. They walked him over to Felicia's clinic. Those ten minutes of silence merged into infinite timelessness.

Brian dragged his feet between them, into the waiting room, past Val's empty desk, and into the hall. He collapsed onto an examination table and stared at white walls while Antoine ran out to find Felicia. D stayed with Brian, holding his hand.

"He ain't dead yet."

This snapped him out of his daze. His eyes moved from the blurry wall to D's face, focusing on it with vivid clarity.

"Vest slowed it down. She used a .22LR. Clipped his rib above his spleen, nicked a blood vessel, and caused a lot of bleeding. It knocked him out. He needs a transfusion, but Felicia don't know his blood type—"

Brian grasped her arm. "I'm O-negative—I can donate to anyone."

D's shoulders slumped. "Well, that's lucky. She was askin' around, but you'd be surprised how many people don't know their own dang blood type—and the ones who do ain't O-neg." She shook her head. "I used to think Felicia was a stone-cold bitch, but I got a lotta respect for that woman after all I seen her do today. She's runnin' herself ragged." She gripped his wrist, violet polish flaking from her nails. "I was with Rod and them, didn't see what happened with y'all. But Red told me. I'm guessin' Eva tried to shoot you, but Louis saw it comin' somehow, took it for you?"

Brian slumped back against the vinyl cushion. He smoothed his damp bangs to the sides of his forehead. "She wanted to hurt us both. She succeeded."

D patted his arm. "You know what? No one got killed. They worn out, dehydrated, but we got the jump on those Stalkers. Even got a few for Felicia to study. A nasty one, a normal-ish one, a kid, and that King mofo himself. She's fixin' to study the rate of decay and... What'd she say? Their 'mental acuity'? Some kinda fancy doctor talk."

The fancy doctor herself burst into the examination room with Antoine behind her. Her normally impassive face crinkled into haggard creases, her smooth ponytail frazzled and half-undone. Blood spatters stained her usually pristine coat, and her glasses tilted across her nose at an odd angle.

"Brian"—she rolled in a rack with an IV drip attached to it—"we need to hydrate you—"

"D said Louis needs blood. I'm O-negative. Take whatever you need." He rolled up his sleeve and flattened himself against the raised table. "If Eva or anyone else needs it, take more."

Felicia's frantic eyes relaxed. "That's a blessing. Thank you. Once you're hydrated, I'll work on it straight away." She jerked open the drawers and withdrew a needle and disinfectant wipe and then tore the wipe open and rubbed the inside of his elbow. After stripping the cap from the needle, she attached it to the drip line and stuck it into his arm, swift and painless like the strike of a snake.

Brian shut his eyes and drifted away. The pain would come later.

White blinded him. White walls, white ceiling, white fluorescent light. A sterile chemical scent wafted into his nose. When Brian tried to lift his head, he felt all ten pounds of its weight. It collapsed against the cushion of a thin pillow.

He lifted his left arm. A blue bandage strapped a square of gauze to it. *Right. They needed my blood.*

Brian blinked rapidly in a bid to fight back the blinding light, but lowered his lids in defeat. *Did Barry get the power running? Or are they set up on a generator?*

A relieved sigh slipped between dry lips. *We did it. Cassandra shot him. The mayor and the rest of us are rid of him. Rid of the Stalkers following him. Eva's here, being watched. Taken care of. Louis...*

Brian drifted in and out of sleep until a knock roused him fully. The door cracked open. Felicia stepped in, more composed than when Brian had last seen her. The bags underneath her sharp eyes betrayed her exhaustion. "Brian, it's a relief to see you're awake. You've been out for eighteen hours."

"*Eighteen?*" he repeated, lifting his heavy head. He scooted into a sitting position. "How is he?"

Felicia sank onto a stool at the side of his bed. He scanned her face for the answer before she gave it. "He's asleep. I think he'll pull through."

The weight lifted from Brian's head and shoulders. "What about Eva?"

"Physically, she'll be fine. I removed the bullet from her shoulder and cut the arrow from her hand. I assume you did it to knock a weapon from it? She wasn't talking much."

"She tried to hurt herself."

"Cecilia's with her." Felicia exhaled. "I can't give her the help she truly needs."

"Does she know he survived?"

Felicia nodded. "She shut her eyes and went to sleep after I told her. Maybe a sense of relief eased her. People are complicated creatures." She patted Brian's uninjured arm and stood. "That's why I study their bodies, not their minds."

"Felicia"—Brian stopped her in her tracks before she could walk away—"what about the Stalkers? Are you studying their behavior? Or just their bodies?"

"Both. We must all take steps to improve ourselves, no?" She slipped through the door and shut it, offering him a tight smile through the crack.

Despite his eighteen hours of sleep, Brian succumbed to exhaustion again until D's voice woke him. "All right, sleepin' beauty, time to wake up—unless you want me to kiss you!"

Brian's eyes opened to her reassuring smile. He rubbed them and scooted up. "I know, I know—I slept long enough."

"They took a good bit of blood from you. I don't blame you."

Antoine crept in through the door. He sat on the stool and spun his way over to Brian. "How you doin', boy? We been keepin' close to you, ain't even been back to our cabin yet. Between you, Lou, and Cill, we got our hands full."

"Felicia too." Brian scratched at the rubber band clinging to his arm. "How is she? How are the mayor and everyone else?"

"Rod's busy puttin' out the fire, and Barry's still patchin' things up at the dam. They got their folks helpin' 'em. Felicia's gonna conk hard, need pamperin' afterward—which I'm more than happy to offer her. I give mean massages." Antoine cracked his knuckles with a lopsided grin. "Cill's been flittin' between you, Eva, and Lou, more worried 'bout y'all than herself, as usual. Her arm's doin' good, though. Once the smoke clears, she wants to head back for Evergreen pronto."

D's bright expression dulled. "The mayor's tough, but keepin' busy's the only thing stoppin' her from breakin' down. She's gonna need some help buildin' things back up when she falls. And who better to help her than Jacque and Marie? Hell, Marie and Halloran could be redheaded stepsisters."

Brian continued plucking at the blue rubber band. "What does Mayor Halloran want to do with Eva?"

"She's cuffed to the bed. She's goin' under house arrest when she heals up. Marched right back to that hotel room and put into timeout. She'll be supervised 24/7. The mayor suggested a trial, but Louis put the kibosh on it. Said he don't want her goin' through it in public—"

"He's awake?" The rubber snapped against Brian's arm with a hot sting.

"Well, that's partly why we was in here—"

Brian swept his legs over the bed before D could finish talking. "I wanna see him."

His legs wobbled when he put weight on his feet. Antoine reached across the bed to keep him from collapsing. "Easy, boy! You ain't been on your legs for a while—you gotta go slow."

Brian leaned against the bed and gave his legs a few minutes to adjust. His eyes swept between D and Antoine's. "I'll go with you to Evergreen. But Louis needs to stay here and heal."

A raspberry rippled through D's lavender lips. "That's completely on you, Sunshine. You really think he's gonna listen to any of us? The first thing he asked when he woke up was how and where you were. And now that your blood is pumpin' through him, y'all's DNA might as well be twisted together." She steepled her fingers. "I can believe he took a bullet for you, but he refused to make a spectacle out of his sister's messy little vendetta. He even asked how *we* were—"

"What D's tryin' to say is we're just as relieved he's alive as you is." Antoine elbowed his sister's arm. "And we want him to stay behind too— not because we don't trust him, but because the boy don't need to add no more scars to his collection."

Brian circled around the bed once his strength returned to him. He leaned in to hug both siblings. "Thanks for having my back. And staying by my side. But sit this one out." He withdrew and patted their shoulders. "Which room is he in?"

"Room four—"

Brian left the Etiennes in the dust. Although he wore underwear beneath it, the flaps of his hospital gown left him exposed as he scurried down the hall. Some of Felicia's assistants asked if he should be out of bed, but he brushed them off and pushed his way into room four.

Louis's eyes opened when the door clicked shut behind Brian. He pressed his back to it, his heart hammering against his chest. The words froze in his throat.

"Don't get out of bed," he finally said, his voice cracking. He scoffed and covered his face. "That was smooth. I'm lucky you already like me."

"I more than like you, dumbass." Louis lifted an arm above the sheet covering him from the waist down. "I heard some of this blood pumpin' through me is yours. I don't know how to thank you."

"You took a bullet for me; I owed *you*." Brian moved to Louis's bed and sat on the edge. He scrutinized the bandages covering Louis's exposed torso and diaphragm. "How do you feel?"

"Like someone hit me with a bat twenty times." Louis winced when Brian's palm cupped his swelling ribs. "What am I at now? Five?"

"I don't care how many scars you get, as long as you're alive." Brian shifted his gaze from the bandages to Louis's eyes. "I can't believe you were willing to die for me."

"What I *wouldn't* do for you is a pretty short list, only has one word on it: nothin'."

Louis laced his fingers with Brian's. Brian exhaled and tightened his fingers around Louis's. *Too much to say, not enough words to say it.*

"After this, we're going back to Evergreen." Brian arched his eyebrows. "But I want you to stay here so you can heal."

Louis's lips parted to protest, so Brian stopped him before he could start. He withdrew from Louis's face, taking care to avoid putting pressure on his wounded torso. "Be a good boy and stay put for once, okay? Your Lord demands it."

Louis shut his eyes, chest deflating with a deep sigh. "I'll try to behave. But don't take too long. Make the mayor and Rod loan you his van and enough gas to get there and back. And make sure you have enough ammo—"

Brian squeezed Louis's arm. "I got this, mon loulou. Just relax." He leaned over to sweep Louis's bangs from his forehead and pressed his lips to it, relishing the heat he absorbed from Louis's skin. "I'll spend more time with you before we go, but let's not do anything *too* crazy. We've had enough for a while."

Brilliant sunbeams streamed through the window, penetrating the austere interior of the room and illuminating all the shadowed corners. Louis opened his eyes and angled his face toward the window. "When you come into the room, it's like a ray of sun breakin' through a sky filled with storm clouds. And any time you leave, they roll right back in. Even that island felt like a pit of darkness without you there."

"This is the last time I'll leave you. Once we come back with everyone from Evergreen, I plan on staying here so I can help you get better."

Louis turned his head toward Brian. "Good, because you're the cure to all my illnesses."

Brian leaned over and pressed a gentle kiss to the bandaged area of Louis's torso. "There. Just pretend I'm a Cleric and I cast a healing spell on you."

Louis caressed the back of Brian's head as he withdrew, dragging his fingers through the wavy locks of Brian's hair. "I dunno. I kinda like you as a Dungeon Master." He snorted. "But don't tell D that. Let my kinks be a lifelong mystery for her."

"Okay then"—Brian leaned his elbows against the bed and steepled his fingers above Louis's chest—"what's our goal now? We found the treasure, but it turned out to be a mimic who tried to kill you with a projectile—two, actually."

"Well, I guess our Cleric will try to heal it, and if she's successful, the mimic will turn back into...hmm...Princess Eva? And once you lead your party to the Dark and Light Wizards, they'll return D's great beast to her..." Louis's lips lifted into the crooked smirk Brian so adored while his eyes darted around the room, lost in his fantastic thoughts. "Maybe once I heal, I'll hunt for some magic rings or somethin'."

Brian laughed and swatted Louis's arm. "Then you really *will* be Gollum!"

Louis clicked his tongue. "I already got my precious, are you kiddin'? I dunno, I was thinkin' of that whole pledgin' devotion stuff..." He caught Brian's dismayed expression. "I mean, I wasn't gonna ask you to marry me or nothin'. I just wanted it to stand for, like, commitment to bein' good and loyal and all that. Put it on a different finger, I don't know. Hell, it can even be some other kinda bauble."

"I'll think of something—but no rings!" Brian's cheeks prickled at the thought. "That's too traditional, and there's *nothing* traditional about us."

Louis's hand slid to the back of Brian's neck. "Tattoos, maybe? Since we know we can both take a few pricks..." He snickered at Brian's skeptical face. "I'm just kiddin'. I know you hate needles. I still can't believe you donated all that blood."

Brian lowered his head to Louis's chest and listened to the steady rhythm of his heartbeat—though it briefly escalated. "You're like a shadow that clings to me wherever I go: I can't get rid of you. And if I did, I'd be incomplete."

"What're you sayin'?"

"That I'm just as crazy for you as you are for me. And that's okay."

A content and steady sigh escaped Louis, making his chest fall beneath Brian's cheek. He stroked Brian's hair until they both fell asleep; at some point, someone stepped in and turned the light off for them.

They both dreamed of an utterly ordinary life of trips to the lake, games and dinner with friends, and long nights spent curled up on the couch or romping in bed. No more magic coins, potential commitment rings, island paradises, or deserted sisters—and if someone else wanted to deal with the bogeymen, they had no interest in being part of the story.

Epilogue

9/3, Diamond City, Arkansas, Sunset at the Shoals Resort, 5:37 p.m.

Louis tightened Brian's tie. "You're way hotter in this than you were in that hospital gown."

Brian glanced over Louis's shoulder into a full-length mirror. "I don't care. I couldn't wait to get out of it, and I can't wait to get out of *this*."

"I'll help you with that." Louis stood next to Brian, examining his reflection in the mirror. He raked his hands through his bangs and clicked his tongue. "D's gonna give me shit about not stylin' my hair, but I hate gel: it makes it sticky and hard."

"Don't tell *her* that." Brian tried to smooth the curls flipping over his ears but failed. He grimaced, understanding now why his father used to shave his hair. "Be honest: do I look like a kid in this? I feel like the sleeves are too long and I'm gonna trip over my pants."

Louis circled behind Brian and buried his chin in Brian's shoulder. "You look handsome as hell. Plus, I know what you look like underneath that get-up, and it *definitely* isn't a kid. I don't really want anyone else to see, anyway—it's bad enough when we go to the lake and you're all wet in that swimsuit... In fact, let me just leave a little mark here so everyone knows you're taken." He tugged back the brim of a stiff white collar and sank his teeth into Brian's neck.

The door opened in the mirror behind them. D barged into the room, huffing as soon as she saw them. "Don't get freaky in those suits! I can't turn them in all stained!"

Louis withdrew from Brian and crossed his arms. "What the hell are you doin' in here? Aren't we supposed to not see you beforehand or some shit?"

"Only if you the one marryin' me!" D moved from drawer to drawer, yanking them open. "I'm lookin' for Red's cufflinks. Either of you seen 'em, or you been too caught up pretendin' *you* the ones 'bout to get married?"

Louis scoffed. "Not in your lifetime. And no, I haven't seen the cufflinks."

"Ugh!" D put her hands on her hips, dressed in a gown Cecilia had sewed and dyed in various shades of purple—D's favorite color. Louis liked to call her "Big Purple" to go with "Big Red." "Antoine done misplaced 'em or somethin'." She kept grumbling and shoved through the door in pursuit of the wayward cufflinks.

"Don't stain the suits... Geez." Louis withdrew something from his pocket. "If she didn't run her mouth for once, I mighta given her the damn things."

Brian eyed the round objects glinting in Louis's palm. He looked at Louis and arched his eyebrows. "You really *are* a Rogue. You should return the stolen treasure to 'Toine before D casts a rage spell on him."

Louis smirked and shoved them back in his pocket. "Just give it a little longer. I'll put 'em somewhere she already looked, make her think she's goin' crazy."

Brian shook his head and snagged the collar of Louis's suit jacket. "Let's check in with the rest of our party before you get up to more trouble."

He dragged Louis out and went to check in with Cecilia while Louis wandered off to see the groomsmen. D and Red had decided to hold the ceremony outside the Sunset at the Shoals resort where the couple lived. Antoine had moved out of their cabin at the lakeside resort and moved into Felicia's two-story house, which happened to be across from his sister's new residence. Cecilia remained in her cabin; Brian and Louis also felt no need to upgrade from theirs, which held too many memories they remained attached to.

Cecilia was in one of the resort's rooms working on a bridesmaid's sleek, jet-black hair. Lavender dresses hugged both Felicia's svelte figure and Cecilia's petite frame.

"What're you doing in here?" Cecilia called when Brian entered. "We could've been naked or something!"

He shut the door and swung a fist through the air. "Darn! Should I go back out and redo the sneak check?"

"Very funny, dork." Cecilia twisted Felicia's hair into a sophisticated bun. Her eyebrows quirked as she stuck a hairpin through it to keep it in place. "I'll worry if the day ever comes where you're more interested in seeing one of *us* naked than Louis."

"Gross." Eva shifted in a chair to the side of the room while she watched Cecilia work. "Where is he, anyway? Doesn't his energy drain when he's away from you? You'll have to go wind him up."

Brian snickered and stuffed his hands into his pockets. Eva met his eyes with a wry smile and a quirk of her eyebrows. Her mannerisms these days resembled her brother's—probably because she'd always been just as damaged and insecure as he had, only better at hiding it.

When Jacque and Marie had arrived at Diamond City, Cecilia had pulled them aside and explained the situation with Eva. The three of them spent a lot of time with her, even setting up therapeutic sessions with Louis when Eva was ready to engage in them. Brian participated in several until they apologized to each other and said the cathartic "I forgive you." They weren't best friends, but they weren't enemies, and the uneasy tension from before didn't linger.

The door popped open. Louis stuck his head in and homed onto his target immediately. "Bri, Jacque needs us for rehearsal." He swept his gaze across the women. "Ladies, you all clean up nice."

Cecilia flashed him a feigned smile. "I might appreciate that if you weren't such an obvious suck-up."

Louis wriggled his eyebrows. "They didn't name that cathedral after me—*I'm* no saint." He pinched Brian's side. "Meet us outside when you're done gossipin'."

After he left, Eva's eyes met Brian's. "Wow—he made it a whole five minutes without you." She shook her head, eyes flitting to stare off into the distance. "I thought he was fakin' it at first, but then I remembered the way he'd smile and laugh with you when we were kids. That's how he is now." She held her hand in front of her, scrutinizing her freshly painted nails and the fading scar left by Brian's arrow. "You've left scars on both of us, but in a weird way, you saved both our lives."

Felicia stepped out of her chair. Cecilia gestured for Eva to take her place and dragged her fingers through Eva's thick ebony tresses, which now reached below her shoulders. "We all have scars now, Eva. They remind us of our mistakes—and that we can learn from them and improve." She tucked Eva's hair behind her ears and smiled at her in the mirror.

Brian retreated to the door, a little dazed by Eva's comment and trying to hide it. "I'm going to go find Louis before his energy depletes. See you at the ceremony, ladies. Maybe I'll catch you changing later."

"Byeeee, Bri," Eva and Cecilia called after him. Their giggles drifted through the door. Cecilia never failed to snap Eva out of her melancholy moods.

The warm summer air tickled Brian's skin as he walked over to the dock. Grimes meandered near the water's edge, content to graze and watch the goings-on, but Jonesy scampered nearby. He avoided LD, not appreciative of the dog's burning desire to chase and lick him.

Once Brian joined the groom's party, Jacque led them through the motions. Although the B.E.N. maintained their beliefs, they had taken D's advice and ditched the robes. Many of them confessed they preferred this. They merged into the society at Diamond City seamlessly, bringing more resources and skills to the fold. With their help, they'd expanded the fence and farm and improved security at the dam. The mayor invited Marie and Jacque to join her council and to open a church for those who wanted to attend services. Arkansas certainly had enough of them to choose from.

Conveniently, both knew how to perform wedding ceremonies, so Cecilia's prediction came true. But D didn't want "no borin' shit," so she and Red compromised with a combination of Jacque and Marie's traditions: Creole and Christian. It promised to be an entertaining union.

Once everyone finished rehearsals, the mayor asked the mingling guests to sit. She stood on the dock between Jacque and Marie, representing the union of Diamond City and Evergreen Plantation. The sun glittered on the lake behind them, resting amidst a bed of cotton-candy clouds. A slight breeze rustled the leaves surrounding them. Earlier, D had held her fist to the sky and warned it not to rain on her parade—like Red and everyone else, it seemed to have listened to her.

The band gathered to the left of the dock played energetic music instead of more traditional pieces. A buffet table to the right of the guests displayed a plethora of foods sourced from the lake and farm and cooked by anyone who had the talent and inclination. The delicious scents of cooked meat, seafood, and vegetables wafted over to the guests and wedding party, making Brian wish they had eaten beforehand.

Louis fidgeted next to Brian, tugging on his sleeves or tapping his foot. Being in front of a crowd made him anxious, but Red had insisted on him joining the groom's party and D didn't argue against it. Antoine and Rod joined them.

Cecilia's lavender gown complemented her fair skin and straw-blonde hair. Felicia glowed with newfound radiance. D had also bonded with Andi during her stay at Lakeside Resort. It delighted her to be up there in a nice dress holding pretty flowers. Eva remained in the crowd, too ashamed of her transgressions to join the party even though D had extended the invitation.

"Ladies and gentlemen," Mayor Halloran called over a handheld microphone. She lingered on the dock with Jacque and Marie. Red stood in front of his groomsmen, tugging at his collar and clearing his throat. The musicians ceased playing. "We're gathered here today to celebrate the union of my dear friends, Dionne Etienne and Al Sanderson. On this lovely summer day, the sun shines down on us as we watch them honor their love and commitment to one another. I'm proud to stand beside Jacque Declouette and Marie Murphy, who have taught us differing beliefs retain many core similarities."

Mayor Halloran stepped away from the dock to join Cecilia and the other bridesmaids, ceding the spotlight to Marie and Jacque. Louis yawned, but a swift elbow to the side cut it short.

Marie took the microphone from Mayor Halloran. "Friends, we thank you for welcoming us into your flock. But we are all our own shepherds now; we walk this path together. And today, Al and Dionne will carve their own shared path."

Jacque took the microphone from Marie. "When the illness spread, we all lost so much: friends, family, lovers. Yet we persevered, and though we can never replace what was lost, we have built something new from the rubble: this town, this community, and the bonds you have formed within it. Let today serve as a reminder and a celebration of human resilience, of the ability to grow together, to share a love which opens our hearts to each other and ourselves. Alone, the path is dark—yet, like Mayor Halloran said, the light shines on us all when we're together. And today is the brightest of all."

Mayor Halloran swept her arm out toward the aisle. "It's time for the bride to enter and to exchange vows. Maestro, the music, please."

The band eased into a delicate tune. Antoine nudged Brian and whispered, "I offered, but she said she didn't need no man to march her down the aisle."

Brian's smile only grew once D emerged from beyond the rear rows of seats. She danced her way down the aisle with her bouquet bobbing and weaving, showering petals on the crowd. "Let's kick this music up a notch! This is gonna put everyone to sleep!"

So much for the somber entrance of the bride. But Brian hadn't expected D to do anything the "traditional" way—it didn't suit her boisterous personality.

A fiddle accompanied D's lively march. She'd poo-pooed the veil ("Why would I wanna blind myself and trip over my own train?") and flashed everyone a dazzling smile. Everyone beamed at her as she made her way to Red's side. His cheeks matched his hair, but he looked just as excited to be there as she was. Louis pressed his lips together; he found Red's serendipitous choice of a white tuxedo and red bow tie unbearably amusing.

Once D reached the dock, the song ended. She clasped Red's hand and stood in front of the glimmering lake. An ethereal halo of light shone above their heads.

Marie and Jacque led them in the exchange of vows. Red tugged on the tie matching his cheeks and hair. "Dionne... It feels funny to call you by your full name. Everybody knows you as D—that one little letter carries all the character you need. D stands for delightful, determined, and delectable—all of which you are. It also stands for devoted, which is what I pledge to be to you. You brought happiness into my life I hadn't known in so long—perhaps a happiness I'd *never* known. When you're in the room, it's impossible to be anything but happy. You're a wonderful friend and an even better partner, someone who refuses to let anyone she loves suffer. You've known pain, my dear D, but you haven't let it defeat you. Instead, you've knocked it to the ground and dug your heel into its face. As long as I live, I vow to help you stomp anything that dares to try and drag you down. I'll share the burden of your pain and the triumph of your victories. I love you, and I thank the Good God He brought you into my life."

D wiped beneath her eyes, already on the verge of tears. Brian smiled when he spied Cecilia's glistening eyes; she caught his gaze and smiled back. Andi kept sniffing and dabbing her eyes.

"I was never any good at writin'"—D gripped Red's hand—"always worked best on the fly. I guess all my life, I been used to changin'. I didn't even know who I was for so long. By the time I found out, I was scared to let anyone know the *real* me. And the one man who broke through to me, who accepted me, was taken from me. I never thought I'd love again. I never thought anyone would love *me* again. Like Jacque said, you can't replace someone—but you can't let it stop you from findin' new folks to love. When I lost Gus, I was all alone, just me and Jones tryin' to make it to my brother—and I was scared he'd either be dead or gone. But the fine folks at Evergreen helped me confront my loss; otherwise, I might not've let Red get to know me. There ain't no point in bein' so scared to lose someone you never let them love you.

"Red, you didn't even worry about livin' up to Gus, said you'd help carry my baggage. And there been so many nights you listened to me talk, held me when I cried, and showed me love—I don't feel scared no more. As long as we together, I know we can take anythin' the universe throws at us. I love you, Al Sanderson, you spicy stick of cinnamon!"

Brian's eyes stung with burgeoning tears. Cecilia, Andi, and Mayor Halloran had given in and let theirs flow freely. Even Felicia had a shine in her eyes, and Louis's (forced, Brian suspected) neutral expression softened into a smile. Brian patted Antoine's arm when he started sniffing.

Because jewelry stores had been looted early into society's breakdown, the exchange of rings didn't occur. D and Red tied a red ribbon to their wrists instead, signifying, as Felicia told them, the red string of Fate binding them together.

A passionate clench between D and Red followed Jacque's declaration of "We now pronounce you lifelong partners!" The audience clapped, and the band resumed playing. Their song accompanied D and Red's descent down the aisle. D eschewed the rice-throwing because she didn't "want to pull pieces of rice outta strange places durin' my weddin' night!"

The groomsmen dispersed into empty seats in the front row, but Louis made a beeline for the punch bowl. D moved to the clearing behind the chairs and held the bouquet in front of her face. "A'ight, ladies: I'm tired of holdin' this thing. Let's see who's gonna catch the bug next!"

The bridesmaids joined the other women gathered in the clearing. They lifted their hands into the air as D turned her back to them. Excited chatter filled the summer air. She lowered her arms and launched the assortment of colorful flowers behind her.

A powerful gust of wind took the bouquet. It soared into the back of Louis's head while he bent over the refreshment table ladling himself a drink.

"The fuck was that?" He turned, glaring at the pink stain on his white dress shirt.

D and the crowd collapsed into an uproar of laughter. "Better get Cill to sew you a gown, Louise!"

Louis's face contorted into a mortified expression. He kept his drink in one hand and bent over to grab the bouquet, contemplating what to do with it. His eyes flashed to a panicked Brian, who dreaded the possibility of Louis doing something impulsive and embarrassing, but Louis merely shot him a wink and directed his attention elsewhere. He walked over to the giggling assortment of women and kneeled in front of Bailey. "Here, kid—now you can get married one day and throw one of these in someone's face."

Bailey grabbed the bouquet with a delighted smile. "Really?" She angled her face toward Cassandra. "Mommy, am I really gonna get married like you an' Daddy an' Aunt Bill an' Uncle Craig?"

A lump formed in Brian's throat, though Bailey couldn't have known her innocent question would evoke such painful memories. He hadn't known Billie and Craig were married; it reminded him of all the questions he'd never be able to ask them and of the void left by their boisterous personalities.

Bailey ran up to her mother while Louis slunk back to his seat. She climbed onto Cassandra's lap and buried her face in the bouquet to smell it while Cassandra stroked her daughter's hair and smiled. The sight evoked a ghostly image of Brian's mother and sister, but Louis squeezed Brian's knee and snapped him out of his brief reverie.

D clapped her hands. "Okay, y'all, it's cake time! I bet you starvin' like I am, and this food smells too dang good!"

Jonesy agreed. He bounded up onto the buffet table and made D run after him with a fist flying through the air. Grimes snorted, watching the proceedings with stoic interest. The ever-whimsical D had even stationed Missus Periwinkle alongside one of the trees.

While most guests lined up for food, the rest shifted the chairs around several circular tables. Brian and Louis sat and waited for the line to die down. Cecilia joined them. "Eva's getting mine," she explained with a yawn.

Louis leaned an elbow onto the table and cupped his cheek with his hand. "Should I have given the bouquet to you, Cill?"

"I hate to break it to you: I'm not a Mormon. You can't have Brian *and* me."

"Ha-ha." Louis arched an eyebrow in response to her deadpan delivery. "Guess my sister and I both have a thing for blue-eyed blondes."

Cecilia swatted Louis's arm. "We're *friends*, Lou. I spent a lot of time with her during her house arrest. She needed someone to show her kindness, to help her accept her own self-worth. It's still too early for her to be alone." She stood with a sigh. Once Eva left the line, Cecilia pushed her chair under the table. "Speaking of Eva: I should go join her. Brian, please keep an eye on your loulou. Don't let him drink much more."

Brian arched his eyebrows. "How did you know I call him that?"

Cecilia held a hand to her chest and affected a dramatic expression. "*Oh, baise moi plus fort, mon amour.*" She made an effective switch from an imitation of Louis's throaty French to Brian's subpar attempt at an accent. "*Je vais vous donner chaque pouce, mon loulou.*"

Brian wanted to crawl underneath the table, then run home and soundproof the walls. The blood rushing to Louis's cheeks betrayed the embarrassment he struggled to hide. Cecilia snickered and jogged off to join Eva with her hands linked behind her back, not as much of an angel as Brian once thought.

Louis's eyes shifted from Cecilia to Brian, and he lowered his voice. "Well, now we *have* to move. Maybe it's time to upgrade to somethin' bigger—with thicker walls."

Brian watched Cecilia and Eva while they chatted with Felicia. Antoine hurried to Felicia's side with two heaping plates of food, making all three women break into bright grins. D and Red fed each other cake, laughing when they smashed it into each other's faces. Mayor Halloran sat at a table talking with Jacque and Marie. Everyone was smiling, laughing, relaxed, and able to enjoy themselves.

Brian reached across the table for Louis's hand. "Can you believe it's summer, the sun is shining, and everyone's safe, happy, and together? Eight months ago, I never even would've *dreamed* of this."

Louis threaded his fingers through Brian's. "It's nice when reality is better than your dreams for once. I still pinch myself when I realize what my life's become—that I'm here with all these people who don't treat me like shit or ignore me, or act like they're scared of me. I never knew what it was like to fit in before... To be accepted."

"It's because all of us have suffered to get to this point. I guess it means we passed the test Cill's always talking about God putting us through."

"I dunno about all that, but I definitely feel like we passed *some* kinda test to get here." Louis stopped watching the crowd and switched his attention to Brian. "Thank you for not givin' up on me. You're the only person who really gave me a chance. Even Cill and 'Toine only did it 'cause you convinced them to. After all the things I did, all those mistakes I made, bein' a melodramatic asshole who threatened to off myself if I didn't get my way... You never doubted I loved you even when you had every reason to. There's so much about you I admire, and I'm proud of you—" Louis's voice started breaking, so he scratched the back of his head and cleared his throat. "Sorry if that comes off as condescendin'."

Brian smiled, his chest warmed like a hot beverage was passing through it. "I'm proud of you too—for admitting your mistakes, for confiding your weaknesses and fears to me, and for working hard to right your wrongs. Our pasts don't define who we are; sometimes they define who we don't *want* to be. You didn't give up on yourself, and now you know how loved you are. Not just by me."

Louis pressed his forehead against Brian's. They both closed their eyes, but their noses brushed and Louis's breath tickled Brian's lips when he spoke. "I don't have to say it, do I? You just know."

Brian's eyes opened to look into Louis's. "I don't know if you've ever heard of this, and you'll probably give me shit for it and call me a romantic dweeb, but I think we're twin flames. A twin flame is someone you always come back to, someone who causes you pain but helps you grow, a mirror reflecting both your weaknesses and strengths—someone who makes you feel complete the instant you meet them. It's not idealized, sappy, romantic bullshit like soul mates and true love—it's messy and it's fucked up and it *hurts*, but it reveals the truth about who you are and helps you accept it. When you said you ached and burned for me, I knew exactly what you meant because I went through the same agony reasoning with my feelings for you—it just didn't click for me until a few months ago when D loaned me a book about this stuff. Our love isn't wrong; it's *perfect*—but only because we're perfect for each other, no one else."

The same dazed expression slackened Louis's features as the time Brian had mentioned creativity and discipline at the rustic corner store. He gently shook his head and smiled that crooked smile, but his eyes melted with affection. "You *are* a romantic dweeb, but you're right: you're also perfect for me." He cupped a hand around Brian's cheek and closed the scant gap between them, his lips caressing Brian's with tenderness instead of passion.

Everyone else converged into a blur around them, talking, laughing, eating. The wind whispered through the tree leaves, rocking string lights that twinkled as day darkened into night and fireflies flickered in the cooling air.

While they kissed, music blared through the speaker system. D's squeal was audible even over the piercing horns of the song's opening. "Oh, I missed me some Beyoncé!"

Louis withdrew from Brian with a wry smirk. "This is my anthem, isn't it?" He bobbed his head and mimed the lyrics, making them both bust up laughing.

D ran around dragging everyone up who dared not dance to Beyoncé. For so long, she'd put up a front, tried to crack a joke in the face of adversity, to be strong for everyone without asking for anything in return—now the humor and happiness were real for her. Brian loved her dearly, loved seeing her arms wrapped around Red's neck, those shades of purple taffeta shimmering in the waning twilight sun. He mentally captured the image of her dancing surrounded by the happy faces of their loved ones: Antoine and Felicia, Eva and Cecilia, Cassandra and Bailey, Jacque, Marie, Gloria, even Grimes and Jonesy. *I'll cherish this moment because of its fleeting beauty, not in spite of it. And the next moment will become a memory I'll treasure, if not for eternity, then at least for the rest of my life.*

Brian swayed in Louis's arms, the heat of their bodies merging until they moved as one. The world around them evanesced into a dizzying haze of sound and color. He tucked his head into the crevice between Louis's neck and shoulder.

It fit perfectly.

Acknowledgements

As always, I thank my husband and mother for their unwavering support.

I'd also like to thank the awesome team at NineStar Press for their work on this novel and its predecessor, and for allowing these diverse voices to be heard (or read).

Finally, I'd like to thank everyone who read *Stalker/s* and encouraged the writing and publication of the sequel. I hope the ending is satisfying— it can't be as bad as the finale to a certain fantasy show on HBO, right?

About the Author

As an only child, I was allowed plenty of freedom to explore my interests—namely reading, writing, and art. My parents encouraged me to pursue these and never discouraged me from the diversity of the world. I like to think my work today reflects my interest in exploring and appreciating such diversity. Ultimately, I wanted to create and inspire as so many others have done in my life, and to tell stories people might take something from.

Compared to the rest of the world, I'm not all that interesting! I love animals, Fall/Halloween/Horror, coffee, board and video games, and the occasional Anime. And yes, I owe the world of fanfiction a debt for being my stomping grounds as a teen. I sometimes call myself the "Mother of Rats" because I own three—they're clever and sweet and don't deserve the bad rap they get! Beyond that, I count myself lucky to be able to share my love of writing with anyone interested enough to read it—so thank you!

Email: ikebukuroinfobroker@yahoo.com

Twitter: @LolaInSlacks69

Website: www.lola-in-slacks-88.tumblr.com

Other books by this author

Stalker/s

Also Available from NineStar Press

Connect with NineStar Press

Website: NineStarPress.com

Facebook: NineStarPress

Facebook Reader Group: NineStarNiche

Twitter: @ninestarpress

Tumblr: NineStarPress